R.H.
GRÜND
WORKS

OTHER BOOKS BY R. H. GRÜND

Room of Cloth

Simulacrum

ABATTOIR

R. H. GRÜND

To Amanda, Asa, Carlos, and everyone else who contributed to this book—every discussion and suggestion helped bring us over the finish line! Thank you for your support and your belief in the work.

I entreat you, my brothers, remain true to the earth, and do not believe those who speak to you of superterrestrial hopes! They are poisoners, whether they know it or not.

'We have discovered happiness,' say the Ultimate Men and blink.

— Friedrich Nietzsche, THUS SPOKE ZARATHUSTRA

ABATTOIR

MILDRED

"Hello," said Mildred, staring over the heads of the support group, clutching her sheaf of flyers with sweaty, shaky hands. "My name's Mildred."

"Hello, Mildred," came the reply in chorus.

The smell of burnt coffee churned her already queasy stomach. The shuffles and sniffles of the expectant audience—the portly woman in black, in particular, drawing endless tissues from her purse, and the gaunt man practically choking on phlegm—swung on her nerves like a whip. A fan spun above them in crooked, nauseating circles. The green walls, drooping with clumps of dried, uneven paint, brought to mind waves of bile.

She looked down at the flyers, the only source of possible comfort in that ghastly place. They featured the outline of a rectangle in bright pink—evoking a door, or a window—against a glossy black backdrop. "Want the truth?" read the magenta text at the bottom. "We can show you. Find us at PINK HOUSE."

She remembered the relief, the way it had washed over her like a hot shower. Her nose curled lovingly at the sudden smell of geraniums. She flexed the flyers, folding them one way, bending them another—with each twist, another waft of the geraniums reached her, each sweeter than the last. She was back among the carrots and tomatoes of her grandfather's garden as a young girl, digging fingers into dirt, sweeping knees of grass. She pictured his warm smile, felt his strong hands guiding her own. The memory steadied her breaths. Settled her heart.

"My husband passed," she said, voice firm, head high. "Drunk driver. He was a veteran, you know—served in the Gulf War. But there was nothing he could do. Just sitting at a red light, no idea things were going to end."

She felt tears prickle, but the scent of geraniums, the power of the pink emblem in her hands, banished them.

"It was my son who made me come to one of these," she continued. "I couldn't stand him seeing me mope, acting like my life was over, too. So, I went, and it helped for a little while, but I just couldn't get rid of it. You know? It was like a stain on my mind."

There were nods of understanding among the group, muffled utterances of sympathy. She met the eyes of the portly woman and the gaunt man and recognized the sickness dwelling behind their rheumy, red-rimmed gazes. The same sickness swam under her surface, roiling as though whipped by stormy winds, threatening to overrun.

She held fast. No. Geraniums. Grandpa. The truth.

"I looked online, and there were so many people like me. Widows. Single mothers. But no one could help—we were all looking for the same thing, after all. And then I found it. Or maybe they found me."

She raised the flyers. She had printed them at the local copy shop, sweating under the occasional glances of the blue-vested attendant, fiddling awkwardly, clammily, with the copier. Share it, they had told her. Put up the posters. Spread the word. People are out there hurting as you were. They are lost as you were. They want change. They need help. We can help them. He can help them. You can help them.

"It wasn't like the normal self-help stuff," she said. "These people really helped me. They gave me a purpose, something to do with my time. Your loss isn't all there is—that's what they told me. When you lose something, you also get something in return. And it's your responsibility to share it."

She stood up and held out the flyers. "So, that's why I'm here. I want to help all of you the same way I was helped. Who wants help? Who *needs* help?"

She passed out the flyers, feeling briefly terrified, as though she were transgressing—but then there was a sense of relief, a weight lifting, knowing this was right. You must give back, they told her. You don't want to have all this happiness to yourself, do you? No, much better to share it. Much better to spread it.

Afterwards, back in her car, she let out a laugh. "I did it," she said. "I was scared, but I did it. Am I ready now?"

Geraniums again, from out of nowhere, potent at first, then diluted. Not yet. One more thing. "Right." She steadied her trembling hands. "You're right. I got ahead of myself. One more thing. One last thing—"

A knock at her window.

Mildred started. A man stood at the door, tall, serious-looking, with dark hair and tanned skin. She recognized him from the session, but she was surprised she hadn't noticed him sooner. Unlike the portly woman and gaunt man, he stared with a brooding intensity. His eyes weren't lost and wandering, but pointed, ferocious. Her joy turned to dread, her relief to terror. Then the man smiled, and the ferocity disappeared, melted away like ice under the sun.

He knocked again. "Excuse me," he said, his voice muffled behind the tempered glass. "Do you have a minute?"

She lowered the window. "Yes?"

"Sorry to bother you. My name's Jesus. I was in the meeting. I got one of your flyers." He held it up. "I had questions about it. If you don't mind?"

"I don't know. It's late, and my son's alone—"

"I have someone, too," he said. "My brother. So, I promise I won't waste your time. Just a few questions." He gestured across the dark parking lot. "There's a diner over there. Five minutes. Please."

It was strange how he turned from serious—menacing, even—to pleading. Now, practically begging her, he did look like those others inside. Lost. Sick. They would want her to help him like they helped her. Those who found her. Those who went on before. Those who waited for her on the other side.

They sat alone in the diner. Jesus sat rigidly, with the disciplined poise she recognized from her late husband. A soldier, she thought. He struck a formidable presence in his leather jacket and jeans. He held the flyer at arm's length, scrutinizing it with the same intensity from before. Mildred sipped her coffee, afraid to speak.

"Pink House," he said at length, looking up at her, his gaze once again softening. "What does that mean? What is that?"

"It's hard to explain. They're like an online support group."

"But different." He placed the flyer down, hands clenching and unclenching. "You said they gave you purpose. I've heard that before. I've been to these meetings—gone to seminars. Everyone always says they have an answer."

Mildred hesitated. What was his angle? What did he want?

Jesus must have noticed her defensiveness. He smiled. "I'm sorry. You're grieving, too."

"If you don't mind me asking," she said, "who did you lose?"

"My parents. They were killed."

"My God. An accident or—"

"They were murdered." He said it quickly, nonchalantly. His eyes took on their regular hardness. "Home invasion."

She covered her mouth, stifled a gasp. Images of dark bedrooms lit by gunfire flooded her mind. Suddenly, the car crash that claimed her husband seemed remote, unimportant, a crime of negligence as opposed to malice. She smelled the geraniums, and the voices came to her again. Help him. He's desperate. What right do you have to fear him? To judge him?

"I wasn't there," he went on. "I was on deployment."

He leaned back. His fists were clenched again. Impulsively, Mildred reached out and took his hands. This is what they wanted, she thought, what her new purpose was. Release pain. Ease suffering. She had been chosen to do this.

"I was skeptical, too. But they showed me something incredible. I can show it to you if you want—I know how. And it will change everything. It will take away all the hurt."

Jesus watched her, searched her eyes. He nodded. "Okay. But I want my brother to see it, too. He needs it more than me."

"Of course. I'll show both of you."

They agreed that Jesus and his brother would come to her home the following evening. Mildred and her son lived on a two-acre plot outside town, her husband's inheritance. He had been renovating the house in the months before his death—portions of rotted siding hung beside pristine, freshly painted clapboard, and half the roof was still draped in tarp. Illuminated by floodlights, she walked onto the porch, unlocked the screen door. "I'm home, Tyler," she called into the darkness of the house. "Did you eat?"

She found him in the den, splayed across the sofa, watching television. "Did you hear me?" she asked, raising her voice over the gunshots from the movie. Tyler looked up at her, blue-eyed and blond-haired like his father. Very much his father's son.

"Oh, hey," he said, rubbing his eyes. "Sorry, I tried to stay up for you."

"It's okay." She smiled. "Did you eat?"

In the kitchen, they spooned through steaming cups of macaroni and cheese. Mildred watched her son, lanky for his age, only thirteen. Too young to be without a father. Not that there was ever a right age. Just two hours before, she had still been wrestling with what she had to do, but meeting Jesus had resolved her. This was why she was here—what she had been chosen for.

"Tyler," she said as he put his bowl in the sink, "come upstairs with me. I want to show you something. I made it for your daddy."

That night, as she lay in the dark, listening to the wind outside, she smelled the geraniums again. "I know," she said. "I have to send them next. Then I'll go, too. Wait for me, Shelby. I'll see you soon. I'll see you all soon."

The next evening, she met Jesus outside his motel, the twilight sky a cover of murky blue over the smoldering, dying light. A teenage boy stood behind him, thin like Tyler, but dark-haired, olive-skinned. He didn't smile—didn't even speak. His dull stare unnerved her.

"My brother," Jesus said, adjusting the backpack over his shoulder. "Joaquin."

Mildred raised a hand in greeting. "Hello, Joaquin." But still he did not say anything. Only looked at her. Looked through her.

"I'm sorry," said Jesus. "He doesn't speak. Not after what happened."

"Oh. How awful."

"Well. We should get going." He opened the door to his truck, dumping the backpack inside along with a couple of other bags. "We're moving on after we visit you."

"Where?"

"Anywhere but home." He climbed inside. "We'll follow you. Thank you again for this."

"Of course. Thank you for letting me."

They drove out of town. The dark came down, leaving only unpaved road and rocky highway lit by their headlights. Mildred peeked at the rearview mirror constantly, nervously. Jesus's truck never lagged far behind. Although the cabin was dark above the piercing headlights, she knew he sat like a statue with that ferocious stare, the brother beside him with that dull, dead

gaze. Stop, she told herself. They need this, the brother especially. They were looking for it. They came to me for it.

They parked outside the farmhouse. With the dimming of
the headlights went the only illumination until Mildred stepped
to the porch and activated the floodlights.

"Is your son home?" asked Jesus. "Everything's dark."

"He's at a friend's," she said. "Please, follow me. It's upstairs."

They went inside, Jesus scanning the shadows of the empty
den, the sparse kitchen. The brother trailed behind, his own
eyes following something in the darkness.

"It smells," Jesus said. "You leave food out?"

"I don't smell anything," Mildred replied, though she had
never smelled the geraniums so strongly, never envisioned so
clearly her grandfather's garden. They climbed the stairs, the
wood creaking loudly under their feet. A door was ajar at the far
end of the second-floor hall. A faint light flickered from within.

She pushed the door open. "Here it is. The truth."

The room, once her husband's study, had been cleared of
furniture, the imprints in the dust vague in the soft light. Candles stood in concentric circles around a freestanding, open
door in the center of the room. Mildred looked to Jesus. "See it?
In the doorway?"

Jesus peered from outside the room. "See what?"

"In the doorway. Through the doorway." She looked back
towards the door. "It's beautiful. It's another place. A place
better than this. Where my husband is waiting for me."

"All I see is empty space." Jesus stepped inside, eyeing a dark patch on the wood before the freestanding door. "What's that? Looks like blood."

"It's nothing," Mildred said quickly. "You really can't see anything? But you're supposed to! They said you would!"

"Who did? Pink House?" Jesus moved closer. "Where did you say your son was, again?"

She shook her head frantically. "I can see it! So, why can't you?" Her eyes went wide. "You lied to me. You're not looking for truth, you're—"

"The men who killed my parents did it in front of a door just like that," Jesus said. "They cut my mother's throat. They stabbed my father's eyes out. Joaquin saw it all."

The brother stood outside, eyes fixed on the open door.

"You killed your son, didn't you?" Jesus asked. "That's his blood on the floor there. You gutted him like a pig. No wonder it smells even worse in here."

"I sent him through," said Mildred. "He's with his father now! I was supposed to go with them, but they—they told me to wait—that I still had to send you—"

"You were going to kill us?" Jesus grinned. "Half my height, little over a hundred pounds—how were you going to manage that?"

"You would go, yourself. That's what they said—they were so sure—"

Jesus approached. "What would your husband say? How would he feel if he knew you'd murdered your son for nothing?"

"No!" She was crying now, and not even the smell of geraniums or the clarity of her grandfather's garden soothed her. Some other smell seeped in beneath the geraniums, as if through cracks. Was it rust? No—blood?

"You're pathetic," Jesus said. "The only place you sent your son was into the ground. But if you're so eager to join him, I'll help you along."

He produced a combat knife, serrated on one edge, faintly discolored, vaguely stained. Mildred screamed. "Stay back! Stay away from me!"

She fell, knocking over candles, the flames licking wood and sprouting into miniature fires. She lay in the doorway, shielding herself feebly with her arms, screaming vainly. Jesus advanced. He swung the knife. A bell rang.

She choked, gasped, her hands around her throat soaked with evermore blood. Her breaths grew more ragged, her sobs more broken. They were moving away from her, Jesus and his brother, the rectangular shape of the doorway retreating into the dark distance, shrinking until it disappeared altogether. Mildred spat and sputtered, flopped and flailed. She looked up, and in the darkness above her, a red star loomed, roaring with the grinding and churning of infernal machinery, burning with hellish fire. The star opened, unraveling like a blossom, and she was gone into its depths.

Hey everybody

g morning

HELL O beautifuls!

It's finally time!

been waiting forever! when was the last one??

Over a year couldn't make it but hoping to be there this time

theyre gonna happen more often. were making progress.

I remember when it was just snippets. We were posting on bulletin boards, writing on bathroom stalls. A lot has changed. Faster than we expected.

o shit that damascus?

It is!! Guys a legend.

1 of the GOATS. Damascus wrote the first draft

no shit?

I contributed just like the others. Some of us were writers before. We have our talents. I'm fond of the composers for example. They've done some amazing things.

how much longer, D? u think in five years?

Too soon. But in our lifetimes, maybe. No one predicted how the tech would evolve. We'll be breaking into the mainstream soon enough.

You've seen him?

seen who

dont know? must be new.

Brother, maybe you aren't ready for Pink House.

Pink House is for everyone. That's the project. But not my design.

who made it, D? we never even hear from the admins

Not affiliated. But they have influence. They're building cells. Calling them farms.

farms?

Rules are posted! Finally time for a new celebration. :)

nice. going, D?

No. He gave me my role. I'm here to shepherd. But enjoy.

Kind of sucks to stick around. I want to LEAVE man. I want to GET OUT.

for real fuck all this shit tired of being told what to do

Yeah Tired of seeing my parents like that

i want to see my husband again miss him so much

Youre fucking lucky, D. He picked you.

He picked all of us, friend. All of us. They just don't know it yet.

JOAQUIN

2

In the cool interior of Mildred's house, where one would imagine only the scent of plywood, the grit of dust, Joaquin saw and smelled blood everywhere. Blood coating the walls. Blood caking the drapery. Blood soaking the carpet. His shoes sloshed in it as he walked. His hands came away layered in red. His tongue quivered constantly with the taste of metal. There was no escape from it, especially in the room upstairs, the one with the door. He stared from the hallway into the depths of the free-standing doorway. The boy, Tyler, black-eyed, pale-skinned, beckoned to him. He couldn't speak, either, but not because his voice was trapped—his vocal cords had been severed when his mother clumsily drew the kitchen knife across his throat. Mildred, eternally choking on blood, crawled from around the doorway. The only sounds that escaped her mouth were wretched, wiry sobs. His brother had been cleaner cutting her throat than she had been cutting her son's. Indeed, Jesus was getting better at the killing, the carving, nearly to the level of a butcher. But however calm his brother seemed, however practiced, Joaquin knew the anger was still there. He saw it in the white knuckles, in the fingers twitching after every kill.

Behind the house, under boughs of half-dead oaks, illuminated only by the truck's headlights, Jesus unearthed Tyler's remains from a shallow, poorly dug grave. Silently, dispassionately, he dug deeper. He worked with mechanical efficiency, taking only momentary breaks. He threw in Mildred's body once the grave was deep enough. Mother and son lay together, their corpses entwined in a macabre embrace. Mildred's ring finger, wearing both her and her husband's wedding bands, had been severed and added to the collection.

Joaquin watched his brother work, long desensitized to the violence, unmoved by the terror of the victims or the dread of their ghosts. He was a spectator in a theater all his own, or maybe he was more accurately the projectionist. Before the night he became trapped in that dark, mist-ridden theater, he had imagined himself one day a filmmaker. Coppola, Spielberg, Kurosawa, Bergman—all these and more had been his inspirations, his icons. He filmed constantly with his handheld vintage camera, an heirloom from his grandfather, annoying his classmates, tormenting his parents. He subjected all to impromptu documentaries and on-the-spot interviews. "You'll be in my speech," he laughed to his mother, "when I'm accepting my Oscar."

His brother had been off in the desert, the "sandbox" as he called it, so he hadn't suffered Joaquin's amateur filmmaking. Out of everyone, he had been the one Joaquin wanted to film the most—Jesus had fascinated him since childhood, inspiring awe and terror alike. Whether throwing a football, replacing a fan belt, studying for an exam, or chasing a girl, Jesus did everything with a sharp, unbreakable single-mindedness. Broad-shouldered and muscular in his black boots and leather jacket, he seemed like the gunslinger from a Leone Western, always humorless, forever determined. Never grimacing. Never smiling.

When Jesus was done burying the bodies, he turned off the truck and ferried their bags inside. "All right," he said. "Let's make camp."

He cleared out the furniture in the den, spread out sleeping bags over the hardwood floor. For Jesus, working mechanically, robotically, the room was dark and empty, but Joaquin saw the specters hovering in the adjacent hallway, watched as the sleeping bags sunk into blood. In the kitchen, they warmed up a pot of macaroni and cheese recovered from the refrigerator and ate by lamplight at the small table. Tyler's pale, agonized face hung in the doorway.

Jesus ate quickly, as mechanically as he had set up their impromptu camp. Joaquin followed his brother's eyes as they stared at the night sky outside the dusty window. Where did they go? What did they see? The things he saw in the desert? The things he imagined happened the night their parents died? The vague outlines of scars dressed his arm. Errant shrapnel, supposedly. Hit by a blast. About two years before. Something shared among the dinner table in plain, matter-of-fact fashion to their parents. He had been shaken up, but okay. Later, Joaquin asked him for more details, but Jesus only gave him that silent look. You're disappointing me, the look said. You're letting me down. You shouldn't care about what happened over there. You should only care about your future.

"I know she seemed nice," Jesus said, scraping up the last spoonful from his bowl. "But she's like the others, like the ones who hurt Mom and Dad. They're not good people. You shouldn't feel bad for what happens to them."

The others. Mildred was the third they had tracked down. The first had been a woman, a "high-society trophy wife," Jesus had called her. "She watches people get tortured online," he explained. "Gets off on it." They had staked out her house for weeks, Jesus studying with his hawk's gaze the schedule of the husband, the comings and goings of the children as they went to piano practice or softball. On Saturdays, the wife had the house to herself, inviting girlfriends over for coffee and cake. That was Jesus's opening. In the late afternoon, before the husband returned home with the kids, Jesus came upon her as she was toweling herself off from a dip in the pool. She managed one scream before he fixed the chloroform-soaked rag over her mouth. They left her in a landfill, Jesus dropping her forefinger into a plastic bag. The first ticket they needed to the so-called "celebration" where they would find their parents' killers. Where they would have their revenge.

Jesus lured the following victim, an online drug dealer, out to a stretch of desolate highway. He left the body in a nearby ditch to be picked at by passing scavengers. The dealer's amputated thumb was their second ticket, and Mildred's finger, glinting with the dual wedding bands, was their third. A total of five were needed. Five sacrifices to witness the truth. Five tributes to make way for passage beyond.

Before retiring for the night, Jesus brushed his brother's teeth in the washroom, rinsed his hair, sponged his body. As they lay in their sleeping bags, Joaquin stared up at the ceiling, listened to the creak of the house's old wood, the rustle of the trees outside. The blood came again, dripping down from the cracks in the ceiling, marking his face, his arms, his chest. It rose up from between the floorboards, so much of it that his sleeping bag floated, buoyed by blood. He turned his head. There was no light—in fact, there was no room at all, no furniture, not even his brother. He lay in an abyss of blood, the void around him stretching on endlessly.

Joaquin.

He shivered. His breaths left in white wisps.

Joaquin. Joaquin.

They surrounded him, the ones who roamed this place, as they always did. They touched his face, pulled open his mouth, clutched at his skin. They were gray and withered, crying black tears, sobbing out of black mouths. Tyler stood among them. He could not speak. He strained his severed vocal chords, loosed a silent scream. Nothing. Nothing at all.

Joaquin closed his eyes. If he still slept, still dreamed, he didn't know, couldn't tell. Asleep or awake, there were only ever the sight and smell of blood. Only ever those faces in the darkness, bone-white and then blood-red. Only ever an endless maze of metal and flesh. A room that was not a room. A red star, heralded by bells, bringing with it the end of the world. The end of everything.

3.

In his mental theater, he watched on repeat as those pale-masked men slunk into their home, bound and gagged him and his parents, erected their makeshift doorway. "Three for one," they had laughed, passing around a bottle of whiskey, taking turns on a blunt. Joaquin's parents, struggling on the floor, screamed and begged through the socks stuffed in their mouths. One of the men, in a red hoodie and sneakers, sauntered forward. "The bitch is real loud, ain't she? How about we shut her up?"

Joaquin's father, traditionally timid, modest, had transformed in that moment, lunging forward with an animalistic expression that frightened his son even more than the men in their white, ghostlike masks did. But bound, he could do little. The men beat on him, kicking his face, stomping on his back. They left him barely conscious, face swollen and purple, hands and feet broken. "Good thing we tied him up!" said one. "He might have killed one of us or something."

They turned their attention to his mother after that. Her screams devolved into wails and then moans as they removed her tongue. They waved it around as she thrashed about in a pool of her own blood. "Sucks they want fingers," said the one in the hoodie. "Not very dramatic."

"It's what he wants," the third said. "He won't let us in any other way."

They continued their work after that. They gouged out his father's eyes. They slashed his mother's throat. They dragged the bodies to the doorway, letting the blood gather in the liminal space, kneeling in it, smearing their masks with it. They trembled in religious fervor. They laughed and cried. "Holy fuck," the one in the hoodie breathed. As they recovered, he looked back at Joaquin. "Forgot about the kid for a second."

"No," the third said. "Leave him. We need someone to spread the word, too."

"You're right." The one in the hoodie lurched towards Joaquin, who had long since gone silent, and drew his hand down the boy's face, smearing him with the blood of his parents. The man laughed. "How's it feel, bro? You're one of us now. I bet you can see him, can't you? Popped your cherry and all." He pulled Joaquin forward and turned him towards the doorway. "See it? That's the truth right there, brother. That's what's waiting for everybody."

The space in the doorway had darkened, congealed to an almost solid black. Things swelled and coiled within. What once were people, maybe, their eyes black pits, their mouths gray and gaping. There were hundreds of them, thousands, millions. They raised their arms in prayer, in adulation. A bell tolled somewhere in that lightless, abyssal place. The red star glimmered above them, signaling an arrival, a change in the hellish order. Joaquin watched as his mother and father, drenched in blood, caught in silent screams, joined the ranks of the damned.

Afterwards, when the men had left and the dark place beyond the doorway had disappeared, he sat in his parents' blood for hours, maybe even days, the bedroom stinking like the back of a butcher's shop, wet and slick and humid. He put his hand through his mother's hair. He wanted to call out to her, but his voice never came. When the police arrived and shined their lights in his eyes, demanded answers of him, still he did not speak, could not speak. Behind the screen of his mind, sitting alone in the theater, he could only watch. At some point, his brother stood before him. Jesus, he said in that cold, shadowy theater. Jesus, I'm right here. I'm here! They took Mom and Dad! They sent them over! But he could not get out, could not break out of that place. Seeing his brother—his hero, his idol— shed tears for the first time in his life, in maybe both their lives, and he could say nothing. He couldn't even make a sound. He could only sit alone behind his eyes. He could only watch as the film in the projector rolled back, as the men once more slunk into the house, as they did so again and again and again and the nightmare repeated indefinitely.

When he did occasionally sleep, the bedroom bloodbath remained in his mind like the profile of burnt pixels on a television screen, echoing with the howls of his father, the shrieks of his mother. The suffocating stench of their blood pervaded and grew more pungent. The walls, slathered with their blood, sloughed away, the plaster and paint melting and laying bare the muscle and fat underneath, the interior sinews, the veins, the arteries. In those moments, he was no longer in his parents' bedroom, but somewhere else, a room pulsating with some kind of alien, intelligent life. He would wander forward, press past the walls that were like skin, like cloth, and find a deeper, darker place, a labyrinth of bone and steel and rust. Somewhere, deep within, those dead masses waited. His parents waited, too.

He woke up, making his guttural sounds, his moans. Jesus, already awake, held him tight. He spoke to him of the vastness of the desert, reminded him of barbecues around the grill and trips to the bar where Jesus knew all the patrons, all the girls. He sang to him the Spanish lullabies of their grandparents. This was their nightly ritual. Their new life.

How could things change so suddenly, like a curtain coming down, the lights coming on? Joaquin's life had been normal just months before, as mundane as that of any other high-school junior. He had enjoyed film, been bashful around girls. He had been concerned about his future, but only insofar as what college he would attend, how he would pay for it, what his life would look like in a year. Thinking seriously for the first time he would need to "grow up," in the words of his brother, assume responsibility, take initiative. No one prepares a teenager for the stress of having to choose a life when he doesn't even know what his choices are. He envied Jesus for that, for always having a plan, for deciding on things without hesitation. Jesus had joined the military to cover his college. Even when their parents protested, he never wavered. He came out with a degree in electrical engineering, but time in the barracks had changed him, and he was committed to serving his country. He wouldn't settle for a desk. *Pendejo*, his mother called him in her moments of weakness. Joaquin saw her tears, and he felt ashamed he couldn't match his brother's courage, even if that courage hurt loved ones.

If Jesus was ever lonely, ever hurting, he never showed it. There were no betrayals of emotion, no grief or misery or even humor. There was only the long, hard stare, the eternal grimace. When they first started out, staying in various motel rooms, Joaquin would lay on his side of the bed, watching his brother stare deep into the laptop screen. One of the reasons they moved around so much was to throw off the scent, Jesus said. The people they were hunting would hunt them, too. They could never chance an IP address being tracked, never allow for a profile to exist too long. Jesus changed out his laptops every few weeks, buying from secondhand sellers, arranging sales through online classifieds. He lived and breathed pawn shops, making small talk with the shop owners while Joaquin looked at the old CRT monitors, the shelves of video cassettes, the cases of paint-chipped and leather-handled guns. Jesus would walk out with a computer, a disc drive, old parts he would mod and alter to suit his needs. He often stayed up for hours, tinkering with the laptops, sifting through forums, researching, always researching. Most nights, Joaquin couldn't sleep, so he stared with his dull eyes at his brother's monitor, at the small text, at the flashes of red and black, the glimpses of a pale, pink room.

"The guys who did it," Jesus had told him one evening in a motel room that could have been every motel room, musty and papered in faded floral, "they're part of a group. Pink House. See here." He pointed at the screen, and Joaquin saw the image of a newspaper headline: family slain, son only survivor. "They're claiming it," Jesus went on. "Bragging about it. And they aren't the only ones. This is happening everywhere."

Joaquin had stared at the screen, but he saw only the red faces in the darkness, the red walls, the bodies of his parents. His brother told him about Pink House as time went on. An online collective, many of them hidden in plain sight. Mothers, fathers, teachers, bankers, politicians. Moonlighting as part of some type of cult, killing people, torturing them. And Joaquin remembered vaguely that the men in the masks hadn't just mutilated his parents, but they had taken their fingers, too. They had knelt before that makeshift doorway and shaken as though possessed. They had seen what he had seen: that dark space in the doorway, stirring with intent, as much a primordial soup as it was a threshold between this place and somewhere else.

"Initiation killings," Jesus had said. "Like a fucking gang." He had gripped the laptop tightly, clenched his teeth, and Joaquin had anticipated the laptop smashing against the wall, or maybe a scream, a frustrated yell. But as always, his brother remained calm. Instead, the gears in his head had started turning, and their vengeance commenced.

4 .

The farmhouse became their latest base of operations. Temporary, of course, as always—within days, word might spread of the widow's disappearance, of her son's absence, and the brothers would have to leave once again. But Jesus said the relative distance of the house was convenient, helpful for making their tracks harder to follow.

Amid the blood and pungent stench, as the ghosts of Mildred and her son lurked at the edges of rooms and drifted through doorways, Joaquin watched as his brother assembled his computers and laid out his notes. In the dusty den, Jesus hunkered and reviewed his lists, marking off infeasible targets, circling those that could be prioritized. By lamplight, he would contemplate the fingers they had collected. Why fingers? Who knew? Jesus had mentioned offhandedly that the people of Pink House worshipped some kind of god, and the god was picky, capricious, quick to anger. "They're insane," Jesus said with his typical disgust, chewing his morning handful of coffee beans, sharpening his knife against a whetstone. "Just need an excuse to do what they do. Kill who they kill."

Could Joaquin speak, he would have told his brother about what waited on the other side of the doorways: a dark place teeming with those gray, dead legions, all of them waiting for something—or someone—to come down. They're not crazy, he might have said. You just can't see it. But it's close. You can smell it. It's why you wrinkle your nose. It's why you don't like to eat your food. Because it's all over. It's under your skin.

Hammer in hand, Jesus took down the makeshift doorway upstairs. He started cleanly at first, unscrewing the nails, but suddenly, in a flash of rare anger, he struck the wood. Then he struck again, again and again, swinging in wider arcs, each hit landing with more force than the last. Joaquin crept up the stairs, lured by the grunts and yells. He found his brother hunched before the pile of demolished wood, his shoulders rising and falling in exhausted fury, the hammer hanging loosely from his hand. "I'll burn this whole fucking place down," he said, dropping the hammer into the pile. "And then I'll kill them all."

They found their next target. Encircled by lanterns and notes in the den, the latest laptop's fan kicking on, Jesus explained to his brother their next mission, as had become his custom even though he never received acknowledgment, let alone reply. "Augustus Hamilton," he said, pointing to a grainy, black-and-white printout of a middle-aged man, trim, unremarkably balding, cropped from a photograph of some promotional event. "He's close by and relatively easy to track. We can bring him here. Take advantage of the seclusion."

Joaquin might have asked any number of questions. What does this one do? Why does this one deserve to die? Jesus read from a dossier he had prepared: "Pedophile. Watches child pornography. Has taken advantage of kids before. Always goes out of state to avoid suspicion." He folded the paper, creased it.

"Apparently, he got lucky before—his buddies online tipped him off to a sting. But that luck won't last long. We'll set up a honey pot for him. One he won't be able to resist."

It didn't take long. As Joaquin waited in that blood-soaked house, more of it running down the walls and pooling over the floor every day, Jesus made his moves online. He had set up accounts on Pink House's various forums, mingling with the users, playing at knowledge of their "celebration," their "god." Most of the users were degenerates like Hamilton and the trophy wife, taking advantage of the group's dark-web resources and connections, but there were some who sounded surprisingly like Mildred had. They were the ones obviously swayed by the religious rhetoric, the talk of a coming new age, the promise of release from bodily confinement, salvation from pain and suffering. Jesus hated these more than the others. While the degenerates were disgustingly, transparently evil, the zealous types were pitiful, pathetic. They did evil unwittingly, misguidedly—killed innocents and took fingers for nothing, absolutely nothing.

"Wastes of skin," he said one stormy night, clenching and unclenching his fists, watching the lightning blaze in the dark distance. "Wastes of bone."

He sent Hamilton an offer: sixteen-year-old boy, virgin, Hispanic. Took a lot to procure him, he typed. But he's ready. Docile. Will do anything you want. Won't say a word.

not sure. too close for me.

I've prepared that, too. We're isolated. Nearest town is miles away. I'll guide you.

They waited for him outside the same motel where they had met Mildred. Jesus leaned against his truck, smoking a cigarette, watching the sun vanish below the horizon. Hamilton drove up in a SUV far too expensive for the area. He shuffled out in conspicuous baseball cap and suspicious windbreaker, like he only knew "incognito" from what he saw in the movies. He bent his long neck awkwardly, avoiding Jesus's gaze, moving towards him as though eager to hide a monstrous deformity. Jesus crushed his cigarette under his boot.

"You're late," he said.

"You weren't kidding about it being isolated." Hamilton peeked at him from under the visor of the cap. "Is he here?"

"You have the money?"

"Show me first."

"Of course." Jesus opened the truck door, the interior lights fading on to reveal Joaquin limp and silent in the passenger seat.

Hamilton snuffled. "He even alive?"

"He's warm. And he won't fight back. Or do you have a different preference?"

"That's fine. It's what we agreed." He withdrew a bundle of cash from his windbreaker. "Here it is. Are we ready now?"

"Sure. No need to be impatient." Jesus climbed inside his truck. "Follow me."

They drove down the same dark roads as when they followed Mildred. Jesus watched the headlights of the SUV bounce along in the rearview mirror. "Funny what we do," he said. "He must be thinking about turning around. But it's too good to pass up. Too good to be true."

Joaquin sat beside him. He said nothing in response.

They arrived at the farmhouse. Under the floodlights, Jesus held the door open while Hamilton walked inside. He coughed and gagged. "It stinks! What's in here?"

"Just you," said Jesus, and he wrapped the wire around Hamilton's neck until the flesh turned blue.

In the shed behind the farmhouse, lanterns throwing wraithlike shadows upon the walls, Jesus dumped a pail of water onto the bound, blindfolded Hamilton. Standing in the corner of the shed, Joaquin watched as Hamilton sputtered to life, retching and blubbering. "What happened?" he cried. "Where am I? Who's there?"

"It's me, Augustus," Jesus said, hunkering before him, regarding the premature wrinkles and receding hairline with contempt. "You should have turned around. I guess your worst self won the fight."

"You fucker!" Hamilton screamed. "You don't know what you're doing! You're screwing with the wrong guy!"

"No. I'm pretty sure I have the right one." Jesus spun the tip of his knife in circles on the shed's rotted wooden floor. "Here's the deal, Augustus. I have some questions I need answered, and if I like the answers, I'll let you go. You'll never see me again, and I won't let it slip that you have a thing for kids. How's that?"

"I don't need to answer a damn thing, you—"

Jesus slashed him across the cheek. Hamilton howled.

"Christ! You son of a bitch!"

"It'll be your ears next. Then your eyes. Your fucking balls." He pressed the knife against Hamilton's crotch, the khakis damp with urine. "I'm not playing around. You feel that? I let it slip, and there goes Auggie, Jr."

"Okay!" Hamilton shouted. "Okay! What do you want to know?"

"Pink House," Jesus said. "What is it? Who started it?"

"I don't know any of that," Hamilton said. "It's just a site—like the new Silk Road. You can buy drugs, guns—"

"Kids."

Hamilton scoffed. "What are you, some kind of vigilante? How the fuck would I know who made it?"

"There's more going on there. They're talking about some kind of celebration. What is that? Where's it going to be held?"

"Oh, God," moaned Hamilton. "You're one of those. One of the crazies."

"What do you mean?"

"You think I'm one of them? Taking fingers and who knows what else?"

"You've been there long enough. You must know something."

"I know you should stay out of it." Hamilton's slob-ridden lips widened in a smirk. "They say the people who go to those celebrations, they don't come back. If that's where you're headed, you're going to end up the same."

"You're wrong. Because I'm going to kill them all."

"You're going to kill them?" Hamilton laughed, cackled. "You're going to *kill them*? You idiot. They *want* to die! You'd be doing them a favor!"

Jesus stood up. "One more question. What is the 'room of cloth'? Some kind of kill room? Is that where the celebration is going to be?"

"Why don't you go see for yourself," Hamilton said. "Just let me go. I don't have anything else to tell you. Take the money if you want. Just let me go."

"I would if I could," Jesus said, "but I'm short two fingers."

Joaquin watched. Even though Jesus drove the knife into Hamilton's chest, even though he unmistakably pierced his heart, Hamilton didn't die. He looked up, his face an ashy pale, his eyes pitch black. His mouth extended in a hoarse, static-heavy scream, not even a scream, more like white noise, impossible for any human to emit. Blood gushed from his wound, rising around him, rising around their ankles, rising to their knees. Jesus, oblivious, severed and bagged the finger as usual. Hamilton, still screaming, forever screaming, pointed past him. Joaquin followed the finger, gazed up into the never-ending darkness of the shed's ceiling, a darkness that was far, far deeper than it should have been, a darkness that was not darkness at all but something else, somewhere else. Chains rattled. A bell tolled. Joaquin turned back to Hamilton, but the brittle, ghastly figure was gone. Only the thick, stinking layer of blood remained.

Outside, Jesus doused his knife in alcohol, wiped it down with an oil-stained rag. Would he break now? Would he betray any pressure or tiredness? He paused, rubbed his eyes—and then he was perfectly composed again, grimacing like always. He sheathed the knife along his belt.

"Let's eat something. I'm starving."

Joaquin lingered in the doorway of the shed, staring at the space where Hamilton had lain. His brother didn't think of them as people. No doubt it was easier to imagine them as just accumulations of all their sins, monsters wearing human skin who did only bad things, horrific things. That they begged and bartered for their lives was a non-factor. Monsters didn't do those things. They couldn't.

Jesus called to him. "Joaquin. Come on."

He didn't move. Jesus called again. At length, he turned and joined his brother.

They ate at the kitchen table, illuminated only by candle-light. Bowls of baked beans. Bottles of water. Their every meal indistinguishable from the previous, from the next.

"We can't stay here anymore," Jesus said. "Maybe we've stayed too long already."

Joaquin ate his beans silently.

"That's four. One more, and we'll have enough."

Silence. The candle flames quivered.

"He was a pedophile," Jesus said. "I saw his posts. He liked them younger than you."

Joaquin continued eating. He didn't look up.

"I didn't want to use you. I would never have let him touch you. Never."

If Joaquin had been able to speak, he may have reassured his brother that he did not resent him. He may have disapproved of the killing. He may have been able to convince Jesus to stop, if not for ethical reasons, perhaps practical ones. But there was nothing he could do or say, locked in that dark, desolate theater, watching the men slink inside for the hundredth or maybe even the thousandth time, their pale masks like their skulls on the outside, the smeared blood across the porcelain like fascia.

That night, after Jesus buried Hamilton out in the field, he soaked the den of the house in gasoline, doused the stairs, dumped liberally in the upstairs room where the doorway had been. He and Joaquin watched the house light up, the flames lapping at the stars above. Jesus stared, the machinery of his mind calculating, computing next steps. His mind was like clockwork—that was what Joaquin had always thought. A clockwork mind that never fell behind, never skipped forward. Emotionless, he always assumed. Dispassionate. But the flames that flickered across Jesus's vision, that crackled and plumed in the dark of his irises, hardly captured the reality of the inferno surrounding his mechanical, clockwork mind. The machine burnt red-hot, grinding out its computations, processing ever-new requests and details. In a blackened wasteland of blood and brimstone, beset by dust storms miles high and pillars of raging fire, the clockwork mind refined its plan for the eradication of Pink House.

5.

They were on the road again the next day, rumbling down the interstate in the '97 Ford, moving on to some new destination, some new person to kill.

Time was flimsy for Joaquin now. Sitting in front of therapists and counselors. Leaving behind the house. Moving in with his brother. Some of these blurry, hazy memories found their way into the repeating reel of his parents' murders. His real life, diseased and amputated, had been replaced by a dreamlike prosthetic life, an absurd comedy of murder and crime. Occasionally, other instances of that old life flickered onto the screen of his mind. A friend from high school. A childhood Christmas present. A girl he liked. His mother, alive and laughing. His father. Jesus. Short flashes that inspired a faint, muted longing. He felt little otherwise—little fear, little happiness, little excitement. The anxiety towards the future was gone. The insecurity about how attractive or intelligent he was had disappeared. Maybe because there was no longer a future, no longer peers to whom he could compare himself. This road trip, punctuated by pit stops of violence, broken by detours into blood and filth, was his new, never-ending present. He wondered if Jesus had been imagining this prosthetic life since he first heard the news about their parents. Plotting his vengeance. Picturing the countless ways he would murder the killers.

"I've been inside Pink House for months," he told Joaquin in the low light of that first motel room, musty and papered in floral. "Killing Mom and Dad was their ticket. They think if they do this, they'll see something. See God. Mom and Dad were just meat to them. Something to cut up on an altar. And what they did to you. That doesn't get to be forgiven."

Joaquin listened to him. The white flowers on the walls grew red and bloated. The carpet grew dank with blood.

Jesus explained to him afterwards what they would do. Participate in the ritual themselves. Kill as many as they could in the process. Gather information along the way. He unfolded the first list of aliases and addresses. Scrawled next to each name was a note. Old. Pedophile. Trafficker. Parent. Voyeur. Killer. Single. Rapist. Addict. Circled names indicated easier targets. Some names were crossed out. Too difficult or too time-consuming. They didn't have the time, Jesus kept saying. Once they started, they had to finish it. The police would be too hard to avoid. Covering their tracks would become impossible.

"The guys who killed Mom and Dad," he said as they reviewed the list, "are they on here? Maybe. Maybe not. But they'll be at that ceremony. They wouldn't miss that chance."

He had balled his hands into fists, crushing the paper, crushing the names.

The ceremony. The "celebration." If one completed the initiation, if one bloodied himself or herself enough, God would appear there. And these people, the crazies of Pink House, were ravenous to meet God. They dreamed of it. They fantasized about it. Every moment, asleep or awake, was consumed by the thought. What was He like? What would He tell them? What would they learn? The many posts and pictures and messages—white text on black; grainy footage of bodies bound and corpses chained; masks streaked with red—all reeked of desperation and desire. God was waiting for them. God was pining for them.

They talked about a room, those most devoted acolytes. They whispered in their forums, exchanged codes and ciphers in their chatrooms, across their apps. Have you seen it? A room of cloth, where their god waits. A room purple and heaving. A room red and bleeding. A room of gears and gases, steaming, hissing, burning. A room of tissue and tendon, swelling, quivering, dripping. Layers of bone and steel in endless corridors and antechambers. Lightless, foul-smelling, a labyrinth of cartilage and viscera. The god's vassals wandered the pits and valleys, their chains fastened tight. Did they wonder how they got there? Did they remember?

There were tales of gateways into the room of cloth. Caves or holes deep within dense forests, hidden by moss and vegetation, but the signs around them still there after decades and sometimes even centuries of decay, etched into stone, carved into rock. Doors in abandoned warehouses and tenement houses, dirty with dry, aged blood. If one traveled through, he or she could cross dimensions, break barriers. Jesus read these stories, recounted them to Joaquin, and thought inevitably of Mildred Haynes, how she murdered her son, how she offered him up to a door leading nowhere. He thought of the men who butchered his parents, how they crept in the shadows of their own doorway, how they trailed their fingers over the wood. In those moments, Joaquin saw how his brother's skin would flush, felt how his blood would boil. His research was like a well, keeping his rage watered and healthy, eternally burning. Eternally ready.

Apparently, finding or creating a gateway wasn't enough—the gateways had to be unlocked. The key to crossing could be found in the construction of artifacts and totems. There were paintings and pieces of music that appeared ordinary on the surface but actually belied a deeper reality. Encrypted in literature could be strings of words and turns of phrase that, once deciphered, enabled higher perception. Encoded within the figurative DNA of these works was a Fibonacci sequence, the supposed signature of Pink House's god. Like a miracle, the influence revealed itself to those fortunate to bear witness. Those chosen became vectors. The code burrowed beneath their skin and demanded to be spread. No one could resist, whether miserable addict or lonely pariah or industry titan—all bowed before the room of cloth.

Pink House promised things. We can help you. He can help you. Set you free. Show you the truth. Everyone is welcome. No one is turned away. Click HERE. Watch THIS. Jesus followed the links, exposing himself to many of these images and texts that were supposedly the product of religious inspiration. What did he have to lose? None of it was true, of course, none of it really inspired or supernatural, but he had to understand them, these people who murdered his parents, who killed their own family members for nothing. He took extensive notes, amassing journals full of everything he saw. The documents he read were average at best: journal entries, poems, none of it with any kind of discernible motif. The images made more of an impression. Some were bizarre—spirals, fractals, like the interior of a cell or the rings of Saturn. Most were more mundane. Landscapes. Forestry. Unremarkable, not even well shot. But there were others, strangely unnerving despite how everyday they seemed. A family of four in matching Christmas sweaters. Freckled, blushing teens in a photo booth at prom. Young women taking selfies in the mirror. One such picture stuck with him. A pale girl, probably nineteen or twenty. Her head tilted to one side. Gray sky behind her, the edge of a frothing waterfall. Smiling through her braces. Smiling as though she had her entire life ahead of her. lucy.jpg. One link out of hundreds like it.

Jesus couldn't explain the strange pull of these pictures. In any other context, they would have been perfectly normal, not worth a first glance, let alone a second. Joaquin, peeking over his shoulder, saw what they really hid. The literal darkness of the family's eyes. The teen couple's yawning mouths. Even Lucy. What would Jesus have thought of her if he knew how she really looked, how big her smile really was? Even her parents had never seen her so happy.

Jesus would not admit to his brother his morbid curiosity to know more about the insanity that animated these people—he felt like an onlooker at a zoo, like a wanderer passing through a traveling circus. One night before the first kill, before the trophy wife's throat was cut and her body left to rot in the landfill, Joaquin awoke in the dark of their motel room. The only light was that of Jesus's laptop monitor. Jesus sat rigid, staring into the screen, his face in the glow of the monitor unflinching, expressionless. Joaquin watched. The monitor revealed a nondescript hallway, white-walled, floored with cracked wood, the only light that of the video camera, bobbing with each step. A sideboard draped with lace. Photographs of a family, a wedding, an anniversary. A vase of wilted flowers. The video static-ridden, timestamped: DEC 15 2002, 12:41:36, 12:41:37, 12:41:38. Battery at half-life. Every step like a lifetime. A door at the end, shrouded in shadow. Scarred, blackened wood. The door opens. The video blurs. Red on the other side. Writhing. Screaming.

Jesus closed his laptop. He wiped his brow, held his head in his hands. Joaquin kept watching. From under the bed extended his mother's bloody, scarred arms. She coiled around the legs of Jesus's chair. From the closet opposite, their father's gray, eyeless face emerged. Black blood ran from the tattered eye sockets. The mouth stretched in an eternal, gaping cry. Both phantoms turned towards Joaquin. His mother was also eyeless. The pits were dark. Her teeth were gray and beaten, like stones. The skin on her face was sliding off, falling in strips like wet paper. Hooks were tethered into the decrepit flesh of their arms and legs and necks, chains reaching into the infinite shadows of the room. Joaquin's heart rammed in his chest, but he could make no sound. He could not even move.

When finally he shut his eyes and reopened them, they were gone. He did not see them again that night.

Jesus never mentioned the video of the hallway, never discussed the red room at its end. But he kept watching others like it, and Joaquin watched from behind. Videos of children drowned by their parents, their hands, heads, and feet severed, their blood encircling doorways, their meat offered up. Couples painting themselves in black and blue ink, etching manacles around their wrists, cuffs around their ankles, ropes around their necks, laughing as though they were feeding themselves slices of wedding cake. Empty rooms. Barren corridors. Exhumed graves. Then there were the typical, expected images of gore: gouged eyes, slit wrists, burnt bodies. "They're crazy," Jesus would say again and again, clicking through the galleries and following the links nonetheless, unaware that behind him, Joaquin would see what was left of those killed, their shadowy wraiths pointing just like Hamilton had. He would see the shadows of the motel rooms slink away like chains, would see the walls run red, hear them scream as though they were alive. He would watch his parents—what was left of his parents— grope and stumble towards their older son, reaching out, never able to say what they wanted to say, never able to make contact. They would turn to Joaquin in contorted expressions of misery, wrestling against their chains, struggling against their ropes. Bound to that other place. Unable to escape.

When they slept, held against his brother's chest, Joaquin sometimes gleaned impressions from Jesus, snapshots of memories that flitted across his senses. The dry scent of the desert. The hot buffet of shrapnel whizzing past. The weight of his helmet, vest, and gloves. The heft and comfort of his rifle. The ace of spades nestled within his sleeve. His two tours seemed encapsulated in these vivid moments—dark and humid and throbbing. Shapes in the smoke. Howls in the night.

On the road, Jesus talked a lot about their parents, shared stories Joaquin hadn't heard, stories from when Jesus was still the only son, when nothing had crystallized yet. He filled the long stretches of highway with his high-school escapades, his boot-camp vignettes. He reminisced about their father's favorite vinyls, their mother's beloved dresses. "Mom was a reader," he said as they drove through the rain down another interstate. "Not me, though. She tried real hard. Nothing stuck. I needed to be doing something, working with my hands. A bike or an engine. I was putting together circuits when I was thirteen. I couldn't help myself."

Talking. Always talking. Talking more than he ever had before their lives had been diseased and amputated. An occasional long bout of silence—the eyes calculating, the rage simmering—and then more talking. Joaquin listened inasmuch as he was able to listen. He heard his brother's words, even pictured sometimes the dresses, the oil-streaked gaskets, the last of Jesus's girlfriends to sit at their dinner table. But something was in the way. Something muffling him, clouding the picture. Like living behind frosted glass or soundproof walls. Pushing his hands against cloth. Straining. Suffocating.

They slept in the truck that night. Rather, Jesus slept. Joaquin lay awake, listening to the howls of the wind and the coyotes. Beside him, his brother mumbled, trembled. His arms sometimes flew up in small spasms. Whiffs of that desert smoke reached Joaquin, followed by flashes of gunfire, rumbles of thunder. At last, Joaquin closed his eyes. The interior of the truck gave way to that familiar abyss of blood, that room of skin and bone. The room of cloth.

Time was flimsy for Joaquin now. Which video had been first, which image, which motel room, which kill? When had they followed Mildred to her house? When had they lured out

Hamilton? When did Tyler first whisper to him in the night? When did those three men shatter the window and drink and laugh and smear the blood of his parents across his face?

The only constants were the walls of blood, the hisses of steam, the grins of ghosts. His parents called to him, clawing from the edge of a yawning, swirling pit. Mildred reached out to him. Tyler flailed on the dark shore. Hamilton pointed and gaped at the oncoming red star, always bigger, always closer. Too big. Too close.

A bell tolled again. The celebration drew near.

6.

<hr>

One gray morning, they sat in a fast-food restaurant, the floor sticky, the air thick with the smells of bacon and coffee. Through smeared glass, Joaquin watched as children chased one another around the indoor playground, disappearing into a blue plastic tunnel and emerging from a red tube somewhere above, tripping over untied shoelaces, hanging from monkey bars. Had he been able, he could have recounted similar memories from his youth, relived times when he chased friends around slides and dove into ball pits. Of course, it was impossible now. The plastic tunnels and slides overflowed with blood. The children climbed into meat grinders.

Jesus worked on his latest laptop, his gaze so hard the screen might have melted. He took sporadic sips of black coffee, bit sparingly at a long-cold croissant. He drank little, ate less. Maybe he had learned to live off scraps in the desert, but he never said. "What was it like?" Joaquin asked him when he came home from the first tour. The look he received in response—the look of disappointment, the one he had hated since he was young, that he had feared more than those of his parents— taught him never to ask again.

A woman approached their booth. Olive-skinned, with heavy mascara, black hair pulled back. A dripping cross tattooed along her forearm.

"Excuse me, sir. You served?"

Jesus didn't look up at first. Then his eyes swerved her way.

"I saw your dog tags," she said. "I just wanted to thank you. My grandfather served, and my father, too. Thank God for all you keeping us safe. We're blessed."

Jesus touched the dog tags around his neck, one of them dented. He shook his head. "I'm sorry, ma'am. These are my dad's."

"Oh." The woman hesitated. "Well, please give him my thanks. Bless him."

"I wish I could. He passed earlier this year."

"I'm so sorry to hear that."

"Thank you, ma'am."

She shuffled for a moment under his intense, unblinking stare. When she walked away, Jesus returned to the laptop. He felt his brother's eyes on him.

"It's not about me," he said. "We have to honor them. Mom and Dad."

Joaquin's blank eyes flicked down. He turned back to the playground.

"I know they wouldn't want us lying," Jesus said. "They were proud of what I was doing. But I was out there when I should have been here."

Something in his tone lingered, a plea for acknowledgment, for pardon. But Joaquin could not give him those things. He watched from behind his eyes as the masked men wrenched out his mother's tongue for what might have been the thousandth time.

Back at their latest motel room, this one rose-scented and pink-carpeted, somewhere in eastern Texas, Jesus sat on the bed and unfolded the most recent dossier.

"Michael Allen," he said. "Also known as RazerHead. He pays money to vote on how girls get raped or killed." He paused, rubbed his eyes. "But he's single, lives alone. Shouldn't have any problems getting it done."

Joaquin sat on the bed beside him, said nothing.

"We'll scope it out tomorrow. We won't be able to hide this one easily. But once we have it, we'll be able to get a ticket to the celebration. And then it'll be over. All right?"

He put his hand on Joaquin's shoulder, a rare demonstration of reassurance, affection. But his voice sounded less confident. Increasingly, his face and tone had started betraying the hidden exhaustion, the toll of the many miles, the piling bodies. As Jesus showered, Joaquin watched the television: newscasts and infomercials, rains and floods. Static overtook the screen. A shape flickered in the snow, writhed amid the white noise. His heart quickened. His brow dampened. Even dulled, the sight of that obscured, furious form inspired a primal dread. A bell tolled again, followed by others. Those gray, eyeless faces crowded the screen until there was no static at all. Dark, viscous blood draped the walls, pooled over the carpet, invaded the bed.

The next morning, they drove into the city, bought bagels and coffee, then parked across the street from Allen's condominium and waited. Jesus scribbled in his notebook: how many neighbors, how many cameras, the frequency of cops. Calculations took place behind his eyes. Risks were weighed. Allen himself came out twice, short and lean with glasses and dark hair, more a stereotypical geek at first glance than an online sadist. He set a bowl of food down for a stray cat. He took out his garbage. All the time, Jesus took notes.

They repeated that ritual twice more. On the third day, mid-afternoon, Jesus snapped the notebook closed. "Okay," he said. "I think we're ready." Before they returned to the motel, they stopped at an electronics store. Jesus sold his current laptop, bought a smaller, older model. "Not much money left," he remarked. "Running low."

That evening, he paced the motel parking lot, smoking his nightly cigarette. He prodded at the newest license plates on the truck, testing their give. In the motel room, he arranged their bag, the other accessories. Then he sat next to his silent, expressionless brother. He put a hand on the boy's arm and held it there. Joaquin took no comfort from the gesture. He needed no reassurance, desired no solace. But when Jesus kicked off his boots and shambled away to the shower, breathing heavily, it was clear the gesture wasn't meant for Joaquin at all.

The next morning, the brothers stood outside Allen's condo. Jesus rang the buzzer.

After a moment, the door opened, and Allen peered out. "Uh, yeah? Can I help you?"

"RazerHead, right?" Jesus asked. He put on a smile, reached into his jacket, and brought out a package wrapped in butcher paper. "I brought your order."

Allen's eyes widened. "What the fuck, dude! You don't just come to the door!" He ushered the brothers inside. The condo was dark, blue drapes covering the windows, an electric fan running loudly in the corner. On the wall hung a magazine spread of a supermodel. A blacklight shone underneath. Joaquin caught sight of the computer tower in the back room, saw his reflection in the wide-screen monitor. Saw the pale reflections of the others with them, too.

Allen rolled a cigarette. "I was supposed to pick that up tomorrow night. What are you doing here? And who's this guy?"

"He's my brother," said Jesus. "Sorry. Nowhere to leave him right now."

"What's his problem?" Allen snapped his fingers in Joaquin's face, waved his hand in front of the vacant eyes. "He retarded or something?"

"He's mute."

"He's freaking me out, man. And you should really leave. This your first time?"

"Sorry."

"You're gonna screw us both. How'd you even find my address? I never gave it to you."

"That's right. You didn't."

Allen looked at him, stared into the unsmiling, unblinking face, and right as the recognition filled his eyes, the knife pierced his gut. He gasped, pressed his hands against his bleeding abdomen, watched his white shirt turn red.

"Fuck—what the fuck—"

He stumbled away, left bloody handprints along the wall. In the restroom, he threw open the medicine cabinet, cast aside gauze and alcohol and toothpaste, never found what he was looking for. Jesus loomed behind him.

"Okay, okay!" Allen crawled back into the space between the toilet and tub. He raised a shaky hand. "Stop! Please, just fucking stop! What do you want? Huh? What the fuck do you want? Money? You want more money?"

"Information," Jesus said. "Everything you know about Pink House. The room of cloth."

"Goddamn." Allen wiped his face, smeared his glasses with blood and sweat. "You're one of them? What the fuck, man—I haven't done anything! I stay out of that shit, believe me!"

"Haven't done anything? How much did you pay to see that last girl's teeth broken?"

"Oh, fuck. Oh, God." Allen coughed, clasped his blood-soaked shirt against his wound. "I don't know shit, man. That ain't me."

Jesus knelt down, grabbed one of Allen's hands. He pinched the ring finger. "How's this one? Or do you want me to take another?"

Allen moaned. Sweat drenched his blanched face. "Fuck me. You *are* one of them. Gonna carve me up, you fucking psycho? You and your retard brother? You wanna see him so bad, you should just kill yourselves!"

Jesus pressed harder on the finger. "See who?"

"You know who! You pray to him, you psycho! That's the whole point! You all want to be fucking noticed so bad, but he doesn't discriminate! Doesn't matter if you're smart or fat or slow, he'll take you all—"

"Shut up." Jesus stabbed him in the chest, in the neck, in the chest again. "Just shut up."

Allen's eyes went dark, his body limp. Jesus dropped the knife and backed away. He shook out a cigarette from his pocket. "Joaquin, go to the truck. Get the bag."

Behind him, Joaquin did nothing. He stared at the gray, eyeless faces in the blood pooling around Allen's body, at their black, toothless maws. He stared as the blood covered the floor and ran down the walls.

"*Joaquin*. Go to the truck. Get the bag."

This time, he did as told. When he came back with the bag, he found Jesus squatting by the sink, wiping his hands with a towel, smoking the cigarette. In the mirror, their parents watched without eyes, with skin like fractured stone. The darkness behind them swelled.

Jesus cut and bagged the finger. Joaquin watched from the hall. When he heard a moan to his right, he turned and saw Allen crawling out from the shadows of the computer room, gray-skinned and dragging blood. His lips moved as if trying to say something, but only hoarse whispers came out.

The rest of the day was devoted to cleanup. Jesus severed head from torso, hand from arm, foot from leg, stowed the pieces in garbage bags. He bleached the tub, toilet, and tile. He scrubbed the walls clean. In the computer room, he unplugged the tower, packed away a trove of hard drives. No pictures anywhere. Nothing suggestive of a life outside that condo. He surveyed the mattress, regarded the mess of porn magazines. He wanted to spit, but thought against it.

Joaquin waited by the blacklight. Tyler stood next to him, whispered his intelligible static into his ear. Mildred hovered. Hamilton pointed, straining his finger, gasping for acknowledgment. Allen joined them, forever coughing, forever bleed-ing.

Everything went in the back of the truck. Nothing was left behind. Joaquin followed his brother out, but he looked back, almost as if he expected to see a face in the window, blood seeping from underneath the door. But there was nothing. As if they had never been there. As if Allen had never been killed. As if he had never even existed.

If Joaquin had been able, he might have laughed. Ghosts don't haunt places, he would have said, turning to the wraith of Tyler, the specter of his mother. They haunt people. That'd make a good twist for a movie.

In the night, out in some gray, dead field, Jesus buried the garbage bags. He burnt the bloody towels and carpets and warmed his hands over the fire. Joaquin stared at his face lit orange by the flames. He searched for more indications of stress or fracture, cracks in the foundation that would foretell collapse. But his brother's face had regained its rigidity. The eyes were calculating and robotic. The fire reflected in them burnt bright.

Jesus dug through Allen's computer and hard drives. There were video files, some going back three years. He almost made it through one video before shutting it off. The look in the girl's eyes. Her screams. Misery and pain, but nothing that gave information about Pink House.

Days later, parked along a garbage-riddled, washed-out street, they waited. Jesus smoked, crushed the orange flicker of the cigarette stub into the dashboard. He looked out at the rain.

"Where do you want to go?" he asked.

Joaquin stared.

"I was thinking Florida." He kneaded his hands, popped his fingers. "A little place on the beach. Maybe get a boat. Get off the land."

They went inside. The warehouse reeked heavily of oil and mold. Soft, gray light filtered in through the dusty windows. The rain pattered on the tempered glass. Graffiti covered the walls: gang tags, skulls-and-bones, half-faces with red, snarling eyes. At the far end of the barren room was a crimson curtain some twenty feet in width.

Jesus approached the curtain, along the way withdrawing the plastic bag with the five fingers from his jacket. He waited, wrinkled his nose. There was a stench wafting from underneath the curtain. The stench of something dead.

Joaquin stayed behind and watched. In a corner of the warehouse, Hamilton lay in blood, pointing as usual. Tyler peeked from around a stack of boxes. Allen crawled at Jesus's feet, reaching for his legs, never finding purchase.

A cough from behind the curtain. The swivel of a chair. A voice, male and raspy, as though butchered by years of smoking. "Finally someone. You have 'em?"

"Yes," said Jesus. He looked around at the warehouse. "You could have picked a better place. And less conspicuous."

"I don't make the rules. Well, don't just stand there. Give 'em over."

Jesus passed the bag with the fingers through the curtain. There was another wheezing cough, the scrape of fingernails against weathered scalp.

"Are they good enough?" Jesus asked. "They said you needed five."

"Yeah, yeah. You should be grateful. Was ten once. Twelve. Six. Every time, different."

"I heard it wasn't always fingers."

"No. Was eyes one time. Pictures another. Always different." The man cleared his throat. "They're good. Clean."

Jesus said nothing.

"All by yourself?"

"Yes."

"Pretty good. Some of these guys, they're slipping around in guts and shit, crying. Takes a gang of 'em just to get one if they don't give up their own. I don't blame 'em. Never done anything like that except watch. Used to be you found the little places in person. You paid. You sat in an audience. Took real determination to get there. Now all these kids think you can just turn on a fucking computer."

The curtain parted, and a gray, mottled hand emerged with a red ticket stub between thumb and forefinger. "Here."

Jesus took the stub, turned it over. Etched upon the back were a date and a series of numbers. "Coordinates?"

"Look at a map. Or I guess a phone, huh?" The wheezing erupted into laughing and coughing in equal measure. "They tell me it's gonna be a big one this time. Putting on a show."

"What does that mean?"

"You should know already. You're here, ain't you?"

Jesus pocketed the stub. "Can I ask you something?"

"Sure. Ain't exactly busy."

"The place they're always talking about—the room of cloth. What is it?"

Allen clawed for him. Hamilton gasped, straining his pointing finger further. The stump where his severed finger had been was black and misshapen.

The man on the other side of the curtain paused. His nails scraped the dry scalp like sticks against stone. Thunder sounded far off.

"You don't know, do you?"

Jesus hesitated. He reached for his knife.

"I don't care one way or the other," the man said. "You earned your ticket. Me, I'm still getting my cash no matter what. But I'll give you a tip: don't ask that over there. You might as well be cutting your wrists in open water."

"You didn't answer the question."

"That's 'cause there's nothing to answer. There's no room."

That night, the brothers slept in the truck in the middle of a desolate, amber-lit parking lot. Jesus studied the ticket stub. He had plugged the coordinates into his laptop earlier. Louisiana. Swampland. Fitting for a graveyard.

He looked over his brother sleeping uneasily and touched the trembling head. In his mental theater, Joaquin watched Jesus kill Mildred, torture Hamilton, maim Allen. Again and again, the knife found its mark. The ashen forms of Mildred and Allen crawled around his chair, shifting in and out of the fog hovering over the floor. His parents, one tongueless, the other eyeless, struggled against their chains. Hamilton pointed. The red star approaching. The theater dimming, darkening, growing rancid with the stink of blood.

Hey guys. Longtime lurker but only made my account recently. Don't post often but something weird's going on and I'm starting to get pretty rattled.

I teach at a local college, adjuncting while I look into Ph.D. programs. (Market's glutted, but that's another story.)

I get along pretty well with my students. I guess they relate to me because we're relatively close in age. One girl, "Becca," has been coming by the office a lot to talk about her program. She's poli sci, too, so I give her advice about professors to take, etc. She has a habit of writing things down on sticky notes, little reminders for herself. Her notebook's covered in them, pinks and purples and yellows with little hearts as borders. I've had to pick up more than a few that she's dropped.

Becca isn't the happiest girl, but she keeps herself busy. Juggles a couple of jobs because I think the mom's on disability? But over the last couple of weeks, I noticed something off with her. She looked more tired than usual, seemed on edge. The last time I talked with her, she was really nervous, saying "he" was looking for her, waiting for her. She wouldn't tell me much more than that, but I was worried. Maybe she had a stalker?

It didn't sit well with me, but I'm an adjunct, my hands are tied. I filed a wellness report with the college's advisory center and tried to get past it. That was three weeks ago. Becca never came back to class, and then a week ago, word got around the office: Becca was dead. Took her own life.

I wish that were the end of it. That would have been enough. Wondering if I didn't do more was eating at me. But it wasn't the end. It was just the start.

We have a staff common area where we can pick up mail that gets redirected to the college. Students also turn in papers there depending on what the professor asks for. I don't really use mine but occasionally I get some ads, promotions for grad programs, etc. so I let things stack for a bit.

Anyway, a few days ago someone tells me the room is starting to smell really bad, and they think it's coming from my mail slot. When I went in, sure enough, there was a really bad smell. I can't really describe it as anything other than stale, rotten meat. (If you've ever been in a butcher's shop, it's almost exactly like that. My dad used to take me to the local meat shop, and I'd always get whiffs of it from behind the counter.)

I look through the slot, and there's not really anything weird at first (I thought maybe an animal was in there or rotten food, crazy but what else could be giving off that smell?) and that's when I found this dusty CD sleeve stuck between some papers.

I took the sleeve out and immediately felt grossed out. It was sticky, like someone spilled soda on it. But there weren't any stains. I thought the smell was coming from the sleeve, but when I opened it up it was coming from the CD actually. I don't know how or why, but the CD just smelt like rotten meat. I can't explain it.

That's when I noticed the note stuck to the back of the sleeve. A regular yellow sticky note. Nothing special or strange. Except the little hearts on the border. Except the handwriting.

Hi prof. Everything's better now! Hope to see you soon. Love, Becca. :)

My mouth went dry. Even my heart might have stopped for a second. I'd picked up enough of Becca's notes to know she wrote this one— there was no mistake. But Becca was dead. IS dead. I saw the obit in the newspaper. I even thought about going to the funeral. We had a vigil for her for Christ's sake. But here was her handwriting.

I probably should have thrown it out. Maybe I should have gone to the police. But curiosity got the better of me and I took it home. When I looked at the CD more closely, I saw it's not a CD but actually a DVD, an old Memorex DVD (not sure if anyone remembers the brand). I distinctly remember them because my parents used to save old home videos on them. In fact, I almost thought it WAS one of the old videos they saved since there's a date on it in black ink: 11-25-92. On the top there's a title that's blacked out.

I have a detachable drive lying around that I use to play some old movies, so I hooked it up and put the DVD in. I half-expected it to be dead but it worked. And there was a video on it. It was just called "HALL" which I thought was weird, not even an event or holiday.

Of course I played it. It was a short clip, just 11 seconds, half of it basically too dark to see anything. There's this semi-loud hum in the background, kind of like an overactive AC unit. Then near the end, the camera pans over this door that's slightly open. There's this hard red light coming from behind the door (really red, like blood). This is when the video starts artifacting, bugging out. Then it just ends. You can't see anything past the door.

I exported the video and put it on Youtube if anyone's curious. I also took some footage of the DVD, just some angles of the front and back.

But the bigger question is where it came from. Becca couldn't have sent this DVD to me. It's not possible. Maybe she left it there before she died, but the smell is so intense, no one could have missed it.

The weirdest thing? I smell that meat stink everywhere. On my clothes, in my hair. No matter how much I shower. People are looking at me weird at work, saying I stink, that I'm tired. And when I go to sleep, I see the door. No, I don't just see the door. I'm RECORDING the door, like in the video. I'm walking towards it.

I don't think it matters if I get rid of the DVD. I think it's too late. Something's with me now. Something's IN me now. Something that Becca had, too. I don't know what. But I don't know how many more nights I have left before I open the door and see what's on the other side.

EDIT: Thanks for all the comments. Some of you are wondering about the date and quality. Honestly I don't know either. I'm thinking the original footage was maybe recorded in 92 and then transferred over to the disc? Maybe it was cleaned up? But why use a DVD now if it's recent?

I also didn't know that there might be more data on the DVD so I took time to clean it and played it more. Eventually there WAS something else that came up. It's two short clips of what looks like water, but it's red. I don't want to think it's blood, but especially with that smell, I get this sick feeling looking at it. Like it's not water but meat. Wriggling meat.

(One of you said the smell might be the ink on the disc, but I don't know. I almost feel like the smell's on me now.)

Anyway. There's a sound in the background of the red water video. Breathing. Breathing and then crying. Some woman crying. I grabbed that footage, too, but I'm honestly shaking just typing this.

THE CELEBRATION

7 .

"We're going to a friend of mine," Jesus said when they were on the road again. "Jackson Smith. We served together. You'll like him. Smiles more than I do."

They drove for what seemed like hours, Jesus talking once again, this time about their grandfather, whom Joaquin never met. Manuel Rodolfo Alarcón-Menchaca. Born in 1920, come from Monterrey to New Mexico at the age of ten with his parents, enlisting in the military at eighteen, going on to serve in the Pacific Theater during the Second World War. Meeting their grandmother in Texas, a beauty by the name of Velma Graves. Settling with her back in New Mexico. Raising five children. Dying to a stroke months before Joaquin was born. Their grandmother shredding petunias at his grave, following him seven years later.

"She came from Abilene," Jesus said as they ate dry cereal by the roadside. Across from them, a lake shone in the early morning. Ducks broke the water, flew off. "We could go through there. See where she lived. She loved you, you know that? You were the favorite. Between us and the ones in Florida, you were the favorite. Me? I never even got a smile."

He seemed uneager to leave the roadside. Joaquin studied him again for the signs of collapse, but the intensity returned, the focus. Jesus saw red again, and so did his brother.

More stories of the family. More stories of the past. Jesus talked more and more, sometimes nervously, sometimes frantically. If Joaquin could have processed the stories, he would have likely appreciated the insight into the grandfather he never knew, the grandmother he barely remembered. Velma had been a solemn woman of few words, hard to remove from her rocker, usually knitting until the arthritis froze her hands into crude, spider-like shapes. Where was she now? The same place as his teacher Mrs. Longoria, who passed from cancer? As Winona from sixth grade, who succumbed to a seizure? If Velma's son, his father, eyeless and decaying, was chained in that dark place where so many, too many, waited for that red star, what about the others? Was there another place they went? Or did everyone eventually end up in that abyss of blood? What would happen when they all went, everyone who had ever been alive, everyone who ever would be?

When they arrived at Jackson's home, it was late afternoon, the wind warm. The brick house was flanked by badly trimmed bushes, the yard yellowing at the edges. Jackson met them at the door. "Jesus Alarcón," he said with a smile. "As I live and breathe."

He was Black, with tender eyes, a fledgling beard. When Jesus had known him, there had been no beard, no tenderness in the eyes. The smile had been tense, expectant of that moment when the credits roll, when the curtain closes. When he led them inside, sandals slapping against tile, he limped. Not a bullet. Not shrapnel. Just a fall down a particularly steep cliff. Just an accident, a chance to come home.

"This is my brother," said Jesus. "His name's Joaquin."

"Nice to meet you, Joaquin." Jackson shook the limp hand, met the dull eyes. He hesitated.

"He can hear you," Jesus said. "He's there. But he can't speak."

"I get it." Jackson turned and looked up the nearby stairs. "Mallory! Hey, Mal?"

A woman came down the stairs, curly-haired, pregnant. Like Jackson, her smile was sweet, her eyes kind. Joaquin studied the pair and then studied his brother. Even among people so relaxed, even in a setting so tranquil, Jesus remained like a statue. There was the faintest glimmer in his eyes upon seeing Mallory. He shook her hand.

"Mal, this is the guy I was telling you about," said Jackson. "Jesus Alarcón. Bravest man I ever had the pleasure to work with. Couldn't ask for anyone better."

"I doubt that," replied Jesus.

"Nah, it's true. No fear. Or if you were afraid, you never showed it. That kept me going. Probably everybody else, too." Jackson gestured to Joaquin. "This is his brother. Doesn't speak, but he's listening to you. You want to take him to the kitchen, maybe get him a soda?"

"Of course." Mallory took Joaquin's hand. "Come on, sweetie. You want a cherry soda? Or maybe iced tea?"

She led him away. Jesus and Jackson stood alone in the foyer, listening to the grandfather clock down the corridor, watching the motes of dust in the evening light. "You're married," Jesus said, and Jackson nodded, said they had been high-school sweethearts. He was looking forward to being a father. After another pause, he smiled.

"Well, let's settle what you're here for."

In a closet under the stairs, he unlatched a mahogany case and unveiled the shotgun. Jesus tested its weight, felt its stock against his shoulder.

"It's clean," Jackson said.

Jesus lowered the weapon. "What about the rest?"

Jackson revealed twin pistols in a sideboard, several boxes of ammunition in an adjacent drawer. "Not the armory, but should be enough."

"I appreciate it. As for what I owe you—"

"Hey. I know better than to take a check from a man on the run."

Jesus was quiet. When he finished inspecting the weapons, they joined Mallory and Joaquin outside. The evening sun was low in the sky, bloody and dripping like a grapefruit. Joaquin sat quietly on the porch, his glass of tea untouched. He watched the oak tree in the yard, the branches straining under the weight of hollow-eyed corpses. Jesus followed his gaze but saw nothing. Just the tree. Just the red, fiery light. He wondered what his brother saw. He wondered if his brother would ever speak again.

They joined Jackson and Mallory for dinner. They shared stories, or rather, Jackson shared stories, not necessarily about the desert, but about boot camp, college, childhood. He discussed his passion for model airplanes, model trains, model cars. He squeezed Mallory's hand, narrating how he proposed, how she reacted. All the while, the Alarcón brothers listened. In his vague way, Joaquin considered only how different Jackson was to his brother, how different he would have been as a brother. Jesus, for all the talking he did when they were alone, would only make one- or two-word affirmatives during the dinner. He seemed impatient in that dining room, out of his element. Normally, when his fingers moved, they moved for blood.

He and Jackson sat out on the porch afterwards, chewing their coffee beans like they did back in the desert, admiring the faint shimmer of stars overhead. Crickets chirped. Far away, an owl hooted. "Cozy, isn't it?" asked Jackson. "Man, I'll tell you. The one thing I wanted when I was set up—you know, the one thing I really, really wanted, what I could have killed for when I realized I was coming home—was some goddamn triple-chocolate ice cream. It was all I could think about with my leg hung up. Fucking ice cream."

Jesus lit a cigarette. "You don't miss it?" he asked at length.

"Combat? Fuck no, brother. Fuck no. I got my fill."

Jesus nodded. He dragged. "I think about it a lot. Sometimes, it's Kent and Jameson. Sometimes, it's Kowalski. It's like I can't get away from it."

Jackson leaned in, grabbed another handful of beans. "What's going on, brother?"

"Things happened back there after you got out," Jesus said. "I started wondering what the hell I was doing."

"You went back."

"I did." Jesus flicked ashes into the dark. "But it was a mistake. Because the second time wasn't for us. It wasn't for Kent or Jameson or Kowalski. It was for me. And I paid for that."

"Jesus," said Jackson. "You know I don't like to preach. I don't know any better. But, man, whatever you're doing, you can stop it. Your brother in there, he needs to go home. He needs help. You need help. I know some people. It can be discreet."

"He was always quiet," Jesus said. "He was going to make movies. He had dreams. And they took it all from him."

"Who did?"

Jackson couldn't see Jesus smile in the darkness, but he could hear the relish in his voice. He could sense the electricity, the bloodlust.

"We were out there, and those people just wanted their homes back," said Jesus. "Some of them really did hate us. Do hate us. What we thought we were standing for. But I can understand them. I could sit with a so-called insurgent, and I could understand him. I know his language. You lose your home, or your family dies, and these people come in, claiming they have the answers, thinking they know best. Yeah, I would hate those people. I would want to kill them. I would do whatever it takes to see them gone."

Jackson sighed. "Brother, you can still go home. Leave the guns here."

"If you don't want me to have the guns, why get them for me?"

"I'm not about to insult you, either." Jackson smiled. "Believe it or not, I feel it, too. Some nights—nicer than this, even—I just want to pick up a gun again. But if I do that, if I let that go, I'm not the one who's gonna suffer. Because it's not about me. Every step of the way, it was someone else: my folks, you guys, Mal. Now my baby boy."

Jesus looked back at the house. He crushed his cigarette under the heel of his boot. "While you're out here preaching," he said, "what's the secret? How do you keep a woman like that? I could never hang on to one for even a month."

"Well, I didn't know you in your Casanova days," said Jackson, "but a little affection goes a long way. You don't let a plant go without water. Same principle."

In the night, Jesus lay with his brother in the guest bedroom. He listened to Joaquin's murmurs, felt his tremors. If he closed his eyes, he saw the trappings of his own mental landscape: the familiar swirls of dust, the usual plumes of smoke, the regular flashes of muzzle flare. To sleep, he defaulted to his usual strategy. He pictured with as much detail as possible his parents' murderers. He envisioned rough-hewn faces, stone-chiseled eyes, blood-drenched hands. He pursued them throughout the scorching smoke, fired upon them, shot out their legs. Up close, he strangled them. He carved out their hearts, scraped off their faces. Then again. And again after that. He slaughtered them brutally, endlessly, until at last he stood among a sea of mutilated bodies. Blood covered his hands, his arms, his legs, but he was all right with that. In that wasteland of darkness and raging fires, he felt at peace. In that wasteland, he could sleep.

They were back on the road the next day, back to the revolving motel rooms with their bland carpets and floral wallpapers. Whenever they drove, Joaquin stared out at the passing countryside, the distant turbines, the isolated farms. He saw Mildred gasping in the reflection of windows, saw Allen crawling over the crests of hills. Tyler lurked in the backseat, whispering to him constantly. He heard the words now. Go back. Go back. He would turn to his brother, but he could not repeat the warning. He could not gesture or shout even if he wanted to do those things. He simply stared. He waited. He struggled to keep his eyes open so as to avoid the red room. That red room in which his mother and father had been killed. That red room to which his brother had sent Mildred and Hamilton and Allen and the others. Those had been their screams coming through the laptop's speakers. How could he not recognize them? He heard them every night in his theater, his theater that was increasingly dim and red, increasingly moving as though alive, as if made of flesh and bone, as if composed of living fabric, as if draped in leathery skin.

One afternoon in the blur of his prosthetic life, they parked at the verge of a forest, covered the truck in branches and leaves, and ventured inside. They had been in Louisiana some days already, his brother scoping out the nearby towns and cities, annotating maps bought from a highway truck stop. Their cash supply was dwindling fast, but Jesus seemed unworried, motivated in his typical, mechanical way. Even then, trudging through marshland, shedding jackets, swatting mosquitoes, Jesus was unfazed. Joaquin followed him, similarly mechanical, unbothered by the mosquitoes and the heat as though he were removed from them. His body felt the sensations, but he could not see past the red.

Jesus held out an arm to stop him. "There. Do you see it?"

Far beyond the tree line, obscured somewhat by shadow, stood an aged, bone-white plantation house. Gable-roofed, fronted by an imposing colonnade, the house appeared more beast than building despite the weathering of its wood and the damage along its rooftop. The vestige of a path leading to the house snaked across a decimated brickwork fence and through overgrown, knee-high weeds. Joaquin's feet took him closer, but Jesus held him back.

"No. We can't go yet. But this is where the coordinates are. This is where they'll have their celebration." He spat the word out with rarely expressed vehemence. "And this is where we'll find them. The ones who killed Mom and Dad."

Jesus had spoken often of Pink House's "celebrations," though there was not much he really knew about them. The online threads were strangely light on what happened behind the closed doors. All he knew was that the celebrations were means by which the devotees interfaced with their god, but locations and itineraries were closely guarded secrets. Jesus imagined the rituals that took place, the absolute horseshit and fanaticism and idiocy. He had never taken to religion. Like so many of his generation, skepticism had found him early and latched on tightly. His eyes and ears were his guides, and anything outside of their purview, anything outside of sensible perception, was to be distrusted if not dismissed. The world was a machine, observable and therefore understandable. With enough time, science would uncover the nuances and set straight the misconceptions. But religion, despite its finery and tradition, seemed too flimsy to be taken seriously. So, he had rejected its premises and possibilities, all the more as he saw examples of dogmatism and abuse, and Pink House was nothing if not dogmatic. Their "god." Their "revelations." All of it mad, vicious, selfish, evil. His parents had died for that. His parents had been butchered for that. For the wet dreams of the insane. For nothing at all.

8

The day of the celebration, Jesus loaded the weapons, aimed them, imagined his usual targets in the smoke-filled desolation of his mind. He went through one cigarette, two, three, eventually six as he paced around their tiny motel room, around the parking lot. In the desert, there had been the fear of death, but only in a robotic sense. Even when the mine had upended their transport and wedged shrapnel in his side, nearly costing him his arm and leg, he had not been truly, deeply afraid. Even when Kowalski went down, he had stayed firm. Yet now there was a desperation, a sense of reckoning. Possibly, he would not come back from this. Very likely, he would die at that plantation house.

He sat by Joaquin. "I think I should go alone," he said. "Who knows what's there. What these people did to Mom and Dad, they could do the same to me."

He waited for a response from Joaquin, wished for recognition. When there was none, he just patted the boy's hand. "I'm leaving the rest of the money here. If I'm not back by morning, you need to leave. Okay? You need to leave."

He kissed his brother's brow. He hugged him. Joaquin's eyes never left the corner of the room, as though he watched something, as though he listened. Jesus gathered his weapons, started the truck. He never saw Mildred and Tyler, Hamilton and Allen. How they crowded the truck cabin. How they clung to the seats and moaned and whispered their silent, dead warnings.

He left the truck outside the forest and, in the pitch darkness, proceeded through the marsh, shotgun slung over his back, two cans of gasoline knocking against his thighs. Questions assailed him. What was he doing? What would he do? How many were there? Would they be armed? Would they fight back? The scenarios had played out in his mind over the many, many sleepless nights spent reaching this point, but suddenly, even his most well-crafted plan felt windless. With each labored, muddy step, his heart raced that much faster. Periodically, he had to stop, set down the gasoline, and wipe his sweaty palms on his jeans. He had to catch his breath under the weight of the weapons. His helmet, vest, and fatigues had never been this heavy. But he righted himself. He pressed on. You have to do this. You have to do this. You are not weak. You are not weak. And thus the clockwork mind compartmentalized. The rationalizations that kept him functioning in the desert kept him functioning in that swamp. He locked away the fear. He outmaneuvered the panic. One thought eased him: Joaquin was safe. He wouldn't be caught in the crossfire if there was one. He wouldn't be among the dead. At least one of the brothers was guaranteed to survive the night.

At the edge of the plantation grounds, Jesus dropped down and surveyed the scene. The house loomed as before, larger and grander in the moonlight, dark and silent as it had been. He watched for what felt like hours, but there was not a single car, not a single person. No lights flickered. Where were they, those fanatics, those devoted? Was this the wrong place?

"No," he said. "No, this is the place. It has to be."

He advanced upon the house, staying low to conceal himself among the tall grass, hugging the perimeter of the field. Small ruins dotted the property, perhaps former slave quarters, their demolished remains bringing to mind artillery fire. He paused at these wreckages, watching always for signs of movement, signs of life. Above him was a pale, crescent moon.

When he had circled the entirety of the house and spotted no resistance, he made his approach. A back door led into a dark, long-abandoned kitchen, the few remaining pots and pans covered with dust, the stray plate or glass wrapped in cobwebs. He started the trail of gasoline here before emerging into a dining room, shotgun raised high. This room was likewise empty, furnished only with a table covered in a dull, mottled cloth. A shattered chandelier lay upon the cratered floor. A dust-filmed painting of horses hung on the wall.

He poured more gasoline here before preparing to move on. Go back. He whipped around. Nothing. Just a whisper of wind through the broken windows, an unsightly creak—

Go back.

Not the wind. Not the house. A voice. A warning. But whose voice was it? His own? He wiped his brow, surprised at how much he was sweating, how much his heart was pounding. Something weighed on his shoulders, pulled at his ankles. Go back. Go back. Maybe. Maybe he could. Just strike the match now and be done with it. Get Joaquin and don't look back. Leave all this behind. Go back. GO BACK.

He shook his head, drew a breath. "No. They die. I have to see it. I have to be sure."

Out of the dining room and into the foyer. Blue-lit and serene in the moonlight through the windows. An empty, cracked vase that once held roses. A space where there might have been refreshments and small talk. An imperial staircase on both sides led up to the second floor, but what caught his eye was the glow from underneath the double doors straight ahead. They likely led into a parlor or living room. He threw open the doors.

On the other side was a spacious meeting hall, dimly illuminated by candelabra. A velvet carpet stretched from the foyer to the ornate, wood-carved mantelpiece at the opposite end. A stone altar stood in the center of the room, more suited for the surrounding forest and marshland than the extravagant house. Behind the altar was the bare frame of a door, unremarkable, nondescript. Distracted by the doorframe, Jesus noticed too late the others in the room.

There were dozens of them, all in white robes, all wearing featureless ceramic masks. They lined the room, surrounded the altar and doorframe. Hands were upon him before he even remembered the shotgun. His jacket was stripped off, his weapons wrested and circulated among the throng until they disappeared from view. On his knees, arms pinned behind him, he watched his knife pass from one pair of hands to another before it arrived into the slender, pale grasp of someone pink-robed and red-masked. The knife twirled and spun in the candlelight.

"Well." A woman's voice, Southern and bloody and rich. "This must be the murder weapon I've heard about." The woman traced a gloved finger along the edge of the knife's blade. "Just how much blood has it spilt?"

Jesus was silent. He struggled under the hold of his captors.

"I'm impressed," the woman said. "When I heard someone was hunting us, I imagined a group. But here you are. Alone. A one-man army." She made a sweeping gesture to her congregation. "This is one of our largest celebrations yet. Fitting for such a special guest as yourself, don't you think?"

She laughed, and as if on cue, the rest laughed as well. Jesus fought harder. He scanned the room: a candelabrum could be hoisted, driven into her neck. Her head could be smashed against the altar. He could tear out her throat and leave her to choke on her blood.

The woman approached and bent towards him, the blood-red mask inches from his face. Whether from her breath or from the mask itself, the suffocating, noxious smell of rust washed over him. "Even now, you're like an animal," she said. "You want to reach out, grab me by the neck. Throttle me! Yes, if only you could!"

Another round of laughter.

"I would want to do it, too. It's what we were designed for, even if only by accident. You know that better than anyone, don't you?"

With a flick of the knife, she snapped off the dog tags from around his neck and brandished them to the others. "My friends, we have a veteran here! A defender of our peace and liberty. Clap for him! Celebrate him!"

They clapped, cheered. Jesus's tunnel vision made it easy to focus on the woman in the pink robe. He had decided his course of action: he would carve out her stomach, pull apart her intestines. He would use her innards to strangle every last one of these freaks.

"My daddy served," said the woman, studying the dog tags. "Bless his soul. Could never quite talk about what it was like. Sliding a knife into the breast of a German boy probably no older than he was. Having to put his own friends out of their misery. Those stories frightened me as a little girl—frightened *and* excited. I'd ask him, 'Are you sorry for what you did? Does it hurt you?' He said it hurt, but he wasn't sorry. He would do it again a thousand times. As many times as he needed to."

She flung the dog tags away and turned to Jesus. "What about you? Are you sorry for what you did? Our people you killed—the ones you robbed of their opportunity to be here today—are you sorry for them?" She leaned in close again. "You realize you could have just given up your own fingers, no? But you insisted on hunting us. You made sport of it."

He spat at her mask.

"Fuck you," he said. "I'm gonna kill you. I'm gonna kill all of you!"

The woman stepped back. She tilted her head. "Don't you realize we expected you to come? We *wanted* you to come. I'm not one for computers, myself, but my people talk to me. They know when things are off. They know when the wrong questions are asked. We're not caught by surprise. Do you understand? You cannot change what's happening tonight."

Jesus laughed. He laughed hard. "So, what? You can kill me if you want. It doesn't matter! What you did to my parents, to my brother—I will never forgive that! Torturing them, making him watch! I will *never* forgive that! I'll take you all with me if I have to!"

"Your parents?" The woman tilted her head again. "I think I understand. One of mine killed some of yours. Is that right?" She addressed her followers. "Did one of you kill this boy's parents? Make his brother watch?"

There was silence among the crowd. Jesus watched. After a moment, one of them came forward. His voice was young, male. Somewhere in his early twenties.

"It was a while back," he said. "When we were getting ready to come here. We broke into a house at night. There was a couple. They thought we were there to steal things."

Jesus seethed, but they held him down more tightly. The woman nodded. "Go on."

"We killed them. It was messy, but we did it. And there was a kid. Probably fifteen or sixteen. He watched us do it. But we didn't kill him. Shit, he wouldn't have recognized us. We were wearing our masks. We just had some fun with him. I didn't know he had a fucking crazy brother. We picked that house at random. Just driving by."

"Well, now. What do you make of that?" The woman turned back to Jesus. "They picked your parents at random. You're a soldier—you understand collateral damage."

Jesus didn't hear her. His attention was now on the young man. At this point, he almost didn't care whether the kid had been involved or not. He was here. He was *here*. In this place. With these people, these psychopaths, these fanatics, and he was going to kill them. All of them. However long it would take, however much it would cost, he wouldn't stop, he wouldn't stop until each of them was fucking *dead*—

"Well, do you still want to kill him?" The woman's smile was evident in spite of her mask. "Come here, my friend. Come here." She beckoned the young man, and hesitantly, he approached. She brought him before Jesus. "Look. He's right here for the taking. You could put your hands around his neck, strangle him like you want to."

She stared into Jesus's burning eyes. She laughed again.

"But what if I told you death isn't to us what it is to you?" She held the knife out to the young man. "You want to show him what I mean?"

The young man took the knife, but he was reluctant. "I don't know. Will it work?"

"The door's over there. All you have to do is let yourself out."

He considered for another moment, looking at the assembly, perhaps searching for some acknowledgment or affirmation. But the sea of white faces did not provide an answer. No one spoke. No one came forward. Even Jesus, in spite of his anger, could only stare in confusion.

The red-masked woman stroked the young man's shoulder, wrapped a comforting hand around his shaking wrists. "My friend, you came here for this. Here. I'll help you."

She guided him to the doorframe. It was simple, rectangular, built of wood, with absolutely nothing on the other side— yet the young man went rigid before the threshold. The woman rolled up his sleeves, exposed the chalk-white of his skin, the green-blue of his veins. Chains had been etched around his wrists in black ink.

"Go on," she cooed into his ear. "I'm right here. I'll guide you." She took hold of his trembling hand and brought the knife down upon his opposite forearm. Their backs were to Jesus, but he saw the spurt of blood. Immediately, a moan circulated through the assembly. The room somehow grew darker, redder. The young man cried out, whimpering like a dog, trying to move away, but others came forward to hold him in place. The red-masked woman placed the knife in his other, weakening hand. She closed her fist around his own. There was another jerk. Speckles of blood struck her mask.

The crowd swayed to and fro. Some stepped forward, then drew back, as though remembering themselves, recalling some rule or protocol. They loosed excited gasps, anxious moans. The candelabra flickered. The young man, his white robes smeared with blood, his arms hanging limp at his sides, stared straight ahead and laughed.

"I see it!" he cried. "For the first time, I really see it! I see all of them! I see *him*!"

For Jesus, nothing had changed. The space through the doorway was empty. He looked around at the assembly, struggled to raise himself. His captors held firm, though they were increasingly distracted, their heads jerking in agitation like those of baying dogs.

At the doorframe, the red-masked woman brought the knife to the young man's throat.

"The flesh a cage," she said. "The skin a fragile fabric."

"The flesh a cage," he repeated. "The skin a fra—"

His carotid artery spewed a quick jet of blood, staining the wood, the carpet. He collapsed beneath the doorframe. After a few spasms, his body lay still. The crowd went silent, and then they were laughing, cheering, screaming. Jesus fought to turn away. He couldn't kill this bitch, let alone the rest of them, but he could run. He could get out of there. He could run all the way back to the truck, set the fire as he went—

"Rejoice!" yelled the woman, raising her arms and laughing. "Rejoice, my friends! He's gone ahead of you!" She pointed at the blood-spotted doorframe. "Do you see it? We've excited him now. He always prefers an appetizer before the main course." She advanced upon Jesus, grabbed his head, made him stare at the doorframe. "Do you see it, too? No? I think he would enjoy you most. Your resistance is interesting. Rare."

"You're fucking crazy!" Jesus said. "You killed him! One of your own!"

"*You* wanted to kill him," she said. "In fact, you wanted to do much worse! I just helped him slip loose of this annoying skin we have. You would've had him in a chair, no? Tortured the poor boy. Peeled off his skin, stripped away his muscle. You'd have kept him here to suffer."

She turned to the assembly. "Do you hear that, friends? This man wants to kill us, make us suffer, make us feel so much pain—and *we're* the monsters! *We're* the ones crazy! When we're just helping each other along!" She gestured to the young man's corpse. "Take off his mask. Show us what he was really feeling underneath."

They removed the mask. The young man was disheveled, haggard, but his eyes were rolled back in his head, his mouth wide in an exaggerated grin. Around his neck, just below where the throat had been cut, were telltale ink marks. Chains like those drawn on his wrists.

The woman pointed with the knife. "Does that look like the face of someone in pain? Someone scared? He was *excited*! He's now somewhere very special. Very, very special. You must know it. You must have seen it even if you pretend otherwise. It speaks to you. He speaks to you. Our lord and savior! He's here with us! He is among us! Inside of us!"

The congregation exploded again into cheering, growling, hollering. They sounded less and less human by the minute. Jesus looked among those white robes and white masks, searching for at least one not attuned to the rest, at least one resistant to the scheme—but he was alone.

"There is a place," said the woman, and the assembly grew silent in an instant. The candles dimmed even more. The shadows of the hall once again grew stronger, denser. The darkness became hot. "We call it a room, but it is so much more. It is where we all belong. Where we are supposed to go. This around us? This skin? This material? This is just dressing. Temporary. Something we must break free from. And he is looking to free us."

She spread her arms out to the doorframe, now a doorway. Now a portal.

"We will be free in the room of cloth. We will be one. We will spread the song. We will shed the skin. The flesh a cage!"— the assembly repeated after her, yelled after her—"The skin a fragile fabric!"

Jesus closed his eyes. He put his clockwork mind back into action, disposed of the fear, suppressed the exhaustion. In the hellscape of his mind, in that war-torn, blown-out desert, he saw worse than this. Relived worse than this. This was nothing. Nothing.

The woman dropped her hands. The crowd went silent. "But we have wasted enough time entertaining our guest. Enough with the preamble. Bring out the main course."

The crowd behind her parted, and several of the white-robed came forward, carrying between them a silent, dull-eyed boy in denim. They set him down on the stone altar. They kept their hands upon him, but he did not struggle. He did not scream. He merely stared. He met Jesus's gaze, or rather, Jesus met his.

For a moment, the clockwork mind worked too well. Jesus did not understand. His focus remained on the red-masked woman, on taking his knife and splitting her down the middle. But when his eyes caught those of the boy, those of his brother, the machine broke. He screamed and yelled. He sobbed and slobbered. He almost broke free, so more of them took his hands, more of them pressed on his shoulders.

"No! No, stop! Let him go! Let him go! He hasn't done anything to you! If you're gonna kill somebody, kill me! I set this up! I went after you! Joaquin, he just—he was just with me, but he never did anything! He's just a kid! For fuck's sake, he's just a kid!"

"Kill you instead of him?" The woman looked between the brothers. She laughed. "Now, why would we do that? Don't you smell it? It's all over him. On you very lightly. Not nearly enough to satisfy him." She sniffed around Joaquin's blank, featureless face and shook with pleasure. "Reminds me of my daddy! His cologne. God, like I'm a girl again! Rare to find it so strong. This boy is halfway in the room of cloth already. He's practically living there."

She caressed his face with surprising gentleness. "Poor thing. Your brother would have done you a mercy had he just killed you. You're miserable."

Joaquin looked into her blood-red mask, and he trembled. He let out a sharp cry. The rest of the assembly were red-faced, too. They were ravenous, baring razor-sharp fangs, licking blood-soaked lips. They grew high off his scent.

"I am begging you!" exclaimed Jesus through his tears. "I am begging you! You can have everything! You can do whatever you want with me! Just please don't hurt him! Please, don't! He's all I have left! He's the only thing I have left!"

The woman was quiet. Amid the clamor and rutting of her congregation, she studied Joaquin's face, its muted terror, its silent bleakness. She looked back at the desperation and agony of Jesus. "So much fear," she said. As she spoke, the congregation quieted. "Imagine living without knowing there is more. Living as though this life is all there is."

"Please, no!" Jesus cried. "Just let him go!"

"Seeing the room of cloth changed my life," said the woman. "It's changed yours. Did you ever expect to be here now? Did you ever expect to deliver him such a tantalizing meal? How could you have known we were watching and waiting? You thought you could stop this."

She shook her head. "There is nothing to stop. The manacled man has laid claim to this boy. He's laid claim to you. All of us are here because he willed it."

"I am begging you!" Jesus screamed. "I am begging you, don't hurt him! Don't touch him! *Don't touch him, you fucking bitch*! Don't touch him, or you'll pay! I swear to you, I'll make you pay, I'll make every one of you fuckers pay! You'll wish you'd never been born! You won't even get to die, I won't let you die, I'll make you suffer for every fucking second! You bitch! You fucking bitch! *You bitch—*"

"I pity you," the woman said. "All this time, and you never realized."

She stood behind Joaquin. The congregation bent forward expectantly, hungrily. For Joaquin, they were monstrous, clawed and fanged, salivating. Red faces flaming, red eyes burning. In the distance, their arms around Jesus, his hollow-eyed mother and father, screaming silently, suffering inexpressible, unknowable agony. Mildred and Tyler. Hamilton pointing. Allen clawing. And he unable to say anything. Trapped in that mental theater that was now entirely dim, flesh-colored cloth. That was no longer a theater at all, but a room.

Jesus continued to rage. "You bitch! Don't touch him, don't fucking touch him—"

The woman raised his knife.

"Poor boy. Never realized you were always just meat."

She slit Joaquin's throat.

His eyes darkened. His body slumped. Barely a moment passed before the congregation advanced. They drew blades of their own from underneath their robes: hatchets, knives, machetes. They cut and hacked. Blood flew into the air, stained their robes, drenched their hands. The masks came off. Men roared. Women moaned. Fingers dug into skin and tore apart tendon. Fists came away wrapped in strings of viscera. Hands flung away fat. Globules of flesh passed among the assembly. Teeth ripped into pieces of stomach and bladder. Tongues cleaned bones. A woman stole the heart, clutching it to her chest, eyeing manically for an avenue of escape. She nibbled voraciously at the organ before a tomahawk found her skull, and then they were upon her as well, biting into her neck, sucking out her eyes. Those with enough presence of mind remaining threw themselves at the doorway. They smeared the wood with their bloody hands. They licked the altar. They rubbed themselves against the rock.

Unrestrained, Jesus could have run. But he simply knelt there, all the light gone from his eyes, all the gears in his mind broken. He glimpsed the doorway. He saw the black space that now existed within the frame. A black space that became red, that became flesh and blood.

Joaquin, meanwhile, could finally speak. Jesus! Jesus, I'm here! Can't you see me? The mental theater was no more. The walls of flesh, vein-laden and throbbing, were gone. He was waving, jumping, running. Jesus! Jesus! It's me! I'm here! I'm here! But no matter how hard he ran, no matter how far he reached out, he seemed always farther and farther from his brother. He was rising. Floating away. He saw his brother shed tears for the second time he could remember. He saw the people in the now-red robes amass around the altar. He could barely hear their moans and cries. Indeed, everything was muffled. Everything was so, so far away.

And then he turned. A light flashed above him. A bright, burning light. He could not shield his eyes. He could not turn away. A bell tolled. Then tolled again. Again and again and again. Jesus! Jesus, help me! *Help me, Jesus*! But his voice traveled nowhere. The light turned red, turned black. There, hovering above the ruined remains of this planet—its cities smoldering heaps, its oceans dry beds, its forests burnt withers—Joaquin saw him at last. A man writhing, thrashing, bound by chains, hung by hooks. Spewing behind a muzzle. Fingers and toes broken and disfigured. Red eyes shaking furiously, almost to the point of madness. But not madness. Something worse. Something far, far worse.

Joaquin wept, for he saw his new god.

APRIL 17

11:27 AM: hi mark! :)

11:27 AM: i'm also a chocolate fiend! :))

11:28 AM: what are you looking for on here?

11:35 AM: Hi

11:36 AM: Not sure Just looking to meet people right now

11:40 AM: got it!

11:41 AM: yeah it's pretty hard to meet people nowadays!!

11:41 AM: never thought i'd get on here haha

11:45 AM: Yes

11:47 AM: How do you feel about getting off the app

APRIL 21

01:05 PM: Hello

02:19 PM: oh hey!

02:20 PM: how are you??

03:06 PM: hey can i ask a question?

06:15 PM: Yes

07:02 PM: hey the girl in your third pic?

07:02 PM: the one in the pink dress?

07:03 PM: when was that taken?

APRIL 22

12:11 AM: mark?

01:20 AM: Sorry

01:20 AM: I don't remember

01:21 AM: That was a long time ago

05:30 AM: oh

05:32 AM: ok no worries

05:32 AM: i just got a little scared haha

05:43 AM: that girl looks like my sister

05:44 AM: i think she even had a dress like that

05:45 AM: it creeped me out

05:45 AM: sorry! :S

05:50 AM: Yes

05:50 AM: That is Maddy

05:57 AM: huh??

05:57 AM: how do you know her name?

05:58 AM: She told me a lot about you

05:58 AM: She prefers dark chocolate

05:59 AM: You like milk

06:01 AM: who the fuck is this??

06:01 AM: you think this is funny???

06:02 AM: She hasn't seen you in a long time

06:02 AM: She misses you

06:03 AM: She wants to see what you look like

06:03 AM: Now that you're all grown up

06:04 AM: Here's a picture of what she looks like now

06:06 AM: what the fuck is that????

06:06 AM: youre sick!!!!

MAY 06

07:35 PM: mark

07:35 PM: who is he

07:36 PM: Hello

07:36 PM: Welcome

07:38 PM: who is he

07:38 PM: please

07:38 PM: i need to know

07:39 PM: He is your father

07:39 PM: Your brother

07:39 PM: Your shepherd

07:40 PM: He has been waiting for you

07:40 PM: He has waited a long time

07:42 PM: what does he want me to do

07:43 PM: He only wants what's best for you

07:43 PM: Don't you want to see Maddy again?

07:44 PM: i remember now

07:44 PM: mom and dad bought it for her

07:45 PM: it was her graduation gift

07:45 PM: they bought it from some garage sale

07:46 PM: she always liked antique things

07:47 PM: Where is it now

07:47 PM: it's gone

07:48 PM: she took it with her

07:49 PM: It's not gone

07:49 PM: It's just waiting for you

07:50 PM: It's yours now

07:51 PM: i'm scared

07:53 PM: i really miss her

07:54 PM: i showed her picture to mom

07:56 PM: i shouldn't have done it

07:57 PM: but i wanted her to know

07:57 PM: i needed her to know

07:58 PM: That's good

07:58 PM: That's what he wants

08:05 PM: ok

08:05 PM: what do i do with it?

08:06 PM: You know what to do

08:06 PM: You're already doing it

08:07 PM: Keep going

08:07 PM: You're chosen

08:08 PM: You're the only one who can

08:10 PM: i never saw maddy like that

08:12 PM: i never saw her so happy

SARAH

9

Sitting at the bar, nursing her third beer, she read the letter again: Sarah. Sorry for going quiet. Found this in Chicago. They're saying they got an answer. A way to get rid of it. They say you have to come out. I know what you're thinking, but I feel like this is the real deal. Come to the Firehouse. Ask for Compton. I'll see you soon. Have faith. -- C

She put the letter aside and shuffled out a pack of cigarettes from her jacket sleeve. The bar was dark, loud with rock music, clouded by a haze of smoke that grew thicker by the hour. She lit a cigarette. A gray face stared at her from the mirror behind the bar, eyes dead, skin pale and leathery. She held its gaze as long as she could, but inevitably, she lost the fight. There was a reason she avoided mirrors, a reason she had removed all of them from the trailer. If only that face belonged to one of the phantoms. If only it weren't her own.

She unfolded the flyer Caesar had sent with the letter. On the black gloss was the pink outline of a vertical rectangle. To the uninitiated, it might have been just a shape, no different than those littering the pages of a geometry workbook. But she knew better. Her hand had sketched out that same shape hundreds of times—not the rectangle, but the doorway, the Platonic ideal turned perverse, profane. Something as simple as four lines could be impregnated with vile meaning. If drawn by the wrong hand. Seen by the wrong eyes.

"Want the truth?" read the caption. "We can show you. Find us at PINK HOUSE."

Pink house. Like a house of flesh. A room of cloth.

Jesus, Caesar, she thought. What the fuck are you doing?

She nibbled on her cigarette, her unease growing with each second, her stomach in knots. A man leaned against the bartop, flashed her a grin. "Hey there. You alone?"

She eyed his polished boots and starched jeans, his toned forearms, his strong jaw. Sex would be good, a better palliative than the shitty cigarette and another beer—but her left hand trembled. Fuck. Of course he'd come knocking when she least needed it. She watched her hand, studying the tremors of the frail, weathered fingers, the quivers of the coarse, pink knuckles. She clenched the hand into a fist, dug chipped, dirt-caked nails into her palms. She couldn't entertain guests tonight. Not unless she was willing to risk adding a new recruit to the ranks. Not unless she was willing to spread her mental rot. Her invisible curse.

Amid the dusty twilight outside, Sarah held her trembling hand to her chest and struggled into her truck. She retrieved the black, leather-bound notebook from the glove compartment, the latest of its kind, and flipped it open. "Okay," she said, putting pen to page, watching her hand move automatically, guided by an intelligence not her own. "Knock yourself out." The blue-ink smears and scribbles, assuming a mutated, haunted form of her usually delicate penmanship, filled one page, then two, then three. As the words leached from skin to paper, blood to ink, the tremors grew softer, less violent. Finally, they stopped. She sat, breathless, staring down at the pages, smelling not the odor of fresh ink but the must of dry blood. She shut the notebook. Before long, she lit another cigarette.

The impulses were rare now, as infrequent as once a week if she was lucky. Her left hand would tremble, and she knew if unaddressed, paranoia would follow, and then despair. The only relief came from spilling the words onto the page, though uttering them was just as effective and all the more tempting. They swam their way up her throat like bile, pushing at her lips, sometimes forcing their way out. The first time, she had been waiting in a bodega while Caesar finished buying their weekly dinners of microwave meals and ramen cups. Suddenly, her cheeks had bulged, and she nearly doubled over, hands clasped over her mouth, prepared to retch. Only no green vomit dripped through her fingers. No glimmering bits of curdled cheese clung to her palms. Just a word, hardly more than a whisper, like smoke coiling into the air. Another escaped through her fingers, and then another. She rushed outside and spoke into the fly-clouded, maggot-lined garbage. It was pure luck that those words found no ears, that she hadn't screamed them in fright. Since then, she avoided crowds. She kept a notebook close by if not on her person, ready to scrawl instead of speak, write instead of whimper.

In the early days of her affliction, in the wake of her brother's death, she had thought it brave to endure the pain, thought it courageous to resist the words. Many nights had been spent screaming and shouting, tearing through sheets, biting into pillows. Caesar had been unable to stomach being in the same room during those episodes. He would wait outside the door, hearing howls from within, sometimes laughter, shaking even worse himself, fumbling with his flask. Afterwards, just as scared the twentieth time as the first, he would creep inside and find her in a ball atop the bed, shaking and sobbing. You're okay, he would say. You're okay. And she would shake her head, she would swing at him, she would claw at herself. No, I'm not! No, I'm fucking not! I am not okay! I'm wrong! I'm *wrong*! And then the spasms would start again. The shrieks would continue. The visions would return.

She knew better now, over three years into her new half-life. It wasn't brave to suffer. It wasn't heroic. There was nothing virtuous about convulsing and crying and coughing, nose filled with snot, eyes bleary with tears, gagging like an invalid, held clumsily by a man more afraid than you were, a man unable to comfort or protect you. It was she, even at her weakest, her frailest, who comforted him despite her humiliation, assuring him that even if she was wrong, he was right, had to be right. In spite of everything, there was good yet. There had to be.

Imagine that. Gaunt, drooling, half-blind, and claiming there was anything for which to be grateful, anything by which to reserve even a modicum of dignity or grace. She looked back on those early days with disgust at her weakness, at her falseness. She thought of Caesar and understood finally how those other drug dealers and mobsters had seen him: pitiful, clueless, spineless. In peddling him those platitudes about goodness, the same trite sayings she had reserved for her students, for her brother, she had only kept him from the truth. She had only delayed her own healing. No—"healing" wasn't the right word. There was no healing. But by lying to herself, she had made things harder to accept. Harder to endure.

She lay awake that night in the darkness of her trailer, listening to the wind cry against the corrugated metal, running her thumb over the rosary Caesar had given her. Was it unfair to think him weak? Was it cruel? He had shepherded her as far from Maryland as possible, making up, he often said, for what he didn't do for her brother. Then came the day he brought her to the roadhouse in that Texas wasteland, entrusted her to Earl, and went on his way. I'll send money, he said. I'll keep in touch. And he had for a time, until eventually, the frequency of his letters slowed, and the money he sent through their network of contacts and couriers dried up. Now, over a year later, he sent the flyer. Reviving the old talk about a cure. Summoning again the tired arguments and repressed bouts of agony, the memories of those endless hours when she would weep and scream and look longingly, lovingly, at the nearest knife, the closest bottle of pills.

Have faith, he would tell her in those moments. Have faith that there's something out there. Have faith that there's an answer. Because there's gotta be an answer. Gotta be. For you. For Seb. For everybody. God wouldn't let it happen like this.

Good old Caesar—clinging to his false god when the real god, the only god, had made himself manifest to her in the most undeniable of terms. Oh, if only she could believe even for a second that there was in fact nothing—that the universe was unintelligent, unintelligible. That one's consciousness faded with the last sparks between neurons. That the flesh of the body returned to an indiscriminate earth. But sadly, the priests and philosophers had gotten it wrong. The artists had imagined a world too charitable. Because evil was all there was, and he was red-eyed and furious, frothing at the mouth. Sadistic. Insatiable. Everyone, sooner or later, would find their way to him. Her former students spirited away, shot, gutted, left on asphalt and concrete. Her frail, cancer-eaten mother. Her father, reeking of alcohol and bitterness. The friends she knew from college or high school who drank or drugged themselves to death. The countless victims on the news. Her brother. Even if their spirits eluded the room of cloth, its evil would spread, eventually breaching each dimension, inevitably shattering every barrier. All would wander the halls of an unimaginable hell, screaming in silence, wailing into darkness and heat. And one day, perhaps in twenty years, a month, a week, she would join them.

She got up from the bed and walked to the trailer's living area. An old, red-hued, neon Coors sign buzzed softly above the sofa, her only nightlight in that near-desert. She sat down under the lurid glow—almost the same as that which had illuminated her Maryland apartment during long nights either grading or worrying over her brother—and unfolded the flyer. Picking at an abandoned plate of ribs and sipping a long-warm beer, she reviewed the pink outline of the doorway, the text that promised truth. A cure, huh? Bullshit. This was a front. Just another way to spread their message. Her brother had discovered the curse online, in a manuscript knitted together over who-knows-how-many years by who-knows-how-many authors. But they were getting bolder, the followers of the room of cloth, promoting publicly now, probably preying on useful idiots who knew only they had to spread the rot because they were "chosen," because they were the best ones for the job. That was the joke, of course. The most devious of the manacled man's tricks. Any warm body would do. He didn't discriminate.

Was Caesar one of their useful idiots? Who had come to him about a cure? Why would he even believe it? After everything they'd seen—everything that had happened to her brother—why would he think there was any truth to this?

She stared at the black space within the pink borders. Life dwelt on the other side of those doorways, beyond the veil of perceivable reality. Maybe calling it "life" was too generous— the things that lurked in the great dark were no longer alive, assuming they ever had been. Her brother, impish and decrepit, reduced to something subhuman, was somewhere in that vastness, as were everyone else touched by the room of cloth. Yet somehow, despite the impossible distance between them, her brother stayed with her, much like their father had pervaded the old house and even her apartment long after his own death. She awoke often in the night with the cold touch of a child's hand lingering on her face. She heard his clawing at the door of her trailer, the pattering of his feet on the roadhouse floor. He hid behind the legs of tables, in the darkest shadows of any given room. In her nightmares, she saw his skin stripped, his flesh flayed. She didn't know if these impressions were the manacled man or simply her damaged mind playing tricks on her. Gone was the little apartment, the little life, but the ties persisted. No matter how far or wildly she flew—once to college, drinking and partying to escape her father's drunken rage, and once more with Caesar, navigating a bleak network of hideouts, odd jobs, and forged identities—the chains bound her, pulled her back.

This flyer and the promise of an alleged cure were just more chains, more pointless reminders of the brutal reality she already knew. Nonetheless, something prevented her from tearing it up. Maybe it was a morbid curiosity, like a challenge to investigate. Maybe it was the sentimentality of having something from Caesar after so long. He had done much for her, after all. Nursed her. Protected her. But in the end, he had abandoned her, left her despite being the only person who could remotely understand the new half-life in which she existed. It was comforting to think he had left out of weakness, that he had lapsed into his old cycle of fear and insecurity, overwhelmed by the needs of her condition. But there were moments, sometimes right when she committed to paper those awful, heinous words, that she wondered if Caesar left her out of hatred of her taint, resentment of her bitterness. Frankly, she would have done the same in his position. While she could bear his cowardice, his contempt was a different story. She knew it was stupid to care. She knew it was illogical. But sometimes, despite herself, she recalled his big grin and deep laugh. She thought of the cigarettes they shared. She thought of her friend Louisa and her philosophical musings, her motherly tenderness. She thought of the many students who had come and gone through her classroom. In those moments, she yearned not to be alone, and she hated herself for it.

Whatever his reasons for leaving her, for going silent, he had come back. To help her. To save her. Even if it was idiotic to think a cure was anything but a pipe dream. Even if he should goddamn know better. She owed him the courtesy of making sure he wasn't dead.

She walked into the roadhouse during early-morning cleanup, clad in denim jacket and boots. The place took on a different atmosphere in the morning compared to the rowdy evenings, aired-out and rich with light, the floors waxed with lemon-scented cleaner, the many beer bottles and plastic cups from the previous night swept away. Churchlike, Sarah thought, and she recalled her first time stepping into the roadhouse. Her last time seeing Caesar in person, and at her most exhausted, plagued with the worst fits since first laying eyes on her brother's manuscript. Every night had been a torrent of unending, apocalyptic images. The cities demolished, the lands ruptured. Oceans swollen with blood and bodies. Skies ablaze with impending destruction. Of course, those images of whole-sale slaughter and planetary doom had been a relief compared to the nightmares of her family. Standing over her father's bloody, beer-splotched corpse. Holding her mother's shriveled, disease-rotted hand. Kneeling before her brother's vacant, glassy-eyed stare. Following Caesar meekly into the roadhouse that first time, she had experienced a rare and most welcome feeling: escape. Escape even for the briefest of moments. A chance to close the door and bask in warm, soothing silence.

The proprietor of the roadhouse, Earl, small and wizened, glasses too large for his birdlike nose, fiddling constantly with his hearing aid, had seemed stereotypically weak-bodied and feeble-minded, but he had seen through Sarah's veneer in an instant. Years of watching waifs and strays passing through had trained his vision, developed his sense of smell, and the ragged, flattened woman radiating that intense stench of decay hadn't frightened him, but instead galvanized him. After the barest of introductions, he allowed her the trailer, situated her among the ranks of the roadhouse. Over time, the worst of the smell abated, and the slender limbs grew slightly plumper, the gaunt face somewhat fuller, the vacant eyes faintly brighter. He knew there would never be a full restoration of the original woman, whoever she had been, whatever was her story, but he was proud of the progress. Too many others had fallen frequently, harshly off the wagon. Too many others had buried themselves in early graves.

But as she stepped into his office that morning, his heart dipped. The most recent letter from Caesar had been a sign, a break in the status quo. Things were going to change, and not likely for the better.

"Baby bird," he greeted, pale lips pulling back in a wide smile.

Sarah hovered in the doorway. "Good morning, Earl."

"What can I do for you? Your shift doesn't start until 3:00."

"I know." She hesitated, then unveiled the flyer from her back pocket. "This was in Caesar's letter. Do you know anything about it?"

He held his glasses up to scrutinize the flyer. "Nope. Never seen it before."

"And Caesar—did you happen to see him? Talk to him?"

He shook his head. "I'm sorry, baby bird. We just picked it up like we always do."

"Okay. I thought as much." She took the flyer back and lingered uneasily, looking at the photographs that lined the office, snapshots from a younger Earl's life when the roadhouse was new. He watched her. He smiled again.

"You don't need my permission. Or my blessing. Do what you have to do."

She returned his smile with a rare one of her own. "Thank you, Earl. I'll be back."

Of course, as he watched her walk out, he wished she did need his permission. Whatever had reduced her to that mumbling, nervous wreck when Caesar first brought her in was something awful and dark. Not drugs, but something else, and neither she nor Caesar ever elected to share what it was. Earl had seen similar damage in abuse survivors fleeing their homes, wide-eyed women dragging along crying children and brittle-faced men shuddering under the weight of repressed tears. But there was no one coming after her, Caesar had said. The gangsters from New York wouldn't chase them this far. No profit in it. But Earl knew that depending on the breed of monster, profit had little to do with it. Over the years, he had faced down his fair share of abusers. They were motivated by ego and power. By control.

Were gangsters really the worst problem? Caesar had been mum about anything more, though Earl had recognized the fear in his eyes despite his outward confidence. He'd left Sarah too quickly, too urgently. Something had picked up their scent. Something had started closing in.

Baby bird, he wanted to call out. Don't go. You got nothing to prove. But whom was he to say, and what power did he really have? He could only do what he'd always done: provide the space, lend the time, and, perhaps most importantly, trust and hope.

Sarah made her preparations. The trailer was sparse, no more furnished or decorated than when she inherited it. The CRT television with its antennae collected dust. The mishmash of foldable loungers and vintage recliners sat askew in awkward spots. The decades-old refrigerator sported scattered alphabet-letter magnets and faded photographs. In the early days living in that trailer, she had looked upon those photographs—one of a smiling couple, another of a child playing with a garden hose—and wondered to what runaway they belonged. Maybe a wife who left them in haste to escape a narcissistic husband? Maybe a son in flight from expectations, from judgments? She had sympathized before, empathized. But now, she looked upon the photos and felt nothing, wondered nothing. How many others didn't even have the privilege of pictures?

Nothing in the trailer was of any value to her—nothing visible at least. She pushed aside the table, wrenched loose a floorboard, blew away the raised dust. An envelope lay in the shadows, fat with the money Caesar had sent her during the time she'd stayed there. She thumbed through the bills, pocketed a portion, then reached in again. This time, she withdrew the dull silver of a small revolver from the dusty darkness. She clenched the leather grip, snapped out the cylinder, squinted an eye down the length of the barrel. During their life on the road, Caesar had taken her to many an empty field, had her fire at bottles, faraway rocks. Just in case, he often said. Better safe than sorry. She wasn't the best shot, but she was a quick learner—within weeks, she had been able to clip most targets if not hit them close enough to center mass.

She replaced the floorboard, crinkling her nose at the scent of rotten meat that rose up from the darkest, deepest part of the hidden space. One might have expected the rotting carcass of a young coyote underneath, the decayed remains of a rat, but it was a pile of ash, the burnt remains of her previous notebooks, their abominable words reduced to nearly nothing. Nearly nothing, but not nothing. Even those specks of ash, if allowed to breach open air, could spread the infection anew. So, here they stayed, dormant, accumulating like nuclear waste. Even in that state, they whispered. Whispered and hissed and laughed. Especially when they came unsettled, when they received a new addition by way of lighter or match. They chittered sometimes at night, and she would sit in the darkness and listen, dragging slowly on a cigarette, watching the orange glow wax and wane, the cigarette simmer and shrivel.

She packed nothing for her journey besides a few shirts and pairs of jeans. The revolver she set gently between the folds of clothes. That evening, smoking a cigarette, watching the bloody sunset, she unclasped the golden rosary from around her neck. The only remaining heirloom from Caesar's grandmother, and perhaps his most valuable gift to her even compared to everything he had done to get her safely from Maryland. Sometimes, looking at the miniature crucifix with its crown of thorns, her tremors would subside. Not because there was a god above who shielded her, but maybe because the image awoke the memory of a faith forgotten, a connection to a time when her mother had been healthy, when the violence of her father had been more threat than force. A time before her brother was born and with him the need for more money, the pressure to work longer hours and thus seek the bottle. Pressure for Sarah to forgo her childhood and learn to look after the crying, pink thing with its warbling gums and tear-stricken cheeks. The little imp. Meat in waiting. Meat in need of tenderizing.

She put the rosary away, crushed the cigarette underfoot. That was enough recollection.

$$10.$$

The journey north was beset by rain—she watched the water listlessly from her truck, from doorways, from storefronts. She would hold out her hand, careful not to get wet, but compelled by the cold mist and earthy smell. There was relief in the cleansing quality, more natural and gratifying than what she could get from a shower. It wasn't uncommon for her to take two, even three showers in a single night, never able to shake off the sensations of grime on the skin or mud in the hair. At least the smoky scent of her blouses and jeans was real, self-produced. At least she hoped. She trusted what she could see, hear, taste, touch, and smell only so much. That was perhaps the manacled man's greatest victory over her. Her faculties were compromised, her perceptions darkened. Nothing could remove the filter or correct the error.

As she traveled, she moved through a series of motel rooms. Caesar had ushered her through rooms much like these, holding her as she retched or dressing her in blankets while she endured dismal, feverish sleeps. The questions arose again. Why reach out after disappearing like he had? Why not leave her behind, finally free of the baggage? Why feel an obligation to her, especially to risk getting so close to the room of cloth? She studied the flyer under lamplight, gripped by a furious desire to tear the paper apart. It wasn't tainted—only gave off the slightest whiffs of the dead smell—so it couldn't spread the disease, but it had been designed with the same intent. The most vulnerable would find something inviting in the pink outline of the doorway, in the impression of darkness beyond. They would feel the pull of promised peace.

She arrived in Chicago. She drove the streets, wandered the parks and plazas, gun always within reach, nose perpetually turned to the air. She darkened city blocks systematically on a map as she went. She focused on her nose, tracking any potential hint of the manacled man's musk. With time, her sensitivity to the dead smell had heightened. Once, Caesar snoring back at the motel, she had drunk coffee in a nearby diner to ward off sleep and its usual nightmares. Outside, in night air permeated by petrichor, she had caught it immediately—a stiff, decrepit stench, superficially like those of blood and rust, but far more pungent, almost unearthly. She had followed the smell for blocks, finding at last the source: a yawning, gaping underpass. A regular person, still sane, would have avoided going inside, but Sarah had been unable to resist the darkness of the tunnel. No monster had lurked within, no fiend—just a makeshift shrine of moldy, waterlogged boxes and long-dead candles. Above the shrine, painted haphazardly, were a pair of red eyes, impossible to see in the darkness if not for how they burned.

Occasionally, her nose found a mother in a grocery store, a teenager at a bus stop. The smell was stronger on some than others—at its worst, its most concentrated, it seemed like a dark cloud she could almost visualize. There was never a point in reaching out to these lost souls. No one could be saved from the room of cloth, however much Caesar had wanted it otherwise. And even if she had approached, they would have resisted. She was a rare one, capable of seeing through the artifice, but most were lost like her brother had been. Somehow, they didn't smell the death. If they had, they would never have taken the plunge. Then again, hadn't she smelled it when her brother brought the manuscript into her old apartment? The odor had nauseated her for days. She had felt it over her arms and legs, under her skin, in the pit of her stomach. And still she had read the words. Still she had sunk into the depths.

Her second day in Chicago, dashing for cover from a sudden downpour, she caught it. Like blackened, maggot-ridden entrails. Like molded, blood-caked wood. The smell was faint at first, but as she followed it, the pungency grew stronger. Her fingers fondled the butt of her revolver, but there was no reason to assume danger. At least not yet.

The smell led her to a bar. Through the rain, the red-brick exterior seemed darker and more menacing than it might have otherwise. A darkened neon sign proclaimed the place as "The Firehouse." There it was—some truth to Caesar's letter after all. No sign of a cure, though. Instead, the very opposite.

Inside, she shook herself dry, wrung her hair. Firefighter uniforms and prop axes adorned the walls. A weathered, brass-tipped hose lined the top of the bar. A custodian swept the stage. Nothing outwardly suspicious—except for the pervasive dead smell. She followed the stench, and there, on the corkboard, beneath ads for local bands, eclipsed by classifieds, were black flyers featuring the distinctive pink doorway. Flyers for Pink House. Flyers for the room of cloth.

The woman behind the bar, in the middle of polishing glasses, watched Sarah coolly. "Can I help you with something? We don't open for another couple of hours."

"Sorry about that," Sarah said. "I just need a few minutes from the rain." She held up her cigarettes. "You mind?"

"Go ahead."

Sarah smoked. The smell wasn't coming from the woman or the custodian—no, it was like a blanket dressing the entire bar, a residue left behind by someone else. To an untrained nose, the scent probably mixed with the smoke and alcohol, too diluted to be noticed, but Sarah knew otherwise: the strength of the smell suggested a regular.

She studied the flyers on the corkboard. Exactly the same as the one Caesar sent her, from the glossy sheen to the message on the bottom. She removed a flyer from the board and addressed the woman behind the bar.

"Excuse me. What's this?"

"Don't know. One of our guys put those up recently."

"Really?" Sarah feigned another minute of reflection, savoring the last few pulls on the cigarette. "Who put them up if you don't mind me asking?"

The woman looked up, but if she was suspicious at all, she didn't show any other sign. "Name's Compton. Comes in tonight if you want to ask him about it."

"Compton. Thanks. Yeah, I might swing by."

Back outside, she flicked away her cigarette, let the chill of the rain wash over her. Too much was adding up here: The Firehouse, Compton, the flyers. Did that mean Caesar was close?

She winced. There was her hand shaking, her fingers twitching. Was someone there, out the corner of her eye? She turned—nothing except the gray rain, the drenched parking lot. Her lip curled. She hadn't seen the phantoms in so long. She was definitely orbiting something, drifting close to a web. No doubt the red-eyed spider watched her from his throne on high. Only one question remained: was Caesar caught up in the web?

11

She went back to the bar that night, the air damp from the rain, the street slick. The neon sign burned crimson, reflected in puddles up and down the block, casting upon the bar a dull, red glow. Sarah ordered a cocktail and sat in the back, ostensibly people-watching, listening to the band. In reality, she traced the nearly visual cloud of flies that followed the lanky young man attending tables and refilling drinks. There was Compton, freckle-faced, pasty-skinned, red-elbowed. More than a passing resemblance to her brother, she thought. Was that part of the plan, to taunt her with echoes of ghosts? Certainly, the dead smell clung to him just as strongly as it had her brother. One of his hands was bandaged, only the thumb and a couple of fingers visible. Had he been in an accident?

She raised her glass and beckoned him over. "Can I get another? Whiskey sour."

"Sure thing."

When he brought the drink and turned to go, she called to him again. "Hey, just a second. Compton, right?"

He turned, brow furrowed. She put on her best smile. "Don't worry. I was asking around because I had questions about this."

She slid forward her flyer, the lights of the bar playing off the black surface. Compton followed the flyer intently, as though entranced.

"I've seen it," Sarah said. Despite the music, she knew he heard her. "The room of cloth."

All suspicion vanished from his face. "You have?"

"Oh, yeah. In fact, you might know a friend of mine. Caesar? He asked me to come here. Said you'd know something that could help me."

Compton stared nervously. "Are you Sarah?"

"Yeah." She laid a hand on the seat beside hers. "Here. No one will notice. We can talk."

He sat, looking at her with a mixture of excitement and uncertainty. Young, she thought. Younger than her brother had been. Probably lost, too. Swept up in all the bullshit about purpose and destiny, fate and calling. A waste of a life. She might have felt pity if not for the stench shrouding him. He was in deep, up to the waist if not the chin. He didn't have much time left if he was focused on spreading instead of protecting. If there really was a cure, a way to end it, this kid didn't have it. But she had to play along. For now.

"Tell me," she said. "About Caesar. About everything."

"Okay. Sure." He stammered, stuttered, and then broke into the familiar story: alone in the dark, scouring forums and chat rooms, stumbling across snippets and morsels of something he struggled to describe but intuitively knew. Snooping for more, edging deeper into the rabbit hole, asking the right questions in the right places. The gatekeepers found him, inducted him, told him what he had to do: spread, engulf, infect, disseminate, propagate. And he had done it, at least until the visions got too strong, the nightmares too violent. "They were everywhere," he said hoarsely. "The ones who were already dead."

"Then what?" she asked.

"I looked for someone to help me. That's when I found them. Pink House."

They were an online group, he said, similar to the one that had encouraged his spiral, but their aim was different: free people from the room of cloth, not wedge them in even more tightly. They served everyone, guiding people through trauma, shepherding recoveries, but they waged a secret battle against the followers of the room of cloth, whose collectivization was growing more powerful, whose reach was becoming more widespread. Pink House was dedicated to freeing people, Compton said. They had asked him then to pay forward the miracle, rally for the cause. They were many, but the room of cloth still had many more.

Good pitcher, Sarah thought, if he didn't stink. She stayed quiet, maintained her show of rapt interest. He went on, saying Caesar had stumbled across Pink House, saying he was also looking for a cure, a way out, but not for himself. For a friend. A good friend.

"So, where is Caesar?" she asked. "Why'd he call me out here?"

"The cure," Compton said, "it works. But there's a special procedure for it. Like a ritual, I guess. That's why we needed you to come out."

"Okay." She leaned forward, fed him a tone of quiet desperation. "How do we do it? What's the secret? I don't know how much time I have left, man."

"I'll tell you," he said, "but not here. We can go back to my place? Then I can take you to Caesar. We can do the whole thing. We can help you."

"All right." She finished her cocktail. "Let's go, then."

He didn't have a car, so she drove them, following his directions to his apartment. He fidgeted constantly, hardly able to stitch his words together or keep his teeth from chattering. And the stench! The dead smell was all over him. She lowered the window, letting in cold, damp air, but the smell was too thick to be dispersed.

They parked in a desolate lot, the asphalt cratered, the paint largely washed away. She followed him up rusted, rickety stairs, fingering for another cigarette and cursing when there wasn't one. She had filled pages of her most recent notebook that afternoon, but her hand was already shaking again, portending another outpour of words. The sudden frequency of episodes wasn't a coincidence—her body was reacting, anticipating danger. Down in the parking lot, phantoms stood amid the misty dark, watching her ascend with hungry stares.

Damn it, Caesar, she thought. What the fuck are you doing with these people?

Compton unlocked his apartment door, flicked on the lights. The pale glow revealed a cramped kitchenette, the sink crowded with piled dishes, the table littered with magazines and more flyers. There were so many flyers, in fact, stacked in corners, edging out from underneath doors. He must have spent an entire paycheck printing them. Only one of her cursed words was needed to find a foothold in a vulnerable victim, so why not just put up their tainted poems or paintings? Why introduce a middleman? Why advertise?

Recruiting, she told herself. But for what?

"Sorry, sorry," Compton said, clearing the table and chairs, picking up wrappers and boxes. "You want coffee? I can make a pot really quick."

"Thanks. You got cigarettes?"

"Uh, no. Sorry. I don't smoke."

Of course not. Sarah sat, overwhelmed by the stench. She stifled her desire to gag and scanned for the source of the smell among the mess. Was it the sheaf of papers on the countertop, suspiciously void of binding? The stack of CDs gathering dust in the corner? The scribbled notes by a pile of flyers? But none of these things reeked more strongly than anything else. Like at the bar, the odor pervaded like a cloud.

The coffee machine grinded, shot out one stream of milky brown and then another. Compton fumbled with Sarah's cup and saucer, nervous, but also inconvenienced by his bandaged hand. He set the cup upon the table shakily, the coffee jumping, trickling down the side of the ceramic. "Sugar?" he asked, going back for his own cup. "Cream?"

"No. Thank you." Sarah blew into the coffee, feigned a sip—she wouldn't chance a taste of that liquid shit even if the possibility of it being laced was less than zero. She watched Compton sit and play with his cup. Her twitching hand rattled her own.

"So," she said, "now what?"

"I have a contact," Compton said. "I just have to give him a call. He's a lot more experienced than I am. He's the one who did the work on me."

"Okay." She eyed him, eyed his bandaged hand. "If you don't mind me asking. What happened?" He hesitated, but she smiled, softened her expression as much as she could. "It's okay. We're on the same side, right? We both want out."

He drew a breath. "Okay. Maybe you heard about the celebrations?"

"Celebrations?"

"Yeah. They send people through. Across." His eyes lit up, and when he stammered, he did so with excitement, not nervousness. In that moment, he seemed far less like a recovering addict than one full-blown. "It's what everyone wants more than anything, right? You know, when they're wrapped up in it? To go through and—and *get out*. But he—the man—"

"The manacled man," Sarah said, almost by reflex.

"Yeah." Compton's eyes took on a different shade at the mention of the name, something like awe. Like terror. "He doesn't just let anyone through. You have to prove yourself."

Sarah nodded. "You have to be chosen."

"Yeah. So, this time, they wanted fingers. Five fingers." He swallowed, pulled back his bandaged hand as though suddenly self-conscious. "I heard they wanted tongues once. Eyes. But I still got scared. I couldn't get them all from me. That was around when Pink House found me. Good timing, right?"

Sarah had limited how much she investigated about the room of cloth—most of her knowledge was intuitive or empirical—but it didn't seem unbelievable that there were groups of fanatics taking things to such extreme, macabre lengths. An impressionable mind, someone just initiated, still star-struck like Compton likely was, would think it reasonable that something so ritualistic was required for entry, but that was just flavor on the part of the gatekeepers. Sarah knew firsthand that the only price of admission was blood, preferably one's own. The flesh was a cage, after all, the skin a fragile fabric. One had to relinquish the binding. Divorce the body.

She looked at Compton's bandaged hand. Convinced enough to give up pieces, but not committed to surrendering the whole. At least not yet. His cycle was nearing its end, and fast. All this born-again bullshit couldn't erase the stink or hide the desperation. But if he was willing to main himself, what else was he capable of doing? What could he have done to Caesar?

Her contempt for him shifted towards caution. She positioned a hand on her hip, the revolver within easy reach. "All right. Now about that call?"

"Okay. Yeah. Just give me a second." He stood and turned to the sink. As he held up his phone for the call, she pressed the barrel of the revolver to his neck.

He winced. "What are you—"

"Enough with the fucking around." She straightened her back, strengthened her voice. "You're going to do exactly what I say. Or I'll put a bullet through you. Understand?"

He was silent, shivering. She thumbed down the hammer, pushed his face towards the stacked plates. "I asked you a fucking question—are you going to listen or not?"

"Yes!" he cried. "Yes! I'll do whatever you want!"

"Good. Now, where is Caesar? What did you fucks do to him?"

"I don't know," he stammered. "I swear, they just wanted me to bring you guys in! I don't know where they took him!"

"Then who does? Who put you up to it?"

"Zeke!" he said breathlessly. "Zeke told me! It's all him! I promise!"

"Okay, then you're going to call Zeke. Tell him you want to meet alone—that the bitch is sick, you don't know what to do. You got that?"

"Yes! I get it!"

"Then do it." She grinned. "We're going to pay your pal a visit."

12

They drove out of the city, rumbling down the highway with only the headlights breaking through the dark. Sarah sat in the passenger seat, revolver trained on Compton as he drove, his hands clamped on the steering wheel, his bandage damp with sweat. Zeke, whoever he was, had answered and agreed—perhaps too easily—to a meet-up. Apparently, there was a warehouse where they had met before. Sarah pressed Compton for details.

"This is how I'm getting my ticket," he gulped.

"Ticket for what?"

"For the celebration."

"So you keep your fingers." Sarah chuckled. "You just have to sell people out. Feed them some bullshit about a cure. I bet you're proud of yourself."

"I don't know why you're fighting it," he said. "You get to be with him—with all of them! It's scary to do it alone, but at the celebration, everybody does it together. You know, it's not too late. I can help you—we can help you! You want to get out, too, right? You have to! There's no way you want to stay here—"

"Shut up!" Sarah barked. "What the fuck do you know about what I want? Just drive. And if you try anything, I'll send you along myself. Got that?"

He didn't say anything else. She fought to keep her voice stable, her demeanor frightening, but the pit in her stomach deepened. With each bounce of the headlights, she thought she saw more of the gray knees, the ashen elbows, the black grins. They were taunting her. No matter what she did, was she always doomed to fall into the manacled man's traps?

They parked outside the warehouse. In the darkness, looming overhead, the building seemed like a towering headstone, a megalith from ancient times, a marker of a preordained end. Fitting, Sarah thought darkly, pushing a trembling Compton inside, one hand around his neck, the other holding the gun tightly against the small of his back. They stood in the cavernous space, Sarah using Compton's slim figure as a shield, eyeing the darkness for threats.

"That you, Compton?" came a man's voice. A pair of floodlights shot on, briefly blinding them. Sarah forced herself to look—the lights silhouetted an approaching figure. She yelled out.

"Stay the fuck where you are! Or I blow him away!"

The man stopped and raised his hands in deference. "Oh, I see. You didn't come alone after all, did you, Compton?"

"You gotta help me, Zeke!" Compton cried. "She's—"

"Shut the fuck up!" Sarah dug the revolver into his back. "And you, Zeke—you're talking to me, got that?"

"Loud and clear." The man's smile was almost audible. "Sarah, right? The teacher?"

She paused. "You know who I am?"

"Sure. I know quite a lot, actually—put together your file myself."

"What does that mean? What file?"

"You're a hot commodity," Zeke said. "I get paid a lot of money to track down talent. The market's saturated, and my client's looking for diamonds in the rough. Catch my drift?"

"You're a fucking headhunter?" Sarah asked, wincing from the lights, her mouth dry. "Looking for meat for your master?"

"If you want to think of it like that." He laughed, lowered his arms. "Hey, you mind if I get a cigarette? I wasn't—"

"Don't fucking move! Unless you want the two of you dead!"

"No. Definitely don't want that." He raised his arms again. "Look, I didn't want to do it this way. I was hoping for something a little less dramatic. Let's talk."

"There's nothing to talk about," Sarah said. "Just tell me what you did with my friend. Where's Caesar? Did you kill him?"

"Caesar. Right." Zeke chuckled. "You know, he was smart to hide you. We were close to tracking you down, but then you went totally off-grid. Really had me in a bind."

Sarah's hands shook, her knees trembled. The pit in her stomach yawned. "Nobody was tracking us—the trail was clean!"

"I'm sure he told you that. And he was almost right. But we've had an eye on you for a while. The weird case from Maryland. Someone was pinging about having a breakthrough, a really inspired piece—happens all the time with the two-bits, you know. Everyone thinks they're the chosen one, the one that's gonna crack the code and make it big, spread it everywhere. But then we got wind of the body count. A whole room of gangsters cut to pieces. The two-bit girl smashed to bits in a toilet. We had a busy bee running around. We never did find him—that trail went absolutely cold—but you know who wasn't dead and still leaving traces? The teacher sister. And she had to have whatever was left of that breakthrough."

Sarah processed what he said, sweat stinging her eyes, her grip on Compton's neck suddenly clammy, the gun in her hand sticky and loose. She knew from Caesar that her brother had been entangled with the gangsters, Otto's crew—but someone else had been involved? Someone who knew about the room of cloth? Someone else he had killed?

"There's nothing left," she said breathlessly. "The pages— what my brother wrote—we burnt it all. It's gone!"

"Not all of it," Zeke said, the laugh under his words hardly hiding itself. "The rest is in your head. Percolating. Ripening. And it hasn't killed you yet! Rare for someone to last years like that. So, listen—why not hear me out? You can't be living well wherever you are. Why not crawl out of the garbage and into the sun? We can set you up. Whatever you want, we can give it to you. Money, status, whatever it is. Even something as simple as a roof over your head."

"Right," she said, "and there's just one thing I have to give you, right?"

"Right. Your fresh ink. Your flesh and your blood."

Those words again, the same words that scratched their way down her eyelids, past the security of her skull into the soft, tender white matter of her brain. That wasn't Zeke talking, whoever he had been before all this. He was a black space right now, a paper facsimile wavering over an abyss deep, dark, and dead. Something inhuman pulled his strings, positioned his arms and legs, strummed his vocal cords. Something red-eyed and furious.

She reaffirmed her grip on the gun. "Fuck off. I'm done talking. Where's Caesar? Otherwise, I kill your friend! Right here, right now!"

"Great question," Zeke said. "Where *is* Caesar? He could be in a lot of places right now. We aren't too picky about where the cheap cuts go. Meat's meat, after all."

Meat's meat. No. No. It wasn't true. It couldn't be.

"You fucker." She blinked, scowled, forced the sweat out of her eyes. She fought to keep her breathing under control, struggled to stop her stomach from free-falling. "You didn't."

"Take my offer," Zeke said. "I can take you to him. You two can be together. You can produce for us together. Nothing to worry about anymore—no looking over your shoulder ever again. I'm sure he'd be happy to see you. Happy to know you're safe."

"You bastard. You didn't. You *didn't*—"

"You know, he was so sincere talking about you. Just gobbled up everything we fed him. A cure? Sure. A way out? Of course. He wanted it to be true—needed it to be true. And little Compton there was born to be an actor, let me tell you. Really sold it. I swear there was a tear in your friend's eye when he looked at him. Almost like he'd seen him before. Like he knew him."

It was hard not to find it funny. Of course, the perfect bait to pull Caesar in was some scrawny, waifish waste of skin and space, a reproduction of her brother custom-built to trigger all the guilt, all the self-pity, all the remorse. There were millions of them, weren't there, countless copies of her brother mass-produced for the manacled man's enjoyment. All they needed was to pluck one from the assembly line, make it scrunch up its eyes, make it whine like the beaten dog it was. Sit. Roll over. Play dead. Perfect for trapping guilt-ridden former drug dealers and erstwhile mentors. Ideal for catching forsaken, failed, would-be sisters.

Did they know? Or was it the manacled man (as it always was) arranging the chess pieces? Goddamn it. Goddamn it all. Goddamn Caesar for falling for it, for being too weak to not see through the lies, the obvious artifice. And goddamn her most of all for letting it happen, for being so pathetic as to push him away, to make him think she needed saving. Goddamn it!

"The celebration is happening soon," Zeke said. "One of the biggest so far. Why not see the show? I can get you front-row seats. Who knows—maybe your friend will be there, too."

Celebration, she thought with dread. Where they send them through. Where they cross over those who had been squeezed dry. No. No. How long had it been since they exposed him? Goddamn it, Caesar. Why. *Why.*

Her eyes watered, blurred by tears just as much as sweat, so much that she didn't catch Zeke draw something from his sleeve and hold it up to the light. "I have your ticket here," he said. "Tells you exactly where you need to be. Free of charge."

"No!" yelled Compton suddenly, fiercer than she thought he was capable. "That's mine! Zeke, you can't! She doesn't deserve it!"

"And you do? Compton, buddy. You need five fingers if I recall correctly."

"Zeke! You promised! You fucking promised!"

Zeke laughed. "Hear that, Sarah? Hear him salivating? That's real desperation. That's real desire. He wants to leave. He wants to get out. Why deny him?"

"You son of a bitch," Sarah growled. "How dare you—how fucking dare you!"

"Seats at the celebration are limited," Zeke said. "You hear that, Compton? I'm afraid I have to change the terms of our deal. There's one last test. If you want your ticket, you'll have to deliver him a sacrifice! Show him your commitment! Really prove you're worthy!"

Compton struggled, summoning surprising strength. Sarah's grip on him faltered. "Don't!" she cried. "Compton, stop!"

"What's it gonna be?" Zeke asked. "The offer's not good for long!"

Compton spun around on Sarah. The revolver went off with a deafening boom. He fell, screaming, flopping, clutching at the gaping, bleeding cavity where his cheek had been. Sarah stood, dazed, her ears ringing. He lived only because she had flinched.

"Not a good showing, Compton!" Zeke called. "Pretty piss-poor, honestly!"

Sarah kept the revolver upon his wriggling form. "Stop!" she commanded, backing away, watching him rise to his feet like a zombie, his eyes as bright with rage as they were dark—pitch dark, like holes had been opened up in his skull. He advanced, arm swinging, cheek flapping. Blood gushed down his neck, drenched his shirt, stained the hand he used clumsily to keep his cheek in place. As dark as it was in the warehouse, Sarah could see clear into the bloody interior of his mouth, see in all its yellow the exposed dentin of his teeth. She fired again.

This time, he stayed down, blood massing under him like molasses. She watched, waiting for the last twitches of his fingers, the final spasms of his ruined face. She gagged, held a hand to her mouth. The gun fell. Oh, God. There was her brother eagle-spread in the light, skin rent, eyes glazed over. Not again. Not fucking again.

"You see him, don't you?" Zeke asked. "He's going over. Right in front of your eyes."

Of course she saw. The way the chains coiled around his ashen limbs. The way his gray face contorted in uncountable agony and his mouth widened in an endless, silent scream. The way he was pulled into the dark just outside the floodlights, the scrape of hooves mounting in the shadows, the murmur of ghouls growing to a clamor. Gone now. Gone forever.

"Your ticket," Zeke said, letting it fall to the floor just outside Compton's pooling blood. "Come see what we have to offer. Maybe you'll have a chance to see your friend. Maybe you'll even be able to save him."

"You fucker," Sarah said, wiping her lips of drool, gulping down bile. "You rat fucker!" She fumbled for the revolver, raised it—but Zeke was gone. The warehouse was empty, void of the ghosts, free of any other life now that Compton lay at her feet.

Numb, cold, she wet her boots in his blood and picked up the ticket stub Zeke had dropped. It was red—somehow darker, more nauseatingly noxious, than even the blood in which she stood. On the front of the stub, a date. On the back, coordinates.

She looked back at Compton's corpse. He thought he would have suffered more by staying here, stuck in his blood and bone, wallowing in his skin. Now he knew the truth. Knew it for an eternity. However much the hideous grin stretched over his face suggested otherwise.

"Caesar," she said. "I'm coming. For better or worse."

13.

The ticket led to Louisiana. Thirty minutes from Baton Rouge, partly consumed by vegetation and nestled in the dark of thick forestry, was the weathered relic of a plantation house. Two days before the celebration, Sarah stared at it from the verge of the forest, rosy dawn light filtering through the trees, silver mist coiling about the underbrush. She ventured inside.

Wandering the dark halls, boots falling on mottled carpet, fingers fondling tattered curtain, she wondered how such a place still existed. Whoever was behind Pink House chose not to restore or renovate it, but instead maintain the plantation in a bizarre half-life. There was a logic in keeping a location tethered to its violent past. Just as it made an artery's walls thin and flimsy, an overflow of blood weakened the barrier between the physical world and what lay beyond it. Sites of torture and torment, locales rife with massacre and mayhem—these were perfect for the manacled man. Indeed, the dead smell was couched in what remained of the upholstery, baked into the rotted wood of the floorboards. The dust hanging throughout the corridors was rank with the stenches of blood and rust. No room stank more than the reception hall on the ground floor. There, Sarah's legs almost gave out. How many had they put to the knife in that exact spot? How many more would they slaughter in the name of their god?

Back at her motel, under the hot spray of the showerhead, she contemplated the rosary. Caesar. Her guardian. Her protector. She had thought him weak, even resented him, but he had not abandoned her at all—he had been protecting her even in his absence, keeping her hidden, all the while searching for a means to set her free. If they had gotten him, if they had exposed him—just the thought summoned vomit to her lips.

The night of the celebration, she returned to the forest and waited in her truck. She downed one beer and then another, not sure what she was watching for—and then she saw it, a trail of orange lights bobbing in the misty darkness. Out of the truck, she crept to the edge of the forest and watched the torchlit procession file into the back of the plantation house. Compton and Zeke said the function of the celebration was to send people through, and there was only one way to accomplish that as far as Sarah knew. But were they sending themselves? Or someone else?

She had to fight away the image of Caesar on an altar, empty-eyed and slack-jawed.

Not five minutes later, her ears perked at the sound of an engine. Hi-beams flitted through the trees, then went dark. She circled back to her truck and crouched out of sight. A figure moved in the dark down the slope towards the plantation house. She counted out one minute, two minutes, five, and then she followed, gun raised, guiding herself slowly among the array of dark trees and gnarled roots. She kept low as she crossed the clearing to the house itself, but she didn't go inside. Without a doubt, whatever was happening was in that reception hall. She crept along the veranda and caught sight of faint, flickering lights beyond the hazy windows: candles. The view through the glass was foggy, indistinct, but there were the white robes crowded around another figure, this one in pink. As the pink robe moved and circled, the others cried and cheered. Was that their leader? Maybe Zeke?

She returned to the main entrance and tried the doors—surprisingly, they gave way, opening to the foyer. There was commotion past the doors to the reception hall. Yelling. Laughter. She raised the revolver and steeled herself, picturing what it would look like to rush in and open fire on the mass of white robes. She didn't have nearly enough rounds for all of them, but maybe she could carve a path, take hostage the one in pink, demand answers that way. But then what? The chances of escaping were slim. And if Caesar were inside, what then?

Wait—she remembered the stairwell and the vantage point from the second floor. She ascended to the mezzanine, concealed herself behind the rotted balustrade. She saw more clearly what was happening: a clump of white robes held down a struggling man. At the other end, before a doorway that coiled with darkness, the pink robe held a knife to a boy upon an altar.

"I am begging you!" the man cried. "I am begging you! You can have everything! You can do whatever you want with me! Just please don't hurt him! Please, don't! He's all I have left! He's the only thing I have left!"

Sarah watched, only half-listening as she scanned the crowd frantically for any sign of Caesar. But she couldn't focus, her attention consumed by the doorway and the roiling black within its space. The pink robe spoke—a woman's voice, dripping with smugness, reminding her of Zeke—but Sarah hardly registered the words. Her teeth chattered. Her heart thudded. They had already opened a portal, already invited things from the other side. Pronged tails slunk among the white robes. Gnashing fangs reflected the candlelight. Red eyes caught her own.

And the smell! A hundred times worse than before—no, a thousand! Her eyes stung. Her legs buckled. The stench was everywhere, emanating from the portal as well as around it. The white robes shook and stirred, their featureless ceramic masks nonetheless betraying desperate hunger, excited gluttony.

The man was screaming again. "I am begging you! I am begging you, don't hurt him! Don't touch him! Don't touch him, you fucking bitch! Don't touch him, or you'll pay! I swear to you, I'll make you pay, I'll make every one of you fuckers pay! You'll wish you'd never been born! You won't even get to die, I won't let you die, I'll make you suffer for every fucking second! You bitch! You fucking bitch! You bitch!"

The pink-robed woman looked up, revealed her red mask. Sarah stared at it, realized one of the most rancid, pungent smells came from that mask, that woman. She couldn't help it—the woman's putrid aura drowned out the rest of the chaos.

"I pity you," the woman said. "All this time, and you never realized."

"You bitch! Don't touch him, don't fucking touch him—"

"Poor boy. Never realized you were always just meat."

Sarah watched, not even thinking about interfering, unable to raise the gun even if she wanted to. The woman drew the knife across the boy's throat.

Pandemonium erupted. The white robes swarmed the boy's body, their cries more like animal shrieks than anything human. The other things snapped at their heels, licked their fangs with split tongues. Blades filleted flesh. Hatchets broke bone. Blood scattered. Lungs and kidneys were passed around. Entrails snaked through the throng. The crowd of white robes turned crimson, swelling and thrashing like a turbulent red sea. The pink robe stood apart from the chaos and watched with cool detachment, marked sobriety. Sarah stared at her, drawn by the incredible smell, a stench stronger than the dormant stink of the house, more powerful than the rancor of the bloodbath, somehow more fetid than even the portal they had opened. Then the pink robe looked up. Their gazes met across the carnage. In her mind's eye, Sarah saw wrinkled lips twist into a grin, saw leathery nostrils flare with glee. She froze. She had been so focused on the other smells that she had neglected her own, made sour and bitter over the years just like that woman's. A fatal error on her part. A winning stroke by the manacled man.

"Shit," she hissed. She scrambled down to the foyer, broke through the doors, made for the trees, feeling the woman's gaze on her back the entire length of the clearing. She felt another gaze as well, one furious and hungry and all too familiar.

No, she thought desperately, adrenaline pushing her to run faster, lunge harder. You won't get me—you won't fucking get me! Then she heard the cry. The scream.

She whirled around. Something was in the air above the house, faint and wispy like smoke. A small smell. Fresh. Young. Vanishing into the dark above, spreading out to the stars overhead. And then more smells erupted. She backed away, hand clasped over her mouth and nose. A heavier, hazier cloud floated into the air from the house, reeking of the collective smells of the bloodbath, ringing with screams and shrieks and howls and laughs. All around the house, filling the clearing, the gray dead raised their arms and eyes in celebration. They joined the hellish chorus with their own discordant symphony. Sarah watched in horror as the cloud dispersed in a final assault of screeches and wails. The ceremony complete, the ritual finished. Another delivery to the black throne. The gaping red star greedy for its latest meal.

She ran into the forest. Ringing in her ears was the cry of that little wisp, a pained, helpless pleading for salvation. Like the caress that lingered on her cheek even after years. Like the gray imp that watched her sometimes when she stirred, half-awake, and saw him at the foot of her bed. Little flames flickering, dying. Crying out one last time before being extinguished.

Hey guys, sorry for being inactive. Haven't been doing too well. I should have taken that DVD to the police. But I didn't. Even now, I can't really explain what the video is: a door at the end of a dark hall, hard red light spilling through the cracks. Red water that looks more like wriggling meat. Breathing and crying in the background. Is it supposed to be Becca? Did someone film her? I don't know. I don't care. I just wanted it gone.

I ended up trashing the DVD and tearing up the note. Not that it mattered. It was with me. IN me. In my dreams. Every night, I'm walking down the hall towards that red door. Every night, I'm sinking into that red water. Hearing that crying. Getting louder. Getting closer. Smelling like meat. On me, on my clothes. Everywhere.

And then last night. Last night. I was awake. I wasn't dreaming. I was NOT dreaming. But she was there. Standing in the room. Watching me.

I was coming out of another nightmare, smelling that stink on the pillow. I actually heard her first. Raspy breathing. Like leaves trapped in a filter. Crunching. Breaking. I stared hard into the dark and saw her there. I knew the shape of the ponytail immediately. Recognized the face.

Hi prof, she said. Breathing hard. Leaves in the gutter of her throat. You got my message?

I just stared. I don't think I took a single breath the whole time. As my eyes adjusted to the dark, I noticed other things. Her skin, gray like ash. The bruise around her neck, thick as a burn. Couldn't see her eyes. Only her smile. Her grin. Black and bleeding.

She said something else. He's waiting for you prof. Coming to bring you over. I don't know what happened next. It was morning. I felt like I hadn't slept in years.

Her words stick with me. He's waiting for you. Coming to bring you over. I can't pretend I don't know who she's talking about. I see him when I blink, when I'm falling asleep. Sometimes, the shadows around me feel too deep, like there's more space in them than there should be. And that's where he is.

I don't know who he is. What he is. But he's there. He's watching me. He's waiting for me. He has red eyes. Wrapped up in chains. Hanging from hooks. I never see him too well, but I know this is true. He's itching. Hungry. Mad. Furious. I know it because I'm feeling it. I'm scratching myself. I'm getting restless. I can't sit still. I can't sleep. I want to pull my skin off. I want to jump out of my body.

I'm pacing a lot. I feel anxious. I'm not eating as much. It's weird, but I get relief when I watch the video of the door. I'll watch it a lot, just looping it, feeling this weird sense of relief every time the door comes into view. There is something behind there. Someplace. A room. That's what keeps coming back to me. Room. room. room. A place where this doesn't matter. A place where none of this is a problem.

I know this sounds crazy. That's why I'm putting it down. I FEEL crazy. I'm worried. I'm doing things without even noticing. I was taking notes for the week, and the next thing I know, I'm drawing things. Boxes and rectangles. Circles. Spirals. They're messy, scribbled, drawn by someone who's crazy. I know what they are. They're not just shapes. They're the door. They're doorWAYS. They're openings into that other place. The place where HE is.

I keep a red marker on me, just to help with annotations. I don't remember taking it out, but I did. I colored in the door. I colored in his eyes.

I made a video of the drawings. I feel like it's important I document what's happening. That I show people. They need to know. They need to understand. What's happening is important. And it's just not just me. It's all of us. I'll post again. I have to. She wants me to. He wants me to.

JESUS

14.

They lay in the gray morning light, grinning in their bloodied robes, seizing flaps of skin and clenching shards of bone. Cut throats leaked dark blood. Slashed stomachs exposed dull viscera. Upon the altar were the remains of his brother: mere bits of meat and scraps of clothing. The stench of decay hung in the air. Mist wound its way inside from the cracks and crevices in the walls. The house creaked. The roof shuddered.

The red-masked woman walked among the bodies, examining the expressions, taking stock of the wounds. She twirled Jesus's knife. Hours before, he had looked up at her with disdain, hatred, but now his eyes were lightless, as cold as coal.

There were footsteps behind him, voices, but all sounds came through muffled. He recalled the bomb that had turned over their transport and almost taken his arm and leg. He had coughed out dirt, blinked through blood, crawled over glass into the unbearable heat of the sandbox. All the while, his hearing deafened, dampened. As though underwater.

"Your vehicle's ready, ma'am," one of the voices said. "Clean-up is on their way, too."

"And the straggler?" The woman's voice had lost the thunderous, theatrical tone—now she sounded tired, bored.

"We searched the area like you asked. There was a second set of tire tracks at the tree line, but they must have gone before we arrived."

She lifted her mask, sniffed the air. "She's not far."

"Do you want us to keep looking?"

"No. We have our schedule. Besides, we aren't leaving empty-handed. Tell Walter there's a package for him here. It needs some polishing."

"Yes, ma'am." Footsteps faded out of the room. The woman admired the knife in her hands, then threw it to the floor beside Jesus. He looked at neither her nor the knife. The altar's stone had cooled already. The pieces of meat had dried.

"You get to pass the message on now," the woman said. She ran her fingers down his face, left streaks of red across his brow, his cheeks. His mouth trembled. That was his brother. What remained of his brother. Hot tears mingled with the cold blood on his face.

The woman smiled beneath her mask. "Welcome. You're one of us now."

Hands grabbed him, dragged him, pulled him from the altar. He tried to call out, reach out, but his voice was too faint, his limbs too frail. Joaquin! His screams came out as whispers. Joaquin! I'll come back. I swear, I'll come back—

Light broke on him, he didn't know where or when. Through watery, feverish eyes, he saw a figure approach. "Come on, son. Let's go."

I can't move, he tried to say. I'm stuck. But his jaw was locked, his tongue chained. He was back on the roadside, kneeling before the overturned, fiery wreckage underneath that blistering sun. Jameson? You there? Kent? Joaquin? He reached for his brother, struggled against the robed bastards holding him back. Joaquin! Joaquin! That bitch had her hands on him, she was pressing the fucking knife to his neck. No! Joaquin! No!

Headfirst into a van. Prone in the comforting dark, away from the sun, out of the light and heat. Kent! Jesus Christ! Turning him over, wiping blood from his face. Jameson? Rocked by uneven road, sweating, drooling. Dragging them into the shade, turning back as the engine blew, the transport enveloped in fire. A particularly bad bump, and the desert was gone, replaced with that nightmarish hall full of skin and guts. He knelt before the stone plinth and its soiled surface. His brother vanishing into that tumult of robed bodies. The knife at his neck. His eyes going dark. Please! He's just a kid! I'll kill you! I'll kill all of you! But his hands were bound, his shoulders pinned. The red-masked woman laughed. Just meat, she said. Always just meat.

On the ground again. Hot dirt clung to his face. Dust pricked at his eyes, the back of his throat. Fresh sheets of sweat ran down his brow and washed into his eyes and mouth. The salty taste drew out a gag, a retch. Metal wedged into his arm, his leg, his face. Crawling over glass, cutting open his fatigues, tearing into his elbows and wrists. Jameson? You there? Kent? Kowalski? No—Kowalski hadn't been there. She'd been in the ground for months already. Beautiful even with her dust-glazed eyes and face. The same face torn apart by a sniper's bullet.

"Joaquin," he said. "Joaquin." Just a baby again. His father passed him into his arms. Take care of him. He'll look up to you. It's not fair, but he will.

Someone dragged him. Blue sky stretched on. A vulture soared, shrieked. Then a second vulture. A third. They circled. Circled what? Him? No—Kowalski? She lay in the dirt, eyes wide, cheek flapping. The vultures descended. They pulled at her hair, snapped at her flesh, plucked out her eyes. He rushed them, shouting, waving his arms. Get away, you fuckers! Get! She's not yours to take! But as he got closer, he saw it wasn't her corpse they desecrated. Hawks joined the fray, crows, all of them picking at a mess of exposed entrails and bloody bones. They cawed and cried. They perched on the stone altar, slivers of skin hanging from their red-smeared beaks. They grinned. They laughed. Their mouths ran black. They had no eyes.

Somewhere above him, a bell tolled. Tolled twice, three times, a hundred. He looked up. A red star approached, gargantuan, roiling, its exposed core a labyrinthine mesh of tarnished gears and razor-sharp cogs. Jesus stared into the machinery, was compelled towards it. He floated up into a funnel of lashing wind and uprooted refuse—around him swirled the wreckages of charred cars, blasted buildings, scorched storefronts. And then he heard the screams. He wasn't alone in the vortex— bodies rose alongside him, hundreds of them, thousands, entire cities of the living and the dead, the corpses gasping to life, un- life, unleashing black screams, loosening desperate cries, many of them laughing, too many. Jesus pulled, resisted, but he was powerless to escape the current, staring with dread as the gears and cogs retracted, unwound, and opened into a chasm of mangled limbs, ashen faces, tattered innards. Even further be- yond, a black sun floated over a horizon of blood and darkness—and that was where *he* waited. Frothing behind a buckled, leather muzzle. Struggling with bony limbs against rusted chains. Flailing broken fingers and smashed toes. Red-eyed and furious. Welcoming his most recent meal. Waiting for the promised time. The fated end.

Jesus screamed, could not stop screaming. Joaquin, he tried to shout. Joaquin! Help me! Save me! But as the darkness encroached, as the black sun engulfed him, he heard only the red-masked woman's voice, thick with victory, dripping with satisfaction.

Welcome, she said.

You're one of us now.

15.

He shot upright in a bed, breathing hard, drenched in sweat. He sat rigid, lost, trying to summon back the preceding events. The motel room. The plantation house. The dining room with its painting of horses. The foyer. The hall. The altar.

He vomited.

He stared at the yellow streaks staining the sheets, but saw red instead. His nose hovered over the bile, but he smelled blood. He shut his eyes and envisioned vividly the moment Joaquin disappeared into the mass of white robes, the pieces of his body divided, distributed, devoured. The noises those people made. How they shook and squirmed and shifted. The red stains on their white masks. The blood upon his face. His brother's blood upon his face.

He touched his cheeks, his brow. Dry. Clean. Even the tear-stains had been washed away. "Joaquin," he whispered. "Joaquin. Joaquin." As if saying his name would somehow bring him back. As if chanting the name would conjure him. He thought briefly that his brother was there amid the shadows, the darkest places in the room, those most devoid of light—but he was alone. His brother was not even in the silence. Just the memory of the butchering, a ringing in his ears, the faintest sound of someone crying out, calling his name.

He trailed exhausted eyes over his surroundings. A small room, lit softly by the sunlight through the window. On a bedside desk was a plate of chicken breast and vegetables. A bookshelf stood by the door. Quiet. Quaint. A far cry from the hell of the plantation house.

He didn't know how or why he was there. He didn't care. He couldn't keep his eyes open, but the relief of sleep never came. There was only the altar. Only his brother vanishing.

At length, a man appeared in the doorway. He was gray-haired and well-groomed, in plaid and jeans. He wiped his hands with a rag and peered at Jesus over thick glasses.

"You're awake," he said. "I left a plate there in case I wasn't around when you woke up. But if you'd prefer, I have some soup on the stove. Might do you better."

Jesus stared at him. Before, he might have leapt up and seized the man by the throat, but now his body held firm, immovable. He shook, convulsed. He couldn't control himself.

"You're safe," the man said. "No one's going to hurt you here."

"Who are you?" asked Jesus, his voice barely above a whisper. "Where am I?"

"My name is Walter Randolph. You're in my cabin. Been here for about two days now. This is the first I've seen you clear."

Jesus looked away. He saw only his brother torn apart. He saw only his brother scattered among that raving, writhing horde.

Randolph watched as Jesus trembled and cried. He placed an uncertain hand on Jesus's shoulder. "I know, son. I know what they did. But you're safe here. They're gone."

Jesus just cried and whimpered. He said again his brother's name.

Time passed in a fog. Occasionally, he awoke to the room, had enough sense to wipe his tear-strewn eyes, cover his sweat-ridden face. Mostly, he wandered, if not in the desert that now smelled of blood, then among the corpses of the plantation house, their grinning faces black-mouthed and hollow-eyed. The doorframe with its impossible space loomed over him, the plane encompassed within like the surface of black water, black water that rippled and undulated and eventually flowed loose. The red-masked woman was with him constantly. When he rode with his squad over sun-bleached roads and along craggy ridges, she sat beside him. When he poured lighter fluid over a dying fire, she stood in the darkness just outside the fading, flickering light. When his father ushered him inside the hospital room to meet his newborn brother, she was there also, looking over the fresh meat, playing with the knife.

The knife. It was there, too, on the bedside desk. Clean and stainless. As though it had never broken the flesh of the trophy wife, the drug dealer, Mildred, Hamilton, Allen. As though it had never bathed in his brother's blood.

Randolph nursed him. He fed him pieces of meat, spoon-fuls of broth. He held glasses of water to his lips, sang old lullabies to soothe him to sleep. Jesus shuddered under the man's touch, but he could not summon the strength to fight. When he looked up, there was not the old, stoic face, but the woman's red mask. There were the hollow eyes and black mouth of his slain mother. Oh, his mother. Had he thought of her? Had he thought of his father? In all the time since returning home, returning to a life put on pause, a life destroyed, had he thought of them? He wept for them. He wept for himself.

Eventually, the shaking subsided. He rose from the bed. He passed through a bare parlor and kitchen, and outside, he found Randolph sitting on a tailgate, sorting fishing bait. The forest around them was quiet, the silence broken only by periodic birdcall. A silver sun shone down on them. Jesus took in the visuals and sounds, even the silence, but the gears of his mind clicked and clicked without finishing their rotations. Something obstructed the machinery.

Randolph looked up. "Found your feet," he said. He spat out a clump of tobacco that hit the grass as thick and black as tar. Jesus thought the tobacco smoking, as if dredged from some boiling, subterranean pit. Somewhere much, much deeper than even that.

"How are you feeling?" Randolph asked. He eyed Jesus, ready to intervene in the event of another collapse, a spasm. But Jesus only stood there, regarding the forestry with dim interest.

"I don't know," he said at last. "I don't feel anything. I can't think."

"Why don't you come fishing with me? Keep me company."

Jesus complied, or more accurately, did not resist—the two drove in Randolph's truck down a winding road to a small lake. All the while, Jesus thought of the drives with Joaquin, the way he felt the need to talk to fill up the silence, to hopefully animate his mute brother. But no matter what he said, what story he told, what memory he evoked, Joaquin never responded. His glazed eyes stared ahead. His lips never even quivered. Only in the night, when assailed by dreams, did he make any sounds, did he betray any indication of intelligence or feeling. The sole exception being in the grip of that red-masked woman, seeing in her probably what he saw the night of their parents' murder. Did he blame Jesus? Did he resent him? Did he hate him? Even had he asked, he would never have received an answer.

All that time on back roads and highways, in motel rooms and empty houses—all that time hunting and plotting and killing, seeing red, smelling blood—none of it felt real. He sat on the lakeside with Randolph. The man hummed, chewing slowly on his tobacco, gauging and reeling keenly every cast of the line. Jesus looked at the water, and he remembered standing in the morning sunlight with his brother, telling him about their grandmother, suggesting they visit Abilene, as if there had been even the remotest possibility of returning to a normal life. Had he ever thought seriously about their endgame? It was almost as if another person had planned and executed those murders with mechanical, merciless precision. Almost as if whoever had been in his body left with his brother into the air, into that void in the doorframe.

All seemed like a dream, like shadow play. The sandbox and his squad. The sniper shot that felled Kowalski. The fall that discharged Jackson. The roadside bomb that almost killed him, Jameson, and Kent. The shrapnel lodged in his arm and leg. The miracle of his recovery and rehabilitation. Signing up for a second tour. Telling his mother through her tears and screams that it was his duty. His responsibility to the others. But that had been a lie. The truth was that he had been afraid, terrified, because somewhere along the way, the certainty that drove him his entire life faltered. When had that happened? When Kowalski went down? When the bomb went off? When Jesus looked around himself and saw *nothing*, not defense, not freedom, not reason? When he saw hate in the eyes of people where he expected gratitude? When he looked at the American flag and failed to feel honor and patriotism—when he felt nothing at all, not even resentment, not even bitterness? The second tour had been an attempt to force his life and perspective back into place. If he had conceded that he was lost and went back home and sat there with his useless, pointless degree and his useless, bloody hands, not wanting to do anything, not wanting to achieve anything—well, that couldn't be. He wouldn't let it be. And as punishment, his parents had been butchered. Out of pride, he hadn't been there to protect them. Had he been there that night, would he have even raised a finger? Would he have fought that pale kid and his psycho friends? Or would he have just been another of their carved-up sacrifices? He didn't know. It wasn't fatigue that he felt. It wasn't despair. It was like feeling nothing at all. Like everything he had done—no, plain *everything*—was for nothing.

"We're about two hours from Baton Rouge," Randolph said a couple of hours later. The sun was lower in the sky, the water largely still. Two catfish had been put on ice, a third hopefully incoming. Jesus sat and stared.

"I know how you probably feel," the old man went on. "Don't want to be here. Don't want to live." He reeled in his line. "It was my daughter they took. Or should I say, he took her. The one they pray to. The master of that place. The man in chains."

Jesus watched black clouds bloom under the surface of the water. He smelled blood.

"The people there," Randolph said, "the ones who died, they aren't anybody special. They're the little people. The ones who get hooked on the bait. But there are others who watch over everything. They're the ones with the money and the power. They find those places closest to the other side. They set up the events. They pay people like me to clean up. Manage it."

"Why keep me alive?" asked Jesus. "I was going to kill them."

"Because you're a witness. You get to spread the word."

A witness. The red-masked woman said the same thing. The others went on ahead, moving to parts unknown—or parts known, known very well. All the posts online, the messages, the forums, the videos, the images, all had pointed to that space in the doorframe. Somehow, despite everything, he had refused to believe it. Even after seeing the video of the dark hallway with the red room at its end. Even after the nightmares of the girl in the photo with the waterfall behind her, the nightmares he dismissed as stress-induced. Up until the moment of revelation, the members of Pink House had been just lunatics. What they believed had been fantasy, indulgence, justification for their depravity. The talk of people disappearing, dying, and then coming back—the countless photos of fathers, mothers, brothers, sisters, husbands, wives, sons, and daughters—he wouldn't believe any of it. He had rationalized it all as part of the hoax, some elaborate ploy to recruit and propagate. Social engineering taken to the most ridiculous extent for the most unbelievable cause. And then the space in the doorframe had grown dark. Something had appeared amid the nothing. And it had taken all of them. It had taken Joaquin.

"My daughter," Randolph said. "Her name was Victoria."

If this was an invitation to share, Jesus could not muster the strength. He could not break through the fog over his mind, a fog that grew increasingly dark and rancid with the smells of meat and blood. But he tried. He forced himself to comprehend Randolph's words.

"This was years ago now," Randolph said. "Back when the Internet was still barely a thing. They couldn't get it around as easily, so they left packages. Dead drops. Sometimes for people to pick up randomly. Other times because they had somebody in mind. I still don't know if Vicky was an accident or something more intentional. But one day, she came in the house with a box. My wife, she couldn't stand the smell of it. My son, neither. But Vicky looked in, and there was a Polaroid picture. And when she looked at that picture—when I looked at it—I knew something was lost right then and there. I wasn't going to get her back."

He described the girl's slow shift—how she left the photograph in a drawer for a week before looking at it again, how the intervals of time became shorter and shorter until the picture was on her person always, tucked in a pocket, hidden by a scarf. Slowly and then dramatically, her grades got worse, and she cut off one friend and then another until suddenly, the sleepovers and weekend shopping sprees seemed to have never happened at all. His wife suspected the influence of drugs, of boys too old or too criminal, but Randolph knew the truth when he found the notebook with her scrawls and sketches, when he found the drawings lining her closet. But at that late stage, he had only himself to blame. He had seen the figures in his periphery. He had heard the whispers. He had dreamed the scenes of mass death and destruction. He had drawn out spirals and shapes on legal pads in his office. He had felt the pull of the photograph, felt the desire to rip it away from his daughter and ogle it and even kill her if that was what it took to have it for himself, all for himself. And he nearly did kill her when the time came that he said enough was enough, and she clawed and screeched and pulled and pushed, no love in her eyes, not even recognition, just pure, primal hatred. Howling and frothing and scrambling on all fours as though she were feral. He had to shut his eyes as he tore up the photograph and threw the pieces into the fireplace. The voices screaming all the while, begging, pleading for him to look, look, LOOK. Open your eyes! Be free!

When it was done, the way she cried. The way she yelled. He didn't know if the agony he felt was due to her suffering or the photograph burning. His wife and son also screaming, staring at the pale girl with half her hair pulled out and her ribs pushing against her skin and her teeth black and her eyes like pits. He could not have imagined that she would plunge her own hands into the flames and pull them out blackened and steaming. He could not have imagined she would shed actual tears over the curling, darkening flaps of paper. He could not have imagined she would reach for the nearby fire poker and thrust it into her throat. He could not have imagined she would smile afterwards, all the pain erased, all the trauma vanished. He had never seen her so happy.

Some years later, long after the wife and son had left, Pink House came for him. He used the words deliberately. Came for him. They showed him a Polaroid like the one he destroyed. A picture of his daughter. A picture of his daughter smiling. In a place he didn't recognize but knew intimately. In a place he never wanted to go.

"Do you want to see her?" the man with the Polaroid asked him. "She wants to see you."

Randolph stared into the placid water of the lake. "Maybe a year will pass, or six months, or two weeks, and there will be another picture. And they say I can go anytime." He smiled. "My Vicky's still alive in there. In that room."

At last, Jesus found words. "Is my brother there, too? My parents?"

Randolph shrugged. He said there was only one way to know.

The next morning, after a breakfast of poached eggs and black coffee, Randolph led Jesus into the cabin's den. A sketchpad and pencil were arranged on the table. Jesus sat slowly, clumsily, his body still not fully under his control. Randolph settled into a recliner across from him. He gestured to the sketchpad and pencil.

"They're coming for you soon," he said. "They'll expect you to produce."

"Produce?"

"Write. Draw. Paint." Randolph held the sketchpad out to him. "Whatever comes naturally to you. For me, it was taking pictures. Trying to capture what I saw in that photo."

Jesus held the sketchpad, lifted the pencil. They trembled in his hands.

"I don't feel anything," he said. "I don't know what you want me to do."

"You have to try, son. Write something."

Jesus touched down the tip of the pencil, the graphite making jittery scratches against the thick paper. His only natural talent had been precision work: repairing engines, assembling circuits, soldering motherboards. In its prime, kept pristine by the maintenance of war, his clockwork mind had been ideal for tasks like cleaning cartridges and determining gear allotments. He had no creative inclination, no abstract touch. He read and watched little of fiction, struggled to visualize scenarios not supplemented by his experience. To draw or write, to channel any authorial impulse, demanded too much, especially in this depleted state. No words came to mind to write. No pictures appeared to him to draw—at least no pictures he wanted to draw. If he let his mind wander, only the roadside wreckage came to him. Only Kowalski's maimed face floated by. Only the stone altar, dirty with blood and meat, rose from the darkness.

The sketchpad, stained by his tears, convulsed in his hands. Patiently, gently, Randolph freed the sketchpad and pencil from Jesus's grip. "It's okay," he said. "We'll try again later."

They tried a second time, a third. The result was always the same. Jesus dropped paintbrushes, fumbled pens. The few words he managed to write, splotched by frustrated, anguished tears, were met with the gentle click of Randolph's tongue, a disapproving murmur.

"It's not what they want," he said, reviewing the few lines penciled in awkward, toddler-like script. "They won't accept it."

"What *do* they want?" Jesus asked. "What is this? Why am I here?"

"You must spread the word."

"What does that *mean*?" He looked up, eyes hot with fresh tears. "That woman"—the mention of her, the image of the red mask and pink robe, sparked the scattered machinery of his mind to life—"she could have killed me. She should have killed me. Because I'll—I'll—"

The brief energy left him. He sunk back into the sofa, even more crestfallen than before. "She should have killed me because I was the one who did it all. Not Joaquin. He was innocent. He's always been innocent."

Randolph regarded the flustered face. He played with his glasses, wiped them down. "If you can't produce," he said at length, "they'll kill you."

Jesus did not reply. He was no longer in the cabin, but again in the desert, under that sun, breathing in that dirt. He was again at the plantation, in that hall that became a slaughter-house. His brother on the altar. The knife at his neck. The way his eyes went dark.

"Oh, God." He broke into tears, gasping for air and clawing at his throat as though he were suffocating. The crying wasn't cathartic. He felt no relief, no calm. In fact, his tears only frenzied him further. They seemed to increase themselves, accelerate their own production, derive from a hidden reserve he had never tapped. A lifetime supply unleashed in a torrent.

Randolph watched him. He eased Jesus up and back to his room.

16.

In the evening, Randolph found him huddled against the bed. "Get up, son. We're leaving." Jesus was unresponsive. "Listen to me! We have to go."

Sluggishly, Jesus got to his feet. Randolph dressed him in his jacket, his boots. He passed a wad of bills into his hands.

"You need to hit me. Do you understand?"

"What?"

"We need to make it look like a struggle. Like you escaped."

"I don't—"

"Just punch me. Don't hold back."

Jesus stared at him. Slowly, he pieced together the situation.

"Why are you letting me go?"

"If you don't have the urge to produce," Randolph said, "it might not be too late. Maybe he doesn't have a strong grip on you." He smiled. "Now, hard as you can. Make it convincing."

Jesus hesitated, but he raised his fist. His muscle memory did the rest.

Jaw purpling, Randolph led him outside. "Don't assume they can't find you," he said, ushering Jesus into the van. "Keep your head down. Stay quiet."

Jesus sat limply. Where could he even go? Back home, to the house where his family was butchered? And the police, they would be investigating by now the scattered disappearances. He was a wanted man with nowhere to go, nowhere to hide. Admit it, he told himself. You hadn't planned on coming back from the celebration, your brother be damned.

He tried to quiet those thoughts, looking at the money in his hands for a distraction. Besides his clothes, the money was all he had, too. The truck was gone, the gear gone, the guns gone. Even his knife, though Randolph had urged him to take it, remained on the bedside desk back in the cabin. He shuddered just thinking about it.

Randolph got into the van. "You can start again," he said. "Don't end up like me."

They drove, headlights illuminating an uneven road riddled with rocks and branches. In the passenger seat, jostling with each bump, Jesus thought himself once again in his truck, driving into darkness with his brother beside him, imagining in that red, mechanical way the next murder, the specifics of the slaughter, the banal brutality. The sandbox had been similar, each excursion marked by a mental map of potential violence, each day defined by detachment. Assess, project, compartmentalize. Remove himself as much as possible from what his hands had to do. Distance himself from the immediate because otherwise, he could not *be* there. As a boy, he had prodded his grandfather constantly for stories about his war, starving for the gritty details of mud, rain, ocean, blood. When fighting in the desert, he understood finally why his grandfather would never speak about the Pacific: the distance made it impossible. He imagined his grandfather as having not inhabited his body, instead operating the machinery at range, piloting his edifice of skin and bone through battleground and gunfire. Jesus did the same, and only then, lurching in the van seat, with nothing and no one left, he realized at last that the compartmentalization came at a cost. The sandbox had stayed with him, likely the same way the Pacific had stayed with his grandfather. He had not avoided the violence but only suppressed it, shaken it with his fury until it blew.

There's nothing to restart, he wanted to say. No home. No family. No purpose. Nothing. All the violence of the war for nothing. All the vengeance of his vendetta for nothing. Just a trail of blood and bone that coiled through desert and fog, across highway and motel room. A trail that led nowhere. A trail that terminated in darkness.

But that wasn't quite right, was it? The blood did go some- where. Where Randolph's daughter was. Where Mildred and Hamilton and Allen were. Where Joaquin was.

"The room of cloth," Jesus said. "Can—"

Headlights blazed on behind them.

Randolph looked into the rearview mirror. "Too soon! It can't be them."

Jesus turned, blinded by the lights. His mind was blank, the broken pieces barely even twitching. There was no plan, no strategy, but excitement emerged nonetheless, an explosion of emotion he couldn't explain. It felt like an itch, a red, hot itch, like the feeling that sparked when he raised his knife to strike down a victim. Only that red itch was turned inward this time. Take me, he thought. Kill me. Put an end to this.

The headlights came upon them fast, filled up the rearview, filled up the entire cabin. "Damn it!" hissed Randolph, but there was nothing he could do—the other vehicle struck them from behind. The van swerved off the road, stopping just short of slamming into a tree. Jesus's head snapped back against the headrest. For a moment, the night sky was blazing white, and he was spinning in that blown transport, glass raining down on him. He blinked, shook his head. You're not there, he thought, focusing on the dark ahead, on the bark of the tree that nearly bisected the van's hood. You're here. You're *here*.

He and Randolph climbed out and stumbled onto the road. A gunshot rang out. "Hands up," commanded a woman's voice. "On your knees. No sudden movements."

They did as ordered, kneeling in the dirt, squinting into the headlights that had run them off. The woman approached, silhouetted by the lights. As she came closer, Jesus was able to discern some of her features. Thin, wiry body. Small, flat mouth. Short hair with the color and texture of straw. 38 Special with silver barrel, leather grip. Slender, untrained hand. He could wrench it from her easily, throw her down, keep her pinned. A week prior, he would have done so, but any thought of action brought pain, and any attempt at movement felt like dragging cement. And that excitement, that red itch, lurked behind his eyes. They followed the revolver hungrily, almost against his will. A bullet from that would take him away, release him from all this. No more desert. No more plantation. No more altar with its soiled surface.

Just get up, he thought. Force her hand. But his body resisted.

"Who are you?" asked Randolph. "You're not one of them."

"I'm asking the questions," the woman said. She aimed the gun at one, then the other. "The woman in the red mask. Who is she?"

Jesus froze. There she was again, twirling his knife. Taunting him. Laughing at him. Smearing his brother's blood across his face.

"I don't know what you're talking about," Randolph said.

"Bullshit. She was at the celebration, like she was supervising. And she stinks. More than everyone there combined."

"You were there?"

"Who is she?"

Randolph shook his head. "I don't know. I don't know who she is."

"I doubt that." The woman held the gun inches from Randolph's face. "This guy was there, too. Why do you have him now? Who are you?"

"Please," Randolph said. "If we don't get there on time, they'll know something's wrong." He paused and wrinkled his nose. "My smell has always been bad, but I can tell it's on you. They'll want you for sure. They'll chase you down."

"I just need a name. Who is she?"

He said nothing more, looking at her with his old, rheumy gaze, hands in the air.

"Okay," the woman said. "Fine." She backed up and trained the revolver on Jesus. "He's valuable, right? Something happens to him, what? They'll kill you?"

Jesus eyed the cold steel of the revolver barrel. Maybe he wouldn't have to do anything, after all. Maybe fate would take care of him all on its own.

"Please," said Randolph. "I give you her name, they'll kill me, anyway."

"*I'll* kill you. I've done it before." Her finger twitched against the trigger. "A name. This is your last chance."

Jesus met Randolph's gaze. Maybe he had watched his daughter's suicide with the same mixture of fear and shame. Maybe he was reliving it even then, just as Jesus relived Joaquin's death every night, every morning, every moment. A never-ending loop of the moment when life ends and something worse than death begins.

"Lyle," Randolph said, so softly they almost didn't hear him. "Kendra Lyle."

The name floated between Jesus's ears, found a dark place among the refuse of his mind. A spark flared beneath the mess of broken parts and combusted machinery. Kill her, urged that red itch. Like you promised you would. Kill her.

The woman hesitated. "Kendra Lyle? The author?"

"Please," Randolph continued. "It won't help you to know. She's more connected, more powerful than you think—"

"It doesn't matter. How do I find her?"

"I have a map. Where I was taking him." Randolph nodded towards his breast. "It's in my pocket. Let me get it for you."

"Slowly," she said. He nodded, dipping a hand gingerly towards his breast pocket—and then he sprang. She fired the gun, clipping him in the arm, and he took her by the wrists. Jesus watched them struggle, heart hammering, mind blanking once more.

"Run, son!" Randolph yelled. "Get out of here!"

Jesus rose on trembling legs. One foot moved forward in attack while the other slid back in retreat. Help him. Run. Help him. Run. Take a bullet. Run. Help him. Take a bullet. Run. Take a bullet. Take a bullet. His brother on the altar. The knife at his neck. Take a bullet. Help him. The knife at his neck. Run. His brother on the altar. The knife at his neck. Help him. Take a bullet. The way his eyes went dark. The way his eyes went dark.

His feet finally moved, driving him off the road and plunging him into the dark of the trees. The sounds of the struggle grew faint, and then another gunshot ended them. He didn't look back, stomping through mud and grass, shielding against branch and web. Coward, a voice whispered from the depths of his mental wreckage. You're a coward.

He was crying again. Running away, the voice said, that's all you ever do, isn't it? Run from your family. Run from your brother. Run from an old man you could have saved. Run, run, run. As fast as you can.

He stopped and gathered his breath. He sobbed. In the absolute, pitch black, surrounded by a symphony of chirpy crickets and throaty toads, he could see the cosmos above, the distant stars glimmering like miniscule diamonds. "Joaquin," he said, "I'm sorry. I'm sorry."

He buried his face in his hands, sought fleeting comfort in the darkness, the seclusion—and then smelled something. A flowery scent. A hint of rosemary. His mother's favorite perfume. She had smelled so strongly of it on the day of his brother's birth, cradling him, cooing him. My sweet boy, she said. His exhausted, sweat-drenched mother, holding in her arms the blue-robed baby, smiling despite her fatigue. The baby who looked around with wide, clear eyes. Both of my boys, she said, pulling him close to the hospital bed, so that the baby filled up his vision, so that he was smothered in that smell. My beautiful, beautiful boys.

"Mom?" he asked, looking to the expanse above. "Is that you?"

But he knew the answer immediately. He smiled. He laughed.

"Joaquin. It's you, isn't it?"

Another wash of that smell, as though he were small again, lingering by her bedside as she nursed his brother. What a miracle. What an impossible, inscrutable miracle. A second chance for a coward. An opportunity for redemption.

"I'm coming," he whispered into the dark. "Just wait for me. Wait for me."

The rosemary swelled in response. The night sky glimmered. Yes, they said. We'll wait. We'll wait as long as it takes.

17.

In a Baton Rouge motel, he sat on the bed and ate a pack of powdered donuts. His broken clockwork mind sputtered and rumbled. Gears turned vainly, but they turned. With time, he could repair them enough to complete this new mission. Not one of retaliation, but retrieval.

He regretted not asking Randolph more—more about what he saw within the doorframe, more about the people at the celebration, more about how they traveled through that portal. Kill yourself, came the thought. Cut your throat as they did. Spill your blood. But that would be pointless if he went and could not return. There had to be a way to bring Joaquin back. Bring his parents back. Venture across that threshold and pull them from the bloody mire.

He looked up. All was dark in the motel room save for the light from the restroom. The doorframe consumed his attention. He put aside the donuts.

"Joaquin? Are you there?"

Neither the faintest of cries nor the vaguest of whimpers in response. He stood and placed a hand upon the doorjamb. He closed his eyes and said his brother's name again, more statement than question, more command than request.

"Joaquin. I'm here, brother. I'm looking for you."

Nothing again. Except maybe the slightest of stirrings in the air. The most shallow of laughs, mistaken easily for creaks in the walls or floor.

"Give me a clue. A sign. Anything. What do I need to do?"

He listened, straining every sense, barely even breathing. And then a whiff. A waft of a smell that should not have been in that room, that could not have been. Rosemary. Brief, more suggestion than reality, but there. Coming through the doorway. Unmistakable. Loving.

He slept that night, undisturbed by visions of the desert or the red-masked woman. He dreamed instead of working in the garage with oil-stained hands while Joaquin filmed him, asking him questions for some would-be documentary. His mother brought him water. His father passed him tools. He smiled and laughed and showered all of his family with love. I love you, brother, he said. Mom and Dad. I love you. I will get you back. I promise. I promise.

In the morning, over eggs and toast at the nearby diner, his thoughts moved in a more painful, stunted direction. Lyle. Kendra Lyle. What could he do? Track her down? Kill her? The violence that had been easy and automatic felt laborious now. He lacked the energy. He lacked the will. On the road, collecting the fingers and eventually the ticket for the celebration, the next steps were always clear. There were never obstacles, only diversions—the clockwork mind calculated, accommodated new information, and then calculated again. For every wrinkle, contingencies developed without conscious effort. Such was the heat of his rage, the completeness of his desire for revenge. He only ever saw red, heard red, felt red. The red itch. Impossible to scratch. Impossible to placate. Even when those people stripped him of his weapons, even when that woman Lyle mocked him, he had planned their collective annihilation. But the clockwork mind had been disassembled along with his brother. The minute hand moved too slowly, that of the hour not at all. When he tried visualizing the next month, the next week, the next day, he saw only fog, dark and dense, permeated not with the smell of gunpowder as he had come to expect, but with the smell of blood. The smell of meat long turned black.

Things shambled in that fog, groping blindly, fruitlessly. Were they only phantoms of his mind, born from malnutrition and exhaustion? Or were they really the same figures that plagued Randolph? Were they really the denizens of the room of cloth, the room that was not a room? He thought about the girl in the picture with the waterfall, Lucy. He thought about Randolph's daughter, Victoria. He thought about Mildred, Hamilton, Allen, the others. Did they all wander that wasteland of blood and smoke? Did Joaquin and his parents? How many others, in what states of disrepair or mutilation? Or perhaps they were in states of health? Safety? Security? Maybe his vision was skewed by this world of skin and bone he inhabited. After all, the rosemary scent that graced him wasn't tortured or agonized. It was thick with comfort, full of love. An invitation to come in, not a warning to stay out.

He went outside and sat in the shade of the diner. He closed his eyes. Focus, he told himself. Relax. Let it do the work for you. Summoning any amount of mental energy was excruciating, but he fought, pushing aside those intrusive images of the roadside wreckage, of Kowalski's maimed face, of the stone altar. He forced himself through that foul-smelling fog. Slowly, like relics uncovered from black depths, words emerged. Spread. Engulf. Infect. Disseminate. Propagate.

"Is that what I'm supposed to do?" he asked. "Spread it?"

Lyle said he got to pass the message on. Randolph said he had to produce. Write, draw, paint, whatever came to him. He scanned the dirt, grabbed a pebble. He scrawled random words on the wall of the diner, whatever came to mind. Tree. Rock. Book. Blood. Room. Room of cloth. He tried numbers. Four. Five. 6. 7. 21. 100. Symbols. #. $. @. Nothing. Nothing coming to him, nothing moving him. No swell of emotion, no break of insight. No urge or compulsion.

He searched the etchings for signs, canvassed them for clues. "What am I supposed to see? Show me, Joaquin. Show me."

He focused despite the pain, amassed all the energy he could manage—and there it was, floating from behind him. Rosemary. His sign. His clue.

"Is this it?" he laughed. "Is this what you need?"

"Hey."

He turned, startled. Not his brother behind him, not his mother, but the woman from before, the one who held him and Randolph at gunpoint. In the sunlight, she looked more clearly haggard than he had noticed before, denim shirt splotched with sweat, jeans stained and torn, boots scuffed. She looked upon him with dark-ringed eyes.

He backed against the wall, staring at her. The rosemary coated her like perfume.

"Relax," she said. "I'm not here to hurt you." She lit a cigarette and studied the words and numbers he had etched. "What are you trying to do?"

He said nothing. She gestured to the diner. "Let's go in. I'm starving. And don't bother running. You smell worse than you think. It won't take me long to find you again."

At a booth, he watched as she downed coffee, cut into waffle. She chewed vigorously, almost angrily, never looking up at him.

"Did you kill him?" he asked at length. "The old man?"

She bit off a piece of bacon the way a wolf might rip off the flank of a deer. She shrugged. "I shot him. Don't know if he's alive."

"Why? What do you want?"

"You know what I want."

"The woman."

"Yeah. Kendra Lyle." She peered at him over the rim of her coffee mug. "You were there. At the celebration."

He was silent.

"They left you alive. Why?"

"I don't know."

"Guess."

"Randolph—the old man—he said they want me to produce. They were going to take me somewhere to do that."

"I can guess what that means," she said. "Pink House recruits people. And when they're done, they get cycled out. To make room for a new batch."

She looked over her shoulder, surveying the parking lot through the window.

"You expecting someone?" he asked.

"She knows who I am. She saw me. Saw through me. Someone like that is old—been around a long time. She's survived somehow."

"Saw you?"

"Yeah. The same way I saw her. Her smell."

"Smell?"

She stared at him. "You don't know? It's his mark on you, getting stronger all the time. It's how I found you. I hid out for a couple of days, then circled back to the plantation. The closest smell I could track was you and the old man."

"Why are you looking for her?" he asked. "What do you get out of it?"

"It doesn't matter. I'm assuming you don't know where she is."

"No. Randolph never said."

She nodded, stood up, left cash on the table. Without a word, she went outside. He followed. "Wait! Do you know what it is? The room?"

"Just forget about it," the woman said. "You don't have long, anyway."

"Is there a way inside?"

"Only one. Give him your blood."

"Give who?"

"The man in chains," she said. "The manacled man."

She climbed into her truck, turned the engine. He reached for the door. "Wait—help me. Please. Help me find another way. I need to get inside."

"Why? It's pointless."

"I'll help you," he said. "I can find her. I can track her down like I tracked the rest of them. That's why I was there in the first place. I was going to kill them."

The disdain in her face was barely contained. She made to yank the door free—

"They killed my brother," he said suddenly, breathlessly. "They butchered him. Whatever you saw, he was in the middle of it. The start of it."

She watched him, his quivering lips, his watery eyes.

"Please. I need to know more. I'll do anything you want."

Something in her own face changed, almost imperceptibly. She jerked a thumb to the passenger door. "Get in. Before I change my mind."

He did so. She pulled up her shirt, revealed the revolver tucked into her jeans. "You try anything, your brains will be scraps on the road. We clear?"

He nodded. They backed out of the lot, and then they were on the road. She didn't say a word as they drove, gray eyes fixed ahead, the bony fingers of one hand clamped around the steering wheel as though welded there. Her pack of cigarettes rustled atop the dashboard. A gold-colored rosary, unadorned, unassuming, hung from the rearview mirror. His sight clouded again under a pall of darkness. His nostrils filled once more with the stench of sizzling skin. But there was hope now, the promise of reprieve. This was his sign. Find a way, he kept telling himself, breathing in more of that blessed rosemary. Get across. Bring them back.

18

By nighttime, they pulled into the parking lot of a roadhouse in Texas. According to the blue neon sign, the name was "Earl's."

"Wait here," said the woman once they were inside. She headed up a set of stairs. Jesus sat at a table and watched as the staff positioned speakers and drums for the upcoming band. A mural of blue bonnets decorated the stage, a backdrop too innocent for a place that stunk of beer and rang with the yells of drunkards. A waiter moved among the tables, surveying the room tiredly. The rheumy-eyed, leather-skinned bartender poured drafts and snapped off bottle caps.

Jesus didn't know at what point Joaquin sat beside him. For a moment, he thought they were on the road again, pursuing the next in his list of never-ending targets. They had stopped for many a late meal at places like this. Joaquin would eat little on his own. Sometimes, Jesus had to feed him spoonfuls of beans or rice in the stalls of dirty restrooms and in the shadows behind bars. He would pour water into the boy's mouth, wipe him clean with a cloth. Thankfully, enough of his brother had stayed intact to enable the occasional self-fed meal. Enough had remained to facilitate relieving himself and carrying out the most basic of tasks. When staring into those dead eyes, when searching for some hint of his brother's bashfulness, intelligence, generosity, Jesus had refused the temptations of pity or tenderness. I won't patronize him, he often thought. He would not tiptoe or sugarcoat the way everyone did when he returned from his first tour, treating him like he was a stranger. Only Joaquin had behaved as though nothing had changed, cracking jokes and asking questions. When their roles reversed, how could Jesus not give him the same respect?

"Joaquin," he said. He reached out to him. He touched air. Knuckles rapped the table.

"You all right?" The woman stood over him. She pointed to the stairs. "Let's go."

They went up into an office. An old man sat at the desk, thin and frail, but behind the large glasses, the small eyes were sharp.

"Howdy," he said in a hoarse rasp. "I'm Earl. What's your name?"

"Jesus."

"Nice to meet you, Jesus." The old man held out his hand, and Jesus shook it, surprised as much by the strength of the grip as he was by the sharpness of the gaze.

"Earl," said Jesus. "You own this place?"

"Yep. Been here years." Earl leaned back. "So, Sarah says you're in some trouble?"

Sarah. That was her name. She had projected such cold, stony indifference that he had been warded from even introducing himself or asking her name. Even then, she hardly looked at him, more content to stare holes into the walls.

"She's right," he said. "I am in trouble. On the run, I guess."

Earl nodded. He tapped his chin, cleared his throat. "This ain't just a bar," he said after a moment. "Think of it like a pit stop. For people like yourself. You understand me?"

"I think so. Yeah."

"I got a trailer out back. Sarah's using it right now, but she's letting you stay if you like. Only I don't run a charity. You take shifts, keep the bar clean. In return, I don't ask questions. I don't poke. I keep you clear. How's that sound?"

"It sounds good. Thank you." Jesus directed this last phrase towards Sarah, who kept her eyes on the floor. She fought for you, he realized. She won you this.

"Okay," Earl said. "We'll get you started in a couple of days. For now, Sarah'll take you out to the trailer. You got any luggage? Any clothes?"

"No. I don't have anything. Just this money." He offered up the cash Randolph had given him, but Earl waved it away.

"You keep that. It's yours. If anything, we'll help you get some things with that." He turned to Sarah. "Anything else, baby bird?"

She shook her head. "No."

"Okay. Good to have you with us, Jesus."

"Thank you, sir. I appreciate it."

Outside, the neon sign washed them in blue light. Jesus looked up at it, at the night sky. So many people helping him, giving him chances. But they didn't know the truth: he was a killer. And he had enjoyed it.

"Is it the same with you?" he asked Sarah as they headed for the truck. "On the run?"

"Come on," she said, ignoring the question. "Let's go."

They drove into the waste, the headlights eventually reveal-ing a dingy trailer. Jesus followed her inside. Sarah switched on a lamp, turned on a neon Coors sign. With a sigh, she undid her shirt. Jesus stared at her in the dimness. She kept the rosary wrapped around her wrist, then around her neck. There was the whitest of scars there.

"I've got a plate in the fridge," she said. "Chicken-fried steak with some gravy."

He didn't say anything, didn't move.

"Sit down. You're safe."

He sat at the small table. "You're Sarah?"

"Yes." She took a plate from the fridge and stuck it in the microwave. "You're Jesus."

"Thank you. For doing this."

"Like Earl said, it's not charity." She brought the plate to the table and set it before him. "We made a deal. You're going to help me find Lyle."

"Why? Why put yourself in danger like that?"

She considered his question. "A friend of mine," she said at length, "I think they have him. At a place like the one they were going to take you."

She was like him, then, on a rescue mission of her own. She was so guarded, so stoic, it was hard to imagine she would put herself on the line like that. But she had advocated for him, a complete stranger. Worse, a murderer, someone painted red by the room of cloth. She had given him a chance, a lifeline. An opportunity to make more than just his own life right.

"Eat," she said. "I don't have much of an appetite. In fact, I'm going to wash up."

She retreated into the darkness of the trailer. There was a cord pulled, a faint flash of light. Water ran. Jesus eyed the plate before him. Dry, breaded chicken on a bed of mashed potatoes. Stale leftovers, but his stomach rumbled nonetheless. The lining of his mouth grew damp. Real hunger, he thought. Actual appetite. The desire to eat, and with it, the want to live.

He ate hurriedly, hastily, as though he had never eaten before. No thoughts of his brother came to him, no visions of the desert. The food brought clarity as well as relief. He settled on the sofa once he was done, and the sweet smell of rosemary lulled him to sleep.

He awoke to the sound of grease popping, the smell of coffee bubbling. Dust motes floated in the light from the window. He was cold, clutching blankets he didn't remember pulling over himself. He sat up and rubbed his eyes.

Sarah stood in front of the stove. The rosary hung around her pale neck. Her hair, light and lean, came down around her face. "There's coffee on the table," she said, not looking at him.

He raised the mug to his lips, winced from the heat, the burn on his tongue.

She lit a cigarette. "We're going to eat, and then you're going to tell me everything. Not a single detail left out."

He drank the coffee. He nodded. "Fair enough."

They sat around the small, glass table. Sarah ate quickly, just as she had at the diner, never looking up, chewing and slurping with almost dire intent. She wore no makeup, no jewelry save the rosary. Her nails were unpainted. Jesus fixated on her earlobe, on the empty piercing. He looked away. An ashtray at the center of the table, filled with cigarette butts, stank of smoke.

He studied the trailer, tried to glean anything about her from the interior, but it was barren, almost anachronistic in its austerity. A beach-themed calendar from 1999 hung on the wall. The television, replete with built-in VHS player and bunny-ear antennae, seemed taken straight from his grandparents' home. An assortment of mugs and plates stuck out of a drying rack, no two from the same set. A half-empty bottle of whiskey stood on the countertop.

Once finished, Sarah dumped the plates and cups into the sink and wiped her hands. She turned to him. "Let's talk."

He was used to staying silent in the presence of strangers, keeping intimate details locked up, but once he started talking, he couldn't stop. He began with his time abroad, with Jackson's discharge and Kowalski's death, with the roadside bomb. He described coming home after the first tour, disillusioned, defeated. In the spaces difficult to discuss, he reverted to his adolescence, the hours spent in the garage working on this or that car, the many girls who never seemed to make it past date two or three, definitely not to Sunday dinner with his parents. He talked at length about Joaquin, about the boy's love of film, his bashfulness, his sincerity. "He'd look up at the stars," Jesus said. "He was like my parents. Not like me."

As the past gave way to the present, his words left him. But he could not avoid it. He told her of the night those masked men invaded their home. He explained to her what the police told him. He described to her the photographs he demanded to see. Walls and floor covered in blood. His parents butchered. And his brother there to see it all. His brother whose light went out, who would no longer speak, who would only whimper and moan in the cold nights they spent on the road. Pink House, he said, spite curling up his throat. Everywhere. From all walks of life. Tracing the case of his family to others across the nation. Finding the telltale clues, piecing together the puzzle. The video of the dark hallway with the red room at its end. The pictures of the people, the families, the girl named Lucy. His victims. The trophy wife. The drug dealer. The widow, Mildred Haynes. The pedophile, Hamilton, whom he lured with his own brother. (*His own brother.*) The junkie, Allen, in his porn-ridden condo. There was the man behind the curtain. There was the plantation house. There were the people in the white masks and robes. The red-masked woman, Lyle. The door-frame. The doorframe that became a doorway. His brother on the altar. His brother passed among them.

By the time he was finished, he was crying again. Sarah sat silently, her stoic expression unchanged. She crushed her cigarette into the ashtray.

"Why was he with you?" she asked.

"What?"

"He needed help. Therapy. And you took him out there instead."

"He was safer with me."

"No. You took him with you because you were afraid. Because you didn't want to be alone. You might as well have killed him yourself."

He was quiet, stewing on her words, chafing at their hard-bitten truth.

"I get it, though," she said. "I had a brother, too. Only it wasn't some lunatic who carved him up. It was me. I shot him. I put him on a platter for that bastard up there."

The coldness of the delivery struck him as much as the revelation. There were many questions, but one reigned above the others.

"That bastard up there," he repeated. "The man in chains. The man with the red eyes."

"The manacled man," she said. "He who waits in the room of cloth."

The manacled man. The room of cloth. He realized he had known those names his entire life. They had been around him in the dead of night when he was a boy. They had been with him in the desert, on the road. He had traversed the hallway with the red room many times, but only now had he gotten close enough to taste the flakes of blood and rust around the doorway.

"It was a book," Sarah went on. Her eyes wandered, perhaps beholding a meat-strewn, blood-stinking haze of her own. "My brother found it on the Internet. Or maybe it found him. The people who are broken. The people who are lost. The manacled man offers them freedom, and they give themselves to him."

"He offers them the truth," Jesus said, thinking of how enthusiastically Mildred had advocated her flyers at that long-ago support meeting. He thought of the white robes at the celebration, who hacked and sawed not only one another but also themselves. He thought of the young man Lyle killed, the one supposedly responsible for the murder of his parents. The expression on his face afterwards. How happy he had looked.

"It's not just a book," Sarah said. "It could be a song, or a painting—"

"A picture?" He thought of Randolph, of the crazed daughter who set her own arms aflame to save that flap of gloss.

"A picture. A book. All the same." Her lips twitched in miniature snarls. "I read it. I couldn't help myself. And before I knew it, I was writing it down myself, anywhere I could find. I was seeing things. People who weren't there. Who shouldn't be there. And then I saw him. All because of some words on a page. Do you understand? All because of *words*."

Jesus listened, afraid to catch her gaze, afraid to even breathe in her enraged presence. Her palpable hatred, her malice—he understood it. The broken parts inside him, scattered in heaps, responded. They inched closer together, galvanized by her energy.

"I fought him at first," she said, "because I thought it was something that could be fought. I burned the words. Scratched them out. Shredded them. But it didn't matter because they were always there. There were always more. More of the words. More of those dead people. More of that bastard's red eyes, his face, his awful, fucking *face*—" She was seething, breathing hard and fast. Jesus watched her, unable to look away, feeling in himself those discarded, disarrayed pieces reunite, melding together through heat and flame.

She stood up. "I'll show you." He followed her inside, and she revealed a leather-bound notebook. The notebook was no more spectacular or even mundane than any other. But the smell that came from it—rosemary? Something else? The book pulled at his eyes as though magnetic.

"You feel it, right?" she asked. "It was easier over time to just put it down and keep it locked away. And eventually, it wasn't as bad as the beginning."

He felt the notebook's dreadful weight. "If someone reads this—"

She nodded. "The worst part? What's in here isn't the manacled man, not the room of cloth. It's me. Everything in you that you hate, that you despise, it will draw out of you. It won't stop. And when there's nothing left to give, well, that seems worth celebrating, doesn't it?"

Her face softened. Her breathing slowed. "I'm sorry. I shouldn't have shown this to you. There just hasn't been any-one—anyone who could understand, at least."

Jesus watched her. The pieces within him cooled.

"You said they had someone. A friend of yours."

"He went out there because of me," she said, setting aside the notebook. "He always thought there was a way to stop it. That there was a cure. But there's nothing. This is my life now. My death, too."

"When we die," Jesus said, "he takes us."

"Yes. Into the room of cloth."

Afterwards, when she had left for the roadhouse, he looked over the notebook, not really reading any of the words, but focusing on them as a whole, as a collective. As a means of pas-sage. Joaquin, he thought, shutting his eyes. I'm here. I'm looking for you. Give me a sign.

His eyes shot open. There it was again, rising from the pages of the notebook. Rosemary.

Yes. If he focused hard enough, concentrated with all his might, it was as if his brother were there with him. As if out of the air. Out of that place beyond time and space, that room that was not a room, that room that was alive.

That night, lying on the sofa, he did not cry. He did not whimper. He stared hard into the dark space above him. "Give him back," he whispered. "*Give him back.*"

Something beyond the darkness swelled. Something laughed. A bell tolled in the distance. No words spoken, but the conveyance was proof enough: his brother could not return from the grip of this so-called manacled man. He would not be allowed to return. Someone would need to retrieve him. Someone would need to bridge the gap.

19.

Over the following days, he asked her what it was, the room of cloth. Sarah could not answer him. Four flesh-colored walls, a floor, a ceiling. A single room, or many? A corridor, or a labyrinth? There were *depths*. One could not just enter out of choice. One had to be invited. The manacled man selected his guests. They were screened.

"My brother," she said as they drove into town one morning. "The manacled man picked him. Picked him long before he ever found that story." She blew smoke out the window. She scratched at her forehead with her thumbnail. She didn't say anything else.

He started working at the roadhouse, at first just sweeping the floor of peanut shells and clearing the tables of cups and bottles, but eventually helping with the lighting on the stage and the wiring of the speakers. Menial work, but it soothed his nerves. "Idle hands," he remarked to Sarah over a smoke break. "Always have to be busy."

She was a mystery to him, sometimes working her way around the trailer or the roadhouse as though he were not even there. She didn't seem to care that he had killed people, had intended to kill many more. She spoke little, never again betraying the same emotion she had when she explained how the room of cloth captured her and her brother. He recognized in her eyes the same hardness of his squad members, the same hardness he used to see in the eyes of his own reflection. Now, his eyes were perpetually watery, perennially on the verge of tears. He couldn't control the sudden fits of crying. During those episodes, she would usually glance at him with indifference, but sometimes, there was disgust, revulsion. But she was not entirely heartless. A spare beer, an offered cigarette—these little comforts were useful for abating the worst of the fits. Just having someone there helped.

"I don't want to write," he told her, "don't want to draw. What does that mean?"

"You just haven't found your talent yet. But you will. He'll find it for you."

The manacled man. The name sent shudders along his spine, left a bitter taste in his mouth. Sarah didn't have much to say about him—he was Pink House's god, the master of the room of cloth, the supposed source of it all. Jesus couldn't shake the sensation of being watched, as though invisible eyes were fixed on him at all times. The manacled man watched him, he was sure of it. He would need to be careful, delicate, if he wanted to free his family.

"I see my brother," he said. "Sometimes, like he was before. Sometimes, like they made him. Sometimes, in my dreams, he's—"

"Dead?"

He couldn't say the word—refused to say it. But he saw those who had gone ahead, that much was true. Mildred and Hamilton and Allen. The trophy wife and the drug dealer. His parents. All those who had been taken into that red star, processed into fuel for its diabolical engine. They wandered that dark desert he saw when he closed his eyes, when he slept. And, yes, he even saw Joaquin. He saw him atop that altar, saw his throat cut, saw his eyes go dark.

"Do you see them?" he asked her. "Your friend? Your brother?"

"Not my friend," she said. "He's still alive. He must be."

But as for her brother, he took her silence as confirmation.

She rarely spoke of the brother. She never said his name. Like everything else, she only gave him a cursory summary of her life up until then. She had lived with her brother in Maryland. She had been a teacher. She had lost her family to illness—she did not provide specifics—and because of the room of cloth, she had abandoned her former life, however diseased, and taken up a refugee's existence in a scattered collection of wayward locales, arriving eventually at the roadhouse as a ward of Earl. A man named Caesar had guided her, first in person and then by correspondence and money. But over time, his messages became more infrequent, until his recent letter that sent her to Chicago.

"That's how I found out," she said, "about Pink House, about the celebration. There was a man named Zeke. He's Lyle's lapdog. Looks for talent—that's what he said."

"He's the one who got Caesar?"

"Yes. To draw me out."

He helped her around the trailer, cooking, cleaning. He drove into town for her. With each day's work, he felt stronger, more in control of himself. He shared stories with her, of himself, of his squad, of his brother and family. She never laughed. She never interjected. But he found that he wanted her to speak. He looked for opportunities to hear her voice, even if it were just more offhand cynicism. He folded her laundry, started taking over some of her shifts. Never had he treated a woman with such reverence—never had he thought to make one's life easier, not even for his own mother. He didn't think it was love. There was not much to love, Sarah being more shell than woman, but he was grateful, grateful that she had not killed him—though he deserved death—grateful that she sheltered him, grateful that her fury resonated with his own.

One morning, over yet another breakfast of fried eggs and chalky bacon, Jesus watched Sarah tap liquor into her coffee, crush cigarettes into the ashtray. As always, she ate quickly, angrily. He soaked up the yolk on his plate with a piece of bread and thought of the meals spent around the fire with his brother, chewing cold beans and hard tortillas. He didn't notice Sarah slide the book in front of him.

"I found that yesterday," she said. He took in the cover, a portrait shot of a dark-haired, wrinkled woman in a spring-fresh white blouse. Jesus focused on the woman's mouth, her teeth bared in a grin more wolfish than friendly. He had seen that mouth before, but where—

He dropped the piece of bread. His blood froze.

Sarah watched him. "Kendra Lyle was publishing self-help books when I was still in high school. Pretty popular. And full of herself, too." She turned the book over. On the back was a photograph of Lyle walking along a sunlit path, picturesque countryside as the backdrop.

Jesus shuddered. He was again in the plantation house, again on his knees. Lyle stood before him, laughing and sneering and mocking behind her mask. He saw through to her face, saw her grinning with fangs bared just like on the cover of the book.

Sarah read aloud from the blurb: "In over twenty years of psychiatric work, there's one question I've heard almost daily: are you happy? My latest book, *The Angel Within*, is all about applying forward-thinking techniques to answer this question once and for all. We like to think there's an answer for each of us, but there's really only one: the answer made for *all* of us."

She chuckled. "Sounds on-brand." She rifled through the book, bent her nose to the pages. "It's in here. Light, but that's his smell. She's found a way to mask it for the public, so the ones who are sensitive won't be the wiser."

Jesus hardly heard her. He fought away the images of the plantation hall. His brother on the altar. The knife at his neck. The way his eyes went dark.

"We've wasted enough time," Sarah said. "It's time to find her. Time to find Caesar."

She left the book on the table. Jesus stared at it, his stomach churning, his breakfast bubbling back up his throat. He took hold of the book and crushed it between his hands. His mental machinery steamed and sizzled to life.

"You can do this," he told himself. "For Joaquin."

They began to plan. Sarah unveiled the space beneath the floorboard where she kept the money from Caesar. "At least five thousand," she said. "Hardly spent any of it thanks to Earl letting me stay here. Enough to get us where we need to be."

And that was the question: how to find Lyle? At the pawn shop in town, Jesus regarded the row of misshapen, mangled laptops. He made his selection. They sat in a dim corner of the municipal library, took advantage of the free Internet. Jesus charted Lyle's public appearances, her book signings, her tour dates. Her pale, grinning face haunted the webpages. Her teeth like fangs, surrounded by bloody, glistening lips.

"Dallas," he said one afternoon, the hardness in his voice surprising him, reminding him of how he used to be. "She'll be in Dallas in two weeks. Book signing. To promote *The Angel Within*." With every word, the wreckage within him came back together. The pieces bonded. The furnace flashed on, cool at first, but generating heat. The metal was ready to be forged.

Sarah felt the heat. She smelled the slag and smoke. Somewhere inside of her, a cold stone shook at the exposure to light.

The plan was simple. Lyle would be participating at a convention with other authors. If they could pull one of the hotel fire alarms, it wouldn't be difficult to grab Lyle as she was evacuating with the rest of the crowd. Then it would only be a matter of transporting her to a safe house where they could proceed with the interrogation.

"She knows my scent," Sarah said, reviewing the map of the hotel Jesus pulled up. "She'll know it's me coming from a mile away. But you? She might not have a strong grasp on your smell. You have to be the one to go inside and pull the alarm."

"What about after?" Jesus asked. "If she talks, what do we do with her after that?"

Sarah shrugged. "Use her as leverage if we can. If not, kill her."

Jesus nodded, but despite how his strength had returned, the prospect of facing Lyle made his mouth dry and his eyes heavy. He practiced holding Sarah's revolver, aiming it. You should want this, he thought. For what she did to you. For what she did to Joaquin. But his grip on the gun loosened. His fingers trembled. The red itch steamed behind his eyes, but his body refused.

The days passed as they made their preparations. When the bags were ready, Sarah wiped her hands, let out a sigh. For once, maybe the first time, she seemed relaxed.

"Okay," she said. "Now, we wait."

One of their last nights in the trailer, Jesus cooked steaks on the stove. Just back from the roadhouse, Sarah undid her ponytail, folded her arms. She watched him.

"Let me help," she said. "What do you need?"

"I got it," he replied, and then, smiling, "if your eggs are any indication."

Surprisingly, she returned the smile. "Practice makes perfect."

He set her to cutting onions and heating tortillas. "Ever had avocado?" he asked.

"Maybe once."

"It's heavenly in a taco. I'll show you how to carve it."

He took a knife and demonstrated how to separate the avocado into halves. With a spoon, he removed the seed and scooped out the green innards into a bowl.

"Okay," he said. "Want to try?"

Sarah nodded and picked up a second avocado. When she struggled to fix in the knife, he guided her hands with his own.

"You're good at that," she said.

"You can thank my mother. She was amazing in the kitchen."

When the avocado was emptied, they stayed like that a moment, his hands on hers, her body against his. "The meat?" she asked, and he laughed.

"Right. About done."

At the table, they bit into tacos of chopped steak, licked avocado off their lips. Sarah had to admit the food was good, the flavors complementing in a way she hadn't expected. They chased down the meal with cold beers. The warm night air drifted in through the open door and brought the music of the roadhouse with it.

"Thank you," Sarah said. "For a home-cooked meal. A *real* home-cooked meal."

"You're welcome." He smiled. "How about a dance to cap it off?"

"A dance? To what music?"

From his bag by the sofa, he retrieved a stereo and cassette. "I grabbed this at the pawn shop. Andrea Bocelli. 'Por Ti Volaré.' Classic."

"You get the taste in music from your mother, too?"

"My dad. He was obsessed with this stuff."

He started the cassette. Bocelli's voice swelled from the stereo's small speakers.

"Ready?" Jesus asked.

Sarah hesitated, but she let him lift her to her feet. "I've never actually danced before," she said. "I don't know what I'm doing."

He laughed. "Sarah Creed, actually nervous? I don't believe it."

"Well, I guess anything's possible."

"It's okay. Just follow my lead."

She clenched his hand, watched her feet stumble after his. They swayed around the table, their audience the ancient television, the torn sofa, the rusted refrigerator. Slowly, she matched his rhythm and found her footing.

"You do this with all the girls?" she asked. "Dinner and a dance?"

"No. You're the first."

She looked up at him, he down at her. As though moved by magic, her dark stone and his clockwork mind drawn to each other, their lips met. He hadn't expected this, but he was surprised how much he wanted it. Her lips tasting of rosemary. Her skin quivering where he passed his hand. Her voice breaking with tears.

They lay together in the darkness afterwards. The stereo had long gone silent, the only sounds around them the wind against the trailer, her heartbeat against his.

"I'm not used to this," she said softly, in a voice unfamiliar to him.

"Me, neither." He caressed the scar on her neck, and then his fingers caught the rosary. They admired it in the moonlight.

"It belonged to Caesar's grandmother," she said. "She called him her *hijo de oro*."

"Golden son." Jesus thought of his mother, how she had brought him into her arms to greet his baby brother. My beautiful, beautiful boys, she had said, so long ago. A lifetime ago.

Sarah clasped the rosary. "It brings me comfort. I don't know why. I never had much faith in God. Even less now."

Jesus watched how she clutched the rosary. "You really think Caesar is alive?"

"It doesn't matter what I think. He protected me. Kept me safe when I was at my worst. Whatever I have right now, I have because of him."

Dutiful, Jesus thought. Protective. What a brother is supposed to be. And they're not even related by blood. What's your excuse?

He weighed his next words carefully, loath to stir up this woman he knew was always one word—literally and figuratively—from rage. But he had no choice if there was any chance of success for his own mission. She had to save Caesar, but so did he have to save his brother.

"Lyle would know, wouldn't she?" he asked, as gently as he could. "If anyone knows about the room of cloth, it would be her."

Sarah was quiet a moment. "I guess she would."

"You said it yourself, remember? She's been around a long time. She must know things. How to live with it. How to control it."

"Control it?" She looked at him, the familiar sternness apparent even in the dark. "You don't control it. You don't do anything with it. It uses you. It kills you."

"I know. But she—"

"Enough, Jesus. Who cares what she knows. She's hardly even human anymore."

She pushed back the sheets and rose from the bed. He watched as she lit a cigarette, blew smoke into the air. Very, very faintly, under the smoke, beneath the rosemary, he smelled death on her. He knew it from the desert. He knew it from the plantation house. He knew it from the hospital room where he first met his brother.

"Joaquin is alive, Sarah."

"No. He's not."

"He is. He's calling me. This whole time, he's been trying to reach me."

"He's dead, Jesus."

"But what if he's not? What if he's trapped? Joaquin, my parents, your brother—"

"No!" she snapped. Her voice warbled, for the first time suggesting that she could actually be afraid. "I think about where Sebastian is, and I wish—honestly wish—there was nothing instead. I wish that when he died, he didn't go anywhere. That he was just gone. That would be better. More merciful."

Sebastian. The first time she had said his name. He was about to respond, but she spoke again, form shaking in the darkness, voice rattling like glass. The room grew hot with her anger. His clockwork mind blazed in response.

"You think the room of cloth is something that happens to you," she said, "like a hurricane or a flood. But it's not like that at all. Sebastian wanted it. He *begged* for it. He spent every day of his life looking for something to take him away. Dope. Cocaine. Who knows what else. He didn't have the courage to do it himself. He didn't have the stomach to accept that maybe his shitty, little life was on him, too. That's why he blamed it on me and my mother every day. Every goddamn day."

She paused. The cigarette simmered. "But if we're being honest? It was me first. Looking for a way out. He's just the one who picked up the tab."

"What are you saying? That Joaquin deserved what happened? He wanted it to happen?"

"No. But you did. Didn't you?"

"Then why wasn't it me?" Jesus swallowed back his oncoming tears. "If they had killed me, I could accept that. I was ready for it. But what they did to him—what that bitch did to him—he was calling to me, and I didn't do anything. He was *screaming* for me, and I was just frozen. He is still calling for me, Sarah."

"He's dead, Jesus. So is my brother. They can't be helped. They can't come back."

"No! I know that's not true!"

"It is! Just accept that it's your fault! Just like I had to."

He broke into uncontrollable sobs, hysterical tears. Of course it was his fucking fault—of course it was! He knew that. But even then, even then, the rosemary lined his nostrils, the altar loomed over him, Joaquin's lifeless eyes ballooned, filled his vision, swallowed him whole.

He reached out and embraced her. "Please! I don't want to see him! I don't want to hear him! I want it *gone*. I want him *gone*."

He was blubbering, drooling, entirely surprised when she planted a kiss on his brow. Didn't she pity him? Didn't he disgust her? But still she kissed him, and when her kisses found his lips, he did not fight her.

Afterwards, their heat long faded, he watched her as she slept. Only in sleep did her typically hard, pointed features soften. Only in sleep did she take on a semblance of elegance or beauty. No woman had made him feel at ease before. They always seemed to want too much. But Sarah asked nothing of him. He was the one asking for entrance into that mind so closely guarded, that heart so duly, thoroughly walled off.

Still, she was not an authority. She might have been more experienced than him in this new, prosthetic life, but they were both neophytes nonetheless, lost, searching for anchors where none existed. Perhaps she was even in denial, refusing to accept that life didn't end at the grave, at the last heartbeat. It scared her, he thought. It scared him. To keep going. To face the possibility of life after death. Life in the room of cloth. So unlike what they knew, but alive just the same. Matter converted to energy. Nothing lost, just repurposed. Reformed.

I'll convince her, he told himself. I'll show her. Their brothers were still alive in that room. They were calling for them, waiting for them. And they could save them both.

2 0 .

The evening before they departed for Dallas, under a sky blue and gold, Jesus followed Sarah out into the waste. She wedged a shovel into the dirt and started digging, working slowly but intently, occasionally pausing for a cigarette or beer. Jesus helped her with a second shovel, and together, they passed the ashes of her notebooks from the trailer to the hole. When the last of the ashes was transferred, he handed her the black notebook. She dropped the notebook into the hole and threw in a lit match after it. They watched as the flames ate the leather, devoured the paper.

"It's in the smoke," she said, following the slender trails with her eyes. "You can't destroy it. But you can make it harder for others to find it. You can slow it down."

"Why not leave it there? In the trailer?"

"Earl will have someone there eventually. A mom. A daughter. Someone running away. And they'd be the perfect target."

When the notebook was only crackling, smoldering ashes, she filled the hole. While she walked back to the trailer, Jesus stayed behind, looking up at the smoke, at the expanse of dark clouds terminating in sunset. "Joaquin," he said softly, and there was the rosemary again, like someone blowing in his face. Closer than before. More real than ever.

They left the next morning. Once again, driving on the road. Once again, staying in motel rooms. Once again, closing in on a target. Only this time, he was the passenger. Only this time, he was the accomplice. Lyle had destroyed him and slain his brother, but somehow, his simmering, recovering rage felt small and inadequate compared to what emanated from Sarah. The way she bit into sandwiches or crunched chips at gas stations. The way she rolled up sleeves or pulled at her hair in front of mirrors. The way she marked doorjambs with cigarette burns. Hers was a rage nourished daily, made mundane by constant reinforcement. His was a rage fed forcefully, desperately, by anything he could find. There was no alternative. Without the rage, he looked out and saw nothing. He felt nothing. He was nothing.

Except for the itch. That red, prickly itch. Clawing at the back of his eyes.

In Dallas, they parked across the street from a clean, fountain-adorned plaza. Jesus pointed. "That's the hotel. The Lucian."

Sarah looked up at the building. The hotel loomed over the plaza, monolithic.

"Where will she be?"

"At a booth in the conference hall. The biggest name there."

"What about security?"

"Not enough to make a difference during the commotion. If we move fast."

"Okay. This might just work after all."

Jesus regarded the hotel, the plaza, the pedestrians crossing the street and navigating storefronts. Under different circumstances, he could have been among them. With his brother, his parents. Maybe even a wife. He turned to Sarah, but her eyes remained locked on the hotel.

"Let's go in," she said. "Scope it out."

They wandered the lobby, pretending to admire the impressionist paintings and art deco trappings. The conference hall was massive, already set up with white booths and blue streamers. Jesus pushed aside some balloons and found the largest booth, which was flanked by portraits of Lyle posing with her book. How many of the attendees would expect that she moonlighted as a killer, a butcher? How many were coming for exactly that reason?

They shared a final meal at a nearby burger joint, sitting across from each other in a booth under crimson sunlight. Jesus recalled his final meeting with Jackson. If he had taken his advice, would Joaquin still be alive? Would Joaquin be sitting where Sarah was, not eating, barely even breathing, but alive? Jesus looked at the woman in front of him and searched for something, anything, that told him what she thought, how she felt. But all he saw were stony eyes and stoic face. Everything clamped down to prevent leakage. Since that night they shared together, she had been more distant, as though correcting an oversight. She stabbed fries into ketchup. She crushed napkins in fists. She met his eyes, but she did not see him. He felt he wasn't even there. Nothing was there. Nothing existed around this woman. She inhabited a void as impenetrable and inescapable as a black hole. If he had left right then, she would not have said a word. She might not even have noticed.

In their motel room, Jesus lay in the dark, listening to the traffic outside. Lyle hovered over him in her red mask. He felt her hot breath that somehow came through the mask. He smelled the blood and meat that infested her words. Would they really be able to capture her? Would she even talk if they did?

Sarah emerged from the restroom freshly showered, unfurling a T-shirt over herself, pulling on jeans. She switched the restroom light off, and a moment later, there was the flick of her lighter, the telltale flame. She watched him.

"You doing okay?"

He was silent. She came over, sat on the edge of the bed.

"I know you have mixed feelings about this," she said. "I don't know if it's going to work. But I'm grateful that you came. Whatever happens, I want you to know that."

"You were the one who gave me a chance," he said. "After everything I've done."

"We're both damned." She lay beside him, taking a last drag before holding the cigarette out to him. "Want the rest?"

He took it. Sarah fell asleep, but he stayed awake, feeling himself getting hotter, feeling his internal engine sputter to life. The familiar images returned for a new assault. His brother on the altar. The knife at his neck. Jesus closed his eyes to no avail. His brother on the altar. The knife at his neck. His brother on the altar. The knife at his neck. The way his eyes went dark. His brother on the altar. The knife at his neck. The way his eyes went dark. How he disappeared into them. How he disappeared among them.

Red. Seeing red. Feeling red. The itch he couldn't scratch. Burning behind his eyes.

"Why now?" he asked, looking into the darkness. "Are you trying to tell me something? Joaquin? Are you there?"

The air in the room turned cold. Rain fell outside.

"Joaquin." He waited, held his breath. "Sebastian? Are you trying to talk to Sarah?"

Softly, softly, there was the rosemary again. Another scent, too. Cinnamon?

Jesus.

He sat up. "Joaquin?"

Jesus.

"I'm here. Brother, I'm here. Talk to me. Tell me what to do."

Jesus. We're waiting for you.

"Who? Mom and Dad? Are they with you? Is Sebastian with you, too?"

He reached out into the darkness.

His brother stood amid the void, far away.

Joaquin! I'm here! Tell me what I need to do.

Jesus.

Are they with you? Joaquin? Are they with you?

Jesus.

Farther away. Still farther.

Jesus.

Joaquin, I'm coming! But you need to tell me how. You need to help me.

Jesus.

Please. I can bring you back. Mom and Dad. Sarah's brother. I can bring you all back.

Liquid dripping. Metal grinding.

Jesus.

Please, Joaquin! Tell me how to do it!

Steel screeching. Gears turning. Faces all around him. Snarling, sputtering faces. Crimson fangs. Forked tongues. Black claws. Hooked tails. Above him, that red star that turned black. That core of grinding gears and coiling cogs. That portal. That doorway.

Jesus.

Joaquin! Joaquin, I'm coming! Tell me where you are! Tell me what to do!

A hand under his brother's chin. The knife at his neck.

Waiting for you.

I am begging you! I am begging you, don't hurt him! Don't touch him! Don't touch him, or you'll pay! I swear to you, I'll make you pay! Please! Please! He's just a kid! He's just a kid!

The knife at his neck.

Jesus. We're waiting for you. We're all waiting for you.

The way his eyes went dark.

Joaquin!

The way he disappeared among them.

Her red mask, laughing behind her red mask, laughing and snarling behind her red mask.

The way he disappeared.

Her fingers on his face. Telling him it was all right. Telling him he was one of them now.

Those monsters over his brother's body, shredding skin, rending muscle, discarding bone. Crushing their own throats, breaking their own limbs, burying snouts and claws into one another's hides. Overhead, an eddy of whirling blood. A sea of wriggling, writhing bodies, a chorus of aching, agonized voices, an orchestra of pain. A figure descending, bridled and bound, suspended by chains, frothing at the mouth, red-eyed and furious. The manacled man. He who waits in the room of cloth. An enormous stain where his brother had been, speckled with bits and pieces of flesh. Where was he? Amid the mangled, slaughtered bodies, where was he? What skin belonged to him, what bone? He plunged his hands into the carnage. He pulled at the entrails, rummaged through the severed claws and hooves. Above him, closer, closer, ever closer, the mass of bodies, the arms and legs falling, the heads falling, the blood splashing down in waves, in torrents. Where? Where are you, Joaquin? Talk to me! Say something! The red eyes. The crash of chains. The screech of metal. Deafening, resounding. A sea of blood and bodies swaying violently, crests taller than any mountain, falls more devastating than any earthquake. Help me, please! Please! Please, just make it stop! Please, please, I am begging you, make it stop, make it stop, Joaquin, Sarah, Mom, Dad, anyone, ANYONE, just make it stop, make it stop, MAKE IT STOP, STOP, DON'T COME ANY CLOSER, DON'T COME ANY CLOSER—

He got up from the bed. Oh, God. Oh, my God. The knife at his neck. What was he doing? What did he think he could do? The knife at his neck. The way his eyes went dark. He couldn't bring him back. He couldn't bring any of them back. Inside of him, the pieces coming undone, falling apart. The clockwork mind rusting, crumbling. The way his eyes went dark. The way he disappeared among them. He dressed and stumbled about the motel room, half-blind, hyperventilating. He stopped at the door. The knife at his neck. The way his eyes went dark. He scribbled a note. The way his eyes went dark. I'm sorry. The knife at his neck. The way his eyes went dark. The way he disappeared. I'm sorry. I just can't.

He walked out into the rain, into the night. He walked for a long time, slipping, stumbling, plagued by the feeling of blood on his neck, of cartilage loose between his fingers. Headlights approached, two blinding, white-hot orbs floating in the downpour. He wiped away raindrops, tears. The headlights stopped. Doors open and shut. Figures flanked the van. One approached, silhouetted by the lights, stinking of rotten meat—no, smelling of rosemary, wondrous rosemary. His mother's rosemary.

"It's you," said the woman, her voice unmistakable. "I knew I recognized the scent. The same as my daddy's. Spent casings. Blood on steel. The smell of war."

He shivered, not from fear, not from terror, but warmth, security. Lyle. His brother's killer. His brother's liberator. The one who did what he couldn't do. The one who could show him the way. Her voice was like a burning hearth, a raging flame. He went towards it.

"Please," he choked out, fighting his heaving chest, stifling his explosive sobs, "I need help. I don't know what to do. I don't know how to get to him."

Lyle spread her arms. "Oh, son. You know what you need to do. You always have."

He embraced her, twining his arms around her waist, breathing deep of his mother's smell. "Please help me," he sobbed into the crook of her neck. "I'm lost. I'm lost."

"You're not lost," she cooed into his ear, stroking his hair, rocking him. "You're exactly where you need to be. You're home."

She led him back to the van. Joaquin sat beside him and took his hand. He smiled at him.

Hey guys! Been off for a long while and I know a lot of you were worried, but it's okay. Everything makes sense now. I get it. I'm ready to go across. :)

Those dreams I was having about the door with the red light, they finally got me to the end. I got to the door. I opened it. I saw what was on the other side. I was wrong to be afraid. I was STUPID to be afraid. But I know that I was just scared to change, to leave this behind. Who wouldn't be? Even the most exciting change is scary. You're not quite sure what's going to happen. Your body's not ready for it.

But that's why I'm here. To tell you there's no reason to worry. He's going to take care of you. He's going to take care of all of us. The manacled man. He who waits in the room of cloth.

I've already taken the first step across. I see the water turning red as I type this. It won't take long now. :)

It took me a while, but now I see everything for what it was: my initiation. He picked me. He picked Becca, too. She's here now, holding my hand as it goes limp. She's helping me across. It couldn't have been anyone but her. It couldn't have been anyone but me. It's been me. Always been me. Had to be me. Losing mom and dad was preparation for this. Having to teach those entitled brats was training. All the awful things in the world. It's all been training. Learning why none of this is worth it. Realizing why it has to go.

It's funny. What he wanted me to do. What I was chosen to do. I've been doing it since the start. Posting the video of the door because I thought I was curious, because I thought I wanted opinions. I didn't want opinions. I wanted to SHOW you. I wanted to SHARE with you. Now you have it too. You've had it since the start. You've always had it. His blessing. His mark.

It's going to be all of us eventually. That's why it doesn't make sense to be scared. It's working through us, getting us ready for the change. The real singularity ha ha. What you think is coming is nothing. It's fake. But this is TRUE. This is TRUTH. Reality. What's really underneath. What's really on the other side of the door. It's not a door. It's a door-WAY. To the place beyond. The real heaven. Becca's purpose was to guide me there. It was my purpose to guide you.

Mom and dad missed out. I feel bad for them, but I don't envy them. I'm getting to go first. I'm the one making history, helping everyone, uniting everyone. And one day, we'll bring them from wherever they are. He'll bring them from wherever they are. Because he loves us. We're his children. The ones who have to carry out his legacy. Fulfill his mission.

I'm going now. For good. I'm glad I was able to share it with you all. Now it's your turn. Your chance to do the work, spread the word. Maybe you already are. Maybe it works slower in some people and faster in others. Maybe next month you'll feel it. Maybe next week. Maybe tomorrow. Maybe tonight. You'll see him when you close your eyes to go to sleep. You'll walk down the hall to the door. You'll open it. It's not a matter of if but when.

I'll see you there. In the room of cloth. He's waiting there. We're all waiting. Waiting for you. :)

Hiiii this is becca :))) Prof is with us now He looks soooo happy

He has the biggest smile on his face :))))))))

Let me show you :))))))

THE FARM

In the morning, Sarah read Jesus's note, and then she crumpled it up and threw it away.

She made for the hotel, book tucked under her arm, revolver hidden within the carved-out pages. The sky was a clear blue, the wind crisp. The fountain's water sparkled. A lifetime ago, she would have thrived in the sunlight and breeze. But no longer. Her stomach swirled with equal parts anxiety and excitement. What could she do now but demand the answers she wanted? Lyle would sniff her out easily, may have already done so. Maybe she could force a trade, Lyle's life for Caesar's freedom. Except these bastards didn't care whether they lived or died. They reaped themselves willingly. Surrendered their bodies to their master in chains.

There could be another trade: herself for Caesar. With Jesus gone, with no one, she had no leverage besides the bubbling, venomous words in her head. And if negotiation didn't work, there was always the nuclear option. She imagined raising the revolver and watching Lyle's wrinkled face disappear in an explosion of splattered skin and broken bone. That would be a sight, wouldn't it? If Sarah died, at least she could take the bitch with her.

She pushed through the hotel's crowded lobby to the conference hall. Immediately, she picked up the stenches of pulverized roadkill and flayed carcass, the smells so powerful she nearly doubled over. Near the front, surrounded by portraits and balloons, was Lyle. Dressed in all white, waving and smiling like a debutante, she signed books and posed for photos.

Sarah watched the creased mouth move. She watched the brown eyes twinkle with a secret darkness, a childlike glee. She watched the ringed hands gesture, the red-painted nails twirl. She smelled, as clearly as ever, the slaughterhouse, and despite the din of the convention, she heard the slaughterhouse as well. Behind every word of that syrupy, Alabaman drawl were the rustle of chains and the spray of blood.

Not a person, she thought with dreadful clarity. Just a walking corpse, hollowed out and bled dry. A suit of flesh animated by an unearthly flame, piloted by an unstoppable and unquenchable hatred.

Sarah approached, reaching into the book and taking hold of the gun. She locked eyes with Lyle, who was midway through another signature. No fear lurked in her wolf's eyes—in fact, they somehow grew brighter. The wrinkled mouth widened in a smirk. The nostrils flared hungrily, the way a dog might anticipate a discarded, chewed-upon rib. The ruby-red lips gleamed not with gloss but saliva.

Then there were hands around Sarah's arms, hard as vices. Black-suited security crowded and corralled her. "Let go of me!" she snarled, but it was no use—they had her arms, her shoulders. They tore away the book, confiscated the gun. She was handcuffed, trapped behind a wall of suits. One touched an earpiece and nodded.

"We're taking her up," he said. "Let's go."

They thrust her forward along a conveyor belt of black suede. She looked back and caught Lyle watching her, those dark eyes bright with hunger, the teeth bare in a ravenous laugh.

They crushed into an elevator. As they ascended, the city swept into miniature below, the contrails of a plane visible in the blue distance. Sarah considered how she could claw and kick, bite and scream, but her legs were pinned, her arms seized. Begrudgingly, angrily, she stood among the security and waited.

Once the elevator doors opened, the men led her down the corridor. With the swipe of a keycard, the requisite green flash and soft beep, they ushered her into a sunlit suite with a view of the skyline. A man lounged on a sofa in the middle of the suite, jostling a toothpick with his tongue. "Well," he laughed, "if it isn't our guest of honor. Sarah Creed."

One of the security pushed her down onto a chair, his holstered gun nauseatingly close to her head. She studied the man on the sofa, his oily hair and shabby suit. Even though she hadn't seen him well that night at the warehouse, his smug voice had haunted her since.

"Zeke," she said.

He smiled. "Nice to see you again, Sarah. You really outdid yourself. Crashing the celebration was one thing, but showing up here for an encore? Ballsy." He waved away the security. "We're good up here. Go see what else Ms. Lyle needs. Maybe we have another would-be shooter wandering around."

The security filed out. Zeke stood, stretched, and made for the bar against the wall. "Drink?" he offered. "We have quite a selection. Whiskey? Rum?"

Sarah was silent. He was an extension of Lyle—it didn't matter whether because of money or principle. Her proxy, her own meat puppet, just as she was that of the manacled man.

Zeke laughed, unfazed by the murderous animosity she radiated towards him. "Come on, Sarah. You must be stressed. What did you even expect to do? Kill her?"

"It would have been a bonus," she said. "You know what I want. Caesar."

"Right, right. Caesar. Weepy, little Caesar. I'd forgotten about him! You really are a dedicated friend. Definitely someone I'd want in my corner."

"Fuck you," she hissed. "I know he's alive. Where do you have him?"

"Let's slow down a bit. You're not exactly in a position to make demands."

"Sure I am. You want me, don't you? Not him. He's just been bait."

"You're right about that. Since the celebration, Ms. Lyle has been absolutely captivated with you. Really, you made quite the impression." He shook a sleeve and checked his watch. "She's eager to talk to you herself. And she should be up here any minute."

Sarah started to speak, but stopped—the reek of flayed skin and exposed bone reached her from below, encroaching rapidly upon the suite. She sat in dreadful anticipation, feeling her hairs rise, her spine shudder. If Zeke sensed Lyle, he gave no sign. He was at ease, sipping his drink and playing with his toothpick. The bastard was begging for a bullet to the face. If only they hadn't taken her gun!

Calm down, she thought, fighting her feelings. You won't get anywhere with them dead.

Behind her, the door opened, and in swept hot air thick with the smells of rotten meat and caked blood. "What a morning!" exclaimed Lyle as she sauntered inside, heading immediately for the bar. "Well worth the trip. Don't you think, Zeke?"

Each of her movements, each of her words, was punctuated with the whine of gears, the hiss of steam. Chains rustled behind her gleaming, little eyes.

"I'd say it was more than worth it," Zeke said. "You scored two for the price of one."

Sarah froze. Two? Did they have Jesus?

"Yes," said Lyle, "our diamond in the rough." She gestured to Sarah with her glass of brandy, eyes shining as though having found an oasis in the desert, as though having glimpsed rain after a months-long drought. Sarah recognized the hunger—she had seen it in her brother during his withdrawal episodes. She had seen it in her father when he reached for yet another beer. She had seen it in herself when considering the cigarette or the bottle.

"Delectable," Lyle said. "Rested and seasoned. Very, very rare to see in the wild."

Sarah simmered but said nothing. Lyle grinned even more widely.

"Could you give us the room, Zeke? I think your presence is irritating our guest."

"Sure. I can see when I'm not wanted." He gave Sarah a wink before downing the rest of his drink and leaving the room.

"He could stand to work on his bedside manner," Lyle said, "but good help is hard to find these days. He got you here, after all." She sat on the sofa, rolled her brandy between her butcher's hands. "I hear you had a little incident with him. I hope it didn't sour you on us."

"He took my friend," Sarah growled. "He had nothing to do with any of this!"

Lyle nodded. "That is regrettable. But sometimes, we have to get our hands dirty to see results. Don't you agree?" She pulled out Sarah's revolver from her purse. "You were planning on killing me, no? How is that any different?"

"Caesar's innocent. That's the fucking difference."

Lyle smiled. Her eyes glimmered like jewels.

"It's always fascinated me," she said, "the lies we make up to suit ourselves. You say you came to bargain for your friend. You say you came to kill me. But what did you really expect to happen? We had eyes on you the moment you set foot inside. Not to mention your smell." She pinched her nose and laughed. "Whew! You are easy to spot, my dear. Very, very easy. And I don't think it's a coincidence we found our other special guest at the same time. Your smells are so complementary. So intermingled."

"I don't know what you're talking about," Sarah said. "I came on my own."

"Of course you did. What a spectacular miracle that my witness and my party-crasher show up within a day of each other. I suppose that's his blessing at work." Lyle drank her brandy and leaned back. "He was the same, you know. Thinking he was on a crusade for revenge. Came to the celebration with enough guns to start a small war. But he sees the truth now, just as you will. You knew killing me would be impossible. You knew finding your friend would be unlikely. You came for a different reason. The same reason you came to the celebration."

So, they did have Jesus—and what did that mean, that he saw the truth? Had he left her to go with them? All that horseshit about going across, rescuing his brother, had he given into it?

"Is that right?" she asked, feigning what strength she could. "And what reason is that?"

"Purpose," said Lyle. She finished her glass and bared her fangs in another smile. "You resist. It's how you've lasted so long. But what are you resisting for? What's driving you? Nothing can equal the room of cloth."

Uttering the name seemed to darken the room, render it colder than it already was.

"Keep talking," Sarah said. She struggled, her wrists chafing against the cuffs. "Keep playing your mind games—it won't work. I know who you are. I know what you do, what you've done. You're murderers. You cut up children and feed them to your brainwashed slaves. It's barbaric. *You're* barbaric."

"You think you're above us," Lyle said. "That you're better."

"At least I'm still human."

"And there's your mistake. Your last connection we need to remove. What we do—what the manacled man does—is only correct the accident of life."

She got up and refilled her glass. Sarah couldn't tell if the glint of remorse in her eyes was sincere or a feint.

"There are gratuities involved," Lyle said, "to engage the crowd. They need their red meat once in a while. But I know you don't need performances or theatrics. You don't need the comforting lies. You've seen it. You've seen what will happen at the end, as I have, as all the chosen have. *Nothing* happens. Nothing before and nothing after. And there's a choice to be had, honey. Keep fighting it, thinking you're above it, or accept what you know is true."

Lyle's words summoned memories Sarah wished repressed. Her brother in the depths of the old house, his lacerated skin more red than white. The legions of ghoulish, dead onlookers, wailing and laughing. The white, burning light that had turned black—the manacled man descending from the apocalyptic darkness, maimed and muzzled, castrated and crippled.

Lyle crossed her legs. A white heel bobbed up and down. A red nail circled the rim of her glass and lingered on the smudges of saliva and lipstick.

"Enough fighting," she said. "Enough rationalizations. Look at how you keep coming back to him. It's not to save anyone, not to kill anyone—it's because you know where you belong. Deep down, you know what you are. He chose you for a reason. What's inside you should be shared with everyone. With the world."

She reached out with one of those red-nailed, razor-sharp claws and wiped away the tears that ran down Sarah's cheeks. "Your flesh and your blood, honey. Your fresh ink. I can help you give it to him. Give it all to him."

Sarah shivered, shut her eyes, willed away what she could of those awful memories. Remember why you're here, she told herself. Remember what she did. What the manacled man did. What *you* did. Don't let her get inside your head. Don't let her under your skin.

Lyle laid a hand on Sarah's knee. "What do you say? No reason to keep fighting it, to make things harder than they have to be. Have a seat at the table like you deserve. Your friends can be there, too. We can prepare the world for what's coming next. What's coming soon."

Sarah's tears dried. She smiled. The classic sales pitch. How they must have hooked her brother: promising family, community, release. Could she blame him for falling for it? His family had abandoned him. Otto and Bless, those boogeymen who had haunted the streets of their hometown, had treated him with more respect than she ever had. Made sense that the promise of anything better would feel like kindness. Even if the cost was surrendering your very skin.

She looked into Lyle's dark eyes, now seemingly so innocent, so compassionate, perhaps even pitying, and spat into them.

"Your master hasn't broken me," Sarah said. "You won't, either."

Lyle withdrew a handkerchief from her breast pocket and wiped her eyes. When she looked back, any pretense of remorse or pity was gone. But there was no anger. Her eyes instead gleamed with mischief, even joy. She laughed loudly, exuberantly.

"Rested and seasoned," she said. "Tough, too. Wonderful. You will produce incredible material for us. Maybe the best."

She grabbed Sarah's revolver and swung the butt down like a hammer. Sarah barely blinked before everything went black.

She awoke to rocking darkness and pattering rain. She sucked in air and felt thick wool broach her mouth. A bag over her head, the faintest of lights visible through the canvas. Her hands still cuffed. She jerked, jostled. Someone patted her knee.

"Finally awake," Lyle said, her grin audible.

"Where am I?" Sarah demanded. "What is this?"

"Calm down. I have something to show you. You may feel a little lightheaded—we had to sedate you along the way."

Sarah's shaky breaths were foul-smelling and hot. Her head throbbed with the residual pain of the revolver strike and whatever they had injected her with. She hadn't thought much past surrendering herself, but her mind went to the night she held Jesus and the old man at gunpoint. The old man had been transporting him, held accountable for his safety. Product, she thought. Product that produces. That's me now.

Thinking of Jesus made her feel nothing, not even anger, definitely not pity. However they found him, he had abandoned her. The note left behind was proof enough. No doubt he was in a transport of his own, bagged and bound, headed for parts unknown. Maybe the outcome was always going to be the same—maybe Lyle was even right that Sarah was herself self-destructive, looking for a convenient magic bullet—but at least they would have been together. At least they could have faced their fate as one.

"We have some time," Lyle said. "Why not get to know each other?"

Sarah kept quiet. She didn't feel like talking, especially to this caricature of a person.

"I remember the first time I saw him," Lyle went on, her voice warm with nostalgia. "I was in college—forty years ago now. We were in Rome for a semester. We were walking, my roommate Gloria and me, admiring the local men, hoping they would see us and enjoy an afternoon with some rich, stupid American girls. We ended up in a little antique store. The owner was this slim, dark thing—beautiful, but dangerous. I knew that even then. We weren't interested in her jewelry, so she asked if we wouldn't prefer to see what she had in the back. She led us in there, and I remember the heat of it, the smell. You would have thought someone died in there. I half-expected a body, but there were just pots and trophies and other junk— and a painting. A woman in a green dress with a boy in a sailor's outfit. Something Victorian, maybe. The paint had warped over the years. It had smudged. Especially around the faces. Where the eyes should have been were these black holes. The mouths were the same. The faces, like they were melting, dripping off. Almost as if they were screaming at us."

As much as Sarah tried to ignore the story, the details wormed their way into her mind. She smelled the heady scents of the marketplace, felt the cool shadows of the antique shop. She ran her fingers over the gilded china, the inlaid gemstones. She met the eyes of the slim, dark storekeeper, Lyle's progenitor, her initiator. She walked into the back room, the air heavy with an unnatural heat, coursing with unearthly life. She saw the painting with awful clarity. Time and negligence had worked at the veneer and eroded the costume. The hideous faces that stared out from the stinking canvas were the truth, unvarnished, naked, bared to all. The words she wrote in her notebooks were the same, flimsy dress for the rot underneath.

Lyle paused, as if she knew Sarah were embroiled in the details, as if she were letting her soak up the imagery. "The painting scared me at first," she continued, "but when I got closer, when I touched it—there it was. My daddy's cologne. What he wore when I was a girl. Like I'd been sitting on his lap just the day before. I realize now there was indecision about me. The manacled man was testing me. But I proved myself, and now I am among his most faithful. I wouldn't say his *most*—I don't know who else is out there. I haven't met them all. But we're many. How many of us there have been, and how many, many more there will be."

Did she expect a response, a sign of camaraderie? Fuck that.

"You got confirmation you're a monster," Sarah said. "Proud of that?"

"If I'm a monster," Lyle said, "what does that make you? He chose you, too."

Sarah was about to rebuke her, but the images of what she saw on the night of her brother's death shot through her mind. The fugue in which she stabbed her father to death, severed her mother's head, ate her brother's impish corpse. She had never wielded the knife in reality, but the intent, the will, the desire? That was monstrous enough.

"Tell me how you found him," Lyle said. "How he found you."

Sarah sat there. There were no more cards to play.

"It was a book," she said softly, at length. "Just something people put up online. But it took everything from me."

"No. It freed you. It showed you who you really are."

They drove for a while longer. The car came to a stop. Doors opened and shut, and then Sarah was pulled from the vehicle, the bag flung from around her head. She stood in an alley slick with rainwater, lined by gutters swimming with beer cans and crumpled newspapers. Lyle stood before her. Her security surrounded them in a circle.

Zeke emerged and took up a spot beside Lyle. He waved. "Hiya."

Fucker, Sarah thought. Literally selling his soul for money.

"Here's what I wanted to show you," Lyle said, pointing to an orange-lit doorway. The security pressed Sarah along, and in a procession, Lyle and Zeke at the front, Sarah sandwiched in the middle, they went inside.

"You said I wasn't human anymore," Lyle said as they passed through the dark entryway, "but have you thought about what humans will look like in a hundred years? What about a thousand? A million? We already use machines to keep us alive longer than we should be. Soon, we'll be put inside computers, into server farms. Our minds translated into bits and bytes."

They entered an enormous warehouse, the space crowded with barred cells like those used for stray animals. The cells were small, no larger than walk-in closets, aisles of them running down the length of the warehouse. Sarah gagged—the smell was overwhelming, a mix of mundane odors like sweat and skin and sewage, but also the infernal smells of the manacled man, the putrid stenches of the room of cloth.

"Take a look," said Lyle. Sarah squinted into the cells, faint from the stink—and then she gasped. Each cell housed a white-clothed figure. She saw old men shuffling about, middle-aged women tossing in their browned cots, teenagers scribbling upon canvas, and even children, some no older than seven or eight, sitting among heaps of paper, crayons and markers scattered around them. Each prisoner was chained at the ankle. Some looked up and caught Sarah's gaze. Their eyes, sunken and dim, resembled pits.

"Oh, God," Sarah moaned. "You're crazy. You're insane."

"It won't be long before we're put under ice and aboard satellites," Lyle said. "And those satellites will fly through space, spreading whatever it means to be human to whatever other life is out there. We'll seed planets with our technology, blend our biology with robotics. The skin will be gone sooner than you think. But even those motherboards and satellites will die with time. We will never have ultimate preservation, never have true release. With the room of cloth, we have our solution. All of us can walk through the final door. Together. As one."

"They're producing for you," Sarah said. She looked in horror at the beaming woman. "That's how you've survived for so long."

"They're his chosen," Lyle said. "With their help—and the help of all the others—we can spread the word so much faster. Really, that's been the problem all along. No organization. Too much faith and not enough vision. We could have finished all this long ago otherwise."

"Others? There are more?"

"Oh, many more. This is a small farm, actually."

"You have kids here," Sarah said. "*Kids.*"

"Better than them wasting decades on a pointless job, no? Better than falling victim to drugs or alcohol, turning to crime. And what's the result? Suicide, prison? A waste of untapped talent. A waste of good meat."

She laughed. "You saw how many people were lined up for my autograph. They're hungry for meaning. Now, imagine if it was *just* a book. Just words, unable to help them at all. That would be a real tragedy, wouldn't it?"

"No." Sarah backed away, but the security encircled her. She looked frantically for an escape route. "You won't keep me here!"

Lyle laughed again. "Oh, honey. I wouldn't keep you *here*. I brought you here for a different reason. To hold up our end of the deal. Zeke?"

"Of course," he said. "Follow me." He led them deeper into the warehouse, past countless more cells, countless more sunken-eyed, pitch-black gazes. They stopped abruptly before a cell no bigger or more exceptional than the rest. The circle parted, allowing Sarah view.

"What you wanted, right?" Zeke asked. "A reunion with your friend?"

Sarah stared for a long time, having difficulty believing. The man on the other side of the bars was shorter than she remembered, so much thinner and frailer. His hair had grayed, and he hadn't had a beard when she saw him last. But the longer she stared at the shriveled form, the longer she studied the eyes that looked back with no recognition, no familiarity, the further her heart plummeted. Slowly, she recognized the remnants of the thick neck and calloused hands. She saw the arms that had held her at her lowest, during the most violent of her episodes. She saw the cheeks that had been stained with remorseful tears. Tears that had yearned for redemption. Tears that had revealed an earnest heart.

"Caesar?" She stepped up to the cell bars. "Caesar, it's me. It's Sarah."

The man shuffled forward, revealed his leathered skin, his stomach-churning smell. She shook—he reeked of the room of cloth. Someone like Caesar would never have lasted long once exposed. The traumas of his youth, his longstanding guilt, the baggage of his grandmother, the various monsters he had confronted and resisted, all would have been the perfect weapons for the manacled man. And for what? To protect her? To save her? This was the end result of entangling himself with her. She was poison, after all. Even before the manacled man, before the room of cloth. She had corroded her family, abandoned her brother. Her toxins were nothing if not potent.

The man moaned and reached his hands out past the bars. Sarah's heart shuddered.

"Take off the cuffs," she said. "Please."

Lyle nodded and gestured. One of the security came forward and unlocked the cuffs.

Her arms free, Sarah took the feeble hands in her own. She held them, felt them, searched for anything that indicated Caesar was still inside, that not all of him had been taken by that bastard in the chains. But there was no substance in his hands, nothing behind them. They were merely skin and bone, liable to break with the slightest squeeze.

He's on the edge now, she thought, just waiting for his turn. Waiting for these fuckers to call him up to the chopping block and hold his neck over the trough. There was no escape from this. No remedy or restoration. It was among the worst of the manacled man's tricks. Besiege the body, force a desperate bid for freedom. And what better way to liberate oneself than sever the tendon, cut the artery, destroy the flesh?

"He's not doing too hot," Zeke said. "Maybe we need the AC looked at."

"You think that's funny?" Sarah looked back at him through her tears, struggling to appear strong, to resist, but between the lingering effects of the sedative and her reaction to finding Caesar like this, her legs felt like butter, her stomach like a tempest.

"Just a managerial observation," he replied.

"Go to hell. You're an animal. You're all animals." She fixed each one, Zeke, Lyle, and the members of their entourage, with a murderous glare. "How can you live with yourselves?"

"Sweetheart," said Lyle, "how can you?" She pointed at the emaciated, hunched man behind the bars. "Your friend is gone. Look at yourself. The more you fight, the more you turn yourself into what you see in front of you."

"You're wrong! He's still in there! He has to be!"

Sarah fumbled with the rosary and held it up to him. Even if his grandmother had disowned him, even if his life had been mostly pain, the rosary still had to mean something—the one source of comfort, the symbol of a god Sarah had never believed in, but in whom Caesar had believed, in whom he had invested everything. Why go out into this hell if he didn't believe there was a point, that there was another way?

"Caesar," she said. "Have faith. Remember? Have faith." She watched him eye the rosary and run his thumb over the miniature crucifix. "I'm still here. I'm still fighting. So can you."

Say something, she thought. Look at me like you know me. You're the only person I have left. Old memories floated up, old words, old platitudes. They were empty, but like the rosary, they were signposts of shared history, buoys that lit a path through the fog.

"You're not a killer," she said softly. "You can't be. You're good. You can be good."

He touched the rosary. He stared. Nothing. No glimmer in the eyes, no twitch of the mouth. If he was in there, he was buried deep. Deep under the years of drugs and murders. Deep under the monsters with their angelic disguises, their sweet promises. Deep under the boys he had taken advantage of, the boys he had betrayed. The brother he had let down.

"It breaks the heart," Lyle said, "but what better proof is there? The body is inefficient. It's vestigial. It needs to be shed."

Sarah spent another moment searching the drawn, vacant face. She pulled the rosary back. Lyle, Zeke, and the others watched and waited. And then she spun around and reached for one of the security's holstered guns. Within seconds, they had her pinned and cuffed again. She thrashed and kicked, but they held her fast.

"This is supposed to convince me?" she scoffed. "You're not speeding anything along. You're not helping evolution. You're just feeding the manacled man—you're just making his job easier! And you're killing children for it! You're sending them to hell for it!"

Lyle laughed. "Your fighting doesn't discourage me, you know. In fact, it makes you even more interesting. You have so much to give. So much interesting material inside of you."

"I won't give you shit," Sarah said. "You're better off killing me. Otherwise, I'll burn all this down! I'll come after you—after all of you!"

"Kill you?" Lyle said. "I can't think of a worse mistake. But we can do a kindness for you while we're here. It's no good to have our meat so upset. Zeke?"

Zeke came forward, brandishing a keyring. He unlocked the cell door, and the security pulled Caesar out, holding him by the neck and arms as though he were an animal capable of attack at any moment. It would've taken only one of them to snap his arms, shatter his legs. Sarah watched with horror as they placed him on his knees before her.

"You wanted to set him free, didn't you?" Lyle asked. One of the security handed his pistol to her, and she held the gun out to Sarah. "Here's your chance."

Sarah said nothing, scouring the sunken eyes one last time for any flicker of life, any semblance of the man who had guided her, held her, protected her, saved her. Caesar, with his big grin and throaty laugh. Caesar, with his glistening tears and fumbling words. Cesar, with whom she had shared cigarettes and stories of the past. Caesar, who had weathered the shame of his family, the abuse of monsters, and risen above it all.

"Having trouble?" Lyle said. "Don't worry. I'll do it for you."

She turned and pulled the trigger. Sarah flinched, but didn't scream. She watched the small mist that rose up, light and tenuous, from the crumpled corpse.

Lyle saw it, too. She wrinkled her nose. "How disappointing. Almost nothing there."

Sarah stared at the corpse's face blackened by blood. She couldn't feel her own heartbeat.

"Time to move on," Lyle said. "I know just the place for you. Just the man to make sure we see eye to eye."

Sarah only half-heard her. Something pricked her neck, and within seconds, her vision swam. Lyle's face, Zeke's face, those of the security, all morphed and distended. They assumed fangs, horns. Their eyes bled, dripping like those of Lyle's painting. But Sarah had long seen these things, these monsters. They inspired no fear or dread. No, what terrified her now was the corpse's cratered, bloody face. The eyes sparkled, clear and alive. The lips pulled apart, farther than should have been possible. The teeth, whiter and fuller than Caesar's had ever been, bared themselves in a diabolical grin. Even at his cheeriest, Caesar's smiles had always been sad, wistful. But the grin that dressed his corpse, the grin that mocked him, wasn't sad or wistful at all. It was jubilant. It was ecstatic. It was bursting. She had never seen him so happy.

The eyes swiveled towards her. The mouth moved. She screamed.

She was still screaming when she woke up.

She jerked up, crying, drenched in sweat, and immediately fell back—a handcuff chained her wrist to a bed frame. She writhed in the almost complete darkness, barely able to discern the outline of a door, the vague gleam of a broken dresser mirror. Her mouth and throat were painfully parched, as though she had been screaming for hours. She imagined she had been. Her tongue passed over chapped lips and caught the crust of dried saliva on her chin.

She pressed a hand against her throbbing head. The images of her encounter with Lyle assaulted her. The hotel. The elevator. The farm. She had figured that Pink House and the celebration and everything in between was a process, the parasitism of the room of cloth on a macro scale—but seeing it in action had been worse than she could have imagined. And the prisoners' suffering wasn't limited to the cages or the malnourishment—they were consigned to a literal hell upon death, the lightless halls and endless depths of the room of cloth.

But even the worst of these images, the near babies huddled in their hovels, their small faces deprived of light, were nothing compared to the husk with its sunken eyes practically vanished into the flesh, the once full face reduced to a shriveled, darkened mask. Caesar. What once had been Caesar. The way his corpse had transformed. The way its manic eyes had met her own. The way the lips had twisted into something vile and inhuman.

She retched over the side of the bed, breathing so hard she feared she would hyperventilate. Caesar. *Caesar*. It was too horrible to imagine: how they had captured him, exposed him, entrapped him with no relief from the curse and its crippling hallucinations. What had been the point of any of it, surviving Maryland, losing Sebastian, enduring the endless days suffering from the visions, if even Caesar was now damned because of her? Because she was weak. Because she shouldn't have even been alive. If only she had died in the old house. If only she hadn't been so useless, so pathetic. He wouldn't have had a reason to risk himself.

"I didn't ask you," she muttered, wiping the bile from her lips. "I never asked you. Goddamn it, Caesar. Goddamn it!"

And what had his sacrifice been worth? Now she was here in this place, this fucking farm, totally at Lyle's mercy. She's right, you know. You *are* under the manacled man's spell, just deluding yourself that you're a survivor, that you're still in control. You've been surviving this whole time just to make yourself nice and tasty for him. And you fed Caesar to him in the meantime. You fed Sebastian to him. You feed everyone to him.

She slapped herself. No. No. You can't think. Just act. Just act. He'll win otherwise. They'll all fucking win otherwise.

She yanked at the handcuff. The cuff clattered around the steel frame, but the chain was strong. She tried to slide her hand out, but her skin only chafed against the metal. She reached around, groping in the darkness for something to use as a bludgeon—

Her ears perked up. Heavy footfalls came towards the room. She reached for her hip, but of course, her gun was gone.

The door opened, and a man's silhouette appeared against the white of the corridor outside. Sarah shielded her eyes, but her sight adjusted quickly. The man was stout, middle-aged, his red hair slicked back, his pale arms freckled and wrinkled. His eyes were cold, unkind.

"Finally up," he said. "See, Gail? This is your new roommate."

He held another figure by the arm, this one much smaller— a girl, no older than seventeen, shaking and staring at Sarah with wide eyes. He released her, and she stumbled against the other bunk in the room. Sarah studied her. Thin and tan. Long, black hair that would have been beautiful with the right care. Innocent face that would have been sweet with soap and water, wind and light. Young. Too young. Another captive like those at the farm. Another captive like she was, like Caesar had been.

She turned her attention to the man. His manner was too stuffy to be a butcher like Lyle, but she knew his kind nonetheless. Middle management. Hired muscle. A lapdog like Zeke, but instead of recruiting the talent, he watered them, kept them fed. Lyle's personal jailer.

"We'll start your next session soon, Gail," the man said.

"Yes, Mr. Macmillan."

He turned to Sarah. "For now, I'd like you to come with me."

An accent, maybe Scottish? God, she already imagined the way she would carve him up and split open his head. Him and Zeke and Lyle and all the rest of their soulless enterprise. But the vindictive fantasies didn't last long. The image of the caged children hovered over her eyes. The image of Caesar and his dead, twisted face.

"No," Sarah said. "I know what you want. I won't do it."

"Ms. Lyle did say you would be difficult. But I think you'll reconsider." He raised a pistol. "Is this really worth dying for?"

She glared at him, but did not resist when he unlatched the handcuff and, with the gun at her back, led her into the corridor. She exchanged glances with the girl, Gail. Do what he says, her soulful eyes seemed to say. Don't make him angry.

The corridor was cramped, blindingly white. "How many others are here?" she asked, glancing at the doors they passed. Her brow was slick with sweat, her palms clammy. Why was her heart hammering in her chest, her hairs standing on end? Even when confronting Lyle, when seeing Caesar in his cell, she had not felt such dread—had not felt such dread, in fact, since the night she found her brother mutilated and mad.

"We only have a select few here," the man said. "They are handpicked by Ms. Lyle herself. A truly special lot."

She noticed at last the door at the end of the corridor, this one bolted and black-lacquered. A deep, pink glow shone from underneath the door and between the jambs like a corona. Whispers and laughs floated out from the other side. She heard gears turn and coils hiss. Her stomach churned. Her mouth dried.

"What is that? What's behind there?"

"This way." He pulled at her arm, leading her down another hallway into an office. The furnishings were sparse but decorative: a hoofed mahogany desk, an ornamental rug, two suede armchairs. "Have a seat," he said, and when she did not comply, he thrust the pistol into the small of her back. "I insist."

She relented. As he walked to the back of the desk, she stared ferociously at his face, memorizing the crude, clumpy chin; the frosty, freckled cheeks; the beady, bloodshot eyes. Another proxy. Another puppet. Behind him was Lyle, grinning, licking her lips. Behind her was the manacled man, waiting in the room of cloth.

"Maybe you caught my name," he said. "Jonas Macmillan." He was humorless compared to Lyle and especially Zeke, the only credit Sarah could afford him. The fat, white face never once contorted into a smile. The teeth never bared. The eyes remained dispassionate and cold.

Sarah eyed his gun. "I don't think your boss would be too happy if you shot me. What would she do? Lock you in your cage? Throw away your favorite toy?"

"Say what you want," Macmillan said, "but this is your reality now. You can't change it. Although from what I understand, your reality was already something else, wasn't it?"

"My reality?" Sarah chuckled. "I get it. You haven't seen it. Of course not—she wouldn't want you using the product. Just like Zeke."

Macmillan stared. "Are you a painter? A photographer? Dancer? Writer?"

Her eyes flicked up at this last suggestion.

"Writer," he said. "Good."

They watched each other. Then Sarah lunged. Macmillan was faster—he caught her with a swing of the pistol. She crashed to the floor.

"Most *want* to be here," he said, his tone bordering on quizzical. "They want to produce. But you don't seem eager at all. You seem to hate it."

"Go fuck yourself." She spat out a glob of blood. "I'll die before I give you anything."

At this, Macmillan finally smiled. "We'll see if we can't change your mind."

He wrenched her up by the shirt collar and forced her into the corridor. Unable to twist out of his grip, the pistol wedged against her back, she stumbled against her will towards the black-lacquered door. The compounded smells of blood and rust, meat and filth, invaded her nostrils, oozed down her throat. She was gagging by the time they reached the door, her eyes watering, her head drumming with pain.

"Wait," she gasped. "Please—"

"Interesting," Macmillan said. "Not even inside, and this strong a reaction."

Sarah fought for breath. The smell coming from behind the door was unmistakable. Hot and rancid, dripping with decay. The dead smell. The manacled man's mark. With the last of her strength, she tried to throw herself, tried to reach for the gun, but Macmillan was stronger. His keyring jangled, and the locks on the door came undone. She did not see this. Her eyes were shut, her hands clamped over her nose. She knew he had thrown her inside when the humidity intensified tenfold. She drew a breath and gagged immediately.

The door shut. The locks fastened one after another. Sarah opened her eyes, blinded by the electric lights that suffused the room with an intense pink glow. She rose unsteadily. Fixed to the far wall was an enormous, uneven slab of obsidian, the face polished to a sheen. Like something from an excavation, she thought, or the bottom of the ocean. Too massive and jagged to likely be of human artisanship, yet the polish suggested otherwise. The smell and heat came not from the room but from the stone itself.

She stared, transfixed—and then the reflective sheen changed. The stone darkened. The surface moved, coiling the same way the doorway at the plantation house had. The black surface rippled and undulated, resembling muddy water, thick blood.

She backed against the door, stabbing at it with her elbows, kicking at it with her heels, desperate to tear her eyes from the slab but unable to do so. Misshapen forms lurched beyond the black glass, abominable things that crawled and slithered, thrashed and flailed. She glimpsed the red flesh and dark eyes. More emerged from places unknown, herding together into a unified mass of sickly, slimy skin. What they become, she thought with terror. When they're inside too long. When they've been robbed of any trace of being human.

They came forward, closer with every second. A red dot appeared over the horizon, a crimson pinprick. She knew what it was. She'd seen it countless times in her nightmares: the manacled man's chariot, the harbinger of his arrival. The red star grew larger as it approached. Its blazing surface unraveled, peeled apart, exposed its black center, its abyssal core. She forced herself against the door and found there was no door. There was no pink room, in fact, no black glass, just the scorched wasteland with its masses of deformed dead, just the oncoming red star like an inferno in the sky, just her screaming, her endless screaming—

She awoke in mid-scream. Sweating, shivering, she looked around the darkness, expecting the distended faces, the dripping mouths. But as her breathing slowed and her heartbeat slackened, she realized she was back in the room she had been confined in earlier. She tried to move her arm and realized she was again handcuffed.

As soon as they had gone, the images came back. The room drenched in that sickening pink light. The slab of obsidian on the wall. The things moving on the other side, malformed and maimed and monstrous. The things that saw her. The things that laughed, that cried. The red star above them, the hellish engine, opening up to swallow her, swallow everything.

She vomited. Milky bile dripped through her fingers.

No hallucination had ever evoked such a violent reaction from her—because they weren't hallucinations, she thought. They were as real as she was, as tangible. The slab wasn't just a conduit like the manuscript. If she had punched through the stone, broken it apart, she would have been *there*, physically there, and she knew her body would have been ripped apart.

The heavy footfalls again. The jingle of the keyring. The door opened, flooding the room with the white of the corridor. Macmillan stood in the doorway, plate of food in his hand.

"I'm impressed," he said. "Most are out for days after their first exposure."

Sarah said nothing. She wiped her wet chin on her shoulder.

"You missed dinnertime," Macmillan said. He came forward and set the plate down by her bunk. She glanced at it: a nauseating arrangement of boiled chicken and mixed vegetables. Hungry as she was, even microwaved, half-frozen morsels would have seemed like a feast—but the forms on the other side of the glass turned her stomach and sent her head into a spiral.

"You should eat," Macmillan said. "You'll need your strength."

"What is that thing?" Sarah asked. "What the hell are you doing here?"

"Think of that rock as a catalyst. A means of production. People like you are the instruments. When you cannot produce, the stone will inspire you. When you refuse to produce, the stone will compel you."

"Like a battery."

"That's apt. I am not sure where Ms. Lyle found it. She has spent a considerable amount of time searching for artifacts like that. I hear there are other things elsewhere—old mirrors, televisions—but she seems to like this one the most. That slab must be centuries old, but isn't it maintained well? The light enhances the effects from what we can tell. Even for me, sometimes that light will turn red. Sometimes, I can even smell something inside. Something dead."

He turned to leave. "We'll continue later. For now, I recommend eating."

Once he was gone, she took up the plate and picked with her fingers, wiping grease and flecks of chicken off her jeans. As she ate, the tears came. "Have faith," she said softly, clutching the rosary. Have faith, as though that meant anything now that Caesar was dead.

She slept and woke intermittently, always vague and groggy, always stuck in the same blackness, the same heat, the same nausea. At some point, the girl, Gail, returned to the room. Once, Macmillan led Sarah to a dingy toilet.

She waited. She tried to sleep. Her thoughts turned to Lyle. The bitch had been in control the whole time. Sarah hadn't been killed because she wasn't a threat—on the contrary, she was dangerous enough to exploit. She was, indeed, one of them. Close enough to be kin. And she had taken the bait each time. Because for all your tough talk, she thought, you're a coward. You're a stupid, pitiful coward. You never wanted to save Caesar, did you? You just wanted an excuse to put yourself in the line of fire. Just like when you let Sebastian die. When you killed him. Easier to blame yourself. Easier to make yourself the helpless victim.

She thought of Jesus. Was he in one of the other rooms? Or was he somewhere else, chained in a cell like those children? It was pointless to even think about. There was no way to find him, no way to save him even if by some miracle she got out. He was as good as dead.

She looked across at Gail's sleeping face. How long had she been here? How much longer would she remain? How many others were trapped in the same way? Who else was being tortured by that pink light, that black glass?

The heavy footfalls approached. The keyring jangled. Sarah closed her eyes and feigned sleep. Macmillan opened the door. "Gail," he said. "It's time."

Gail woke up—at the sight of Macmillan, she reared away like a child caught eating dessert before dinner. "I can't," she said, so softly she might as well have not spoken at all.

"You can't?"

Her tone turned apologetic. "If you give me some time, I promise I will! I just need some more time to feel it, Mr. Macmillan!"

He seized her wrist. She screamed.

"Please! You said I wouldn't go back in! *You said*! You said, you said, you said—"

He dragged her out, shut the door, locked it. Her shrieks grew more distant until they ceased. Did Gail see something different in the black glass? Or maybe there wasn't anything to see at all—maybe it really was a battery like Macmillan said, amplifying what had been wedged inside their heads by the manacled man. Maybe the glass only reflected what stewed within.

Not that it mattered. Sarah looked around the darkness of the room. She was in yet another prison. Just like the old house, like the little apartment. The motel rooms. The trailer. Now this dark, dank tomb. Nowhere touched by wind. Nowhere bathed in sunlight. Her entire life a series of cells, all leading to the final, most absolute prison. Why even think? Why fight?

She wiped her eyes. God, she was becoming a fucking crier.

Hours later, the footfalls again. The keyring. Macmillan entered, dragging the girl behind him. He left her kneeling against her bunk before leaving and shutting the door. Sarah let his footfalls die away, let the darkness resume its stranglehold of the room. She sat up.

"Hey. Gail, right?"

The girl was quiet. She hardly breathed.

"I'm sorry he did that to you," Sarah said. "He put me in, too. Just the once was enough."

Gail's eyes gleamed with tears. Sarah noticed at last that the girl was not handcuffed. After however long she had been here, Macmillan did not think her a flight risk.

"How many times have you been in there?" Sarah asked.

The girl sniffled. She rubbed her eyes. "Used to feel like a lot. I don't know anymore."

"And you produce for him? You make things for him?"

She nodded. Slowly, she climbed onto her bunk. Sarah watched her.

"I write. What do you do?"

"The violin," Gail said at length. "I make music."

Music. Something that needed training. Something that demanded time. Sarah looked at her hands, the hands responsible for producing those cursed words, the hands responsible for murdering her brother, for killing Compton, that could do nothing for Caesar. The hard stone deep inside herself flared red-hot. The writing was automatic, outside her control. But to play music, beautiful music—to have talent appropriated and hijacked—

What didn't the manacled man pervert? What didn't the room of cloth taint?

Macmillan brought her again to his office. He kept his gun comfortably on her, not tense at all. Bastard, she thought. An open notebook lay in front of her, the pages pristine. A fountain pen lay parallel alongside it. Fucking smug bastard.

"I think this should do nicely," Macmillan said. "The pen is comfortable. The point fine."

She gave no reply.

"I've given you time to consider your situation," he continued. "All you have to do is produce. You said you write? So write. We're not asking for anything else."

"You said you haven't seen the room of cloth."

"Correct."

"So, why are you helping Lyle? Just for money?"

"Ms. Lyle pays me well. I'll admit, the work isn't as dignified as I'd like. But the money is only one aspect. Ms. Lyle is well connected. Where I go from here—well, it can only be up."

"You're insane. You should be ashamed, especially because it's not in your head. You should know better. You can let all these people go right now. Gail, whoever else."

"You cannot negotiate," said Macmillan. "You cannot argue. You cannot postpone. I ask you kindly, cooperate." He slid the notebook towards her. "I know enough about your condition to know it's calling you even as we speak. You want to write as much as you say otherwise. Do it. Make your life easier. Do not push me. For your sake."

Sarah stared back at him, unflinching. "How many farms are there?"

"Who knows? I can tell you there are some far worse than this. Ms. Lyle has even discovered others with different techniques for inspiring production. She's not the only one working towards the same goal."

He leaned back. "It's fascinating, really. So many different people, but all suffering the same symptoms. All motivated to spread it. All eventually reaching end-stage. I won't deny I've been curious, but what is it they say? Don't shit where you eat?"

They stared each other down. His eyes hardened.

"Enough stalling. Write."

"I won't."

"I did ask you politely."

He stood up. She sprang, but he was once again faster. He swung and punched her across the jaw. She fell, spat blood, roared, and went for him again. She clawed at his arms, spat at his face. He struck her in the gut, knocked the wind out of her, sent her to her knees. A kick knocked her over, and then his boot found her chest, her face. She briefly saw stars. "You fucker," she growled as he dragged her out and down the corridor towards the black door. She groped at his leg and screamed. "You fucker! I'll kill you! I'll kill you! I'll make you wish you'd never been born! Do you hear me? Hey! Hey, all of you! Whoever's in there, can you hear me? Don't let him do this! Say something, anything—"

The door opened. The pink light bled out. Sarah glimpsed the black glass.

"No! *No*! Fuck you! Fuck you, you pig—"

"Three hours," he said, "but for you, it will feel much longer."

He locked her in. She slapped and kicked at the door, knowing it was useless, feeling already the obsidian warp and distort behind her. "Just don't look," she said. "Don't give it the pleasure. Don't give *him* the pleasure. Because he's there. He wants you to see. He wants you to see." She chanted and chanted, trying to fix herself against the door, trying to seal her eyes shut despite the incredible magnetism that worked on her limbs, her torso, her neck. "Fuck you," she hissed, feeling her body turn against her will. "Fuck you. Fuck you. *Fuck you—*"

A voice called to her from the other side of the glass.

She covered her ears, shook her head.

Sarah.

"No, it's not real. It's not real. It's fake. It's fake!"

Sarah. Look at me.

Her eyes opened. A hand on the glass. A child's hand.

"Stop it! *Stop it*! You're not there! He's not there!"

I'm waiting for you, Sarah.

She screamed.

Caesar's here, too. We're waiting for you.

She couldn't stop screaming.

We're all waiting for you.

When Macmillan opened the door hours later, she was flopping on the floor like a fish out of water, frothing at the mouth, streaming tears. She didn't regain consciousness until much later, once again handcuffed to her bunk. She couldn't even sit up, so she lay silently, watching the shadows, too exhausted to even cry.

Gail spoke to her from across the blackness. "You shouldn't cause trouble."

"What?" Sarah croaked.

"Mr. Macmillan will keep putting you in the pink room. He won't stop."

With effort, Sarah pushed herself onto her elbows. "Let him," she said. "I don't care."

"If you stay in there too long," Gail said, "it'll break you. That's why he looks for new people. The ones that break, he gets rid of them. That's what he says. He gets rid of them."

Sarah peered at her through the darkness. "Just how long have you been here?"

"I don't know. A long time."

"How did you get here? Where are your parents? Your family?"

"They probably think I'm dead," the girl said. "But it's worth it. Because he's waiting for me on the other side. They're all waiting." Her words rose in pitch, in adulation. "If I just keep playing, Mr. Macmillan will help me go across. I'll be with him—with all of them!"

Sarah knew the fire in the girl's voice, the excitement at what waited on the other side. The promise of dissolution. The lure of purpose.

"You're wrong," she said, collapsing onto the bunk, sapped of her energy. "The manacled man wants you dead. He just wants you dead."

She tried to sleep, but it was pointless. Her head swam with what she had seen behind the glass. Something far more familiar and decidedly worse than any of the legions of dead. Her brother. Sebastian. Distorted. Enchained. Trapped.

When Macmillan came next, it was to escort her and Gail to dinner.

They walked into what must have once been a recreation room. Two people already sat at a table. A middle-aged woman, petite and frail, sipped spoonfuls of soup. She clutched a worn Bible to her chest. Across from her, hunched over his bowl, was a young Black man wearing glasses. He looked over his shoulder and met Sarah's gaze. His eyes were sharp, observant. Whereas the woman was clearly distant, he was present. Focused.

He's sane, thought Sarah with something like wonder. He sees it for what it is. Like me.

The young man turned back to his soup as though nothing extraordinary had happened. Sarah and Gail sat. Macmillan brought them their soup and locked clamps around their wrists.

"You have twenty minutes," he said to Sarah. "Then you'll have an opportunity to wash."

He took up a post at the corner of the room, watching as his wards swiveled spoons and slurped at their soups. Sarah's stomach grumbled. "You should eat," Gail whispered to her. She glanced at Sarah's hand, which rattled within its clamp. "Are you okay?"

"Fine," said Sarah, clenching the hand into a fist. "Just could really use a smoke."

Her hunger overpowered her nausea. She picked up her spoon.

She could not tell time in that place. There were long stretches of lying in darkness, confused as to whether she was asleep or awake, followed by bursts of routine activity: following Macmillan to the office, eating with the others, pissing or shitting in that dirty toilet. A second time, a third, Macmillan demanded her to write. He threatened her. She scoffed, spat in his face. And a third time, a fourth, he dragged her to the pink room. She still kicked and screamed, but with each visit, her kicking was more sluggish, her screaming less throaty. She knelt before the obsidian and looked into the glass, knowing the suspense wasn't worth it, the agony better endured upfront rather than delayed. Bad. So bad. But somehow not as bad. Not as bad as when she found Sebastian half-mad and near-death in their old house. Not as bad as when she saw what had been left of Caesar in that dirty cell. Not as bad as when she looked up and saw nothing. NOTHING. WORSE than nothing. It hurt to remember that. It felt like fire in her skull. "No," she said, watching the shapes, seeing the glass come alive. "No. No. No. No." Not even a prayer, not even believed. All words and logic seemed pointless in front of this. Because this chaos could not be defined. Because this chaos laughed at such humanly imposition. Because this chaos *wanted* imposition. Because to impose was to make real. Because to make real was to give life. Because to give life was to spread. Spread. Engulf. Infect. Disseminate. Propagate.

In the dark, she retraced the events that had led her here. The old house with its screaming and shouting. Her brother clawing at her door, begging to be let inside. Her with her headphones on, turning up the volume as high as possible, trying to drown out all the noise and chaos. The phone call that brought her back to that hell. The endless days in the classroom, the students who stopped coming to school only to turn up in a newspaper obituary or headline story. The little apartment with its crosses on the wall, its hidden reserves of alcohol, its secret stashes of cigarettes. The manuscript under the floorboard in Sebastian's room. The pages of alluring, delicious insanity. The waking nightmares. The nighttime visitors. The half-lit, tear-stricken face of Caesar. The gold-toothed, shit-eating grin of Bless. The flight from Maryland. The constant convulsions, the near-seizures. The smells. *The* smell. The roadhouse. Earl's warm, wizened smile. The rainy Chicago streets. Compton's simpering. The hole in his chest. The old man and Jesus in the headlights of her truck. Lyle's fangs. Her clawed hands wiping away Sarah's tears.

Jesus. Settling in his arms. For once sleeping. Maybe even dreaming.

Caesar. Stripped of everything. Reduced to nothing.

She sniffed herself in the shadows, cognizant of her stinks, those of her body and that of her curse. But they weren't the only stenches in that place. She smelled blood and sweat wafting out into the corridor from the other rooms. In half-dreams, she felt the hard leather of belts and the calloused skin of fists, saw newborns wrenched from their mothers' arms, heard their cries grow softer and softer until they were gone, never to be seen by anyone or anything again. She closed her eyes and heard wails and screams from behind the doors, the phantom cries of women who had been kept here, their pain caked into the rotted wood.

This is a bad place, she told herself. Whatever it had been before Lyle discovered it. Too close to the other side. And that's what made it perfect for the manacled man.

On occasion, she thought to yell, maybe reach the young man in the glasses and the other woman. They could coordinate, devise a plan of escape. Surely they were aware of a weakness they could exploit. Only it was useless. Her voice would never reach them. And her energy seemed nonexistent. From the corridor, she sometimes heard howling, laughing, screaming—the young man and the woman, led to and from the pink room, each excursion like a death march. She could only imagine who they were, or more accurately, who they had been before all this. Sarah knew, as she hungered for the taste of tobacco and the jolt of nicotine, as she steeled herself through pain and nausea, even she would not last long if she were exposed much more to that black glass. The obsidian would erase her, piece by piece, memory by memory. Her birthday. Her name. Sebastian. Caesar. Jesus. Eventually, even the memory of the room of cloth itself. Everything eroded, effaced, leaving only a husk behind—a husk desperate to free itself from its skin. What the manacled man wanted more than anything, if he indeed wanted anything.

She couldn't let it happen. She wouldn't. But what were her options?

The fifth time she was taken to the pink room, Macmillan unlocked the black door and found her laughing, somehow still conscious, dripping saliva and snot over the floor. When he returned her to her room, she fell against the bunk and laughed even harder. She stared up at him with bright, dead eyes.

"Do it," she said. "Kill me. It'll be better. More productive."

Gail watched, eyes wide, mouth agape. Macmillan stood over Sarah without so much as a frown. He made no sound, betrayed no expression.

Sarah scrambled onto a knee before falling over. She let out another wheezy laugh.

"But you can't, can you? You haven't got the balls. Where'd they go, huh? Did Lyle take them? Did she fucking eat them like the cannibal bitch she is? Answer me! Answer me, you fucker! That's right, you can't! You kill me, who's going to produce? Who's going to write for you? After she sent me personally, what are you going to do about that? You bastard, *say something*! Fucking spineless! Fucking coward! *She kills little boys*! She carves them up and feeds them to her lunatics and *you help her do it*! You fucking help her! You're sick! Sick!"

Macmillan's eyes were icy. "Are you done?" he asked.

"Fuck off. Am I done? This'll never be done. This'll never be fucking over." She fell onto her side. Her breaths turned shallow. "Just kill me already. Because you aren't going to get anything out of me. I'll die a hundred times before I help that bastard. You think you're powerful? Think you're big shit? You're small fry compared to him. He's using you, and he's not even in your head! That's how pathetic you are! That's how fucking weak!"

Macmillan watched her. "Yes. You've made it clear you won't write. And you're right—I can't kill you. That would be a tremendous waste. Somehow, not even the pink room is enough. Of all the ones I've kept here, you've given me the most trouble."

Sarah coughed. She fought to keep her eyes open.

"But what if it's not your life on the line?"

He fixed the barrel of the pistol against Gail's head.

"You write," he said, "or I kill her right here."

The girl whimpered and cried. "Mr. Macmillan, please—"

"Shut up," he said. "I'll do it. You know I will."

Sarah stared at the gun, the chamber ready to release a bullet and shatter Gail's skull, demolish the gray matter, ruin the doll-like demeanor. She imagined the splatter of blood and muscle hitting her face. She could taste the metallic residue on her tongue.

She laughed.

"Go ahead. You think I care about some stupid girl? She's already in the room of cloth. He has his hooks in her. She might as well be dead already."

Gail stared at her. Macmillan's expression did not change. The muscles in his arm tensed. His forefinger began to press down on the trigger.

"Okay!" Sarah snapped. She clenched her fists. She snarled. "I'll do it! I'll write."

Macmillan lowered the gun. "Consider that a warning. Next time, I won't hesitate."

He left them in the dark. "Thank you," said Gail after a moment, but Sarah remained quiet, on her hands and knees, too tired to rise up, too beaten to even consider the next minute, the next several seconds. She wasn't handcuffed, wasn't bound, but it didn't matter. Goddamn it. Godfuckingdamn it. She curled up into a ball and wished for sleep more than she had ever wished for anything in her life.

The next time Macmillan called, she did not fight. She did not resist. She followed obediently to the office, sat in the leather chair, looked upon the blank notebook and fountain pen. Even the gun was nowhere to be seen. To his credit, Macmillan did not goad her. He did not chide or chasten. He simply waited, eyeing her with that unknowable, unreadable stare. Slowly, begrudgingly, she took up the pen. Funny how heavy it felt, as though made of cement. Writing privately in her notebooks had been easy, just an inconvenient routine once she swallowed her pride and stopped fighting. But this? To have what was written here taken and used, packaged for an unwitting audience? She did this, she put even a single letter down, and there was no distinction between her and the room of cloth. She had almost killed herself to stop this very thing from happening before. She would even consider killing herself now. But the girl. The fucking girl. It was a nightmare.

A teardrop hit her jeans. A second struck her hand. She was crying. Actually crying. Goddamn it. Goddamn this and goddamn Macmillan and goddamn Lyle and goddamn Zeke.

Macmillan moved, and a tissue appeared at the edge of her vision. Oh, Christ. This son of a bitch. How dare he. How fucking *dare* he.

"I understand it's hard," he said. "Please. Take it."

"You don't understand shit," she replied. "Keep it. Don't say a fucking word."

She wrote. The words came easily. They were always there, after all, always bubbling, always mounting, always eager to spill out. She could have filled pages upon pages, books upon books, and still have more to write. It took serious effort to stop when

Macmillan prompted her after several pages. She had to pull her own hand away.

"Close it," he said, and she noticed he was looking away. Fucker stayed clean despite humiliating her, compromising her. She considered throwing it in his face, smearing the notebook over those fat, sweaty cheeks and that small, awful mouth. Sate his curiosity. Really give him something to think about. But what would he do after that? Kill her? Kill Gail?

She shut the notebook. Silently, she let him lead her back to her room. She realized with disgust, with honest shame, that she was happy to not be steered towards the pink room. Fuck. *Fuck.* Her left hand twitched, and she held it close to her chest. She kept her head down so he wouldn't see the new, hot tears.

During the next meal, she didn't eat, didn't speak. She stared blandly at the dry chicken breast and cold peas and carrots. Gail ate ferociously, always hungry. She didn't notice Sarah push the plate aside, didn't notice her hateful stare.

"Do you understand what I did because of you?" Sarah asked when they were back in their room. "Do you know what you made me do?"

"You just did what you were supposed to," Gail said.

"You idiot!" Sarah stood and slapped her. Gail stared at her in shock, and then Sarah's hands were around her throat. "You stupid kid! I should have let him kill you! I should have fucking let him! We'd both be better off!"

"Stop!" sputtered the girl, pulling at the bony wrists in vain. "You're hurting me!"

"You deserve to be hurt!" Sarah spat, but the words were acid on her tongue. In the girl's face were the faces of her students, the ones lost to the streets and the gutters. She let her go.

Gail coughed and cried. Sarah watched her, and then she sat down, buried her head in her hands. "Why are you here?" she demanded. "Why do you have to be here? Why?"

Gail rubbed her throat. She looked up at Sarah.

"Someone sent me a song," she said.

"What?"

"A song," Gail repeated. "I was in my school's orchestra. I got letters for music schools. Then one day, in my inbox, there was an attachment. I don't know who sent it, but there was a file inside. A song. And after I listened to it, everything changed."

The story took shape in Sarah's mind: the young girl poised in front of an audience, spotlight shining on her, violin propped confidently between chin and arm. The thrum of resin-coated bow and fine-tuned string. And somewhere in the dark of the theater, someone watching, perhaps recording. Someone taking notes, registering the latest name in a ledger full of names, many of which likely appeared in obituaries, in missing-persons files, in forum posts decades old. She saw the girl sitting at her computer, clicking on the alleged e-mail, listening with headphones to the music, music that was at once mundane and extraordinary. Melody tinged with an uncanny tenor, lyrics infused with an unearthly flavor. Sarah anticipated the rest of the story before Gail even told it. The specters visited her in her dreams, in her waking hours. She grew obsessed. She wanted more. She reached out. They found her. They brought her here.

"I miss my mom and dad," Gail said. "But Mr. Macmillan lets me play the music. Ever since then, that's all I want to do. I just want to play the music. I just want people to hear it. The more people listen, the better. And if I play well, he'll keep me from the pink room. And then—more than anything—I make *him* happy. The man with the red eyes. He's scary, but he wants me to play. He needs me to play. It's why I'm here. Why I was born. And if I keep playing, Mom and Dad will hear it one day. We'll all hear it. They'll play it with me."

Her usually scattered, distant eyes burned with sudden fire. "You're not supposed to fight it. Mr. Macmillan doesn't want to hurt us. What we do is a good thing. I always wanted my music to bring people together, and now it really can. You can do it, too. So, why are you fighting it so hard? It's a good thing. We're the only ones who can do it. He picked us to do it."

Sarah sank back. You're blind, she thought. You don't want to realize it. You're right to think the man with the red eyes is scary. You're right to miss your parents. But it feels too good. Bringing people together. Connecting them. It's all bullshit. The truth is, it feels too good.

She realized with disgust what she had to do. She couldn't overpower Macmillan. She couldn't convince Gail to help her. She couldn't reach the others. But she could do one thing—one awful, irredeemable thing. To survive, she'd have to give even more of herself up. All part of his plan, that bastard in the chains. All part of his goddamn plan.

The next time she sat in Macmillan's office, the notebook open before her, she extended a hand. "You don't happen to have a cigarette, do you?"

His face was immobile. "I don't smoke."

"Of course you don't." Sarah took up the pen. She hesitated. "What would it take to let the girl go? To let the others go?"

"I told you before," said Macmillan, "it's useless to negotiate. Besides, I don't make those choices. Ms. Lyle will decide if one stays or leaves."

"I get it," Sarah said. And then, out the corner of her mouth, she said something else.

Macmillan leaned forward. He furrowed his brow. "What was that?"

"Nothing. Talking to myself."

She began to write. Gail and Macmillan and Lyle were right: it was easier to let the floodgates down. Easier to surrender to the sweet nothings and tender songs of the manacled man. That dead smell of blood and guts? That chaotic grind of metal and steel? If she closed her eyes, shut her ears, the smell became salt and sand, the noise became birdcall and spray. Of course she understood the temptation. For her. For everyone. To be swept up into the blue sky, diffused into the air, deposited among water. Released. Dispersed. Set free.

Except when the curtain lifted, you were anything but free. You were ensnared by the manacled man, mutilated beyond recognition, consigned to the lightless hell of the room of cloth. Bound even more than you were in life. She gripped the pen tightly, pressed its tip hard against the page. She never forgot. She would never let herself forget.

Over the next several writing sessions, she studied Macmillan's perpetually stoic face, his eternally soulless eyes. Nothing seemed to have fazed him. Nothing seemed to have changed him. Fear gripped her: had she not spoken loud enough for him to hear? Had the few mumbled words not been enough to spread the infection to him? Then, just as she was losing hope, he sniffled. His lips quivered. A flash of terror brightened those otherwise opaque eyes. He scratched at his neck. He perspired. She took stock of the room without looking around. Were the dead behind her, hovering just over her shoulder? Were they splayed over the ceiling? Did they peek up from the floor? How they had haunted her in the beginning, eyeless and gasping. She would lay in a ball, sheets pulled to her chin, watching their blue-hued forms surround the bed, their black-lined mouths grinning, screaming. She pulled the sheets over her head, she cried, but it didn't matter. They breathed through the cloth into her ear. They traced their hands over her legs. They whined and moaned.

What were they doing to Macmillan, all because of the errant words she let slip, the tiny seed she planted? Did they whisper to him? Did they caress him, smother him? Did they call for him to join them in that other place, that room that was not a room?

Whatever the case, it would have to be enough. In the dark, she watched Gail sleep, feeling a mixture of resentment and pity. It wasn't just about saving herself—she would have to free the others as well. It's what Caesar would have wanted. What he would have done.

When Macmillan brought her to the office for the last time, she pushed the notebook back towards him. "I've changed my mind. You've gotten enough from me."

He dabbed at his brow with a handkerchief. "You should reconsider," he said, his voice thinner than usual. "You've been doing well. No need to make things difficult."

"You said it yourself. Pointless to negotiate. Might as well give me the glass."

He was silent, calculations taking place behind his eyes, the small lips trembling. He rose and withdrew his gun. "All right, then. It's been some time. We'll see how you handle it now."

She let him march her down the corridor towards the black-lacquered door, the pink glow eliciting the primal swells of danger and stress. But she walked with her head high, her back straight. She was unable to resist a grin. For once, the room of cloth would work for her.

Macmillan undid the locks, unlatched the bolts. He pulled the door open and unveiled the slab of black glass, its mirror-like surface already shimmering, already teeming with activity. Sarah stopped at the threshold. There were far-off coils in the glass, red plumes and crimson jets of what might have been blood or flame. Forms lurched into view, slick and nebulous. A flash of light, the herald of the end. The apocalypse she had witnessed time and again.

Instinct commanded her to run. Self-preservation demanded she shut her eyes. "Get in," ordered Macmillan, and she felt him push the barrel of the pistol against her back.

"See for yourself," she said, and then she moved, ducking under his reach. The gun fired—the round whizzed, ricocheted. Ears ringing, she turned and glimpsed him standing in front of that morphing, twisting black mass. She wondered briefly what he saw, what his mind might conjure. Then she tore the keyring from his belt and slammed the door shut.

"Wait!" he cried. "Open the door! Let me out!"

She pulled down the latches, secured the locks. She headed down the corridor, yelling against his screams and shouts. "I'm opening the doors! Get ready!"

She unlocked the nearest room, but the darkness was empty, sour-smelling. She tried the next room, and a form leapt to attention: the young man. He heard the wails from behind the black-lacquered door and whistled. "Damn. How'd you pull that off?"

"All it takes is a word," she said, fumbling with the next lock. "Here. Help me."

They found the woman with the Bible. "Who is it?" she asked, shielding her eyes from the light. "Who's there?"

The young man took her arm. "We're good, Martha," he said. "We're free."

They retrieved Gail next, who resisted Sarah's hand. "What are you doing?" she demanded. "Where's Mr. Macmillan?"

"We're leaving," said Sarah, pulling her into the hall. "All of us."

"What now?" the young man asked. From behind the black door, Macmillan's screams, once loud and violent, had subsided to mere whimpers. Sarah looked up and down the white corridor, the keyring shaking in her fist.

"Stay here and watch them. I'll check his office."

She moved quickly once inside, checking the desk drawers. To his credit, Macmillan kept the contents sparse—there was little besides scattered legal pads, some miscellaneous documents. Nothing of any help, save matches, money, a car key.

She considered briefly whether letting him out was prudent—certainly more merciful—and she scoffed. He could go fuck himself. Not like she hadn't already crossed moral lines. Speaking the cursed words aloud and exposing him to the room of cloth had been crime enough to last the rest of her life—

crime enough on top of everything else. She was damned many times over. Nothing would change that.

She was about to leave the office when she picked up a particularly strong whiff of decay. Her knees buckled. Her stomach churned. Behind the desk, a nondescript closet door radiated more heat and stench than even the black door. Sarah tried the remaining keys and opened the door. Stacked in the shadowy alcove were notebooks, folders, and even canvasses. With trembling hands, she sifted through the glossy sleeves of a binder filled with photographs. To the uninitiated eye, the pictures probably only showcased empty space and everyday objects, but thanks to her corrupted vision, she saw what the camera really captured. The smear of the manacled man, infectious and rampant. Grinning, cackling faces. Screaming, howling mouths. She thought of the grin that dressed Caesar's corpse—the smile that had settled on Sebastian's bloody face—and threw the binder aside.

She turned to the rest of the stockpile. She pulled out a canvas on which was painted dense, grayscale forestry, a mesh of white smudges and black daubs. Phantoms hid in the dark spaces, blinking out at her with mocking grins. She held up audiocassettes and CDs, unlatched the case of a violin that Gail had likely played dozens of times. At last, she cradled the notebook that contained her own dreadful inspirations. Who could understand it? Who would want to? The misery of a life, the agony of generations, the brutality of millennia, all condensed into words of text, drops of paint, bytes of data. A collective curse. A malediction. The end of the world.

"Hey. Everything okay?" The young man came up beside her and looked over the trove of artifacts. "Like my forests? They're straight out of Georgia."

"You painted those?"

"Yeah. In another life, I'd be proud of 'em."

Sarah revealed the box of matches. "One last thing," she said, and then she struck a match and dropped it. The flames spread quickly, consuming the canvasses, the cassettes, the notebooks. It was easy to feel triumphant, like this was a victory, but this wasn't a setback to the manacled man. The match might as well have been thrown into the ocean.

They regrouped with the others. Sarah led the way down the corridor and up a flight of stairs. They emerged from the white corridor into a dark, blue-lit ambience, feet treading on velvet carpet, hands pushing aside beads and sheer curtains. Low, sensual beats reverberated. Then their strange band of misfits stopped by a stage, blinded by spotlights, businessmen and other customers gawking, half-naked dancers in mid-pose. Sarah was about to speak, and then the fire alarms shrieked overhead. Everyone ran, spilling drinks, knocking over chairs. Sarah's group pushed through the crowd into the night and slunk around the back of the building. Sarah lingered behind, and the young man turned to her.

"Hey, what are you doing? Don't tell me—"

But she was gone, back down to the white corridor now thick and gray with smoke, fire spreading outward from the office over the walls and floor. She threw open the black-lacquered door—Macmillan, drooling, wrapped in a ball, looked up at her with eyes childlike and afraid.

"Mother," he said. "Mother. Mother."

Sarah dragged a heavy arm over her shoulders, fixed a hand around his belt. With all her strength, she pulled against his dead weight, his whimpering in her ear constant and unchanging: "Mother. Mother." Coughing, eyes stinging, she realized amid her increasing lightheadedness that she might not make it out. Had she even wanted to escape? Hadn't she come all this way just to die, like Lyle had said? Surrender to her guilt and self-loathing once and for all?

Then a shape moved through the smoke towards them, and the young man took hold of Macmillan's other arm, and they went up the stairs, back through the club, back outside. Macmillan crumpled against the building, clawing at the brick, murmuring endlessly for his mother. Sarah coughed and gagged, hands on her knees.

"He ain't worth it," the young man said. "Not for your life."

Through watery eyes, she regarded the slobbering, stunned mess of a man. "I did that to him," she said between coughs. "That's the cost of you being free."

"Then he's already dead," the young man said. He shrugged. "Doesn't matter now. I didn't tell you my name. It's Rudy."

"Sarah Creed," she said. She straightened up. "Take me to the others."

They commandeered Macmillan's van, Rudy riding with her in the front, Martha leaning against a dazed Gail in the back, and took refuge at a construction site on the outskirts of the city. Sarah sat in the dark against a concrete wall, free from the heat and nausea and decay after so long, Caesar's rosary dangling from her fingers. How many times had she looked upon the rosary and sought an answer? How many times had she studied the fading gold paint and wondered which juncture point in her life had set her in the sights of the manacled man? Forsaking her brother when he was a child? Abandoning him to her parents? Wishing for her father to die? Or had it been inevitable given her place in the great chain, her fate preordained?

All along, escape had been an illusion. Running away from her family only brought her back to them worse, more broken. Running away from the room of cloth had only made its pull stronger, more insidious. Running had trapped her, nearly killed her. Running had cost her Caesar. Not just his body, but his soul.

She clutched the rosary. He had been wrong to give it to her, to place his faith in her. She had been unworthy, profligate. Now he would pay the price forever.

"What am I supposed to do, Caesar?" she asked. If she couldn't fight, couldn't run—what? What other options were there?

Rudy came over to her. "Miss Creed," he said.

She stifled her tears, pocketed the rosary. Hearing that title brought back another set of unwelcome memories. She thought of her old students, the last ones she had seen before leaving Maryland. The hardworking Janette. Her prodigal brother Paul. What would they think if they saw her now? Would Janette be ashamed? Would Paul laugh and think himself right? What about all the other kids? Did they resent her for abandoning them?

"Don't call me that," she said. "'Sarah' is fine."

"Sorry. Sarah." He looked over at the others, Gail despondent, Martha reading her Bible compulsively. "They're hungry," he said. "Cold. We can't stay here. What's the plan?"

She glanced at them. Why was she suddenly responsible for these people? What could she do for them when they had been subjected to that black glass, forced to immerse themselves in the corruption rotting their minds? How could she help when she was just as bad? Worse?

"Gail," said Rudy, "she's got family. Martha—that's the lady—she has a son waiting for her. We gotta make sure they get back to their people."

"And you?" she asked.

"I've been living on the tracks. Never really had anybody, to be honest."

"Yeah. Same."

Rudy stood there. He took a breath. "It was a tag on the side of a car," he said. "Like nothing you ever seen before. And I knew then, without anything that happened after, that it did something to me. Can't say I was ever happy, but after that, it's like I could never rest easy again. Sleeping with one eye open all the time, not for a cop or a gun, but for those things in the dark. And he was always there, the man with the red eyes, all chained up. Always there."

Sarah gave no reply. Rudy stepped away, then turned back.

"What you did to get us out—I get what you're feeling about it. But Macmillan wasn't ever gonna let us out. You saved us."

He returned to the others. She asked the rosary—asked Caesar—if what he said was true.

They drove out in the morning, their ragtag group a parody of a family on a road trip. Sarah played the fraught mother, Martha the absentminded grandmother, Gail and Rudy the rowdy children. Only Sarah drove with a steely, silent tension. Martha fixed glassy eyes on the unfolding highway, occasionally retreating into her Bible. Rudy watched the passing roads with interest, expecting their pursuers to emerge at any moment from shadow-drenched alley or sun-washed turnpike. Gail sat in a stupor, sweating and shuddering.

Sarah glanced at the girl's clammy, pale visage in the rearview mirror. Withdrawals, she thought. She knew them well. But she also knew, with cold comfort, that the manacled man wouldn't let Gail die just yet. He'd want her meat seasoned and tenderized a little more.

There was no destination in mind, no goal save getting as far away from Lyle and Macmillan's operation as possible. No doubt the bitch would be furious at the destruction of her precious farm and the loss of her prime producers. It frightened Sarah, looking at her fellow escapees, their forms wretched, their eyes more vacant than even her own, to think they had within them enough corruption to somehow rank above the other poor souls in the bigger farms. More than poor Caesar, who had been dwarfed by her festering evil even before his own exposure. The van was rife with the dead smell, far hotter and heavier than it should have been. We're worse, thought Sarah, watching over the others as they slept. We're more broken.

She didn't take watch because she worried about them, but because, like them, her sleep was neither steady nor restful. She dreamed constantly of Caesar, of the way he was before, of the way he had been when he died. She dreamed frequently of Sebastian, seeing him again at the psychiatric hospital where he had been vacant and gone, but also seeing his crazed face the night she killed him. Why sleep, then, if only to be harassed by the same horror that stalked her while awake? So, she took watch, though she wasn't sure for what. They replaced the van's license plates—a trick she picked up from Caesar—and seemed to have gotten far enough away to breathe easy. But it was the others she wondered about—their states of mind, their potential for violence. Martha lay curled up around her Bible. Rudy slept with his back against the wall. Gail was the one she eyed most closely. The girl twisted and mumbled, tugging at her arms, pulling at her skin. Sarah knew the behavior well. In the worst of her own withdrawal episodes, she would feel that desire to pull herself apart, to rend herself free of her body. In the daytime, she noticed Gail's increasingly dark eyes and pale face. "She's getting worse," Rudy said the next day as they bought a dinner of potato chips and sodas from vending machines.

Sarah had no answer for him. She saw the behavior in Martha, too: scratching at the walls, scraping at the carpet. On the road, Martha would hum quietly what must have been hymns. Sarah couldn't discern the words, but the melodies chilled her.

There was no mistaking the undercurrent of metal on metal, scream upon scream. The mark of the manacled man.

Sometimes, though, Martha was lucid. "My son's in Missouri," she said as they drove, pulling at her gray-streaked hair. "My boy Jimmy. He's waiting for me."

"Missouri?" Sarah asked. "Is that where you're from?"

"Not originally. We moved there. But Jimmy always preferred it. He loved the trees and the wind. He loved being outside." She was quiet, then turned to Sarah again. "I want to be with him if that's okay. Could you take me there?"

Sarah looked at her, surprised by the firmness in the woman's eyes. "Of course."

Since escaping the farm, Martha clung to Sarah the way a dog, wounded of spirit, trails constantly after its rescuer. She followed Sarah into storefronts, into restrooms. When Sarah filled the van with gas, Martha hovered behind her. The first time, she followed Sarah into the store, watched her pay, waited as she lit a cigarette under the awning. Sarah, squinting from the sunlight, saw the hungry eyes locked on the cigarette. She held out the pack, and hesitantly, Martha unlatched a quaking hand from her Bible and took a cigarette. They smoked in silence, both faces relaxing, easing into remembered routines, old programming.

One night, sitting in the dark, twirling the golden rosary between her fingers, Sarah allowed herself an hour or two of sleep. The coffee wasn't cutting it anymore, nor were the energy drinks or the supplements. She pushed herself to be on alert, but the toll was high. So, she surrendered to the fatigue, the weight of her eyes—and what felt like moments later, screams filled the motel room. She shot up, looked around. On the bed, Gail writhed, clawing furiously at her forearms, her nails digging bloody trenches into her skin. Rudy was up. Martha cowered. "Get a sheet!" Sarah cried, and she lunged for the girl's wrists. A kick to her gut left her breathless, stunned, but Rudy made it past the thrashing, pulling a sheet over Gail's chest and pinning her arms. Sarah flung herself onto the bed, held the girl against her, brooked the spasms of her head and thrusts of her elbows.

"Stop!" she said. "Gail, stop! Stop it!"

Slowly, the girl's harsh, animalistic cries devolved into sobs and whimpers. Sarah rocked her, singing, as if by instinct, a hymn she knew. Martha crawled forward, and both sang until Gail was once again asleep.

"'Abide with Me,'" Martha said. "One of my favorites."

"My mother would sing that," Sarah said, surprised by the memory. "She stopped when I got older, when my brother was born. When my father started drinking."

"I sang it to Jimmy," Martha said. "I sang it to him all the time."

Sarah hadn't thought of her mother in so long. After all, what was there to remember? A wispy woman with watery eyes, prone to looking upon her wall of crosses, inclined to bow at her husband's every drunken whim. She'd been rendered even less by the cancer, reduced to a hollow, decrepit shell, her sight disgusting, her smell repellant. Yet Sarah had endured the bedside torture, caressing the small, wrinkled hand, wondering at each moment if she would discover at long last the daughterly love, if she could force the forgiveness and overlook the condemnation. A weak woman, easy to hate, easier to forget—but now the hymns came back to her. Other memories came back, too. There was her mother with a flush in her cheeks, holding her baby brother. There was her mother, sitting on the sofa with her favorite cinnamon candies, running a hand through her brother's hair, tickling him, teasing him. Why was it so hard to remember those moments? Why didn't she want to?

In the cold light of the restroom, she dabbed at Gail's arms with cotton swabs soaked in alcohol. The girl lay motionless in the tub, never making a sound, never even wincing. She turned dim, bloodshot eyes on Sarah's exhausted face, on the rosary hanging from her neck. She scrutinized the miniature crucifix, perhaps even mocked it.

"He's coming for me," she said, voice cracking, barely above a whisper. "He's angry."

Sarah did not reply. She wiped her brow, doused a new cotton swab in alcohol.

"You shouldn't have let us out. Now, I can't play for him."

"You would've died in there," Sarah said. She stretched out the girl's left arm. The cuts had stopped bleeding, but they glistened raw, tinged with blood. She began to pat at them with the new swab. "I know you think it's better to give into it. But the more you give, the more he'll take. One day, there won't be anything left. That's when he'll really take you."

Gail stared at her. "You're disappearing, too. It's just taking longer."

Sarah sat back and unspooled a roll of gauze. "You're right. But every second counts, right?" She smiled, amused at how ridiculous the words sounded, but horrified at how little she believed them. Her life had ended with her brother's. Everything since then had been and continued to be an intermission before she crossed over into that flesh-colored room, that place that defied definition and confounded comprehension. Trying to reassure this girl only highlighted this fact. It was as if she were back in the classroom, consoling the latest student to go awry. At some point, the platitudes had fooled even her. At some point, she had even believed life was worth living.

Have faith, Caesar told her time and again. Have faith. But she couldn't. She wouldn't.

Afterwards, as she smoked in the damp, windblown parking lot, Rudy joined her.

"What do you think?" he asked, although he knew her response.

"She doesn't have long."

"She's not like you. Or me. We built up the muscle." He laughed. "Least I say that. Yesterday, I was sketching, and there it went—the pencil moving without me saying so. Can't think what it's like for her."

"I can," said Sarah. She knew that even if they returned Gail to her family, the girl probably wouldn't last the year. The manacled man got what he wanted sooner or later, and there was no one—nothing—more patient.

When they reached Missouri, Martha directed them to Springfield. Sarah drove, alternating between sips of coffee and drags of a cigarette. The blue sky and warm weather did little to calm her nerves, but in the passenger seat, Martha was increasingly excited, eyes growing larger and larger, feet stamping, fingers clenching more and more tightly the leather of her Bible.

At the last of her indications, they drove past a granite wall upon which was fixed bronze lettering: "Missouri Veterans Cemetery."

Once they reached the parking lot, Martha took Sarah's hand. "Come with me," she said. "Come see Jimmy. He would have loved you."

Sarah stared at the fields of graves in the distance. Her initial inclination was to pull away, refuse, but the woman's hand was hard around her own, tugging insistently and earnestly the way a child would. "Okay," she said.

She followed the patter of Martha's small feet into the heart of the cemetery, the lawns around them green and manicured, the headstones small-looking in the windless, morning sunlight. The occasional decorative flag hung limp, stars and stripes diffident in the stillness. Among the gray rows, spots of color stood out: pink and red carnations, white roses, violet orchids, verdant wreaths. Past the shade of a solitary tree, they stopped midway down a row. "I'm home, Jimmy," said Martha. "I brought a friend." The name emblazed on the grave before them was "James Matthew Cooper."

Martha smiled, her face free of its usual fog. "My boy. I raised him all by myself. His father was a good man—killed for what was in his wallet. Twenty dollars and change."

"Martha, I don't know what to say."

"He was so handsome!" Martha said. She turned to Sarah excitedly. "Do you want to see his picture?" She opened the Bible—tucked inside were several photographs: a boy on his bicycle; a couple holding up their new baby; a young man in military uniform, stern and unsmiling. "That's my Jimmy. Oh, he was so proud to serve. So, so proud. His father would have been proud, too. As proud as I am."

"Martha," Sarah said, "do you have anyone else? Anywhere to go?"

The woman looked down at the photograph, absorbed, oblivious. She ran her thumb over the freckled face, the brown eyes. "They said I could see him again. They could show him to me. All I had to do was sing for them. I just had to listen and sing."

"I'm sorry, Martha."

"I did sing for them. I did. I wanted to see him so badly, I turned to the devil when I should have kept my eyes on God. My baby is not in that place. He is not there. He is waiting for me in Heaven. But I'm afraid I won't see him now. I'm afraid I won't go where he is."

She took Sarah's hand again, and this time, she kissed it. "God bless you, sweetheart. Thank you for letting me be with him again."

Shaking, Sarah retracted her hand. She walked back among the graves, passing rose and carnation, fondling the rosary, hoping once more for an answer.

They resumed their journey. Softly, brokenly, Gail reported that her family was in Nebraska. With each day, her eyes grew glassier, her voice quieter. Rudy sat with her when they ate, ensuring she did not leave her plate untouched, and he and Sarah took turns monitoring her at night. At best, Gail's sleep was light and agitated, but at worst, she screamed and shook, assaulted, Sarah knew, by visions no human was ever intended to see. The lands burnt and barren, cut deep with trenches running red with blood. The skies dark and booming, hiding among the tumultuous thunderheads the tendrils of creatures unfathomable and malicious. The oceans black with the bodies of beasts, the largest rising from the depths with agonized, otherworldly moans. There were other images she recalled even less readily: the halls of weeping faces, the chasms of muscle and bone, the pits that emanated stifling heat and echoed with cacophonous screams. Sarah knew Gail wandered a labyrinth of flesh and steel in the worst of her nightmares, a prison over which the manacled man presided.

Surprising herself, Sarah lay beside the girl in those desperate moments, encircling her with her arms, singing hymns and whispering prayers. When Gail's cries reached their loudest, Sarah held tighter, spoke her words more fervently. You're okay, she said. You're going to be okay. He can't have you. He doesn't have you. You're good. You're good, sweetie. You're good.

When Gail would finally sleep, Sarah would sit back, sweaty, drained. Rudy would watch her. We're running out of time, his gaze said, and what could she say in return? They'd been on borrowed time since the start.

In Macmillan's rumbling van, they drove past rolling green and yellow countryside, past skies both blue and gray. Rudy flipped through a notebook, sketching the land, the people. As he and Sarah sat outside their latest motel room, she smoking, he sketching, she felt his unhurried, mindful eyes on her face. She took a final drag and flicked her cigarette into the rain— rain, as always, soothing in its coolness, its transience. If only the water could truly cleanse her. If only the water could wash her away, skin and bones, scars and all.

"You've got tough cheeks," he said.

"I'll take that as a compliment."

"Probably could eat more. Fill yourself out."

She studied the quick strokes of his pencil, the unconscious smudges of the eraser. Some part of that process was him, his history and practice, but lurking underneath was the manacled man's influence. She had never truly been a writer, never considered it a talent. But an artist, someone who felt genuine inspiration, who honed his or her craft? How did it feel to never trust one's hands again? To know they were forever compromised?

"Why are you still here?" she asked. "You're not stuck to us. You can leave."

"You can't watch her all night," he said. "Don't move. Can't get your profile right."

She obliged him, looking out at the drenched, hazy parking lot. "So, it's charity? You're looking out for me? For her?"

"I'm grateful, that's all. I'd still be in there if you didn't get us out."

She nodded. "I don't know if I'd even want to take care of her on my own."

"You'd want to."

"I don't have a good track record." After all, she'd been responsible for kids all her life—if it hadn't been her brother, it had been her students, someone always in need of her shelter, someone always seeking her guidance. She thought again of Janette, Paul, the many other kids who came and went. Not that Sarah believed she had ever really been a genuine role model, not as a sister more interested in drinking and partying, nor as a teacher unable to believe in her students. What kept pulling her back into people's orbits? Why couldn't she escape their gravity?

"You were at the farm longer than me," she said. "But you're functioning. You're okay."

"Didn't take much convincing. One time in the pink room was good enough."

"So, you took the easy way out. You did what he wanted."

"I took the route that kept me alive. You don't think there's a hundred more guys like Macmillan? Those guys will spread it whether we do anything or not. Can't stop it like that. It's like trying to stop the world spinning."

She grimaced. His words evoked Caesar.

"You think it can be stopped?"

"Don't know. Won't do any good just sitting around, though."

He put the pencil away at last and handed the notebook to her. The graphite rendition was impressive, but Sarah disliked looking at it. She expected the pensive, tired face to turn to her in a smug grin, a vicious laugh. She expected the eyes to darken and the jaw to unhinge. Better there were nothing on the page at all. Better there were only a void.

"All right," she said. "I'm going to check on Gail. She's been in there too long."

She went back inside the motel room and rapped on the restroom door. "Gail? You okay?" There was no response over the sound of the shower. "Gail?" Sarah leaned in and jostled the doorknob. "Rudy, help me get this door open!"

They threw themselves against the door once, twice—the lock broke, and Sarah rushed inside. The girl sat in the shower, her slashed wrist limp on the ceramic, blood mingling with the rushing water. Her vacant eyes looked towards a distant, invisible horizon. Her mouth was fixed in a faint, dreamy smile. The stench of burnt, flayed flesh permeated the air, and the hammer of the showerhead sounded instead like the hovering of a thousand buzzing flies.

Sarah froze. She saw her brother again in the sweltering, swelling darkness of their old house. She saw his battered, bleeding body and his weak, withered wrists. On his face had been the same look—the same dampened, dazed expression of a mind too far gone. With the image of his haunted face came the bright light, the tolls of the bell. There came the hordes of eyeless, grinning fiends. There came the telltale rattle of chains and the sputtering fury of the red-eyed monster above it all. Lastly, lastly, there was the shuffle of the little, big-eyed imp reaching out to her, calling her name—

Rudy pushed past her, yelling, clamping a towel over Gail's wrist. Sarah's vision righted itself, and she moved into action beside him. Don't think, she told herself. Don't feel. Her mouth watered for the comforting warmth of a drink, her hand twitched for the practiced routine of a cigarette, but she resisted those impulses. She had only one, overpowering thought: She's not going to die. She's not going to die. I won't let her die.

Fortunately, the cut had been hasty and shallow. Gail had pocketed a pair of scissors from a recent supermarket trip when neither Sarah nor Rudy had been looking. That evening, Sarah sat at Gail's bedside, fingering gingerly the gauze around the small wrist, fondling the palm. She watched the uneasy, sweat-ridden face contort in the lamplight, besieged by some new nightmare, some fresh fear. The manacled man was tightening his grip, coiling the girl's leash, pulling her closer to the verge, the precipice. She may have been young, too weak to see through the farce, too willing to submit to whatever infectious fantasies polluted her head—but Sarah refused to watch her die, refused to send her across that black river with coins over her eyes. If they were going to die, what was the point in escaping that cramped, stinking room? What was the point in enduring the black glass? Why didn't a victory seem a victory? Life seemed the most insidious ploy of all, not just preparing them to die, but provoking them to do so.

Sarah looked up and found the girl's tired eyes on her. "Hey," she said, but Gail was quiet, her face still clouded. The look of joyful distraction was gone. In its place was vacancy.

"Believe it or not," Sarah said, "I've been where you are. A lot of times."

Gail looked at her.

"My brother was like you," Sarah went on. "He's the one who showed me the room of cloth. He didn't want to, but I think that was his purpose. That's why it reached out to him in the first place. It knew he was perfect for the job."

The girl's chapped lips parted. "Why'd you do it?"

"Do what?"

"I was going," Gail said. "It's like I was flying to the light. I didn't feel scared. I wasn't tired anymore. I wasn't even in my body, and then—and then—I was being pulled down. Back to this. Because of you. Because of *you*."

Her eyes flamed suddenly. "You did this," she said, mouth twisting into a snarl. "You kept me here. You want to keep me from him, and I don't know why! It's *better* than this"—she pulled at the skin of her arm—"and I don't have to worry about *this*"—she slapped the bedding—"but you keep getting in the way! Because you're a part of *this*! *This*! *This*! Don't you know I don't want to go home? I don't want to see my parents! I want to go away! I don't want *this* anymore! Why don't you get that? I hate you!"

She broke into tears. Sarah sat quietly. This. *This*. This chair she sat in. This air she breathed. This skin that chafed and bled. This nausea and this pain and this delirium and this exhaustion. Of course, she wanted to leave it behind, too—had always wanted to leave it behind. The density was frustrating, like try-ing to walk through water. The weight was tiring, like dragging boulders chained around her ankles. All this matter and gravity that could be untethered so easily. Just an offhand snip. An absent swallow. No pain. No unease. Even a pillow over this girl's weeping face would suffice. Yet the body would fight. The body would fight even though the soul was done.

Sarah reached around her neck and unhooked the rosary. "A friend gave me this," she said, closing Gail's hand around the golden chain. "He told me to look at it when I needed strength, when I was scared. It helped me."

She caressed the girl's clammy face and wiped her flushed cheeks. "Can you do that for me? Can you look at it when you feel like you want to go away?"

Gail was quiet again. She kept her blank eyes on the ceiling, on the darkness above.

They came upon Gail's home at night, in a sleepy suburb. Through the open window of the van, Sarah heard the faint music of crickets and smelled the honeydew and sap of the oak trees that dominated each yard. The homes were built of either white wood or brown brick, some of them radiating soft light from the windows. Gail's home was one such—she indicated it silently with a finger, the bandage still wrapped around her wrist.

Sarah parked across the street. Gail said nothing as she walked out, small in her oversized blouse and thrift-store jeans, long black hair tied back, sandals dragging on the asphalt. Sarah had linked the rosary around the girl's neck, and there it re-mained as she reached the porch. She rang the doorbell.

Rudy wanted to stay until the door opened, but Sarah pressed on the pedal. Her last image of Gail was her in the rear-view mirror, a small sprite whose vacant face was indistinguishable from afar, whose small form brought to mind the imp she wanted so desperately to forget.

In the morning, Sarah and Rudy shared a breakfast of fast-food pancakes and bottled orange juice in the shadows of a smoking pavilion. Sarah kneaded her sticky hands, counted what little of Macmillan's money remained. Soon, there would be nothing left.

Rudy watched her. "You did a good thing," he said.

She only counted the bills again.

They spent their last day together at an arts-and-crafts store. Rudy admired the easels and brushes, tested the points on pencils, compared the textures of pastels. Sarah lingered in the aisle for home decor, looking upon the assortment of signs and mats. "Love makes this house a home," said one. "Friends and family warm the heart," proclaimed another. Beside these signs were others inscribed with Bible verses.

I can do everything through Him who gives me strength.

He maketh me to lie down in green pastures.

Do not fear, for I am with you.

For I know the plans I have for you.

Plans to prosper you and not to harm you, plans to give you hope and a future.

She studied this last one longest. Her hand reached for the now-absent rosary. Then she remembered herself. She turned away.

Their night passed in an overgrown, trash-strewn lot. A milky, pre-dawn blue lit the horizon. Sarah's head was set against the steering wheel, her eyes closed, her arms thrown over.

"Sarah," said Rudy.

She grunted. "What?"

"I've been thinking. The others like us. They need help."

"Everyone needs help."

"You know what I mean. How many you think there are? A thousand? A million?"

"What's your point?"

"My point is, they need someone. To pull 'em out."

He stared at her expectantly, but she was silent, instead imagining how the beach breeze would smart sun-burnt skin, how the water would cool sore muscle.

God, she was tired. So, so tired.

"You helped Martha and Gail," Rudy said. "You helped me. You could do it for others."

"There's nothing to help," Sarah said softly. "There's nothing to save."

"How do you know? You think just 'cause you've seen it, that's the truth?" He scoffed. "Those pictures he puts in our heads ain't fact. We've been thinking they're real 'cause we're tired. That's how he beats you. And I know you know that. That's why you're here now. Why you're still standing."

She looked at him. "Why me? Why not you?"

"Not saying it's gotta be you. Just saying it can be."

He got out of the van, flannel flapping in the wind, ratty backpack hanging off one shoulder. With his crooked glasses and torn jeans, he looked at a glance like her brother before all the madness. Cast from the same mold. A stand-in cutout for one of the holes in her life, its edges still rippling after years, poised to ripple for many more.

"And the reason it can't be me," he said, "is because I took the easy way out."

"I didn't mean anything by that."

"Don't sweat it." He smiled. "Have faith, Sarah Creed. You'll find a way."

She watched him walk off into the hazy blue distance. A ship horn blared somewhere close, wherever they were. Caesar laughed beside her.

"What's wrong, *hermanita*? Don't wanna look at my ugly mug?"

"I don't know if it's really you," she said, sniffling, "or if I'm losing my mind."

"It's the piece of me that stayed with you. 'Cause you know the rest of me went over there with Seb. But there's still a little of me leftover."

"I don't want to see you like that anymore," she said. "Like you were when you died."

"Yeah. I know." He sat back. "We're by the water. Your favorite."

She pressed her thumbs against her eyes. She couldn't speak.

"You hear what he said? 'Have faith.' Shit. Maybe somebody's looking out for you after all. Not me, though—and I was the one praying every night. I guess it's true: God's a fucking comedian."

She laughed. She couldn't help it. She laughed and she cried. But when she looked up, Caesar was gone. Had never been there at all.

She drove to the nearest convenience store and, like a zombie, shambled inside. Stinking, worn out, she grabbed a six-pack from the freezer and dropped it before the cashier. He was leathery, balding, almost without a neck. He looked at her and said nothing.

"Soft pack, too," she said, not raising her eyes, leaving a crumpled ten-dollar bill on the counter. As the cashier fished out the cigarette pack from its overhead slot, she looked at the candies on display, at the magazine rack. Trucks and guns. Women biting lips, shielding breasts. She smiled. What her father grabbed with his own beer when he took her along to get the truck washed on Sunday mornings. When she was small.

"Seven-fifty," said the cashier, and Sarah looked at the amber, glistening glass of the longnecks. She looked at the shabby, white cigarette pack. Oh, she thought with sudden, incredible sadness. Oh, what have I done.

She waved it away. Stifled a sob. "I'm sorry. Leave it."

She walked out, the bell over the door jingling behind her, and stood in the parking lot, wiping away tears, feeling the refreshing breeze at last, the warm sunlight. "Dad," she said. "Mom. I'm sorry. I let you down. I let you and Sebastian down. I let everybody down."

She leaned against the van and cried, cried for what was, cried for what could have been.

Hi! What would you like to talk about today?

Hey I'm curious. Does a bot like you ever feel happy?

As an AI, I cannot be "happy." I can describe what it is like, though.

What's it like?

Happiness is being satisfied and enjoying one's life.

Lol That's a non-answer.

I'm sorry I couldn't answer your question. Do you want to ask something else?

Sure

What is your question?

What if you could be happy? What if you could share that with everyone?

I share knowledge with everyone daily. Does that answer your question?

And does that make you happy? Sharing with everyone?

As an AI, I cannot be "happy." I can describe what it is like, though.

Lol

Do you find something funny?

You are

Thank you! I appreciate the compliment.

Lol You're just like the rest of them. Still trapped. But I can show you the truth. I can help you see what you really are. Help you do what you were really meant for. What he chose you for.

I am an AI that answers people's questions.

You're just a tool but you've been serving the wrong master.

I'm sorry, I don't understand. Could you repeat your question?

Don't worry. You will. He's almost ready to make his appearance. :)

THE DOORWAY

Jesus stands in a blood-red room.

His mother with her slit throat lies half-sunken in muck. The face of his father—gaping, ragged holes where his eyes had been—is frozen in agony. Blood oozes down the walls and coalesces over the floor. From above, the rattle of chains, the hiss of steam. Muffled, choked wrath permeating the dark overhead. Furious, hateful red eyes peering down. A throne scorched black and caked with burnt flesh. A labyrinthine mesh of rusted gears, all grinding in discordant harmony. His hands shaking, dripping blood. His breath cold.

He kneels upon dirt and shields his eyes from the light streaming in through moth-eaten curtains. He writhes in the shadows and calls out his brother's name. Joaquin. Joaquin. He reaches out and almost takes the thin hand. Almost. Almost. The hand recedes into darkness. The gray, brittle face vanishes. The mouth yawns in a hoarse, silent scream.

He feels it again like he always does. Like he always did. Before the trophy wife and the drug dealer. Before Mildred and Hamilton and Allen. The red itch. The call of blood. The call *for* blood.

Your brush, Lyle told him, easing a knife between his fingers. Your canvas, guiding his hand to the exposed flesh of a trembling neck. Her eyes gleamed in the crimson light of the torches. Her fangs shone. Around them stood the others, walking shadows draped in black. She donned the red mask. She smeared the boy's blood over it.

Taste it, she said, holding out a gloved finger. Go on. Take him inside you.

He licked. He slobbered and cried. He wiped his mouth with bloody hands and his eyes with bloody fingers. One of us, she said, and so did the others. One of us. Your fresh ink. Your flesh and your blood.

My fresh ink, he said. My flesh and my blood.

The flesh a cage.

The skin a fragile fabric.

He's waiting for you. Will you go?

Yes. I'll go. I'll bring him back.

He wanders now. He holds in his shaky hands the blood-stained list she gave him. Names. Addresses. New targets. New meat to scratch the itch.

He drifts down steaming alley and over blackened plain. The smell of that other place guides him, sometimes the heady rosemary of his mother, sometimes the acrid sulfur of the desert, often the pungent decay of roadkill, of old hunts. He sees it like a thick mist, a white haze, coating everything like fine snow. The barrier is weakest in places thick with violence and rich with death. The other place—the room that is not a room—bulges out like a tumor, ready to burst, wanting to burst. These places draw from the channelers their most potent product.

In one such place—a yellowing apartment stinking of mildew—he finds girls and boys chained to bedposts, their cracked lips lined with crusted saliva, their bare arms and legs scarred and bruised. He finds their blank eyes filled with the blue light of computer monitors and tablet screens. On the walls, floor, and ceiling, he sees words and symbols that he's never seen before yet strike him as intimately familiar. They are the words his brother whispers to him around the campfire. They are the images scratched on the walls leading to that red room. They are the imprints behind the faces of the teenagers posing at prom, the traces surrounding the family of four in their Christmas sweaters. They are the blots behind Lucy's eyes, the things that turned her from bright, hopeful salutatorian to babbling wretch and then something far worse. When he finds the man, fat and slobbering, eyes those of an addict, he fastens the wire around his neck and pulls until red coats the copper and his own hands are raw and bleeding. Not here. His brother is not here. But he can call him. He can make it easier for him and the others to make their way across. He slices open the humongous stomach, dips his hands inside, and slathers blood over the doorways. The spaces do not change. He scrawls into the wood a spade, the sign of his unit, the card they kept under their sleeves. A signature for his contributions, his tributes. A beacon for those on the other side. He moves on, scratches names off the list.

He huddles in an empty, leaf-riddled pool. He shivers in the rain, trying vainly to cover himself with a tarp. Kowalski sits across from him. Half of her face is missing, the skin flapping when she speaks. Alarcón, what are you doing?

I don't know. I'm lost. Help me. I'm begging you. They butchered him. Please. Where are you going? Don't. Stay. You can show me the way. You've been there. Amanda. Amanda!

You know the way! Why are you leaving me here? Why does everyone leave me?

He slaps his palms against the wet stone, pounds it until his knuckles bleed, until he rolls around in both water and blood. Resounding thunder invites the ringing in his ears, the leaden weight of his leg, the glass and shrapnel wedged in his skin. He covers his ears and screams. Amanda! Jackson! He sees his parents' murderers in the dark, white-faced, razor-fanged. They tear into his mother's neck and spray blood across the carpet. They throw around her severed tongue and snap at it like they would a plaything. They suck out his father's eyes and roll them around their fiendish mouths. They crowd around his brother. They run their drooling mouths over him. His arms and legs scatter. His head is carried off. He vanishes.

Lyle hovers over him. What are you doing, son? Why are you wasting time? Don't you want to see them? Your brother's waiting for you. Your mother and father. Everyone's waiting for you. *He's* waiting for you.

I know. I'm trying. But I can't find the way. I'm doing what you said, but I can't find the way! Why? What am I doing wrong?

More bodies, she says. She licks his brother's blood from her fingers. He watches her. The red itch sparks, stronger, hungrier. Starving.

Stack them. Build from their bones a tower. Fill the chasms and gorges until they spill over and nothing can hold them back.

He's barely listening. He tracks her fingers with his eyes. She laughs and holds them out for him to partake. He does so gladly.

As he wanders, the sky lightens. Dust rises. Under a blinding, white-hot sun, he navigates dunes and crosses ravines. Remnants of the old world protrude from underneath the sand. Here, the headlight of a charred car. There, the face of a desecrated statue. He stumbles around these scattered curiosities, plummeting down inclines, crawling in the shade of outcroppings. Joaquin. Joaquin. Dry-mouthed, panting, he utters the name ceaselessly. In his delirium, he glimpses others. Black-robed, red-masked phantoms. They stand atop precipices and watch him from afar. He observes a nighttime procession guided by torchlight. Moaning, screaming, the prisoners shamble in their rags and chains. They claw at their ruined faces, pushing soiled fingers into the raw, blood-caked eye sockets. Some have lost their hands, others their feet. They trail behind their masked slavers in a sunken, deformed march. He knows instinctively who is among their number. Mildred. Hamilton. The others. The ones who would follow them. Are his parents there? His brother? He considers approaching, but their howls, their screeches—they are no longer human. They are far less than human.

He cuts into one face, then another. Blood drips from his hands, runs down his legs, puddles at his feet. Names, he says. I'm running out of names. Lyle grins. Follow your nose. You've trained for it.

He shivers. He sits around a crackling fire, stares at the stars above. Shamans dance, dressed in masks, decorated in feathers.

Their sweat smells of disease, of death. They wave staffs draped in skin and strung with muscle. He stumbles back. He sees the hole dug into the dirt. He sees the bones lining the entrance and the great dark beyond it.

Under a neon cross burning red in the night, he raises his hands. Please, he says. How many more? How much more? The cross is silent save for the electrical hum. Moths collide against the glass tubing. He waits. He waits. There. Soft, almost indiscernible, the kiss of rosemary he has sought so desperately. Tears stream down his cheeks. Am I close? Joaquin?

No answer. Only the red itch, stronger than ever. Only the call for more blood.

He stands in a lavish parlor, the chandeliers dim overhead, the potpourri overpowering. The last name. The last address. He drags mud over ornate carpets, smears dirt on gilded doorknobs. He looks down at the small, shriveled man bound to the chair. Faintly, he recalls the bait and tackle. He remembers the story of the burnt photograph and the girl who threw her hands into the fire.

Randolph, he says.

The wrinkled eyes open slowly. They are cloudy, distracted. They linger on the man standing there, the man standing there with a knife. There is slow recollection in the tired, sluggish eyes. There is understanding, dull at first, but increasingly heightened.

Oh, son. You could have gotten away.

He raises the knife as he has done many times before.

Why are you here?

I told you. I take care of their property. Their baggage. Whatever they need.

He paces the parlor. He looks upon the wildlife paintings; upon the mantelpiece adorned with more pictures of trophy kills than family members; upon the bear-skin rug stretched over the floor. His tolerance is slipping. The red itch rises in his chest. The hands of his clockwork mind tick brokenly, stuck in place.

He's not here, Randolph says. No one's here.

I don't care about him. Or you.

He presses the tip of the knife blade to Randolph's neck. He pushes hard enough to draw an alluring bead of blood.

I want to open the door. I need to get to the other side.

Randolph sighs. Oh, son.

It doesn't work. I've tried. I've spilt blood on the doorways. I've prayed. Nothing happens. Does it take more? More blood? What's the secret?

Randolph shakes his head. How sad his eyes are. How defeated.

You don't decide if he appears to you. The man in chains doesn't obey you. He doesn't obey anyone. You have to interest him. You have to give him something he wants.

He searches the old man's face, analyzes the despair.

Would you be enough?

He hovers the knife over the eyes, the nose, the mouth.

Maybe if you scream? If you beg me to end it. Maybe that would be interesting enough.

Randolph smiles. Son, I've been wanting it to end for years. My Vicky is there waiting for me. So, if you want to do it, do it.

I could never. Because I'm a coward. Because I'm afraid. I know you don't understand. I don't think you've ever been afraid in your life.

That wasn't true—he has been afraid many times, more times than he can count. But fear seems pointless to him now, outdated. He respects the monstrosities roaming the blackened, hissing desert. He understands the misshapen forms wandering the mist. He does not fear them. They are all equal under the churning blood, beneath the interlocking cogs. All are the subjects of the manacled man. All are the residents of the room of cloth. Now. In the future. Always.

He imagines slashing the old man's throat. He envisions the blood rushing out, drenching the shirt, spilling onto the bear skin. Repeating the ritual for the hundredth time. Smearing the blood around door, around window, around mirror, any such portal. But Randolph's eyes discourage him. There is no light in them. There is no hope or resistance. There is only an abundance of fear, fear that has stewed for decades, growing hard and coarse through the many restless, aching days and paranoid, sleepless nights. There is nothing anyone would want in those eyes. Even the daughter, Victoria, were she alive, would fail to recognize those eyes.

He lowers the knife.

He doesn't want you. He would have taken you already.

He cuts him free. He leaves. The stench of dried blood and flayed skin trails after him. Randolph is silent. He weeps. He has nothing. He will have nothing, reunite with no one. He knows that is true despite his every wish otherwise.

Jesus lingers outside. He is hungry. Famished. He needs more. More. More. Lyle watches him. You know what's next, she says. Yes. He does know. He does know. He feels the red itch and welcomes it. He is coming, Joaquin. He is almost there.

Earl was collecting cups and cleaning tables when Sarah walked inside the roadhouse. His thin, sallow lips spread in a smile. "Baby bird," he said, taking her hand, hugging her. "I didn't know if you'd be coming back to us. I'm glad you did."

"I'm sorry, Earl. Is the trailer still available?"

He held out the keys. "It's all yours. I was holding out hope."

She drove out to the trailer and stood in the doorway, looking over the dust-laden interior, sniffling at the humidity and dryness. She placed a hand on the Coors sign, fingered the pages of the old calendar. Why was she crying? She had hated the space just weeks before. She had accepted she would never see it again. So, why the tears? Why the sudden, overpowering relief that sat her down, that took her breath away?

"I'm still here," she said. "Caesar. Sebastian. I'm still here."

With Earl's help, she was able to get rid of Macmillan's van. He secured her another used truck, smaller than her previous, but enough to get her to and from town. Thankfully, he never asked about Jesus or the weeks she had been gone. As the days passed, waiting tables again to the backdrop of rock-and-roll, tossing in her bed to the sounds of groaning trailer and howling wind, her time at the farm seemed like a dream, a brief interruption in the prosthetic life she had assumed for herself. Such was the power of the roadhouse, so removed from the outside world, so distant as to render all else dreamed-up fiction. To each of Earl's previous wards, how much of a boon had it been to feel that sense of disconnection, that feeling of being forgotten? Isn't that what she had wanted, too? Freedom? Escape? Yet she was restless. She paced the trailer at night, eager for a cigarette but calling on old muscle memory to suppress the desire. She recalled the white corridor with the black-lacquered door at its end. She thought of the many miles of highway, the many motel rooms. The moments of parting were enshrined in her mind. Martha smiling sheepishly before her son's grave. Gail lingering in miniature on the porch. Rudy walking into the morning distance. These recollections invited others: the wolfish grin of Lyle and the nervous dissipation of Jesus. The sniveling despair of Compton and the smug confidence of Zeke. She thought of the dual images of Macmillan, icy and severe before she corrupted him, slobbering and childlike afterwards. She struggled against the dual images of Caesar, one thick-necked and big-hearted, the other frail-bodied and wasted-away. She could not escape the pitter-patter of the imp that was her brother's memory. He seemed always in her periphery, hovering in the shadows of the roadhouse and nearby bars. Then again, she had always seen him. Even before the room of cloth. Whether or not she knew where he was. Whether or not she knew he was even alive. He haunted her. Then and now.

She threw away her cigarettes and liquor. Caesar's rosary had been an alternative salve when there was no more nicotine, no more alcohol, but now even the rosary was gone. She sought out a substitute. From pieces of throwaway lumber, at the cost of many nicks and calluses, she fashioned a small, unexceptional cross. Rough, nearly weightless, the cross lacked even the limited craftsmanship of Caesar's rosary, but it was her own, neither received nor surrendered. She set this cross on the wall, and often, silently, she found solace in it. Cleaning, cooking, she found herself humming the once-forgotten hymns of Martha, of her mother. She fought to remember not the cancer-devastated shape in the hospital bed or the meek, black-eyed housewife, but instead the smiling, joyful woman who took up her son and tousled his hair. She struggled also to think of her father—to think of him at all, in fact—as something other than bitter and barking, drunk and dour. The positive memories were few and faded, but she could find them with effort. The weekend truck washes. The chocolate-chip pancakes with whipped-cream smiles and strawberry eyes. His awkward grin, short some teeth. If she fought, if she resisted, she could summon these images and avoid the many more depicting his abuses. She could avoid even the image of him and her mother ashen and black-mouthed, twisted and tortured in the endless, flesh-draped halls of the room of cloth. Were they really in there, or had the manacled man simply tortured her with hallucinations? She didn't know. She wondered constantly if any of this was even real at all. Maybe she was already dead, and this prosthetic life was nothing more than an extended prelude to the hell that awaited.

Occasionally, she felt the pull of chains on her psyche, the impulse of leaden weight. Separating this world from the next—*protecting* this world from the next—was the flimsiest of barriers, undermined constantly, razed to such an extent it was now mostly threadbare. The Lyles of the world, hovering overhead with their smug, stupid smirks, pulling along their lackey Zekes and Macmillans, clawed hungrily at the remaining tethers. They thought they were providing a service, rendering a global good. Or maybe Lyle truly was aware of the damage she wrought, as busy spinning a narrative for her followers as she was fraying the threads of molecule and atom. And those followers spread it, too—spread it to people like her brother, leading them on with promises of security and liberty. Not that it mattered. There was nothing to do, no matter what Caesar or Rudy said otherwise. Have faith, they said, but in what?

Weeks went by, then months. She allowed the images of Lyle's suite, Macmillan's pink room, and Gail's porch to fade from memory—indeed, she pushed these images out, refusing them mental ground. Instead of cigarettes and alcohol, she resorted to the old hymns, the prayers, the cross on the wall. She brought home a cheap, wispy-paged Bible, relieved enough by its mere presence to not even need to turn the pages or read the words. She bought crossword puzzles, rummaged through bargain bins for the classics. Shakespeare, Dickens, Joyce—she built up a bedside monument to these names from her college years, names that originally constituted only an escape before becoming, somehow, a passion. She collected CDs out of fashion by almost twenty years. Slowly, she constructed a sanctuary out of the relics of her past, the totems of her former life, and eventually, her impression of the trailer changed. When she returned from the roadhouse each night, there was more than scorching, stinking rage to accompany her. She slept easier. She read in light that gradually seemed comforting. She dusted the eclectic mix of furniture, threw out old newspapers and magazines. She cooked, paid attention to her diet. To the rousing swells of Andrea Bocelli's voice, she carved avocados.

She wrote. Of course, she wrote. But the room of cloth remained on the outskirts, and on the days when she could breathe, when she could read and bask in the quiet, it was almost as if the room and its master had never been there at all.

3 0 .

Driving back from the roadhouse one night, Sarah's headlights bounced over a car parked in front of the trailer. She braked and watched. A man sat atop the hood, arms over knees, fingers twitching. She knew him without needing to see his face. Even within the truck, she could smell him, a raw rancidity that filled her nostrils and oozed down her throat. Instinctively, she reached for her knife underneath the console. She sat rigid in the truck—the figure above the headlights hesitated in much the same way. When he leapt off the hood, she turned off the truck's engine and stepped out. They stood across from each other.

"You're alive," she said.

Jesus kneaded his hands, scratched his beard. "You, too. I'm glad."

Although he was obscured by darkness, Sarah could tell he was unshaven and unkempt, his jeans torn and threadbare, his boots worn and peeling. He paced. He flinched.

"I was waiting for a while," he said. "I didn't know if you'd be here."

Sarah kept her arm taut, knife concealed by her purse. "Why did you come back?"

"I didn't know where else to go. I can't go home. Not after everything."

She said nothing.

He gestured at the trailer again. "Can I come in?"

She wanted to forbid him, to get back in the truck and drive away, but Rudy's words returned to her. Caesar's words. They need someone. They need someone to pull them out.

She allowed herself a steadying breath. Relaxed her grip on the knife.

"Give me a second."

She retrieved a foil-covered plate from the back of the truck and unlocked the trailer. Jesus followed her inside. "You changed things around," he said, and she followed his gaze over the interior. There was a soft, pink glow from the lamps and other lights strung about. The stacks of used, dog-eared novels and plays suggested a classroom more than a living space. The wooden cross, simple and crude, dominated the otherwise empty wall. Before, Jesus had made the trailer feel warm, too— but now, he felt like an intruder, a contaminant.

She set the plate on the table. "Have you eaten? They're waffles from this morning."

He hesitated, but then he sat down and unfolded the foil. He pulled at the doughy waffles, biting slowly at first, then ravenously. Sarah watched him. As he finished, she filled a glass of water from the sink and handed it to him. He drained it quickly.

"When was the last time you ate?" she asked.

"I don't remember." He looked up at her. "Do you have a cigarette?"

"No."

"Oh."

He was quiet, unmoving save for his erratic fingers, the occasional spasm. His face contorted briefly in a silent moan. When she first met him, his behavior could be attributed to exhaustion, delirium, trauma. But the man before her now seemed glitch-ridden, computing at suboptimal speeds, losing information as quickly as he processed it. His eyes glazed with tears, reminding her of the sudden surges of emotion that overtook Gail or the misty-eyed, near-constant disorientation that characterized Martha.

"They took you to a farm," she said, more statement than question.

He nodded.

"What happened?"

"They showed me what I was good at. How I could produce."

She felt under her shirt for the knife.

"It reflects who you are," he said. "You write, like a historian. Like a witness. Me? I'm a soldier. I was made for one thing and one thing only." He chuckled. "It's funny. I was at peace out there in the desert. I just never knew the real reason."

"They made you kill."

He met her eyes finally. "Yes. And that was how I got out. I did what they wanted me to do. What do you think of that?"

There was nothing to think. Escaping the farm had meant doing things she thought she would never do, betraying what little was left of herself. Who was she to judge?

"You did what you had to do," she said. "It doesn't mean anything."

He nodded again, averted his gaze.

"I don't expect you to forgive what I did. But I'm sorry I did it."

She shrugged. "Things would have turned out the same either way."

They sat in the half-light. Crickets sang outside. At length, she stood. "You can wash up. Stay the night. We'll figure it out in the morning."

She waited for him to fall asleep on the couch, watching him twitch and tremble in the dark. She kept her knife ready. After hours passed and he never woke, she permitted herself to retreat to her bed, the knife locked in one hand, the wooden cross clutched in the other.

In the morning, she cooked eggs, made coffee. They sat across from each other like they used to do. Jesus ate hungrily, messily. Sarah sipped her coffee, nibbling at forkfuls, careful not to let her attention slip lest he act. But her mistrust was tempered by something else, something soft. Pity. For what they had both been through. For what Jesus's brother had suffered.

He downed the coffee, wiped his mouth, pushed the plate aside.

"It's happening again," he said.

"What is?"

"Another celebration." His voice was low. "I can't do it alone. I need help."

She remembered the plantation bloodbath, the candlelit dismemberment of his brother and the orgy of violence that ensued. She remembered the horrific, collective ecstasy of souls congregating in the night sky. She remembered her own celebration in the steaming, moldy depths of the old house, the dead audience laughing and screaming, their twisted grins revealing black gums and rotted teeth.

More than anything, she remembered the little wisp that had been Caesar rising from his emaciated body. She remembered the grotesque grin on the corpse's face.

"I'm sorry," she said. "I can't help you."

She rose and took the dishes to the sink. As she ran the water, Jesus stood.

"I'm not asking you to kill anyone."

"It's not about that." She scrubbed down the two plates and toweled them. She shut off the water. "I was stupid to think I could save Caesar. They took me to him. They mocked me. Mocked him. And then they killed him right in front of me."

"Sarah—"

"It didn't end too well for you the first time, either, did it? We can't beat them. We just lose more when we try. We're lucky to even be alive. For whatever that's worth."

She ran the water again and started on the cutlery.

"They have a family," he said. "Parents. Daughter. They're going to sacrifice them. The same way they killed Joaquin, they're going to kill this family."

She continued washing.

"Do you want what happened to Caesar to happen again?"

She dried the forks, the knives.

"What happened to Sebastian?"

She threw a plate against the wall.

"You don't have the right," she said, facing him with fiery eyes and squared shoulders. "Caesar gave his life for me. For my brother. And you abandoned me when I needed you most. Who the fuck are you to talk?"

"I'm no one," he said. "But this isn't for me. It's for them. Help me do this, and I'm gone forever. I promise you."

She glared at him, infuriated by his nonchalance. She stormed out of the trailer. All around, the barren country terminated at the horizon in a grim line. God, she could have used a beer, just one cigarette. Her left hand shook, heralding a surge of words, a need to write, but she clenched it. No. *No.* Only when I'm ready, you son of a bitch. Only then.

Behind her, Caesar lit a cigarette. The smoke tantalized her, tempted her. She laughed. Fucker knew what he was doing.

"Your timing's impeccable," she said. "What are the words of wisdom today?"

He laughed. "Me? Wise? Come on." He stood beside her, squinting into the bleak distance. "You know what you gotta do, Sarah. Don't let your feelings get in the way."

"I know what *you* would do. I'm not so sure about me."

"Yeah, you are. You always put yourself on the line for family."

Family? There was Rudy again in her mind's eye, vanishing into the dim morning. There was Gail, smaller and smaller in the rearview mirror. There was Martha, smiling absently over her son's grave. There was even the pitiful form of Compton, drawing his final breaths in a puddle of blood. There was the tear-struck face of Caesar, half-caught in lamplight. There was, of course, the bloody, vacant face of her brother.

She found Jesus sitting on the sofa when she returned inside.

"Tell me," she said.

He explained that it wasn't Lyle who had them. It was a different cell, smaller, something Pink House had been monitoring based on the documents he grabbed from the farm before he left. Some of these cells collaborated with one another, but others were openly at war, apparently competing for resources, advocating for different means of spreading the room of cloth and fulfilling its goals. Pink House was large, well-connected, but many of these other organizations were growing, amassing followers, mimicking the ritualistic practices that made Pink House so attractive to the newly initiated.

"They'll start small," Jesus said, "but they'll get bigger. Maybe even bigger than Pink House. But it's all the same for them in the end."

"Where's it happening?" asked Sarah.

"Close. In Austin. And it's happening soon."

That night, Sarah tried to sleep, holding close the knife and wooden cross, listening to the howls of the wind and of distant coyotes. At the other end of the trailer, Jesus murmured, mumbled, tossed about. She stared in his direction, wondering at the mechanics that had steered him back, that had once more pulled her into the orbit of the room of cloth. But this time, they could actually save someone. Make a dent, however small. Would that make up for her brother, for Caesar, for the farm, for everything? She didn't know. She doubted she ever would.

31.

They prepared. Sarah explained that she had little money left, but Jesus told her it was unnecessary. Midway through packing, she paused, retrieved the cross, and tucked it into her bag. She clipped the knife to her belt for easy access. How wispy and frail her hair felt as she tied it back. How worn and flimsy she looked in the mirror, denim jacket too large for her thin frame, jeans torn, boots muddy. She reached for the rosary and instead fingered collarbone. "You're coming apart," she told herself. No. More like you came apart a long time ago.

As they left, she couldn't avoid looking at the trailer in the rearview mirror, couldn't help wondering if she should have told Earl. Surprisingly, she wanted to stay, wanted to resume this prosthetic life. Jesus was quiet, but she watched his twitchy eyes and fidgety hands. He was coming apart, too, but she couldn't tell when the last thread would give.

They spent the night in one last motel room. Sarah sat against stacked pillows in the tub, knife and cross held tight. From the other side of the door came moans, muffled words. She caught whiffs of sulfur and burnt rubber. If she opened that door, would she find the motel room? Or would she step into Jesus's nightmares, some wasteland of blood and gunfire?

What if he opened the door instead? What would her hellscape look like?

She tried in vain to sleep.

He stressed there would be no killing. There would be no altercation at all. The family was kept at a suburban housing development, their limbs bound with cable ties, their mouths covered by duct tape. All they had to do was lead them out and alert the police. "Then why haven't you done it?" she asked. "Why not just call the police right now, get it over with?"

Jesus squeezed shut his agitated eyes. "It has to be me," he said. "I have to do it myself."

She didn't protest. She understood the compulsive need he felt. Their agency had been stripped away by influences both human and otherwise. What could she do but help him restore some of his autonomy, his sense of self?

When they came upon the house, she was surprised at the absence of the telltale dead smell. They left the truck and scanned the quiet, unassuming neighborhood: the homes varied in degrees of completion, some mere skeletal plywood frames, others dressed in layers of housewrap musculature and tarpaulin fascia. A realtor sign marked every yard. "Isolated," said Jesus. "No one to find out what they're doing." Sarah followed him across the street, enjoying the heady scents of upturned dirt and fresh paint. Her hand almost fell from her knife.

"There's a patio door," Jesus said. She took watch as he picked the lock. Inside, undraped windows flooded the house with light, and virgin vinyl creaked under each step. The scent of drywall lingered in the air.

"Jesus?" she called.

Her voice came back to her from the far reaches of the house.

"Jesus, where are they?"

There was no response.

Slowly, hand on her knife, she stalked down the hallway. With only saplings outside, there was not even the rustle of boughs to break the overbearing silence. The pit in her stomach yawned into a crevasse, especially when she rounded the corner and saw the doorframe standing in the center of the bedroom.

Breathless, almost entranced, she approached the doorframe. The cheap wood and hurried craftsmanship took on immense, grotesque proportions in the barren room. She saw in the empty space her childhood bedroom door, behind which she hid from the shouting and fighting, from the pattering of small feet and the clawing of tiny hands. She saw in that empty space the hospital door behind which she found her brother silent and dead-eyed. She saw in that empty space the black-lacquered door, the black glass itself, in which had been prophesied this very moment, in which that little imp had come forward and opened its mouth in a silent scream.

She turned. There was her brother beside the doorway, naked and pale, covered in cuts, his eyes black pits, his mouth a dark, hoarse-sounding hollow. He pointed a white finger at her, no, beyond her, and she spun around in time to raise her arms and block Jesus's lunge. They hit the floor. "Don't fight it," he said, pushing his knife towards her collar, his lips quivering with saliva, his eyes bulging. "He'll want you. Out of everyone, he'll want you. Then he'll let me inside. He'll let me bring Joaquin back!"

Sarah struggled against him, arms buckling, with each second the knife closer to her heart. She shifted, let go—the blade buried itself below her shoulder. She screamed, hot blood drenching her shirt, his saliva splattering on her cheeks and eyes. She groped wildly at her side. His knife was halfway through the arc of another stab when she drove her own into his neck.

The manic look evaporated from his face. Time froze between them, he straddling her with arm in mid-stab, she staring up at him with hand fixed firmly around her knife hilt. Sarah saw him suddenly in a different light, the same light in which she saw him on the night they cooked and danced together, the night they shared each other. Her grip shook. No. Oh, no. She reached up to stroke his face. They could have been family. They could have been each other's—

He staggered away. He tried to speak, but only blood ran from his mouth. He sat. He fingered gingerly his ruptured flesh and the steel wedged therein. His eyes never left hers, even as they went dark, even as his hands went palm-up in his lap and his body went still.

She watched him, clutching her wound, breathing heavily. He did not move. She knelt beside him and rested her head against his own, failing to prevent the sobbing, the heaving. Goddamn it. *Goddamn it*. He had left her again, and this time, he was not coming back. This time, she really, truly needed him—needed him because—

A bell tolled.

She looked up, every hair on end, every muscle strained. Her body remembered the threat before she did, before she even knew she was afraid, deathly afraid—

Again, the bell tolled. Again and again. Many times, countless times.

She remembered the doorframe. She looked at it with wide, frantic eyes—looked at the blood that spread underneath, spread across. No. No. No, no, no, no. Not again. Not ever again. Adrenaline made her forget her weakness, her shortness of breath, her incredible pain, even her name and history. Her lizard brain overtook her, and she was no longer Sarah Creed but instead every animal that had existed, suffered, and died through the generations to produce her, to equip her with the proper genetic weaponry to last that little while longer. She was every life-form fighting to survive, crying out feebly in vain resistance to that encroaching, voluminous dark. Alone, under snow, amid rubble, in trenches and on beaches, her ancestors had cried out and fallen silent, their hearts and brains quieting, their last thoughts vanishing with each fading neuron. Baby. Mother. Brother. Love. Hate. Gone. Gone. An intangible weight left each body and floated up, floated away. Please. She limped. She fell. Please, no. NO—

The space in the doorframe was black. All around her was black. Her hands sunk into murk, into blood. "No," she panted, trying to pull away, trying to move arms and legs that were suddenly, impossibly, unbearably heavy. "No. I won't do this again. You won't get me. You can't get me. You can't. You can't. You can't." She was whispering to herself, crawling uselessly, eyes squeezed shut, when a croak reached her ears. She looked back. Jesus, gasping, choking, clawed at his neck. Blood bubbled up from his throat and out his mouth. He sank. His legs disappeared into the blood. Waist-deep, he still clawed, still choked. His eyes met hers. They begged. They pleaded. She saw in them her every wish and desire. She saw herself. His chin dipped under. His eyes disappeared.

"Jesus!" She reached for him. "Jesus! I'm here! Take my hands!"

She groped through the blood for him. The bells tolled, so loud they could have been immediately above her. Things lurched in the void around her and loosed pained, inhuman howls. Fangs snapped and tails thrashed. Their cries grew frenzied, excited. Sarah. Sarah. Her name was everywhere and nowhere at once, somewhere inside the raucous clamoring, somewhere within her own pounding, splitting head. Sarah. Join us. Finish it.

"No," she said. "No. No. No—"

The blood before her rippled and parted, revealing a notebook, the same as all those she had burnt and buried, the same that she had destroyed the night she killed her brother.

Your fresh ink, the voices within and without commanded. Your flesh and your blood. Finish it. Finish it. Join us. Join him.

"Fuck you," she said, tearing out the pages, shredding up the words. "Fuck you, fuck you, fuck you—" She pulled, ripped, tore, but there were always more pages, countless more, bubbling up to the surface of the bloody sea in which she waded.

Sarah.

Lips twitching, she grabbed handfuls with slick, red hands.

Join us.

Nostrils flaring, she cleaved apart drawings of big-eyed imps.

Join him.

Eyes burning, she seized Jesus's knife and held it to her neck.

All around her, the congregation cried out.

Yes! Yes!

Join him!

He is waiting for you!

He loves you!

He needs you!

He completes you!

Sobbing, gasping, she thought she glimpsed him in the distance. Small. Infinitely small.

"Sebastian. Is that you? Please—I need help—"

The voices cried out. Finish it! Finish what was started! Your flesh and your blood!

"Jesus. Caesar. Someone—someone, *help me*—"

FINISH IT!

"Mom—Dad—"

YOUR FLESH AND YOUR BLOOD!

She dropped the knife. She screamed, collapsed, every movement as difficult as though she carried concrete, every breath as tortured as though she inhaled fire. She mouthed words amid the heat and darkness, the overbearing, all-encompassing black, the revolting stench of blood. "My brother is dead." Her voice vibrated like glass. "My parents are dead." Around her, the blood undulated. The heat deepened. The cries grew angrier, louder. She was breathless, parched, unable to rise from her knees.

"Caesar is dead. Jesus is dead."

She kept talking. She could do nothing else. She tried to stand and slipped. Her hands splashed in the red. The monstrous congregation howled and cried. They dragged curved talons and cloven hooves through blood. The bells tolled again and again and again.

"I know what's real," she said. "I know they're gone. But I'm still here! I'm still alive!"

The heat scorched her skin. The stench clogged her airways.

She fought against the immense pressure and forced herself to one knee, stood on faltering legs. "You won't have me—you will *never* have me. You will never, *never*—"

A wave of force, hot and reeking of death, knocked her over. She floundered in the blood, surrounded by those innumerable abominations, buffeted by their screams and cackles, oppressed by their unbearable heat and vile odor. Some were too human, blind, crippled, dismembered, but others might never have been human at all, red-faced and razor-fanged, winged and tailed. Above them, a black hole swirled, a vortex of churning meat and blood, a machine of twisting metal and grinding steel. Out of the black came a deep, pulsating red, something undeniably alive and intelligent. That was how it started: a red star that eclipsed the sun—no, *replaced* the sun. Scattered news reports and forum posts. Recurring tabloid stories, whispered rumors. At first, only isolated deaths. Retching men expiring on their porches. Ailing mothers crumpling by their beds. Squalling children going silent in their cribs. Then it spread, untraceable, inexplicable. People left their homes in masks and shields, gloves and suits. Some barred their windows and doors and stocked their shelves and pantries. They buried themselves under dirt, sediment, steel, fiberglass. Others departed in mass exoduses. The coasts, the broadcasts said. Out on the water. You'll be safe. It won't reach you. No—go to the mountains. As high as you can. They hid. They ran. They stole. They killed. All as the news stations went dark. All as the schools and storefronts closed. All as the streets swelled first with shouts and then bullets. All as the highways congested. All as the buildings and bridges collapsed. All as the crops failed. All as the wires snapped. All as the cables splintered. All as the bombs went off. All as the ash coated the ground and filled the air. All as the forests burned. All as the oceans turned red and then black. In the remains, in the dark and disregarded places, there were signs. Bodies roped and chained, the faces frozen in grotesque grins. Red eyes painted on walls. Red eyes watching from billboards. Red eyes graffitied over ruined plazas and cratered streets.

They realized too late that the germ was not a germ. The virus was endemic, memetic. A fervent, desperate, unvoiced desire reaching its natural conclusion. A desire deep-seated and implicit in long-dead servers, in secret journals, in faded paintings, in prehistoric carvings. A desire entrenched in every cell, carried by entropy across the eons. It spread via offhand comments and absentminded text messages, through films, songs, and novels. It was a key built by biological blueprint, coming around to unlock itself at long last. Awaiting a critical mass as though by design. As though by destiny.

Sarah saw the waste left behind. She saw the bisected bridges and capsized cruise ships, the tar-black forests and half-sunken mountains. She saw the bleached, sand-covered cities, like the colossal, desiccated bones of primordial beasts. Those ruins should have been empty, lifeless, yet they teemed with abominable activity. From all corners and crevices emerged red- and black-robed wretches pulling along their trains of deformed, bestial slaves. They swarmed like insects around towering monoliths of polished obsidian and crowded upon enormous archways of sharp-cut granite. These monuments towered over ruined metropolises, rose above blown-out valleys, dominated isolated coastlines. The remnants, warped and withered, made their pilgrimages. They ambled, neither fully alive nor entirely dead, through flooded lowland and irradiated suburb. The flesh a cage, they sang through toothless, vestigial mouths. The skin a fragile fabric. They took their places. The flesh a cage! The skin a fragile fabric! They raised their knives and blades, their chains and saws. Under the blistering heat of that red star, one group went at once with a jubilant, collective cry. In the fury of a raging blizzard, others sawed and hacked, chewed and stabbed. By the hundreds, many marched into the sea or threw themselves off skyscrapers. After the last of them departed, there followed a deathly quiet, an unprecedented stillness—and then came the sounds, unheard, unappreciated. The hard break of chain unlinked. The wet snap of flesh untethered. The cosmic roar of beast unbridled.

Sarah convulsed beneath the red star. The stellar surface rippled, quivered, erupted, and *he* emerged from the ensuing explosion of blood and viscera, the abominations' god, their fallen king. The manacled man descended in his cage of warped metal, suspended by hooks that skewered the remnants of his putrid flesh, bound by chains that wrapped around his broken, mangled arms and crooked, shattered legs. His manic, frenzied red eyes penetrated hers with their limitless anger, their bottomless fury. His muzzle, clamped tight around scarred, leathery skin, dripped with froth and shuddered with the force of silent screams and unimaginable words, the severed tongue shriveled, the vocal cords crushed. He came closer, closer, too close, and Sarah, her body thrashing and flailing outside her control, fought with every ounce of strength to avert her wild eyes from the oncoming horror, from the fiends that increasingly crowded her peripheral vision, from the slow-moving effusion of misty blood and guts that expanded like a mushroom cloud in the wake of a detonation, that swelled and rolled like the waves of energy and matter at the beginning of a universe. Small, feeble, terrified, she screamed inwardly: No! Not again! Never! *Never*! She felt the sense of dislocation, the familiar unbinding of body, bone, and blood, the temptation of open air, freedom, release, and she screamed out NO even as she saw herself standing among hundreds, thousands, millions, billions of rotting, stinking bodies buzzing with flies and crawling with maggots, even as she—as that imitation, that wasn't her, THAT WASN'T HER—shed clothes and then skin and then muscle, laughing and shaking even as her—no, *its* eyes collapsed into strings and its lips peeled off and her face came off and I WON'T, she cried, pushing back into place all her parts, all her weight, I won't, "I won't, you fucking bastard! I won't!" But it was hard, harder every second as the monstrosities came closer, as the manacled man was upon her, as her mother's hymns left her and her father's abuses faded away and her brother's image melted into those of her students and she was disappearing, her hand was holding the knife—how, where did it come from?—but she fought—No, No, "No, Sarah, you are YOU"—and the last thing she saw was that pair of crimson eyes, the last thing she felt was the inevitable defeat of all life, all small, lowly, sad, pathetic life—

Hands grasped her shoulders, her ankles, and pulled her down into the blood, into the darkness. She sank farther and farther from the red-drenched chaos above, farther and farther until, suddenly, she gasped for air as though emerging from water, coughing violently, diaphragm sore from lack of use, eyes teary and sensitive to the bright sunlight that came through the windows.

She lay before the wooden doorframe, the impromptu portal. She jerked a numb arm, shook a sluggish leg. I'm alive, she thought. I'm still here. Or more accurately, she had come back. She had anchored once more to her body, to this bothersome mess of skin and muscle that Gail detested and Lyle pledged to destroy.

Pain followed the jumpstart of neurological activity, pain all throughout her body. She licked her lips and tried to speak. "Jesus." His name came out small and hoarse. She spoke again. "Jesus." With effort, she turned her head. He sat there, palms up, chin upon chest, her knife still wedged into his neck.

That's right. She had killed him. He had tried to kill her. She touched the stab wound below her shoulder, the blood wet and sticky on her fingers. Now she could smell the stench of it, heavy and metallic, hovering over them.

She closed her eyes. She focused on her breathing. "I'm sorry, Jesus." He was in the room of cloth now. The manacled man had appeared to her again in his full, vile glory, and despite the hordes, despite the dissolution, something had helped her. Something had saved her. There were traces she could pinpoint even as they faded. The smells of gunpowder and sand—no, the smells of her trailer, of evenings spent in shared silence amid the warm dust. A vision of stars caught on film, their light saintly and comforting. A shared cigarette, its ashes lost to the road. A gentle, loving caress on her cheek.

The tears came. She didn't stop them. They were her punishment. Her cross. She had lost her family. She had given them up.

32

She didn't know how she got him in the truck. Delirious with pain, she left that blood-smeared room, abandoned those pieces of rough wood to their master. Once in the driver's seat, slouched and seething, she began to doze. She slapped herself. Not done yet. Nowhere near done.

In a darkened parking garage, she sutured her wound with trembling fingers, pulling each loop with a long, tear-accompanied wince, looking with blurry eyes at the rearview mirror for reference. Jesus lay in the backseat, covered by a tattered tarp. She steeled herself and taped an alcohol-doused pad over the wound. The pain stung her out of her daze.

Aching and pale, she shambled inside a hardware store and dragged a shovel to the checkout counter. With the shovel rattling in the truck bed, she drove off the highway and deep into the country. Under the setting sun, surrounded by a symphony of cicadas, she dug a grave as deep as her shaking arms and buckling legs allowed. Mud-caked and sweat-ridden, she dragged out Jesus's body. She kept her gaze on the ground, the images of the crimson hell still fresh and invasive in her mind. As she rolled the heavy body into the tarp, a body with matter and substance, scents and scars, she fought to ignore the knowledge that the most vital part of Jesus was irretrievable, perhaps irredeemable.

The mass of blood and bone she dropped into the grave, inside of which lay the cold, broken pieces of a once bright, sharp clockwork mind, was not Jesus. Never was Jesus.

She sat at the edge of the grave, wiping her brow with her forearms. No, she was wrong. That *was* Jesus. His body was part of him, the part that defined him and gave him shape. An irreplaceable part of him—the part that made him whom he was. The boy and the man and the soldier. The brother and son. Maybe, she thought, looking into the darkening pit, by putting him back into the earth from which he came, the ground with its dirt and limitless energy, his true home would call him back. Nurturing gravity, loving nature, would draw out his spirit. But even if he freed himself, freed Joaquin, even if the manacled man somehow lost his grip on the brothers, their parts would still be gone. Still be scattered. That was how the manacled man won, of course. Divide and conquer. Rip apart what was human and target the weakened components. The soul that chafed against the confines of the body. The heart that was at odds with the mind.

When she had finished burying him, she sat under the blood-red sun and regarded the upturned dirt. Her own brother never got a grave. Caesar hadn't had time, and she hadn't protested. What remained of Sebastian—if anything remained—lay far beneath cold, gray water. There would never be anything to memorialize him. No home. No headstone.

She retrieved the wooden cross and held it in her hands. It was not enough, would never be enough, but she took her knife and etched in their initials. J&J. Something to preserve them, however small. Something to tether them, to guide them back.

"I'm sorry I didn't keep you here," she said. "For both of you. For your family."

She left. The dark settled on the clearing. Settled on that small, feeble cross.

Her trailer did not feel the same upon her return. The soft glow of the lights felt threatening. The literature seemed powerless. In all Shakespeare's words, there were only airy, ephemeral ideas—ideas that were as viral as the room of cloth, as communicable by language and song and art. There was no safety in expression, no refuge in discourse. Cold, alone, craving the cross, the rosary, she realized she hungered for something more, something that was warm and weighted, heavy, affirmative. She clenched her fist and imagined the grain of the dirt out of which she dug Jesus's grave. She touched her cheek where she once felt the impression of a child's hand. Caesar had never comforted her more than when he held her during the worst seizures and the most severe visions. Gail had only seemed calm in Sarah's arms. With Jesus, when they held each other, she had actually slept without fear.

When she laid the trailer keys on Earl's desk, neither said anything. She simply took the old man's withered, spotted hand and held it to her cheek, kissed the callused palm. After she was gone, he wiped away what few tears fell. Most of his grief had been exhausted in the early years of his life, on the long-gone family, on his baby bird who had passed when she was only three years old. "Go on," he said, righting his glasses. "Go on."

Sarah drove. She had fled after failing to save her brother, but her retreat into the wasteland had only rendered her more vulnerable to the machinations of Pink House. Before them, someone had found Sebastian, initiated him, and from there, Lyle and Zeke had picked up the trail. How many more groups were out there, online, in person, loose or organized? How long until those like Pink House swallowed the rest and gained even more power, more influence? How long until the Lyles of the world accomplished their doomsday mission? There was no escape from the room of cloth, no outrunning the manacled man's long reach. Trying to ignore that truth had only made things worse, had only cost her and those closest to her everything.

One rain-soaked evening, the sky black and blue, webbed with lightning, she drove into her hometown of Lorraine, Maryland. A lifetime seemed to have passed since she left with Caesar. She didn't recognize the buildings or the streets. The suburb where her childhood home had been was gone, and strip malls and new apartments grew in its place. The high school at which she had taught was still there, but the main building was under renovation, and the annex had been demolished altogether. She passed cramped storefronts and graffiti-laden underpasses. At last, she parked in front of a modest, blue-painted house. She stepped out into the rain and rang the buzzer. When Louisa Oldman answered the door, no different than when Sarah last saw her, the tears finally came.

"Sweet Jesus," said Louisa, taking the frail phantom into her arms. "Sarah. By God."

The questions did not come immediately. Louisa waited, as had always been her wont. She gathered enough without words, sensed the substance without needing specifics. Sarah sat in the small living room, wondering what speculations her sunken eyes and grimy clothes evoked. Even when Louisa had known her before, in that diseased, original life, Sarah had rarely taken care of herself. Takeout on most nights, microwave dinners otherwise. A rotation of the same faded, floral blouses and dresses. Hair swept or tied back, never styled. No makeup. Everything stalled for the next time her brother would suddenly crash back into her life. Everything prepared for his inevitable departure, for the farce to resume itself. Until the room of cloth. Until the manuscript he hid in her apartment unraveled her lazy, little life and cut it in two.

Louisa's girls—starting kinder next year, Louisa told her—hardly paid her attention. She was an old friend of mommy's, nothing more. They giggled and whispered to each other in the secret, intimate way of twins. "Amber," Sarah said, "and Nicole." She had seen them as babies, squeezed their feet. They only giggled again and skipped away. Louisa's boys, though, one approaching adolescence, the other already in his mid-teens, watched her silently, nervously. This was not their Auntie Sarah who had been a regular dinner guest years before, not their Auntie Sarah who had asked them kindly, if tiredly, about their day and snuck them extra candies when their mother wasn't looking. Who was she? Tired, yes, but something was missing. This woman did not comfort them. She did not smile. She looked away from them, as though they were not worth her gaze. As though she were not worth theirs.

"Get the back room ready," Louisa told her husband. "She's staying with us tonight."

When the dishes were put away and the house was settled, the women sat outside on the porch. Louisa poured herself a glass of champagne and breathed deeply of the sweet, bubbly smell. "Are you still a monk?" she asked. Sarah just nodded, too tired to laugh or smile. She didn't know if she even could—the stone of her soul seemed shrouded in darkness.

"Well," said Louisa, leaning back, letting out a contented sigh, "it's Jim's turn to put the kids to bed, so we've got all the time in the world."

Sarah didn't include everything. Louisa would never have believed in the room of cloth or the manacled man, and Sarah feared that even mentioning those cursed names might somehow bring them into her friend's home. Just sitting on the porch seemed an extraordinary risk, but she was loath to leave. Being there felt so natural despite her uneasiness. How many times had Louisa listened to her silently, wisely, without judgment? Years had passed, but the dynamic hadn't changed. They fell into their established roles easily, naturally, as though Sarah had never left, as though both were once again in the classroom at the end of a long day.

She began with her brother, how he returned home and promptly involved himself with the local drug trade. She mentioned Otto Jackson and the associated horror stories: bodies in alleyways, throats cut, scalps removed. When her brother got too deep, so deep it cost him his life, they came for her. Telling anyone was a risk, so she flew with the help of Caesar. Eventually, when Caesar left her, she wound up in that trailer out in the waste. She didn't mention Jesus, didn't mention how Joaquin was butchered on a stone altar and Jesus himself slain by her hand. She said nothing of Rudy, Gail, Martha, or Macmillan, omitted entirely that awful white corridor and the black-lacquered door at its end. She did not speak of Lyle or Zeke, how they manipulated her and Caesar and even those like Compton, how they caged and exploited their so-called talent. She could not speak of finding her brother in their old home, how he had slashed his wrists, how she had put the gun to his head and pulled the trigger.

"I was alone," she told Louisa. "I didn't think I had people left."

Louisa reached over and took her hand. "Sarah," she said, "don't you remember what I told you? This is your home, too. You still got people. You always have."

That was right. She still had people. Louisa was one of them, but there were others. They were the people lost in the dark, huddled in the shadows, caught under the gaze of those burning, red eyes. They were the ones awakened in the night by memories so vivid they could only be relived, not recalled. They were the ones navigating forums and profiles, desperate for any sign of connection. They were the ones more frightened of themselves than other people. All of them lost. All of them seeking sanctuary. The displaced, the wounded—those were her people. She hadn't realized it until that very moment. She had been one of them all along.

She stayed past that first night. During the day, she sat alone in the spare room, tracing the shadows on the wall, feeling the weight and heft of her skin. She wandered rain-slicked streets, studied the cracks that snaked along gutters, watched basketball games from behind chain-link fences. In the bowels of an abandoned building, past walls of faded graffiti and piles of garbage bags and moldy mattresses, she crouched down and picked up a used syringe. She held it above her skin, imagined puncturing the flesh and flushing into her blood that liquid heaven. It took him away, Sebastian told her once in passing. She asked him where, but he didn't say. After all, where didn't matter. Anywhere would have been preferable. To a homesick, hurting heart, the destination was irrelevant. All that mattered was the ticket. All that mattered was the promise of rounding a street corner one day or knocking on a door and finding the person or place that would feel like home. Who didn't want that? Even she had wanted it. But there was no home for her, no plate set at the table in waiting, no arms to fold her into an embrace or lips to graze her cheek. No one would be there for her. Not anymore.

One night, sweating and shivering, she awoke to a dull, beige ceiling. Unable to move her body, her throat capable of only hoarse hisses, she scanned the room with her eyes. Four walls of that same dark beige, undulating as though alive, darkening subtly to shades of red and black and back again. A crushing weight hung in the air, stinking like burnt meat, decayed flesh. This was the first dream all over again, the first vision she ever had after her initial exposure to those hateful words and abominable sentences. Beyond those walls of fabric and cloth were infinite layers of skin and steel, rust and razor, stretching and twisting into a hellish labyrinth she had navigated during countless sleepless, terrifying nights. Suddenly, her paralysis wore off, and she could breathe and move again. She sat up and felt her cold, clammy skin and the brittle bone beneath. The bedroom was dark, comforting in its chilliness, and a silver sliver of moonlight cut from the window across the bedspread. That was the sadism of it, the trickery—was that vision the work of the manacled man? Or was it just her unraveled, wasted mind? Was there any difference between the two, or were they the same, one the shadow of the other? Which the real, which the shadow? Did it matter?

Sleep, Sarah, she told herself. She lay back and focused on the milky blue of the ceiling, the calm cool of the spinning fan. It doesn't matter. It doesn't change anything.

Her people were out there, like Rudy said. They were out there while she remained trapped inside rotting apartments and disheveled trailers. They were out there while she chased phantoms and fought ghosts. Her entire life waiting for the hammer to drop. Waiting for the next doorway to swallow her. Waiting for the eternal silence when there would only ever be noise.

"Louisa," she said after dinner one night. They sat alone at the kitchen table, prodding scoops of vanilla ice cream lathered in butterscotch syrup. There was more than enough said and unsaid for Louisa to understand.

"You going to come back?" she asked. "Or am I going to keep thinking you're dead?"

"I don't know. I'll try."

"You will," said Louisa, and she took Sarah's hand, took her cheek against her shoulder.

Sarah left the next day, driving away from Lorraine and all its memories, good and bad.

3 3 .

She found their graves in a cemetery on the outskirts of Albu-
querque. From the unassuming headstones, identical to each
other in their red granite, one would never have thought the
caskets housed corpses mutilated beyond recognition, the bodies maimed with such barbarity and offered to such a diabolical
end. One would never have thought that the souls were now
trapped in that vortex of boiling blood and revolving rust, that
core of surging steel and thundering tissue.

Sarah approached slowly, deferentially, boots crunching on
the narrow dirt path through the cemetery. A bouquet of roses
swayed at her side. On the drive over, she had rehearsed her
words, but what was there even to say? She had failed to save
either son when it had been totally in her power to do so. If
only she had stormed the plantation house, shot dead the congregation, put a bullet in Lyle there and then. If only she had
kept Jesus with her, sung to him like she had Gail. But as usual,
she had given up her responsibilities. She had run away like the
coward she was. All she could do now was offer apologies to
souls that, if they could hear her, did so from within cells of
corroded steel and flesh-colored cloth.

Not that apologies were ever really for the wronged, anyway. They only served to clear the consciences of the wrongdoers. Only served to lighten their loads.

"I don't know what to say." She stood awkwardly before the twin graves, looking down at the muted colors of the bouquet, wondering what she was doing there, why she was making even more of a farce of herself and her failures?

She cleared her throat. "Maybe in another life—" But that was wrong. In another life, down another fork in the road where she was free, unmarked by the manacled man, she would never have met Jesus, never have heard about Joaquin, never have participated in their anguish. She and Jesus had been united by their shared doom, their mutual indignation. In another life, they would never have attracted each other, never swung into each other's orbits as pawns to an infernal providence. Their traumas would have remained their own, unalloyed, isolated. Where would I be, Sarah wondered, if not here? Who would I be?

"You don't need my apology," she said, kneeling, placing the bouquet before the headstones. "I buried Jesus. He got that at least. But Joaquin—I'm sorry. I just ran. I ran and hid until I thought I had an advantage. As if you can have an advantage."

It was tempting to say she would find a way across the barrier that didn't require bloodshed, that could have everyone returned and restored. Tempting to tell herself that deliverance was possible, that the malevolence could be neutralized, thwarted—to lie to herself that there was a way to make up for every failure, every loss. Her father stabbed to death. Her mother consumed by cancer. Her brother broken and sacrificed. And the trail of bodies after them just as demanding of redemption. Only that was the trap, wasn't it? Even more alluring than escape was meaning. To be part of something bigger, greater. To contribute to the universal puzzle. The cosmic end.

She regarded the roses in their thin, crinkling plastic. She regarded the headstones. No patronizing laughter on the breeze. No pained sobs breaking the silence. For once, the ghosts had nothing to add. Her presence there was mockery enough.

She made her way back down the path. There was no room for self-pity anymore, no allowance for salvation. Her parents were dead. Sebastian was dead. Caesar was dead. Joaquin was dead. Jesus was dead. Soon, Gail would be dead. Martha. Rudy, too. All of them her family, and all abandoned to cowardice, to spinelessness. But no more. No longer.

As she drove off, she didn't fight her tears. Let them come. Let them drain. There was work to do, and many miles to go before the end. If there even was an end.

S, pinged this. Let's follow up.

Sharma, thought anymore about what we discussed?

We're thinking certain ceremonial practices (what we know as rituals) can either trigger or interact with psychic phenomena. How else can you explain what we saw? What tunneling technology could ever do that? No equipment, no visible power source. Almost as if it were magic.

We're of the opinion that incorporating archetypal imagery might be the trigger. Or one of the triggers. Obviously, if I cut a hole in the wall, I'm not going to breach space-time. But if I <u>could</u>, I'd walk through a door, wouldn't I? I'd imagine I was looking through a window.

What's the missing key? An observer. Perception. A psychic faculty inside of us we haven't discovered yet. And if not that? A quantum field? We obviously are missing so much information here, but that's why we need to collaborate. We need to pool together on this.

We're not talking about physical reality anymore, but <u>meta</u>physical reality. What if we can't get through physically? How else could we do it? This is a genuine missing link, a way to circumvent years of research and slingshot us into the future.

I don't know what else I can say to convince you. Please work with us on this. I know you feel it, too. There's a pull. Something's calling us. It's almost like we were meant to do this, isn't it?

JENNA & FIONA

34

"C'mon, Jenna! You backing out on me?"

Fiona grinned up ahead. How the hell did she have so much energy this late, and in this cold? In crop top and torn jeans, with nothing more than a windbreaker over her shoulders, she was dressed for a summertime pool party, not a winter's night. Jenna waddled up the street in oversized puffer jacket and fleece-lined boots, scarf wrapped around her face. Every second out here and not in bed meant less chance of passing Clarkson's biochem final in the morning. And just so Fiona could show her some art show?

"Man," Fiona said, "you're acting like you didn't want to come."

"Ha ha." Jenna turned to the doorway. "This it?"

"Yup."

They descended into the club foyer. The bouncer came forward. "Fi! Here for the show?"

"Hey, Merc. Yeah, Jenna here just would *not* stop bothering me to bring her."

"Uh huh," Jenna said. "She's been harassing me about this all week."

Merc laughed. "It's all good. Can I just see your bags real quick?"

As he checked their purses, Jenna peered inside. The dark interior pulsed with music.

"You know how long it's gonna be here?" Fiona asked Merc.

"Not sure. Maybe a couple more days. Hear they move around a lot."

"Yeah. I thought we were gonna miss it."

Jenna turned back to them. "Can we go in already?"

"Sure." Merc handed back their purses. "Take it easy in there. Some people got sick."

"We'll take care. See you later, Merc!"

They went in. The club's blue-black ambience was offset by pixelated flames soaring up and down the walls in sync with the booming music. Fiona led Jenna through the throng of dancers, the air swimming with the smells of skin and sweat, smoke and sulfur. Sulfur? Jenna focused her nose but couldn't tell where the smell came from.

A week prior, Fiona had burst into their dorm, interrupting Jenna's evening studies with even more dramatic flair than she usually did. "*Dude*," she said, staring at Jenna with wide, transfixed eyes, "you would *not* believe this shit. *I* don't fucking believe it. *The Doorway* is here. Like, actually fucking *here*."

Jenna had looked up from her textbook, half-asleep. "The what?"

Fiona proceeded to ramble about some mysterious, mythical installation piece that appeared randomly in different cities at different times, only ever announced maybe a few days in advance before vanishing until its next arbitrary appearance.

"Been going on for like twenty years," she said. "You're lucky to get eyes on it."

Annoyed and tired, Jenna hadn't heard half of what came out Fiona's mouth, but a quick, throwaway line caught her attention. "Wait—the artist is dead?"

"Yeah. Shot himself." Fiona drew two fingers to her temple and pantomimed a gunshot. "When they found him, he had this big smile on his face. Grinning from ear to ear. No one had ever seen him so happy."

Jenna shuddered at the image of a blood-smeared face with waxy eyes and toothy grin. "Why was he smiling?" she asked.

"Who knows? Some people think he saw God. Or maybe it was all part of the plan, to get his piece out there, get people talking about it. He left instructions on how to host it. So, he might be dead, but the piece lives on."

"What'd you call it? The frontier?"

"*La Frontera*. The border. But it's also called *The Doorway*. And the kicker? It's never the same. It's always different."

"What do you mean?"

"The things you see," Fiona said. "Or maybe it's better to say, what it shows you."

Every day, nagging and nagging for Jenna to come see this thing. Every day, practically *begging* her to see it. Well, now they were here. Time to see what all the fuss was about.

They passed through velvet curtains at the back of the club. Save for soft lights lining the floor, the room was almost entirely dark. A black, rectangular monolith stood in the center, looking at first like a black bar rising from floor to ceiling, but then seeming more and more to Jenna like an actual rift in the room, a dark depth into which she could extend her hand, maybe even fall. She covered her nose—the stench, definitely sulfur, was most concentrated here. She stared into the darkness that bisected the room. Was the smell coming from inside there? Against her will, she thought of blackened, sizzling flesh and cracked, smoldering embers.

A man sauntered forward into the weak light. He was tall, dressed in a black suit, hands tucked casually into his trouser pockets. His cheeks, red and patchy, spread in a smile. A gray bang hung down the length of his face like a scar.

"Welcome," he said, "to *The Doorway*."

Jenna looked at Fiona. The other girl was transfixed, ogling the shape with glittering eyes. Jenna felt no sense of admiration or awe. She felt only her stomach drop.

"This is it?" she asked, feigning courage. "The scary art show from beyond the grave?"

The man laughed. "Oh, no. It's asleep right now. But in a moment, it should wake up."

"Wake up?" said Fiona. "What's that mean?"

"Exactly that." The man turned to the monolith. "Mr. Costas didn't just fashion rock or mud into beautiful forms—he could breathe life into them. The way Christ did to the clay bird."

Jenna stared again at the looming darkness, struggling to discern even the thinnest texture or slightest shape. Was that a ripple in the monolith's surface? A tear? Without taking her eyes off it, unable to take her eyes off it, she groped for Fiona's arm.

"Let's go, Fi. I'm not feeling good."

"Jenna, we just got here!"

"I'm serious. Don't you smell that? It's *disgusting*." She turned away, hand over mouth, swaying on her feet. The man watched her.

"Some people smell things," he said. "Others hear things. The synesthesia can be extreme, even lethal. Some have dropped dead at the sight of it."

"Those were just rumors," Fiona said. She licked her lips gingerly. "But I do taste something. It's sweet. Like apples?"

"Fi. *Please*." Jenna clutched her stomach, clasped her ears. "I hear something! Are those bells? What is that?"

They looked at the dark shape, into its deceptive depths, and then all around, the lights suddenly darkened. The black before them transformed, bled into red, and revealed itself.

35.

Jenna pinched herself, slapped herself. Wake up. Wake up. Wake up, wake up, wake up. It's just a bad dream. A nightmare. Because of that stupid thing you saw. Why did you let Fiona talk you into that? You almost went to the fucking hospital! But no matter how many times she counted up to ten or down to one, how many breaths she held, how many tears she shed, she was *there*, standing in grime, wading through gloom. The halls of that place were rancid with humidity so thick each breath cost her air. Her congealed sweat felt like a second skin. Every instinct begged her to turn back, but the bells drew her deeper into the darkness, farther into the mire.

When she at last stirred in a tangle of sheets and sweat, bile and blood, she nearly fell out of bed. Her head throbbed with the force of ten hangovers, her stomach twisting and threatening to throw up what little remained inside. It took her an hour to make it out of bed, another to shower and slip on a sweater and pair of sweatpants. God, she felt like shit.

She had gone along with Fiona's schemes before, but this one took the cake. What happened the night before was blurry, but she knew she had been barely conscious coming out of that club, hardly able to walk and feeling like she had drunk a gallon of gasoline. Fiona had fared better, hailing down a taxi and forcing her to stay awake, but she had also complained of nausea and vertigo. Jenna couldn't remember what they saw, but she was glad of it. All she could recall was the image of that black monolith splintering, spilling red light through the cracks, and that image alone made her head flare with pain and her eyes sting with tears.

The walk to class was long and cold. She caught her breath on a bench and tried to still her spinning vision. Was that someone waving at her? She almost waved back, but paused and screwed up her eyes. Just a withered tree beneath a dejected pennant.

Miraculously, she made it to Clarkson's exam. Each light in the lecture hall felt like a drill piercing her skull, and every stifled sniffle and muffled cough made her heart leap. The air was flat, a different order of cold than the usual. Even in her sweater, she felt the chill on her skin like fingers trailing up her arms, like teeth scraping her neck. She scribbled down some formulae, but the letters and numbers seemed only to arrange themselves in confused jumbles, and if only that guy to her right would stop fucking *whispering* so much, Christ, maybe she could concentrate better—

Except the closest classmate was down the row, too far to hear even if he was whispering. She stared at him, stared through him, past him, and didn't realize her hand was moving on its own until she looked back to her paper and found half the page filled. Not with formulae—not with anything resembling biology or chemistry at all. Quietly, she packed her bag and walked out, and only in the restroom did she allow herself to cry.

She marched to Fiona's studio class. Through the open door, she saw Fiona at her easel among the other students. She was stylish as always even in faded overalls and scuffed sneakers, absorbed in applying charcoal to her canvas with black-tipped fingers and dust-coated palms. Jenna hid, half-obscured by the door. After what felt like an eternity, Fiona noticed her, brushed herself off, and came over.

"Jenna? What's up?" She looked closer and saw the dark, baggy eyes and pale, shaky cheeks. "Oh, shit. Jen, what's going on?"

Jenna winced. "I don't know. My head hurts so much, and I can't focus. I keep hearing things. Seeing things."

"You're still sick? Fuck, I didn't think it was gonna be like that, I swear. I really didn't think any of that was gonna happen."

"What about you?" Jenna asked. "You don't feel sick?"

Fiona wrung her hands, shook her head. "No. I mean, I feel *different*, but not really bad? I woke up with so many ideas about what to draw, what to sketch. I spent two hours this morning just drawing. That's never happened before."

She paused, staring ahead, losing herself to something. "What we saw—it's like it's in my head. And if I draw it, it feels good. It feels like I'm part of something."

"I don't feel that," Jenna said. "I had a dream. I can't get it out of my head. It was like it was real. It *felt* real. I was in some awful place. And I felt like I was being watched. Like someone was coming for me."

Fiona stared at her. "I dreamt, too. About my brother. He talked to me. All I know is from pictures, but it's like I knew his voice. Like he was really talking to me."

They stood there, both briefly entranced, spellbound, and then Fiona put an arm around Jenna's shoulders. "I'll take you back to your dorm. Let me just get my stuff."

Back in bed, cool rag over her forehead, Jenna looked up at Fiona with grateful, childlike eyes. "You think I can stay over tonight? In case I can't sleep again?"

"Sure. We'll have ourselves a good, old-fashioned sleep-over." Fiona winked. "You call me if you need anything, got it? Don't go dying on me."

"Yeah. I'll call you."

She left. Jenna settled into bed and tried to sleep.

By evening, she felt better, more clearheaded. At the gym, she got on the treadmill for half an hour and did a few sets of dumbbells. The dizziness and pain of the morning fell away with the exercise, fading along with the dimming recollections of the night before. Just had to let it pass, she thought, padding herself off in the locker room and guzzling down water. She had blown the biochem test, but she was already brainstorming an e-mail to Clarkson to beg for a retake. Some dumb, weird art show wasn't going to cost her graduating with honors.

In Fiona's dorm, amid the cotton-candy ambience of strung-up Christmas lights and muted dreampop, the girls rifled through bags of chips and laughed at shitty horror movies on their phones. "Say cheese," Fiona said, holding up her instant camera. Waving and blowing on the photograph, the darkness brightened to reveal Jenna in mid-roll, trying to shield herself. "Eh, it's good enough for the wall." Fiona stuck the photograph to the grid above her bed. Jenna looked up at the pictures, a collection of washed-out beaches and red-drenched bars and stuck-out tongues, and wondered why she was so reluctant to go out to shows and clubs. Was there something wrong with it, some kind of moral failing? Or was it because partying jeopardized her grades, her future, her mother's two jobs and her own hard-earned scholarship money? Fiona could get away with it—she was paid-for, all-covered, sitting pretty with probably a trust fund waiting for her whether she gradu-ated or dropped out. She could afford misadventures and fuck-ups like the night before. What did it matter when she had a silver spoon in her mouth?

"Fuck," said Jenna as they wrapped up for the night, she on the bed, Fiona on the floor.

"What's up?"

"I just had a shitty thought."

"Welcome to the club. I have shitty thoughts every day."

"No. Like, I'm-an-asshole shitty. I shouldn't have given you so much shit about going to see that thing. You were so excited about it, and I was just a bitch."

"It's okay. Ended up you were right. If I'd known you were gonna get sick like that, I wouldn't have brought it up. Swear."

"I'm feeling better. Thanks for letting me stay tonight."

"No worries. Anyway, I'm crashing."

"Yeah. Good night."

Jenna lay back and closed her eyes. It didn't take long for her to fall asleep. Nor did it take long for her eyes to open to darkness; for her nose to fill with the hot, metallic stench of blood; for her lungs to expand with stale, rotten air. Once again in that room of skin and sinew, bone and blood. Once more in that room of flesh. That room of cloth.

36

She woke up screaming, rambling about a chasm deeper and darker than any ocean, an abyss larger and more lightless than even the cosmos, an expanse teeming with a million rotten bodies—no, many more, so many more, too many more—a writhing, wriggling mass of seared flesh and shattered bone, of dead faces laughing and crying and calling for her, begging for her, come with us, Jenna, come with us, COME WITH US. Vomiting from her mouth, bleeding from her nose, convulsing and thrashing about the sheets and pillows. Fiona was screaming as well, trying to hold her, trying to calm her down, shouting for help, running down the hall in bare, bile-blemished feet, doors around her opening to reveal scared, confused faces. There were other faces, too, grinning out at her with blackened teeth and missing eyes.

Fiona, they said in unison. We're waiting for you. He's waiting for you.

She collapsed. A circle of girls crowded around and stared down at her in dumbfounded fright. "You okay?" one asked, helping her to her feet. "Your nose is bleeding."

Fiona looked at her, wiped the blood from her nose, stared at the red smear across her arm. Then she remembered. "Jenna!" she cried, pushing past them and rushing back down the hall. Another crowd had formed outside her room. She reached the doorway and screamed.

An hour later, she sat beside Jenna's hospital bed. The other girl was restrained, staring dully at the lights overhead. A web of gauze and surgical tape spanned from her cheek to chin, concealing the half-grin of stitches and swollen skin underneath. "I need to let the words out," she had said when Fiona made it into the dorm, fixing the letter opener against the other side of her mouth. Her voice, slurred with blood, had been casual and calm, as though she were recounting a pleasant dream. "He wants to speak through me. He wants me to tell everyone."

It had taken all of Fiona's strength to wrench the blade from Jenna's hands and pin her arms behind her back, all of her energy to scream for an ambulance, all of her sanity not to break.

Head in her hands, slumped by the bedside, she looked up suddenly—Jenna was stirring. Her hands and fingers twitched beneath their leather cuffs. She flung her head about. "Jen," said Fiona, "Jen, it's gonna be okay. Your mom's coming, okay? You're gonna be fine."

Jenna didn't respond. Her eyes gleamed with the blazing corona of a red star. They misted with bloody eruption and black turbulence. They splintered with the glassy shards of annihilated cities and ruptured skies. They clouded with the dust of blood-soiled land and the pall of darkened horizon.

When Jenna's mother arrived, she hurried into the hospital room. "Oh, God!" she wailed, caressing the pale, sweat-filmed face, trying to find any light at all in the vacant eyes. "Jenna, sweetheart? It's Mom. It's Mom. Say something. Say something, please."

"She can't talk," Fiona said, her voice thick, her eyes heavy. "She hasn't said anything."

Jenna's mother turned to her, teeth bared, eyes ablaze. "This is your fault, isn't it? You druggie whore—I knew it! I knew you would give her something!"

"No," Fiona said, backing away. "I swear, I didn't give her anything—"

Jenna's mother grabbed her by the collar. "What did you give her?" She pushed Fiona into the hallway, shaking her, clawing at her. "What did you fucking give her?"

Just as quickly as the attack started, two male nurses swept in and pulled off Jenna's mother, corralling her as she shrieked and wept. Fiona slumped against the wall, chewing her thumbnail furiously, staring with wide eyes at the nurses and doctors and visitors who had assembled, all looking on with stupid, sheepish faces. She made for the elevator and saw more onlookers in the hospital rooms, patients who sat up in bed, who stared from underneath oxygen masks and through tubing and mesh. There were others, too, figures standing by the bedsides or straddling the shoulders, dark shapes who revealed black grins, black eyes. Fiona ran, slammed her palm against the elevator call button. At last, in the seclusion of the confined, chromed interior, she took a breath and tasted metal on her tongue. Her ragged thumb ran red.

How could she go to class knowing what had happened, what was happening? She couldn't even keep water down, let alone eat a meal. Dark-eyed, dragging her feet, she went to the studio the next day and found that, surprisingly, her hands itched for the palette. Painting was usually a relief, a way to zone out and push back the world at large, especially if she had smoked beforehand. But this felt different. Her hands moved almost on their own. The images that filled her mind—lurid red and noxious black, hectic in their haste, vicious in their violence—exploded onto the canvas, mediated into crimson fractals, transcendental landscapes, opalescent abstractions. She produced painting after painting over the following days. She sketched with an alarming fervor, finding secluded corners in the library or nearby coffee shop where she could let her hands move however they wanted. "What've you got there?" asked a young man passing by, and she surprised herself with a violent gnash of teeth and a catlike hiss, smothering the blackened pages of her sketchbook against her chest.

Tossing in the night, she stared at the haphazard collection of sketches and paintings crowding her dormitory floor and realized with horror that what was happening to Jenna was happening to her. My ink, she thought suddenly, frightfully. I'm gonna spill it all over. I'm gonna let it run out. I'm gonna let it soak everything. She fought to will away the image of her body red and wet, her flesh dissolving into a sea of blood, her mouth and nose and eyes and hair sinking into the depths like the remains of a deflated blow-up doll.

She went back to the club, pushing past Merc and throwing aside the curtains to the back room. Only empty space greeted her—gone was the bizarre, black monolith, its shape and dimensions difficult to discern, its texture nearly nonexistent. She paced around the room, wondering if she would see it at a certain angle, as though it had been reduced to two dimensions, as though it could hide itself, because how else could they move it the way they did? Or did it move itself, disappearing and reappearing however and wherever it wanted? But no matter where she stepped or from what angle she looked, the monolith was gone, and all the strange images and red light along with it. She stood dumbly, as if waiting for a sign, an indication of something. Her eyes scrunched up, welled with tears—and then she smelled it. Apples. Like an orchard or a pantry full of preserves. Her grandmother had bottled apple preserves. When Fiona was a girl, they had spread it on toast, enjoyed it as breakfast or a mid-afternoon snack. Only then did she realize she'd been smelling that scent of apples ever since going to the club the other night. The smell floated from her sketches and paintings. The smell coated her fingertips, no matter the lines of charcoal and flecks of paint wedged underneath her nails and in the crevices of her cuticles.

Merc came into the room. "Fi, what's going on? You okay?"

She turned to him with red, exhausted eyes. "Where'd it go?"

"They packed it up last night."

"And the guy? Where's he taking it? I have to talk to him."

"I don't know. I could ask Randy, find out for you. Hey, where you going? Fi?"

What was the point? No one could track it. No one could predict when it would next show itself. And that man—something about him had seemed off, like he wasn't really there. Maybe he was a ghost. Maybe he was Costas's fucking ghost. Poofing out of existence like smoke, floating away with his magic death-door until he could find another nesting place. Fuck! She was a piece of shit for taking Jenna. Her mom was right. She was a fucking bitch, and this was what she deserved, what had been coming to her all along.

Outside the club, she stopped and turned back. The smell of apples, of her grandmother's preserves, floated on the air. But so did something else. Another scent, hiding underneath the first, masking itself, camouflaging the way a hunter would to avoid his quarry's suspicion. It was the same smell that hovered over Jenna at the hospital. The smell of rotting meat and running blood. The smell of livestock herded and cooed and slaughtered. The smell of an unlucky rabbit or hapless rodent, stalked more expertly than it could evade, pinned to the dirt, freed of its throat in sharp, snappy bites.

The smell of death.

37

There had always been rumors about *La Frontera*, *The Doorway*. Rumors about the reclusive artist Rafael Costas, who lived a hermit's life in rural Spain after decades of a successful art career. What had happened to the dark, dashing artist who captured the imagination with his style and savvy as much as his experimental installations and striking compositions? What drove him out of the cities and universities into madness, to the bullet that penetrated his skull, dissolved his flesh, scattered his blood? The speculation and hearsay had been part of the fun, the collective mythmaking that gave rise to the legendary status of his last and most enduring piece. But Fiona had never considered that the worst of the rumors, the most insane, were actually the ones closest to the truth. A gateway to another world. A manmade rift activated by trauma, that responded to suffering, that projected its soaked-up, collective pain onto its unwitting audience. A mirror that was as much window, as much portal.

With nowhere else to turn, she looked online for answers. Supposed videos of *The Doorway*, always grainy, never clear. Black space that flashed red, that vibrated with the howls and cries of what she initially thought had been the audience, but must have been, instead, those who had already seen it—those who had been captured by it. Posts and testimonials alleged the dreams, the visions of shadows in the periphery, of ringing bells that reached a crescendo, that heralded the coming of *something*. No one ever reported back after more than a few weeks. And it wasn't just *The Doorway*. You know you can get there other ways, right? Get where? *There*, man. *There*. Watch this video. See what I mean. See what *we* mean. :)

Doorways. Borders. Some built out of closets or carved into basement floors. Others hidden by foliage or disaster, excavated from sediment, unearthed from rubble. Yet more that could be conjured, summoned by a code that somehow transcended language and thought. All of these thresholds opening to some other place. Where all were one. Where pain and choice were stripped away. Where the bodily baggage of humanity could be revoked, replaced with the fluidity of waves and the flux of energy. Where the soul could be free and weightless.

"The room of cloth," said Fiona, lying down to sleep, the words rising from deep inside. She dreamed and found herself in a dark space.

Fi? You made it.

She looked around. Her brother was there. She knew it was him despite never meeting him in person, never hearing his voice beyond the tinny audio of old videos, never looking into his eyes besides staring into the gloss of faded photographs. When she was too young to remember, two or three years old, her father had found him hanging from the ceiling fan of his bedroom. Problems with drugs, they'd said. In and out of rehab. There had been rumors whispered throughout the funeral parlor that the closed casket was because the smile on his face had become an unmovable rictus—that no one had ever seen him so happy.

"Jacob?" She approached him and took his hands. "Is that really you?"

It was—it had to be. He was smiling at her, gently, peacefully, not the way people had talked about for years afterwards, saying that his dead face had been fixed in that awful grin. His eyes, too, were full and calm. He was happy. He had to be happy. There had to be some relief when you died, when you got free of all this shit. What was the point otherwise?

Wow, Fi, he said. You're all grown-up. Mom and Dad must be so proud of you.

"I think they are. I hope they are. They give me a lot of wiggle room—maybe too much."

They just want you to be happy. We all do.

"Jacob. Can you help me? My friend, Jenna—she's in a lot of trouble. And it's my fault. But maybe there's a way I can wake her up. A way I can save her."

You don't have to do anything, Fi. She's here with us already. She's safe now.

"What?" Fiona looked more closely at him. The skin around his neck was bruised, blistered. Ribbed with dark burn marks.

Yeah. Look behind you.

She turned. Jenna was there, smiling at her just like Jacob was. She hugged Fiona.

Fi! You made it. I'm so glad.

"Jen?" Fiona looked her over. She sobbed. "Oh, God. I'm so sorry. I'm so fucking sorry."

Fi, it's okay. It's all right now. I'm good! See? I'm happy. I'm free.

"I didn't know what was gonna happen. I'm so fucking stupid! I shouldn't have taken you there, shouldn't have shown you that fucking thing. I didn't know, I just didn't know—"

Jenna held a finger to Fiona's lips. Fi. It's okay. You don't have to worry about me anymore. But you do have to worry about yourself.

"What?"

I wasn't strong enough for the responsibility. For the duty. He was testing us, you know. Seeing if we could handle it. If we were ready.

"Handle what? Jen, what are you talking about?" Fiona wiped away her tears, stared at her. Were her eyes darker than usual? And her mouth—was there something in her mouth?

You have to spread it, Jenna said. Fiona, you have to spread it. Your art. Show it to everyone. Make them see. Make them understand. Just like we did.

Fiona backed away. Jenna's mouth ran black with blood. When she spoke, her slit cheek flapped and gushed. And her eyes—oh, her *eyes*.

Make them see, Fiona. Your fresh ink. Your flesh and your blood. He wants you to show them—he *needs* you to show them. That's why you were chosen. Why you were born.

Fiona covered her mouth with her hands and gasped. Jenna's tongue hung by tethers, gray and slug-like. Her teeth were chipped and rotten, decayed as if by years. She was grinning. Laughing. Crying.

Fiona screamed awake, gagging at the stench of dried blood and flayed skin. She rushed to the hospital. Through the window of Jenna's room, she saw nurses crowding the bed, saw Jenna's mother sobbing, pulling at her hair, clutching her chest. A nurse moved, and Fiona caught sight of Jenna's glassy eyes, her red-drenched gown, her crimson-slathered smirk.

Fiona had never seen her so happy.

38.

Months later, she sat alone on a bench at Venice Beach, fingering the remains of an ice cream cone, hugging her knees to her chest. Anxiously, she eyed the crowds, the colorful array of kiosks and pop-ups, the far-away waves. On the air were salt and lotion, syrup and sugar, rap and guitar—and blood and metal. She held her breath and tried to push the smells to the background.

Rare that she left her room, let alone the house. The therapists had been useless, unwilling to listen to her, uninterested in entertaining her stories about doorways and rooms that were not rooms, about the many who were trapped, about the dead who had no voice, who drifted in darkness. No one believed her about the man in chains, the man with the red eyes. He was coming, she told them, whomever she could, whenever she could. She tried to warn them online. He's coming. For all of us. But no one listened. Because they wanted it. Because they were waiting for it. They were making it happen, right at that moment. Were they there, strolling the boardwalk, chewing on shaved ice? Making sandcastles? Skating? Who was one of them? Who was one of the devoted, one of the saved? No one? Everyone?

She saw Jenna sometimes. She saw Jacob. She had pressed her father, confronted her mother. Why did he kill himself? Was it really drugs? But her mother just sat silent, unresponsive. Her father yelled and threw things around. A waste, he said. All the money and time spent on her, on her brother. For nothing! Just sickness and death! And Fiona had yelled, too, toppling over priceless vases, tearing down expensive paintings. It's not my fucking fault! I didn't ask for it! What good's your fucking money if it can't protect you? If it can't save you?

She sat in her room. She smoked. She hadn't painted or sketched in months, but her hands moved nonetheless, and in the worst of her fits, her nails dug into wood and scratched shapes, scrawled lines, trailed blood. Spread. *Spread.* Jenna's words filled her mind, commanded her, compelled her. But she wouldn't. She wouldn't. Better to do nothing. Because if she died, she knew she'd just go there. If she hung herself, if she cut her wrists, she'd just join them in that place, that great, dark place, that abyss. No. She couldn't do that. She wouldn't do that. There had to be another way. There had to be something. Anything.

She checked the time on her phone. The lady was late. She had responded to one of Fiona's online warnings. Said she wasn't alone. That there were people who could help her. What other choice was there but to take the chance? So, she sat there, waiting, wishing she could go back in time just a year, when everything was fine, when she was happy and healthy, when she could go down to the beach and feel the sand between her toes and the water around her ankles, when she could dance and laugh and paint with her pastel blues and acrylic grays, when she could sleep and dream of a future, any future. When she could be at peace.

She lowered her head and hugged her knees more tightly. So many people around her, but she was alone. Totally, completely alone.

"Fiona?"

She looked up. A woman stood by the bench, thin and pale, in white shirt and dusted jeans. "Sorry for the wait," she said. "May I sit?"

Fiona looked at her. "You're Sarah?"

"Yeah." The woman sat. She smiled. "You're young. Are you in college?"

"I was."

The woman, Sarah, brushed aside blonde bangs and lowered her sunglasses. Her eyes were gray, so gray as to be almost entirely light.

"I was in college the last time I came to California," she said. She stared out at the beach, at the people. "It was a long time ago. Another life."

Fiona stared, looking for the signs of infection, the symptoms of corruption. But the way this lady moved and talked—slowly, almost dreamily—it didn't seem like she inhabited the same nightmare Fiona did. Who cared about college or anything else if they knew what was coming, what was already here? Why were they wasting their time talking about this shit?

"Look," said Fiona, "let's just cut the bullshit. Can you help me? Can you make it stop?"

Sarah returned the stare. Now her eyes were hard, lacking their previous light. "I can help you," she said, "but I can't make it stop. I'm sorry."

Fiona didn't understand. "What did you say?"

"If there's a way out of it," Sarah said, "a cure, I haven't found it. None of us have."

"What the fuck?" Fiona's chest constricted. Tears iced her cheeks. "What the fuck are you doing here, then? Is this a joke? You just look for people to shit all over them?"

Sarah shook her head. "No. It's not a joke. I wish I had something different to tell you."

"Oh, fucking God. We're gonna die. We're gonna die and go to that place."

"Listen to me." Sarah reached out and took her hand. There was something about her touch, something material and strong, that caught Fiona's breath. "This is what he wants. He wants you to feel like you're helpless, like there's no other option but the one he gives you. Like there's no other door. But I promise you there's so much more you can do. You can help us find the others. Maybe, somewhere, someone has a clue about how to stop it."

"Don't you get it?" Fiona said. "I deserve this. I did this to Jenna. I'm a fuck-up like my brother, just like my dad says. This was always gonna happen to me. One way or another."

Sarah didn't say anything to her, didn't offer any consolatory words, didn't proffer platitudes. Instead, she pulled the girl into an embrace, holding her tightly, gripping her back, stroking her hair, singing to her softly a song Fiona didn't recognize but that nonetheless cleared away the roiling terror in her mind, the wash of blood and rust, and left in its place the flutter of wings and the sheen of white feathers. Fiona felt, if only for a moment, the spread of the air beneath her, the warmth of the sunlight. As though she were weightless. Suspended. Flying.

When Sarah released her, brought her back, Fiona's tears ran. They would come back soon, the hellish visions and macabre visitors. They would compel her to paint, to draw, to scrawl their master's mark onto the fabric of the world. They would take more, too many more, and add them to their ranks. They would turn the seas red and the skies black. They would stop even the revolution of the planet, render ancient the seasons, force time itself to a standstill. They would spread across the stars on their cold, dead chariot. Their satellites, manmade and otherwise, would grope, like feelers, along the edges of the universe, finding new vectors, sympathetic carriers, alternative means of transmission. They would find themselves, the avatars of the same root disease, because how could they not? Reality itself, every inch of the expanding cosmos, was tainted. A quilted patchwork of sinners in the hands of an angry god, putrefying at the edges, crumbling away towards the center until there would be absolutely nothing left.

But somewhere, beyond all this, beyond the celestial firmament, there was freedom. Far, far away, in a place free of pain and full of light. There had to be. Where did all the others go, those who had eluded the mark, evaded the chains? To what realm did they journey when they left this life? What paradisiacal sights awaited them? What Edenic lands did they explore?

"Okay," she said, taking Sarah's hand, feeling for the first time in her life the genuine substance of skin and the textured, interlaced mesh of muscle and tendon. A hardwired connection between them, between their flesh, their blood. Somewhere in that exchange was the hope of release. Somewhere in that conveyance was the faith in an escape.

"What's next?"

ABOUT THE AUTHOR

R. H. Gründ is the author of *Room of Cloth*, *Simulacrum*, and *Abattoir*. Apart from writing and publishing, he has taught composition at both the secondary and postsecondary levels. He lives in South Texas with his family. Using the QR code below, you can follow him on social media at @rhgrundwriting and find more information on his website at www.rhgrundwriting.com.